Praise for the Coroner Jenny Cooper series

'Fasten your seatbelts for a quality thriller . . . Hall's Gold Dagger-nominated books, quite simply, get better each time. Part of it is the former barrister and TV producer's ability to structure and deliver a thriller that keeps you turning the pages. But Hall has also hit upon a genuinely fascinating aspect of the justice system . . . The most compelling element of Hall's books, however, is Cooper herself . . . It is wonderful stuff, chillingly plausible'   *Independent on Sunday*

'As premises go, this one's a killer . . . It's a terrific series, meticulously researched, sharply plotted and peopled with sympathetic characters, led by Cooper, who is always aware of the human consequences of failure'   *Financial Times*

'Ed McBain semi-inaugurated the forensics genre, but Patricia Cornwell and Kathy Reichs parleyed his innovations into stratospheric sales. But the field has not become an exclusively female sorority – or an American domain. A highly talented male writer has offered a challenge'   *Independent*

'An edge-of-the-seat thriller . . . this fourth novel in the excellent Jenny Cooper series should come with a health warning'   *Irish Independent*

'As complex and impressive as his debut *The Coroner*'   *Sunday Telegraph*

The Chosen Dead

M. R. Hall is a screenwriter, producer and former criminal barrister. Educated at Hereford Cathedral School and Worcester College, Oxford, he lives in Monmouthshire with his wife and two sons. Aside from writing, his main passion is the preservation and planting of woodland. In his spare moments, he is mostly to be found among trees.

THE CHOSEN DEAD is the fifth novel in M. R. Hall's twice CWA Gold Dagger-shortlisted Coroner Jenny Cooper series.

m-r-hall.com
facebook.com/MRHallAuthor
@MRHall_books

M. R. HALL

The
Chosen Dead

PAN BOOKS

First published 2013 by Mantle

This paperback edition published 2014 by Pan Books
an imprint of Pan Macmillan, a division of Macmillan Publishers Limited
Pan Macmillan, 20 New Wharf Road, London N1 9RR
Basingstoke and Oxford
Associated companies throughout the world
www.panmacmillan.com

ISBN 978-0-330-52662-3

Visit www.panmacmillan.com to read more about all our books
and to buy them. You will also find features, author interviews and
news of any author events, and you can sign up for e-newsletters
so that you're always first to hear about our new releases.

The Chosen Dead

Nature has provided us with a spectacular toolbox. The toolbox exists. An architect far better and smarter than us has given us that toolbox, and we now have the ability to use it.

(Barry Schuler, from his TED lecture, 'Genomics 101')

ONE

THE LAST THING ROY EMMETT HUDSON was expecting on the eve of his forty-first birthday was a bullet in the head, but life and death are only a single breath apart, and as a biologist, he appreciated that more than most. Even as he strolled across the company lot to the Mercedes Coupé he had driven all winter without once raising the roof, his killers' thoughts were already moving on to where they might dump the body so that it might never be found. They were from out of town, and unfamiliar with the wilderness into which the city merged only a few miles away from the Airpark business zone.

Unaware of what awaited him, Hudson counted himself a lucky man. There was no other word to describe the turn of events that had placed him in the ideal position at the perfect time. Aside from the gifted few who had secured comfortable professorships in Ivy League schools, most of his peers from the Brown class of '66 were grinding out their best years in the labs and offices of the giant pharmas back east. They had become company men and women who had left their scientific ideals behind to climb the greasy pole and save for a retirement they might never reach in sufficient health to enjoy. He, on the other hand, had taken a chance. Or had

3

chance taken him? He couldn't decide. Either way, it had all come down to an ad in the appointments section that had lain discarded on the seat of a commuter train which he rode no more than three times each year. If he hadn't chosen that particular Tuesday morning to put his car into the shop, or if he had arrived on the platform thirty seconds sooner in time to catch the earlier train, his working days would still have been spent on the fifteenth floor of the Meditech Building, wondering what had happened to the young man who was going to save the lives of millions and collect a Nobel Prize.

The ad had simply read: *Biotech start-up is seeking gifted and motivated scientists with experience in recombinant gene technology. Full details on application. Résumé to Box 657.*

The few colleagues to whom he had shown it dismissed the ad as having been placed by some gimcrack outfit trying to hitch up to the latest bandwagon. Either that, or it was a sneaky ploy by one the big corporates to test the loyalty of its precious R&D teams. Hudson hadn't been so sure. He had had an instinct, a stirring in his gut that he hadn't felt since he'd first stepped off the Greyhound and hauled his grip through the front gates of Brown. And he'd been right to trust it. The three directors of Genix, all young and visionary men, had wanted to attract only those curious and adventuresome enough to leave comfortable careers behind for an exciting and uncertain future. They could guarantee only twelve months' modest salary, but offered generous share options to be taken up after three years' service. If by that time the company had filed no patents nor had any realistic prospect of doing so, their backers would pull the plug. Simple.

It had taken Hudson's team of fifteen less than a year to splice human DNA into E. coli bacteria and start producing human growth hormone at a level which showed potential for future industrial production. This early success had made real the possibility that all manner of previously rare and expensive therapeutic drugs could in future be grown cheaply and in bulk by genetically altered micro-organisms. The investors piled in with more money than Genix knew how to spend. Five months down the line Hudson was running a team of fifty and racing Eli Lilly, Smith Kline and Johnson & Johnson all the way to the US Patent Office. By the time he picked up his share options he figured they'd be worth more than ten million dollars.

Beneath the ice-blue desert sky, in this brand-new city where anything felt possible, Hudson marvelled at how close he had come to letting his dreams slip away. Back east, his vaulting ambitions had seemed more absurd and delusional with each passing year, but out here in Scottsdale, 'The West's Most Western Town', nothing short of shooting for the moon was expected of every single employee of the new biotech businesses that were taking root in this burgeoning oasis. It had been a long sixteen-year journey with several false turns along the way, but one year into the second half of his life, Hudson believed that he was about to arrive; and he wasn't just going to become a big name in the science of gene technology: he was going to change the world.

The Mercedes' white-walled tyres (a little splash of ex-hibitionism he had allowed himself, along with the $200 sunglasses) made a pleasing squeal as he swung the car round to the exit and turned out into the light, pre-rush traffic heading for route 101. He had fifteen minutes to make the journey to McDowell Elementary, where his daughter, Sonia, was about to play in her first softball match. In the past, his wife, Louise, had taken care of school events, but now four months into studying for a doctorate in political science at Arizona State, she had started to insist he share responsibility. Hudson secretly resented the fact that his wife's focus had shifted outside their home, but he had to concede that she had made more than her share of sacrifices to facilitate his career. They had been students at Brown together, but as soon as they had married, her ambitions had taken a back seat. While he scaled the corporate ladder, she had bottled up her intellectual frustration and made do with a series of part-time teaching jobs. The move west had been the final catalyst for change. 'This isn't just going to be about you or the money,' she had declared, 'this is my time, too.' 'Sure, sweetie, it's time we both stepped out into the sun,' he had said, and at that moment, he had even meant it.

He followed the 101 due east for several miles towards the mountains, the land either side of it one huge construction site: entire neighbourhoods were going up as fast as the sunburned Mexican labourers could build them. Scottsdale was on the move. Businesses were flooding in. Thanks to the domestic air-conditioner and vast water-capture schemes, a town which in the 1950s had only a handful of residents had mushroomed to over 100,000. Just like the micro-organisms he had spent his professional life studying, human beings had an uncanny knack of bringing life to the most unlikely corners of the planet.

Hudson recalled some of the pot-smoking humanities students at Brown talking about 'life force' as some abstract idea drawn from mystic Eastern philosophy, but to him, a microbiologist studying living things in their most elemental form, life was a measurable *physical* force just like any other in the universe. But whereas light or heat would penetrate indiscriminately wherever it was able, in accordance with fixed and unaltering constants set at the beginning of time, the force of life was strengthening and accelerating. There was and always would be the same amount of gravity in the universe, but while the conditions remained to sustain it, life was relentlessly increasing in complexity, ability and ambition. Viewed from this perspective, a city in the desert made perfect sense. As the most advanced form of life, human beings were the fullest expression of the elemental drive to survive and proliferate however and wherever possible. It was beautiful to behold. *Beautiful* – another word he couldn't improve on. Life in its myriad forms was *beautiful*, but, as he always made the point of stressing to his few non-scientist friends, beautiful does not imply *nice*. Life is not a benign force; in fact, it is unique in the cosmos in being calculatingly ruthless.

The 101 swung south into the suburbs. The construction smells of concrete and bitumen now gave way to the sweet scents of cactus blossom and fresh-mown grass drifting over from Horsemen's Park. Hudson leaned forward and switched on the stereo. The auto-tune clicked into a local country station, Lester Flatt and Earl Scruggs on slide guitar and banjo, belting out one of their chick-a-chack old-time numbers: '*I'm on a big black freight train, and we're movin' on* . . .' He smiled as he tapped his fingers on the rim of the wheel. Man, those guys could pick.

Leaving the 101 at 38, he followed East Raintree Drive for a mile or so, before heading south two blocks to the ball park opposite the school. Only three minutes after four: he was almost on time. The lot was already crowded with the outsize air-conditioned suburbans his fellow Arizonans felt compelled to drive, and there were no places left in the shade. He made do with a spot in the full sun and laid his linen sport coat over the passenger seat to save Sonia's bare legs when it came time to go home. Hudson approached the mothers gathered on the bleachers in the shade of a row of palms. Aside from Coach Brewster he was the only man present. He nodded to the few women he recognized from the PTA barbecue Louise had hosted the previous fall, but no one invited him to join them. They seemed a little embarrassed by the presence of a father during office hours, and he sensed a trace of pity in their awkward smiles. He found a space on the bench at the end of the row as the first ball of the game was pitched. The little boy on the plate swung hard and got lucky. The ball sailed into the outfield and he scrambled to second base. Sonia was manning third and didn't even twitch. Beneath the wide brim of her cap she was wearing a frown of intense concentration just like her mother's. Hudson waved, but if she had noticed, she pretended not to. This was serious business, she was telling him; frivolity could wait.

'Excuse me, sir—'

Hudson turned, a little startled. The quiet, polite voice belonged to a young man in a suit and tie who had approached unseen from his left.

'Am I right in thinking you're Mr Roy Emmett Hudson, R&D Director at Genix?'

'That's right.'

The man's gentle tone made it sound like a social inquiry, but he looked too youthful to be a parent at a private school.

'Have we met?'

'No, sir.' He reached discreetly into his pocket and flashed an ID card held in a cupped palm.

Hudson made out the initials 'FDA'.

'FDA? You're kidding me.' The bureaucrats of the Food and Drug Administration were a constant thorn in his flesh – every individual piece of research involving gene manipulation required a licence that involved paperwork of near-incomprehensible complexity – but even by their intrusive standards this was a new low. 'Son, this is hardly an appropriate place—'

'We'll only take a moment, Mr Hudson. We want to process your application as swiftly as possible.'

'What? . . . Which one?'

'I have the documents in the van. I've been told to obtain your signature by close of business – it's a new privacy clause. The Administration's getting anxious about who's sharing what with whom.'

'Why would my company be sharing its research?'

'I promise it'll only take a moment, Mr Hudson.'

Hudson sighed impatiently and stood up from his seat. 'I have a ball game to watch. You have five minutes.' He strode off towards the parking lot planning the stiff phone calls he'd be making to the FDA's Washington HQ first thing in the morning.

'I can't apologize enough for disturbing you, sir, but I'm sure you'll accept this is only a formality.'

The young man sounded embarrassed, making Hudson feel guilty for snapping at him.

'Where are we going?'

'The black Chevy.'

The minivan was parked in the centre of the lot, the engine idling to keep the air-conditioner rolling. Another young official was rifling through papers in the driver's seat. Seeing them coming, he climbed out and opened the door on the far side of the vehicle – the kind that slid open sideways on runners.

'What's this – a travelling office?' Hudson said, with more than a hint of sarcasm.

'As a matter of fact, it is. You want, you can call your attorney or even fax him.'

Hudson made no comment and walked around the rear of the van. 'OK, show me what you got.'

He glanced through the open door and saw black plastic sheeting on the floor of the empty interior, and in the sliver of a second between sight and thought felt a cold sensation at the nape of his neck accompanied by a brief metallic click.

TWO

'DO YOU WISH TO GO STRAIGHT to Dr Keppler's house or call at the apartment first?' Dagmar spoke in perfect Russian.

Professor Roman Slavsky said, 'I have a choice?'

'Of course. But you should bear in mind that it's a thirty-minute drive. You are invited for eight. It's just past seven.'

'No one expects a Russian to be on time.'

'Then you don't know Germans, Professor.'

Slavsky smiled and lit one of the Marlboros he had hidden in a packet of Doinas. 'I think I do, even if your language continues to confound me.' He opened the window of the BMW a crack, still enjoying the novelty of the electric motor that propelled it smoothly up and down, and tossed out his spent match. 'No, I think I'll look into the apartment first, if you don't mind.'

'As you wish.'

Dagmar turned right out of the Institute's driveway and headed through the moonless evening along an empty street lined with dismal apartment buildings. Somehow the bleakness of East Berlin was more pronounced even than Moscow's, Slavsky thought. The atmosphere of depression here felt more acute than chronic. Russians were naturally gloomy, never happier than when staring into the abyss; but his colleagues in the GDR seemed less reconciled to their lot, a condition no doubt aggravated by the uncertainty of the times. The military scientists in his lecture room at the symposium had been greasy with nervous perspiration. During the coffee breaks he had sensed that every last one of them was bursting to discuss 'the situation', not least the matter of their many professional associates who had slipped across the open border from Hungary to the West during the previous month, taking God knows what information with them. But no one had dared say a word. Rather they had silently sweated their anxiety out through their pores.

'A good day?' Dagmar asked.

'Mmm?' Slavsky pulled back from his gloomy thoughts.

'Were your lectures well received?'

'Oh, I think so. Although I'm not sure how much I can teach your countrymen that they don't already know. We Russians like to think we're ahead of the game, but your people have been quietly unwinding the genomes of exotic bacteria for years. Some I've never even heard of until this week.'

It was a good line, and his minder seemed to buy it.

'You're too modest, Professor,' she said, 'your knowledge is critical. Why else would you have been invited?'

Why indeed? It was a question he had pondered for the entire three months since the official letter of invitation had arrived at his Moscow laboratory. Throughout his fifteen years working for the Soviet Ministry of Defence all foreign travel had been explicitly forbidden – his work was classified as 'ultra sensitive' – but with only a day's notice and in the midst of political upheaval, he had been requested to address fellow military microbiologists in the GDR on his innovations in gene-sequencing technology. No one in the Ministry had volunteered a specific reason, but Slavsky had picked up rumours that his presence was one of a hastily arranged series of gestures designed to make the Germans feel they still belonged under the Soviet umbrella. The unspoken message conveyed by his visit was that if they could be trusted to share in the most sensitive of Soviet military secrets, there would be no more playing second fiddle. After four and a half unequal decades, they were all comrades now.

If that was the case, it was an empty gesture offered far too late to achieve its purpose. The Soviet heart had grown hollow, and the Germans and their Eastern European colleagues sensed it even more keenly than Slavsky's countrymen. Gorbachev and his glasnost had merely served to accelerate the loss of faith that had taken hold while dear old Brezhnev was fading. Without the rhetoric of a charismatic leader like a Stalin, or even a Khrushchev, no one knew for certain what the project was any more. Slavsky's own moment of disillusionment had come in June 1982. He had been barely thirty-two years old and placed in charge of an entire research programme with an unlimited budget and a hotline to the KGB. He had expected his colleagues in the Lubyanka to overwhelm him with information from their spies buried in the universities of the West, but instead they came him to like schoolboys asking for instruction. Whom should they approach? Where was our knowledge lacking? Which international scientific conferences should they attend? They were men of straw looking for guidance to a young scientist who had never travelled further than Leningrad. He had whipped them into some sort of shape, and used them to garner a number of valuable secrets from his foreign competitors, but from that day onwards he had known that he was riding an exhausted horse; and as a logical man he had begun to plan for the time when the empire he served would finally crumble.

Ironically, the closer the end appeared to be, the more

confused his once-solid plans became. He blamed his wife, Katerina. They had no children – who could remain intellectually productive and spare time for children? – but she worried for her elderly parents. Her mother was showing signs of senility and her father's heart was enlarged. The prospect of abandoning them was tearing her in two. When, in the week before leaving for Berlin, Slavsky had angrily pronounced that the old had no right to fetter the young, she had denounced him as callous and turned him out of their bed. During three long nights spent on the hard couch he had wondered whether concern for her parents really was the reason she had recoiled from him. Slavsky had spotted expensive black-market French cosmetics on her dressing table and noticed that she had taken to shaving her legs most mornings. He speculated that her fear of the future had led her to seek the distraction of a lover. Could he forgive her if she had? Would she allow him the opportunity, or would she desert him if he confronted her with the truth? So many awkward questions of the kind he hated: those with no rational answer.

'The streets seem very quiet tonight,' Slavsky said.

'Everyone is watching television. The government is holding a news conference.'

'Have I missed something important?' He had been so preoccupied by the wretched symposium that he hadn't looked at a newspaper in days.

'The border issue,' she replied. 'There's to be some sort of announcement.'

'Are we allowed to discuss such things?'

'In theory, but it might be wiser not to.'

She glanced across and unwittingly caught his eye. Dagmar wasn't a classically attractive woman, but for a member of the secret police she was remarkably appealing. During their three days' acquaintance he had observed something in her expression, a knowingness that told him that she possessed intelligence and a degree of perceptiveness far beyond that required for her regular work. He supposed these were the qualities that had singled her out for accompanying a senior military scientist: she was watching him, recording his moods, reading his unspoken thoughts as intently as he was discerning hers.

They continued their journey across the unfamiliar city in silence, Slavsky smoking another cigarette and trying to think of subjects for conversation that would see him through his evening with Dr Keppler. Tell them as little as possible, his director had instructed him, techniques, yes, but the substance of his research, the implications of the genetic code he was deciphering, absolutely not. Occasionally Slavsky felt Dagmar's eyes flit to her right and register his expression, searching out the features of his inner landscape. He pretended not to notice: a woman was inevitably intrigued by a self-contained man. He had secured her interest on the first day; yesterday he had deepened it, and now, he sensed, they were reaching the delicate tipping point. It must be she who makes the first move, Slavsky told himself, only then would he be able to reconcile his infidelity with his conscience.

As they drew closer to the centre of the city, Slavsky became aware that people had start to emerge onto the street, not just in trickles, but in streams that became a river as they turned into a wide boulevard a short distance from the apartment block in which he was staying. They spilled off the sidewalks into the road, prompting Dagmar to lean on the horn.

'There is a soccer stadium nearby,' she said impatiently. 'A big match, I think.' She turned left across the oncoming lanes and drove down the ramp into the basement car park. 'Do you follow soccer, Professor?'

'No. Only boxing. As a student it was the one sport I excelled at.'

'Isn't it rather a brutal sport for an intellectual?'

'I like its honesty – the strongest wins. Chance rarely plays a part.'

'You dislike ambiguity?'

'I avoid it where I can. But a certain amount is unavoidable, don't you think?'

'Perhaps.' She pulled into a space near the elevator. 'Shall I wait for you here?'

'Absolutely not. You don't think I'd treat you like a common driver.'

She smiled. 'Thank you.'

In the intimate space of the elevator Slavsky caught her scent. A trace of perfume and the heat of her body. They avoided one another's eyes, the tension between them increasing with each illuminating number above the door. As they arrived on the seventh floor Slavsky stood aside to let Dagmar step out ahead of him. She brushed his shoulder as she passed.

Slavsky crossed the hall and unlocked the door. 'I have Brazilian coffee – shall I make you some?'

'I can help myself,' she said. 'I'm familiar with the apartment.'

'Of course.' She had probably bought the coffee herself, personally planted every bug and hidden camera. They stepped into the narrow hallway. 'Make yourself at home. I shan't be long.'

He showered quickly and thoroughly and cleaned his teeth with the unpleasantly sweet Western toothpaste his hosts had provided along with the scented soaps and effeminate deodorants. He was perfectly aware that this could not possibly be a secret encounter, but in the headiness of the moment he longer cared. He studied his torso in the mirror. He was pale but carried no fat, his body the envy of his middle-aged friends at the Moscow *banya*. Yes, he could be rightly proud of his body. Reassured that he had no need for self-consciousness, and his conscience eased by the thought of his wife's infidelity, Slavsky pulled on a towelling robe, and slid back the bolt on the bathroom door, his heart pounding in his chest; he hadn't touched a woman other than Katerina for nearly sixteen years.

Approaching the sitting room he heard the sound of the television, and then Dagmar speaking in an urgent whisper into the telephone. He paused to listen, trying to unscramble her rapid German. He moved closer to the door and looked through the crack. Her jacket and shoulder holster were hanging from the back of a chair, her black shoes on the carpet beneath them. She had begun to undress for him.

He caught only a word or two: 'Yes, yes . . . I understand . . . of course, sir. Right away.' He could see half of the television screen. A news programme was showing pictures of an impatient crowd. Hundreds of policemen stood in their way, their arms linked together forming a human chain, and then, as if surrendering in the face of some supernatural power, they seemed to lose their will to resist and let go of one another. A torrent of bodies flooded forward and consumed them. At first Slavsky assumed it to be an incident at a football stadium, but as the camera drew back to a wider angle he saw that the multitude was heading for a familiar landmark: the Brandenburg Gate.

His intake of breath must have been audible inside the room. Dagmar pulled open the door and stared at him, all colour washed from her face.

'We have to go, Professor. Now. Get dressed.'

Slavsky looked past her to the television. People were

running through the border post with no guards to stop them.

'What's happening?'

'The government opened the borders,' Dagmar said. 'It's no longer safe for you in Berlin. I've been ordered to take you to the airport.' There was panic in her voice.

The words escaped Slavsky's lips even before, it seemed, he had consciously formed them. 'And if I don't wish to leave?'

'You have no choice.'

She glanced across to the holster hanging from the chair.

Propelled by an elemental force, Slavsky pushed her aside and went for the gun. He seized the holster and spun around as Dagmar threw herself at him, knocking him backwards across the table. He felt the holster fly from his fingers and heard it skitter across the thin carpet. Dagmar chased after it. Slavsky forced himself to his feet and kicked her hard in the stomach as she leaned down and closed her fingers around the pistol grip. She jerked forward, extending her arm to steady herself on the back of the sofa. Slavsky punched the side of her face. Blood exploded from her nose. The gun fell from her limp hand. He snatched it by the barrel, and beat her once, then a second time across the face with the butt. As she slumped, bloody and semi-conscious, to the floor, Slavsky turned the weapon in his hands, aimed it between her shoulder blades and fired.

Third Secretary Gordon Jefferies climbed the stairs to his office on the second floor at the British Embassy in Wilhelmstrasse, having spent fewer than two hours in his bed. Although the East Germans' lifting of border restrictions had not come entirely as a surprise, the overwhelming events of the previous night most certainly had. The Embassy had primed itself for a gradual transition, a steady flow of Easterners and a cautious warming of relations, but no one had envisaged tens of thousands demolishing the Berlin Wall and swarming into the West in one spontaneous orgy of liberation. It was both thrilling and terrifying to behold. Jefferies was sharply aware that he was witnessing a great moment in history, and yet felt numbed to it, as if he were merely reading a news report from a distant continent. There was too much to absorb to be able to react meaningfully. The best he could do was to observe, to take note and record for posterity.

He swiped his security card through the electronic reader and pushed through the office door.

'Mr Jefferies?' The voice belonged to one of the local temps who'd been called in overnight to deal with the deluge of phone calls from the British press and citizens anxious to know if West Germany was about to descend into anarchy. He tried to recall her name.

'Yes?'

'The front desk has been calling for you – they say it's urgent.'

'Oh?' He noticed her badge, *Ingrid*, that was it. 'Did they say what it concerned?'

'A Russian. He's seeking asylum.' She handed him a note. 'He says his name is Professor Roman Slavsky.'

'Tell them I'll be down in ten minutes.' He passed through the glass door into his office and reached for the phone. He dialled the switchboard of the Foreign Office and asked to be put through to the Soviet desk. It was his old friend Tim Russen who answered. Just like him to be on the night shift. They'd been at Oxford together, Tim a layabout linguist who acted in a succession of pretentious experimental plays, while Gordon struggled through a law degree, entombed in the library for ten hours each day.

'Gordon – I've been thinking about you. It's unbelievable. What's the scene on the street?'

'Like Notting Hill the morning after the carnival – ankle-deep in trash and bodies in every doorway – except the party's still going strong. Thousands of Easterners wandering the streets, gawping through shop windows and stroking the cars like holy relics.'

'You're a lucky man. I'd give my right arm to be there.'

'We may well be needing someone from your desk.'

'Oh?'

'I'm told we've a potential Soviet defector downstairs – a Professor Roman Slavsky. Any idea who he is?'

'Hold on. God, I hate this thing . . .' Gordon heard Tim stabbing one-fingered at a computer keyboard. 'Don't hold your breath, it takes a while for it to flip through the directory or whatever the hell it does.'

While Gordon waited, there was a knock on his office door. A messenger was standing outside holding a briefcase. Gordon motioned him in and pointed to the desk. The messenger set the case down and handed him the delivery docket to sign. He scrawled an illegible signature. As the messenger left, Gordon wedged the phone against his shoulder and sprang the catches, noticing that the inside carried a heavy odour of cigarette smoke.

'I tell you, it was a damn sight easier with a filing cabinet,' Tim was saying. 'At least you could bloody well see what was in there.'

'Yes,' Gordon said distractedly, his attention switching to the contents of the case. On the left-hand side was a stack of cardboard wallet files, and on the right four bundles of 5-inch floppy disks bound together with rubber bands.

'OK, here we go,' Tim said. 'Professor Slavsky . . . Yep, looks like there's only one with that name.'

Gordon pulled out the top file and opened it. The documents were in English – some sort of complex scientific data that looked like computer code.

'You lucky bastard,' Tim said. 'Roman Slavsky? Are you sure that's who you've got?'

Gordon scanned the page and spotted company details printed at its foot: *Genix Inc., 1050 West Bronco Drive, Scottsdale, Arizona.*

'Why, who is he?'

'Your ticket to the stars, my friend.'

THREE

Present day

JENNY COOPER WAS FREE. Eight years after she had frozen mid-sentence in front of a bemused courtroom and felt the walls close in, she had emerged from the long dark tunnel of recovery and completed her last ever appointment with Dr Allen, the psychiatrist who had become such a troubling fixture in her life. He had seemed almost disappointed that she hadn't suffered a panic attack for more than a year and was coping well with her job as the Severn Vale District Coroner. In the absence of symptoms to analyse, he had been reduced to sermonizing and platitudes: 'Remember that life is precious, Mrs Cooper. It exists by chance but thrives by will. Always keep hold of your purpose.' She had promised that she would and had stepped out into the bright morning to feel the warmth of the sun on her face as if for the first time.

No more pretending. No more deceit. No more shame. She was well again. It was official.

Jenny drove her Land Rover out of the car park and turned towards Bristol, saying goodbye to the Chepstow Hospital for the final time. In future she would drive past on her journeys to and from the office not with a sense of dread, but with only a fading memory of the years in which she had struggled to put her shattered life together. She felt like the sole survivor of a bomb blast; a woman who had emerged whole from the wreckage but couldn't quite understand how or why. Don't question, Jenny, she told herself, you're done with all of that. Just live.

Just live. What did that mean?

Driving over the mile-wide expanse of the Severn Bridge, the sharp, fresh air of the estuary blowing in through her open window, she allowed herself to believe that it meant no more than being an ordinary, forty-something single woman, with mundane worries of the kind millions of women like her coped with every day. She was anxious about her future with Michael, the man who only sometimes referred to himself as her 'boyfriend'. She fretted about the lines appearing in her still-attractive features and about the few pounds she was struggling to shed from around her middle. And she was missing Ross, her son, who was at university in London and who she feared would have grown even more distant when she went to collect him tomorrow. Ordinary worries. Nothing that couldn't be overcome; nothing that need defeat her. After nearly a decade of being a 'case' she had rejoined the common flow. She felt an unaccustomed sensation: was it happiness? No, it was something even more precious than that: it was contentment.

Her brief moment of peace was rudely interrupted by the phone. The display on the dash behind the wheel said *Unknown Caller.*

'Hello.'

'Mrs Cooper?'

'Speaking.'

'Detective Inspector Stephen Watling, Gloucestershire. We met last summer – the kids in the canoe.'

She felt herself crashing back to earth.

'I remember.' Images of swollen, drowned teenage bodies

invaded her mind. She pushed them away. 'What can I do for you?'

'Body on the M5. Male. Thirties. Looks like he jumped from the bridge into the traffic – he was lying just along from it.'

'Are there any witnesses?'

'No. He was found at the roadside this morning by a verge-cleaning crew.'

'Right.' So far it sounded like an unremarkable suicide. She waited for the rest.

'We think we know who he is. A two-year-old boy was found early this morning about a mile away in Bristol Memorial Woodlands. He's the man's son. His car was still parked there.'

'What's happened to the child?'

'He's alive. Hypothermia but no injuries. He's been taken to the Vale Hospital. Mother's on the way.'

Now she understood. DI Watling was trying to pass the awkward conversation with the child's mother over to her. Satisfied the dead man had killed himself, it had become the coroner's problem.

'Won't you be talking to her anyway?' Jenny said.

'I'll send a family liaison along – Annie Malik, she's good. I'm tied up on a drugs inquiry.'

What could be more important than that? Jenny wanted to answer, but held her tongue. She had made enough enemies in the police.

'What's the mother's name?'

'Karen Jordan. We think the guy was called Adam. Adam Jordan.'

'All right. Tell your officer I'll be ready to speak to Mrs Jordan in an hour, but I'd like to see the body first.'

*

It was a task most coroners would have left to their officers. The days of being obliged to view the body *in situ* were long past. The coroner had increasingly become an office-bound official who kept contact with the bereaved to a minimum, but Jenny had never been able to operate that way. Having spent the first fifteen years of her legal career in the family courts dealing with the fallout from domestic violence and abuse, there wasn't one human emotion that she hadn't learned to cope with. Death was far easier to manage than a bitter struggle over a damaged child, her role so much more clearly defined than that of an advocate fighting an ugly case: gather the evidence and determine the cause of death. She was to the legal profession what the pathologist was to medicine: the last word.

Some things she never got used to. The heavy perfume of the mortuary – pine-scented detergent and decomposing flesh – was chief among them. A warm day in July was guaranteed to be close to intolerable. A virulent outbreak of hospital infection had been killing elderly patients at three times the normal rate for the past month. Superbugs loved the summer, and their victims were lined up on gurneys in the long straight corridor, two deep. Jenny instinctively covered her mouth as she hurried past and pushed through the swing doors into the autopsy room.

Dr Andy Kerr glanced up briefly from his work, then carried on, his muscular arms bare beneath the elbow save for a pair of blue latex gloves. He was dissecting the body of an emaciated young man with a shaved head, separating the lungs and removing them from the narrow ribcage. Two others, each wrapped in a shroud of white plastic, were waiting their turn for the knife.

'No locum today?' Jenny said, nodding towards the empty second table.

'Called in sick.'

'Coping?'

'No,' he said, in the unflappable Northern Irish way of his she had come to find so reassuring. 'Maybe when they can smell us in the staff canteen they'll hire in some more fridges.'

'I just wanted to check on a suspected suicide – Jordan. I doubt you've had a chance to look at him.'

'Only a glance.' He placed the lungs on the steel counter alongside the liver and heart, and rinsed his bloody gloves under the tap. 'It's that one there.'

She waited for him to dry his gloves on a paper towel and come over. He tugged his mask down beneath his chin and smiled. At thirty-five he still looked unnaturally youthful for a senior pathologist, his eyes bright and keen. His work was clearly suiting him.

'You told me you weren't squeamish any more,' Dr Kerr said. 'Have a go.'

Jenny shook her head. 'Please?'

He lifted the plastic by the corner and pulled it back to reveal a face that had been staved-in by an overwhelming impact. Jenny felt an involuntary shudder travel the length of her spine. There were no visible features remaining above the lower set of teeth. The torso was spectacularly bruised and most of the ribs were broken. The right arm lay straight, but the left was dislocated at the shoulder and broken in several places, fractured ends of bones jutting through the skin. Dr Kerr drew the sheet all the way back and revealed another massive set of injuries around the waist. The pelvis was shattered and both legs showed every sign of having been driven over by a large, heavy vehicle. Jenny's eyes went to his hands: they were almost untouched. The fingers were delicate and slender like a pianist's. There was one ring: a plain wedding band.

'Jumped from a motorway bridge,' Jenny said.

'Looks like it,' Dr Kerr said. 'I'd say he'd been run over several times. Look at the crushing injuries across the lower legs – that was done by big wide tyres.'

'No one stopped.'

'They never do.'

Over the initial shock, Jenny leaned forward for a closer look. She ran her eyes over the forearms, looking for the tell-tale signs of an addict, but there were none.

She noticed the skin was deeply suntanned above the waist and below the knees, and the man had been slim and muscular. No tattoos or other jewellery; no powerful smell of alcohol that usually accompanied male suicides.

'Anything in the clothing?' Jenny asked.

Dr Kerr shook his head and reached beneath the trolley for the list of effects that was kept alongside the bag containing the bloodstained clothes. He handed it to Jenny. It revealed that Jordan had been wearing jeans, a T-shirt, cotton sweater and canvas shoes. The police had retained his wallet. There was no record of a phone, money or keys – the usual items that men carried in their pockets – nor was there any evidence of prescription drugs.

Jenny said, 'We'd better have a full suite of tests on bloods and stomach contents. I've never known a suicide be entirely clean.' She turned away, Dr Kerr's cue to draw the plastic over the body.

'Is something troubling you?' he asked, reading her frown.

'No,' Jenny lied. 'I'm sure I'll learn a lot more from his wife. When can you have him ready?'

'Give me a couple of hours. We'll clean him up best we can.'

'Maybe a mask?'

Dr Kerr nodded. 'Don't worry.'

Jenny left the mortuary and crossed the car park to the main hospital building. She was dreading the encounter with the widow, not for all the usual reasons, but for the unusual ones she knew were coming. Fit, good-looking, well-dressed young men seldom jumped from motorway bridges; less still did they leave their two-year-old children to spend a night alone outdoors. It felt like the worst and most unsettling kind of death: a suicide that had come from nowhere.

Jenny heard the woman's anguished cries even before she had pushed through the door. They emanated from behind a curtain drawn around a bed in the children's ward, and were disturbing everyone within earshot. Staff exchanged glances, parents at other bedsides attempted to distract their fragile sons and daughters from the sound. Jenny was momentarily paralysed, overcome by the widow's all-consuming grief. She stopped and gathered strength, reminding herself she had to appear strong even if she didn't feel it.

A nurse appeared carrying an IV bag. Jenny intercepted her, fishing her identity wallet from her pocket. 'Jenny Cooper. Severn Vale District Coroner. I'm looking for Mrs Jordan.'

'I'm not sure now's a good a moment.' She nodded towards the curtained-off bed.

'Is the child all right?' Jenny asked.

'Mild hypothermia. It's not life-threatening.'

'The police said he wasn't found until this morning.'

'He was admitted just under three hours ago.'

The woman's cries grew louder. The nurse responded to the anxious faces up and down the ward. 'Excuse me.'

'This isn't helping him, is it?' Jenny heard her say patiently. 'Maybe it's best you come with me. Just for a while.'

Mrs Jordan was younger than Jenny had imagined, perhaps not yet thirty, with long, crow-black hair and wide blue eyes that her anguish did little to dull. There was no question of talking to her in her current state, but curiosity caused

Jenny to wait a moment longer while another nurse drew back the curtain to reveal a cot bed containing a tiny child. He was barely more than a toddler and was hooked-up to a heart monitor and several drips. He had his mother's eyes and they were wide open, staring unfocused into space.

Jenny felt the silent buzz of her phone. She fished it out of her pocket and saw her officer's name, Alison, on the screen. She headed out into the corridor to take the call.

'Mrs Cooper. Did DI Watling get hold of you?'

'Yes. I'm at the hospital now. I tried to call you.'

'Sorry. I was out of the office for a while.' She paused. 'How's the little boy?'

'Fine. Physically, at least.'

'Oh . . . Good.'

Jenny registered a flatness in Alison's voice and sensed that something was troubling her. 'What is it?'

'Nothing. Would you like me to visit the scene of death? We ought to have some pictures.'

'Won't the police have done that?'

'They've already emailed them. They're not very clear. What about where the boy was found?'

'Anything you think would be helpful.'

'Righto. I'll see you back at the office.'

'Alison?'

She had already rung off. Jenny held the phone in her hand for a moment, unsure whether to call back to tease from her whatever it was she had failed to say, but was interrupted by the nurse, who had appeared from a doorway to her right.

'Now might be a good moment, Mrs Cooper.'

Jenny looked at her, taking a moment to reorient her thoughts.

'I've told her you're waiting,' she said with a trace of

impatience. 'She's calmed down a little.' The nurse started back towards the ward.

Jenny approached the door. Pausing outside it, she glanced through the observation pane into an unoccupied side room. Beyond the empty bed, Karen Jordan was standing at the window looking out over rooftops to a line of distant hills. She wore jeans and a plain T-shirt that hugged her slender frame, and dabbed at her eyes with a wad of paper towel. Even with a door between them, Jenny felt her bewilderment like a radiating force. She knocked lightly and stepped inside.

'Mrs Jordan?'

The young woman turned, a sob catching in her throat.

Jenny moved cautiously towards her. 'Jenny Cooper. I'm the coroner.'

Karen Jordan stared at her with eyes frozen in an expression of shock.

'Would you mind if I asked a couple of questions about your husband?'

She shook her head, her lips clamped tightly together.

'His name was Adam Jordan?'

She nodded.

'His age?'

'Thirty-two.' The words came out in a hoarse whisper.

'Occupation?'

'He worked for a charity. It's called AFAD – Africa Aid and Development . . . He came back from South Sudan at the end of May.'

'Is there anything about your husband's state of mind that I ought to know?'

She shook her head violently, her hair sweeping across her face and clinging to her cheeks. 'No.'

'I was told he had parked at the Bristol Memorial Woodlands – that's a cemetery, isn't it?'

'A natural burial ground. Adam's father died last autumn. He'd gone there with Sam, that's all. I was working.'

'Sam's your son?'

She nodded.

'Was your husband close to his father?'

'I suppose—' Her voice cracked.

Thinking it better to get the painful conversation over quickly, Jenny persisted. 'Can you think of any reason why your husband may have taken his life, Mrs Jordan?'

'He didn't!'

'I see. And how do you know that?'

'He was my husband.' She stared at her with wild, enraged eyes. 'Don't you tell me I don't know my own husband!'

Jenny wanted to tell her the agony would pass, that as despairing as she felt now, it would not get any worse, but she was unreachable. There was no question of putting her through the ordeal of an identification. She turned to the door and quietly left her to cry herself out.

FOUR

FROM THE MOMENT SHE HAD ENTERED the mortuary
early that morning, Jenny had felt something intangible, a
deep, uneasy sensation that had stayed with her and intensified after her unhappy encounter with Jordan's widow. As
hard as she tried to be rational, she couldn't help acknow-
ledging her instinct that something about the dead man
hadn't *felt* right.

Dr Kerr, along with every other pathologist she had ever
met, seemed able to deal with each set of human remains
with the same degree of clinical distance: the flesh on the
table was nothing more than a forensic puzzle to be solved.
But for Jenny, each body carried its own complex atmospheres and stories. There were those empty shells from which
the soul had passed peacefully; those that still carried the
pain of a protracted struggle to cling to life; those that
seemed still frozen in the violent moment of suicide; and
those, like Jordan's, that hurled confusion at her. She had
dealt with more than a handful of bridge jumpers in her five
years in post, and all had had a history of depression or
worse. As suicides went, they were at the considerate end:
they had chosen an emphatic death away from the intimacy
of the home. Nearly all had jumped into water from either
the Severn or the Clifton Suspension Bridge. But a leap from
a motorway bridge was something altogether different. It

was an enraged choice made by someone intent on inflicting their suffering on the innocent strangers who would have the misfortune to run over their bodies. It spoke of a fury that bordered on the murderous.

Jenny carried these thoughts with her during the drive across the Downs, wearing thin and brown at the end of a dry spell that had lasted nearly a month. Descending the hill, she entered the bustling street-life of Whiteladies Road: crowded cafes and music throbbing out of a reggae record store, kids with waist-length dreadlocks dancing outside on the pavement and bemused old women stopping to watch.

The Georgian terrace in Jamaica Street where Jenny had her modest, two-room ground-floor offices was drenched in unaccustomed sunlight that showed up the cracking paint on the window frames and the rivulets in the ancient panes of glass. There was a faded grandeur about the slowly crumbling sandstone facade that might even inspire a level of awe in the casual visitor, but beyond the front step, the building she shared with three other sets of offices on the upper floors was tired and uncared-for. A worn carpet covered creaky boards in the hallway, and unclaimed junk mail spilled from a shelf which none of the tenants ever cleared. Jenny made her way along the passage to the heavy oak door that bore a dull brass plaque that read simply, 'Coroner'.

The reception area – the inviolable domain that belonged to Alison, her officer – was deserted. The magazines set out for visitors were neatly ordered. Jenny's bundle of messages and overnight death reports were precisely clipped together and sitting squarely in a brand-new wire tray. The papers that usually cluttered Alison's desk had been filed. Gone too was the array of sticky notes that invariably decorated the surround of Alison's computer monitor, along with the postcards and photographs that had covered the noticeboard behind her chair. Alison had done more than merely tidy. It felt like a purge. Jenny instinctively scanned the desk for some clue – there was always a reason for her officer having one of her irregular clear-outs; it was her way of imposing order on churning emotions – but all personal traces had been swept away.

Unsure whether the fresh sensation of unease she felt steal over her had been carried with her from the hospital or stirred by the unquiet atmosphere left in Alison's wake, Jenny moved through into the comforting disorder of her office on the far side of the connecting door. Files were stacked in heaps either side of the desk, books and papers covered every surface and much of the floor. It had been a more than usually hectic summer and Jenny sensed it was about to get busier.

A computer groaning with unread emails was waiting for her. Much of the mail was made up of the tedious circulars and bulletins that were spewed out daily by the Ministry of Justice, but one email was from DI Watling's station at Gloucester. Attached to the cursory message were scans of the papers in their file: statements from the traffic officers who had found Adam Jordan's body, several photographs of it lying *in situ*, a statement from the female officer who had discovered his child wandering in the memorial woodlands, and two photographs of Jordan's car as it was found, an elderly black Saab parked on a grass verge. Jenny noticed that the passenger door was open, there was a child seat in the back and what appeared to be a small wooden figurine hanging from the rear-view mirror. The final document was a scan of two petrol receipts found stuffed in the Saab's cup-holder, one several days old from a Texaco garage in Bristol, the other bearing yesterday's date from a filling station in

M. R. HALL

Great Shefford, Berkshire. The time code showed it was paid for at 5.45 p.m., along with a sandwich and several soft drinks.

Jenny clicked back to the photographs of the inside of the car and increased their size. There was very little to see. She homed in on the figurine and saw that it was a slender female form carved in dark wood, naked from the waist up. Recalling the one piece of useful piece of information Karen Jordan had managed to give her, she ran a search on AFAD. The Aid Agency's website popped up at the head of the list. Jenny opened it and surfed through its pages, learning that it was an organization operating chiefly in South Sudan, Ethiopia and Chad. Partnered with a host of environmental charities that shared the 'small is beautiful' philosophy, it seemed to concentrate its efforts on digging wells and setting up sustainable agriculture programmes in areas that had been ravaged by drought and famine. All the photographs were of Africans working for themselves; barely a white face featured. She searched the site for Jordan's name, but AFAD didn't appear to be an organization keen on personalities. Jenny quickly gained the impression that one worked for AFAD as you might for a church: for a higher purpose.

The agency had an office in central London and a contact number was listed. Professional etiquette dictated that it was largely the job of the coroner's officer to gather evidence, but in a small provincial outpost like Jenny's, the load tended to be shared a little more evenly than it would have been in better-funded jurisdictions. Jenny didn't need an excuse, however; she was impatient for an insight into Adam Jordan.

The phone was answered by an earnest-sounding young woman with an accent Jenny guessed to be Dutch.

Introducing herself, Jenny asked to speak to whoever was in charge.

34

'You can speak with me,' the girl said, 'we all share responsibility.'

'I see. And your name is—?'

'Eda. Eda Hincks.'

Jenny hesitated. 'I don't know if you've heard about Adam Jordan—'

'We have,' the young woman interjected. 'We are all very shocked.'

'The police are satisfied it was a suicide, but I now have to carry out my own inquiry. I appreciate it's very soon after the event, but would you be able to provide a statement for me?'

'I have no idea what happened.'

'I'd appreciate just a little background. The nature of his work, any personal details that you think may be relevant, or observations on his state of mind. Anything that might help me understand what was going on in his life.'

'I don't know what to say,' Eda replied. 'Adam was here last week. He was perfectly fine. It's such a shock . . .' She tailed off.

Jenny said, 'You don't feel there's anything immediately obvious I should know about?'

'No. He always seemed so happy. That's what we thought.'

'You knew him well?'

'Professionally, yes. Not so much socially.'

'Did he have a close colleague, someone he'd been working with abroad? His wife said he'd recently come back from Africa.'

'Yes—' Eda sounded hesitant.

'I assume he wasn't working alone?'

'No. He was in South Sudan with Harry. Harry Thorn.'

'May I have Mr Thorn's details?'

'I can give you his number, but I couldn't say for certain where he is. He's out of the office at the moment.'

'The number will be fine.'

Eda read it out to her, and then explained that he and Adam had recently completed a four-month tour of duty working on a trickle-irrigation project. They'd turned parched scrub into maize fields using buried pipes that drip-fed stored rainwater into the soil. It was a huge success, she seemed keen to emphasize; Adam had been delighted with it.

Jenny ended the call feeling that there was a subtext to Eda's account that she had failed to grasp. It was as if she had been apologizing for something. She tried Thorn's number – a mobile phone – but it was switched off with no voicemail.

Forced to wait for answers, Jenny turned to the pile of other cases that sat accusingly on the corner of her desk. July, along with January, was the most popular month for death. Pneumonia took the old in winter; in summer it was heart attacks and infection. But it wasn't only the old and sick that accounted for the rise. July was the month when the sunshine tricked the unwary into feeling invincible: they fell from ladders, crashed their motorbikes, tumbled drunk from balconies and drowned in rivers. Senseless, random deaths of the kind to which Jenny had never reconciled herself.

She was studying a photograph of a young woman's body – an evening of heavy drinking had caused the rupture of an undetected stomach ulcer, from which she had bled to death in her sleep – when she heard Alison's familiar footsteps pass her window and stop at the front door. Jenny listened to her movements. She heard Alison hang up her raincoat and step through to the kitchenette to make tea. She seemed to open and close the cupboard doors with a forced measuredness that told Jenny she was working hard to keep whatever she was suppressing firmly under control.

Her concentration disturbed by the tension, Jenny was eager to dispel it. She got up from her desk and went through to find Alison returning to her desk.

'Good morning, Alison,' Jenny said brightly.

'Afternoon, I think, Mrs Cooper. Nearly one o'clock.' Far from appearing depressed, Alison looked convincingly cheerful. Her face glowed with natural tan after a recent holiday in Cyprus, making her eyes appear startlingly white. Slim, tastefully dressed, she couldn't have looked more vital or any less like the former detective she was.

'Was it worth the trip?' Jenny asked. 'I didn't get much joy out of Mrs Jordan. She was in no fit state for anything.'

'Not much to see at the motorway. He was found about thirty yards from the bridge. He must have been swept along. Probably a lorry.' She settled at her desk, surveying its tidy surfaces with a smile of satisfaction. 'Did you notice I'd had a clear-out?'

'Yes,' Jenny said. 'Any particular reason?'

'You don't realize how much rubbish you've built up until you come to get rid of it.'

Jenny waited for the subtext to emerge, but Alison changed the subject and slotted a USB stick into her computer. 'I got some good photographs of Jordan's car, though – got there just before the police took it away.'

She called the first image up on to the screen: an unremarkable shot of the abandoned Saab.

'Should I be seeing something significant?' Jenny asked.

'Where he left it, for one thing. He hadn't gone as far as the car park. There's a snaking driveway off the lane. He'd pulled up on the verge.'

'What's in the field behind it? It looks like an orchard.'

'It's been planted with young trees – each one's a natural burial plot.'

'Is that where the child was found?'

'That was several fields away. It's a large site. I think he must have wandered. The passenger door was left open – maybe to let air in. He might have managed to undo his seatbelt and climb out.'

'But he's tiny—'

'The child seat was found with the buckle undone – look.' She clicked to an image showing the child seat in perfect detail, the restraints hanging over its sides.

'Or Jordan took the child with him out into the field, then went off alone,' Jenny speculated.

'Possibly.' Alison was dubious. 'It's odd, though. You'd think he would either have made sure the kid was safe or have taken him with him. Look, he left his keys in the ignition.'

Jenny scanned another picture of the front seats. On the passenger side were a sandwich wrapper, an empty carton of juice and two crumpled plastic water bottles. Suicidal, but not so thoughtless as to toss his rubbish out of the window.

'I forgot to ask his wife where home is,' Jenny said.

'Bath,' Alison replied. 'I think Watling said she's a post-grad at the university.'

She clicked to the final photograph: a wider angle of the whole interior.

Jenny studied it, aware of something feeling out of place. 'There was an object hanging from the rear-view mirror – it was there on the police photographs.'

Alison scrolled back through her pictures. 'Was there? I didn't see anything.'

'Hold on.'

Jenny walked back into her office and called up the email

from Gloucester CID. She opened the pictures taken by the police photographer, time-coded at 9.48 a.m. Hanging from the rear-view mirror was a wooden figurine. 'Look – here it is.'

Joining her, Alison peered at the monitor. 'No, I didn't see anything like that. Perhaps the police took it? It's possible.'

Before Alison could come up with an alternative explanation, the phone rang on her desk. While she hurried out to reception to answer it, Jenny zoomed in further on the figurine until, blurring at the edges, it filled half her screen. Close up it looked crude, something whittled at the fireside rather than a precious object. It hung from a rough leather thong attached to a small metal loop screwed into the crown of the skull.

'It's Mrs Jordan, for you,' Alison called through. 'She sounds a bit fraught. Shall I deal with her?'

'I'll take it.' Jenny picked up the handset on her desk. 'Mrs Jordan?'

Karen Jordan responded in a dull yet determined, heavily medicated voice. 'I want to see my husband.'

'There's no hurry. An identification can wait until tomorrow. Or perhaps he has another close relative—'

'I want to see him now,' Mrs Jordan said. 'I have a right.'

Jenny was in no position to dispute that.

'Where are you now?'

'At the hospital. Where else would I be?'

'I can you meet you at the mortuary at two o'clock.'

'Fine.' She rang off.

Jenny put down the phone to see Alison at the doorway. 'You don't have to do that, Mrs Cooper. I'll go.'

'I'd like to speak to her anyway.'

'You've got more than enough to see to.' Alison nodded

at the untidy heap on Jenny's desk. There was a hint of desperation in her offer, as if she couldn't bear to be left in the office alone.

'She's expecting me. She's very fragile.'

Alison nodded, smiling so widely it threatened to crack her face, and turned back to her desk.

'Is everything all right?' Jenny asked.

She glanced back. 'Perfectly, thank you, Mrs Cooper.'

They both knew it wasn't true.

Karen Jordan was waiting alone outside the entrance to the mortuary, her pretty face as grey as winter. Jenny drove past in the Land Rover and parked behind the building, out of sight. She knocked at the service entrance that was used largely by undertakers and was shielded from the hospital car park by a pair of painted metal screens. It was a tawdry spot, littered with broken plastic cups and cigarette ends that the caretakers and cleaners seemed to have forgotten existed. The junior technician who opened the door looked surprised to see her there.

She skipped the explanation. 'I need to see Dr Kerr.'

'He's in his office.'

Jenny stepped through into the loading bay, passing several bagged bodies stacked on the floor awaiting collection, and continued on into the main corridor. Andy Kerr came to the door of his office wiping crumbs from his mouth. How he could eat lunch at his desk with cadavers lying on the other side of the door was beyond her understanding.

'Ah, Mrs Cooper. I was just about to call you.'

She closed the door behind her, shutting out the worst of the mortuary's nauseating aroma.

'Did you find anything? His wife's outside – I wanted to check.'

'Nothing. That's the oddity. No alcohol in the blood, no

sign of drugs in the stomach. I got hold of his medical records, but apart from some harmless anti-malarials, he's had nothing prescribed in five years. No depression either, as far as I can tell.'

'Cause of death?'

'Massive crushing injuries, and multiple haemorrhages. I'd say there's more than a sporting chance he struck a vehicle before he hit the road.'

'Had he eaten?'

'A few hours before – maybe three. All that was in his stomach was water.'

Jenny pictured the empty bottles on the passenger seat. 'How much water?'

'A cupful. It's hard to say. It can take time to be absorbed after death.'

'He'd walked a mile and a half from his car. There were two empty 300ml water bottles in it. Does that make sense?'

'That seems about right.'

Biologically perhaps, but Jenny wondered about a sober man who calmly drank water before hurling himself from a road bridge. The two actions seemed incompatible somehow.

'He was an aid worker. He'd spent a lot of time in Africa, apparently. Might that make you look for something out of the ordinary?'

Dr Kerr shook his head. 'Forensically, all I found was trauma. Injuries aside, he was a perfectly healthy specimen.' He gave an apologetic shrug. 'The boys have tidied him the best they could.'

'Thank you,' Jenny said. 'I know you're crowded, but if you don't mind, I shan't be releasing the body for burial just yet. Not until I have some answers.'

He gave a resigned smile. 'What possible difference could one more make?'

*

Jenny led Mrs Jordan in from the main entrance. The long walk down the corridor to the refrigeration unit took them past trolleys stacked two, sometimes three deep. At times such as this, when the mortuary was overwhelmed, the technicians employed what they called a carousel, giving each body that was more than a day old a turn in the fridge until it chilled down to below five degrees. Mrs Jordan passed them without a sideways glance, the light stolen from her eyes by sedating drugs.

They arrived at the fridge. Joe, the junior technician Jenny had met at the door, slid open a tray on the bottom stack of three and gave Jenny a look, awaiting her instruction.

Jenny turned to Mrs Jordan. 'I'm afraid you won't be able to identify your husband facially. I'd like to ask you to do it from his hands, if that's possible.'

Karen Jordan shook her head. 'I want to see all of him.'

Jenny glanced at the technician. 'Can you show us the hands, please?'

He leaned down to pull back the flap of plastic at waist level.

'I said, I want to see all of him,' Karen Jordan insisted.

'I really wouldn't advise—'

'Are you telling me I can't see my husband's face?' She spoke with a level and determined assurance that didn't seem to come from the same woman that Jenny had met outside the paediatric ward. It was as if the drugs had allowed only the coldest part of her to remain conscious.

'If you're absolutely sure.'

'Show me.'

Jenny nodded to the technician, who pulled the flap back a little more.

'All the way,' Mrs Jordan said.

The hands and arms came into view, and then the savage, crudely stitched autopsy scar than ran from neck to navel along the midline. A separate, oval-shaped piece of plastic covered the staved-in features.

'I said *all*,' Mrs Jordan said. 'Do I have to do it myself?'

She moved half a step forward. Jenny touched her arm, holding her back, and indicated to the technician to do as she requested.

He lifted the covering clear. Jenny glanced away, but Mrs Jordan's gaze held steady. She took in every detail, forcing herself to record the image that would never leave her.

'It's Adam,' she said, then dipped at the knees and touched his still-perfect fingers with a whispered goodbye. As she straightened, she turned to Jenny and said, 'I suppose we should talk. You probably know more than I do.'

They sat in the staff section of the hospital canteen where they served strong, rich Italian coffee that wasn't for sale at the public counter. Karen Jordan glanced out of the window, her expression saying she was trying to find something that would make sense of it all.

Jenny said, 'I spoke to a girl called Eda – at the office in London. She said your husband was there last week and in good spirits.'

'He always was,' Karen said. 'He was laughing and fooling about with Sam when I left yesterday morning. He doesn't—' She paused to correct herself: 'Adam *didn't* get depressed. It wasn't in his nature.'

'Nothing had upset him recently?'

She shook her head. 'Not that he told me.'

'No arguments?'

'No . . . No more than usual.' She pushed her hair back from her forehead, a nervous gesture. 'We're both busy with work, we've a young child – you know how it is.'

'Was Adam good with your little boy?'

'Always.'

They lapsed into silence, Jenny beginning to feel that maybe it was too soon to push Karen for reasons. She had yet to encounter a suicide of a grown man that defied explanation, but sometimes it took a bereaved wife a little while to admit to herself that she hadn't read the signs. The best Jenny could do was to ease the process along.

'You should understand, Mrs Jordan, that people determined to kill themselves don't want to be stopped. The pathologist found no alcohol or drugs in your husband's system. He died in full control of himself.'

'He hardly drank anyway. He certainly didn't touch drugs.' Karen Jordan seemed offended at the suggestion that he might have done.

'I'm sorry. I didn't mean to imply anything.'

'We've known each other four years, been married for two, and for half that time he's been in South Sudan. When he's home we get along, and when he's away . . .' She faltered, aware that she'd mixed up her tenses again. 'We didn't know everything about each other, but who does? We didn't choose to live in each other's pockets, but Adam was very committed – to his work and to me. We trusted each other completely. We had no reason not to.'

'And your marriage—'

'We didn't sleep with other people, if that's what you mean,' Karen Jordan said sharply.

'It isn't.'

'Really?' Karen looked at her accusingly. 'It didn't happen. The plan was that when I'd finished my PhD we were going to find an African project to work on together. We didn't choose to live apart deliberately, it was just how things worked out.'

She felt guilty. Jenny could feel it seeping its way out from beneath the chemical layers.

'Eda Hincks told me your husband had been working with a man called Harry Thorn.'

'That's right,' Karen answered flatly.

'Were they close?'

'They'd worked together for the best of three years. Ethiopia, then Sudan.'

'You sound a little . . .' Jenny searched for the appropriate word, 'ambivalent.'

Karen shrugged. 'There's no rule saying that only saints can work in the aid business.'

'Would you like to tell me about him?'

'About Harry? What for?'

'I ought to talk to him, Mrs Jordan. It would help me to have some background.'

She gave a reluctant sigh. 'He's worked in the field for over twenty-five years—' She stopped herself mid-sentence. 'I don't want to talk about him. You can judge for yourself.' She turned her gaze out of the window, retreating inwards again.

Jenny said, 'There was a wooden figurine hanging up in the car your husband was driving.'

'What about it?' she said, from far away. 'It was just something Adam brought back from Africa.'

'The police haven't given it to you?'

She shook her head, still distracted.

'Does it hold any significance?'

'It's just a Dinka doll. I think someone out in South Sudan gave it to him.' She breathed out sharply.

'Do you know who?'

'No. He didn't say.' She was growing impatient. 'I should be with Sam now. I have to go.'

'Of course.'

Karen pushed unsteadily to her feet, leaning on the table

for support as she fought against the light-headedness caused by the drugs.

'What's "Dinka" mean?' Jenny asked.

'They're a race of people who live in South Sudan.'

'I suppose I should know that.'

The widow looked at her for a moment as if there was something more she wanted to say but couldn't find the words. And then, just as they seemed to form, a silencing shadow appeared to pass over her. She turned away, and walked quickly to the exit.

FIVE

JENNY HAD BECOME USED TO sleeping alone. During the rare nights Michael stayed over she would often find herself lying awake, disconcerted by his presence and unsettled by his fitful dreams. But after several weeks without his company the lonely ache returned and she wished he were next to her again. They had never settled anything that could be called an 'arrangement', but had simply fallen into an irregular routine of spending the odd night at each other's homes, and somehow it seemed to work. Dr Allen had, of course, isolated the one problem that was nagging at her during their final appointment: she and Michael didn't talk, or at least not in the way that lovers were meant to. When she had been married to David they had found themselves with less and less to say to each other except during their frequent and eloquent arguments. Her former lover, Steve, had been the opposite: sensitive and concerned, almost too eager to prise her open and share her most intimate thoughts. Michael was neither intrusive nor hostile; like her, he was naturally self-contained. And there was the nub: they ran on parallel rails. Both damaged goods, both healed just enough to get by, but both frightened of taking the next step for fear of missing it and finding themselves floundering in midair.

Drawing back the curtains, Jenny blinked in the piercing morning light and looked out over the valley falling away from her window all the way down to the River Wye. Here and there clusters of stone-walled fields interrupted the ancient woodlands that had hugged the hills for millennia. A memory surfaced: she had been looking out at the same view on another summer morning with Steve. *It's all there waiting for you, Jenny, you just have to reach out and take it.* For a moment she could almost feel his hands resting on her hips and the warmth of his breath on her neck, and she wished she had never let him go. He was living happily in France now with a beautiful young wife and a newborn; he had moved on, but she remained behind the same glass, still looking out. She caught her reflection ghosted in the pane: time was tugging at her face. She stiffened with defiance. She had to resist; she had to do something.

'Michael? It's Jenny. Are you free this evening?'

'Mmm? I think so . . .' His voice was still thick with sleep.

'Sorry. Have I woken you?'

'It's all right, I should be up. I've got a round trip to Le Mans.'

In the height of summer he was at his busiest. As a pilot for a small commercial firm, when he wasn't flying jockeys between race courses, he was ferrying wealthy businessmen and their over-indulged families between their summer playgrounds and the city. It was hardly the adrenalin rush he had experienced in his twenty years flying RAF Tornadoes, but it had its dramas. When the phone rang at unexpected times, she would often find herself worrying that it was a call to say his Cessna had failed to arrive at some obscure airfield, that he was missing.

'You won't be able to come to dinner then?'

'I didn't know I was invited.'

'I'm picking Ross up from university today. He's staying for a couple of weeks. I thought you might start getting to know each other.'

Jenny waited for his excuse, expecting him to avoid anything that sounded like a dangerous step on the road to commitment.

He surprised her. 'Sounds good to me. Is eight all right?'

'Great.' She hesitated. 'And you'll stay over?'

'With your son there?'

'He won't mind.' She added, 'It's been ages.'

'Nearly two weeks.'

He'd been counting. She was touched.

Jenny had arranged to collect Ross from the Goldsmiths student halls at four, and planned to spend the early afternoon shopping for clothes in Covent Garden, a luxury so rare and indulgent, the prospect felt almost sinful. She told herself she would be looking for a suit to replace the tired two-piece she wore to court, but as she headed out onto the motorway, she was already putting together the outfit she would surprise Michael with: she pictured herself slim, stylish and elegant, looking ten years younger. Absorbed in the fantasy, she didn't notice the miles passing. Alison's several phone calls barely registered as she enjoyed the heady rush of a day unchained from the office. Freedom. As she approached Heathrow the phone rang again. She glanced at the caller display, expecting another query from Alison designed to make her feel guilty for deserting her post, but it was a number her phone didn't recognize.

'Hello. Jenny Cooper.'

'Are you the woman who left a message this morning?' The man spoke with a thick, deep South African accent.

'I'm the Severn Vale District Coroner. Who am I speaking to?'

'Harry Thorn. I worked with Adam Jordan.'

'Ah yes. I did leave a message.' She proceeded delicately. 'I presume you've heard what's happened to him.'

'Of course. What do you want from me?'

'I spoke with Mrs Jordan yesterday,' Jenny said tactfully. 'I'll be conducting an inquest into her husband's death. When you're able, I was hoping to meet with you – to get a picture of what he'd been doing recently, his state of mind, whether anything had been troubling him. Might tomorrow suit you?'

Thorn said, 'I've no fucking clue why he jumped off a bridge, if that's what you're fishing for.'

'I appreciate now's not the time.'

Thorn gave a low grunt. 'Your office said you're in London today. Why don't we get it over with?'

'If you're sure.' Jenny felt her day darken. 'Where will I find you?'

'15a Quentin Mews, off Portobello Road.'

Jenny's hazy memory of Portobello Road was of the Saturday antiques market, the narrow street crammed with stalls selling Victorian prints, cracked china and the kind of old trinkets that used to fill her grandmother's house. But on a weekday it was almost deserted. All that remained of the market was a handful of fruit-and-vegetable stalls.

Quentin Mews was off the poorer, dirtier end of the street within yards of the Westway, the thundering flyover that carried four lanes of traffic between White City and Marylebone. Picking her way over its rough cobbles in her narrow heels, Jenny realized that the outward scruffiness was an illusion. There were no electric gates guarding the mews entrance or neatly clipped bay trees either side of the front doors, but money, even the kind that tries to hide itself, has a smell, and it leached out of the artfully soot-stained bricks.

15a was at the far end of the cul-de-sac, the house furthest from the street. She rang, and waited for some time for Harry Thorn to come to the door. Closer to fifty than forty, he stood barefoot in jeans and a crumpled linen shirt; his thick grey stubble was longer than the hair on his broad, sunburned scalp. He was tall, with square shoulders that suggested he had once been well built, but his muscles had withered onto a bony frame, and his yellowing eyes were those of a man whose lifetime of hard living was fast catching up with him.

'Jenny, is it?'

She nodded. 'You're Mr Thorn?'

'Harry.'

He turned and led the way through the short hallway into a compact sitting room with French windows that opened onto a tiny courtyard barely big enough to hold a table and two chairs. A set of louvred doors divided the room from a galley kitchen. Thorn had been smoking marijuana; Jenny could smell it on his clothes, as distinctive as leaves on an autumn bonfire. He pressed a heavily veined hand to his forehead as he surveyed the furniture: a low-slung sofa and several African floor cushions, none of it appropriate for conducting a formal discussion.

'Guess we'd better sit outside.'

Jenny heard footsteps from the floor above, then music: a slow heavy bass rhythm that pulsed through the whole house.

'Will you turn that damn thing off, Gabra,' Thorn yelled. 'I've got a meeting here.'

'Fuck you, Harry,' a relaxed female voice called back.

He waited, looking thunderous. When she had made her point, the woman upstairs lowered the volume slightly.

Thorn shook his head. 'Sorry about her. She can be a pain in the ass.'

Jenny said nothing and followed him outside, where they sat on iron chairs at a marble-topped table.

'Mind if I smoke?'

'Go ahead.'

Thorn took a soft leather pouch from his shirt pocket and proceeded to roll a joint.

Jenny glanced away, thinking her time would have been better spent shopping after all.

'What can I tell you?' he said.

'Were you close to Adam Jordan?'

'Shared a tent with him for the last year, and most of the two years before that.' He twisted one end of the cigarette paper and put the other to his mouth. Jenny noticed the tremor in his fingers as he struck a match.

'Sounds like you were somewhere pretty remote.'

'South Sudan. I guess that's about as far off the trail as you can get outside of the Sahara.'

'Putting in irrigation, I hear.'

'No,' he corrected her. 'We subsidize the kit, show them how to dig the trenches, hook it all up to a well. They do the work.'

'Helping them to help themselves.'

'Only way.' He dragged the fumes into his lungs and held on to them, the tight lines on his forehead starting to slacken as the dope seeped into his blood.

'Does it work?'

'Like a dream – until some bastard comes along and rips it all out again.'

'Who would do that?'

'That's Africa. Tribal factions slitting each other's throats since the dawn of time. It's like a bad habit.'

Jenny felt his anger buffeting against her like a hot wind. She waited until she sensed the flare of emotion had burned itself out.

'Something must keep people like you and Adam Jordan going back.'

'You get to save a few, sometimes even a whole crowd. It's a numbers game: life in your average East African village is plentiful and cheap.' He leaned back in his chair and slowly blew smoke towards the sky like an offering. 'If you're keeping more above ground than beneath, you're ahead.'

Jenny said, 'Did Adam enjoy his work?'

'Oh, yeah. He'd talk irrigation like a born-again talks Jesus. He was going to help them bypass all the industrial crap we've been through the last two hundred years and lead them straight to eco-paradise. I'm not making fun of the guy – it's what you need out in the field to keep going: a vision.' His eye was caught by something inside the house. 'Shit.'

Jenny glanced round and saw a tall, slender woman strolling naked across the sitting room. She was beautiful and graceful, her skin the colour of oiled ebony.

'Will you put some clothes on, Gabra, for Christ's sake,' Thorn shouted.

Ignoring him, she continued into the kitchen. Her voice travelled through the open window. 'You two want something to eat? I'm making eggs.'

'I want you to get fucking dressed.'

Jenny shrugged, as if to say she had no problem with Gabra going naked if that's how she liked it.

'I must be getting old,' Thorn said. The tension lines reappeared on his face. He sucked hard on the joint. 'What else?'

Jenny said, 'Any indication as to his recent state of mind?'

'He was a serious guy. Motivated. Had a Master's degree in environmental science. The kind who's always in a book or at his computer. Drank a little beer but never so much as you'd see any change.'

'Was he happy?'

'He seemed to be. We had a good project, left a village

with green fields where there'd been a dust bowl. We had to quit a little early because of some local trouble, but that's how it goes. It doesn't get much better than that out there.'

'You didn't notice anything upset him?'

Harry thought about it and shook his head. 'Not in Africa. He couldn't wait to go back. We were due in Chad next month.'

'On a similar project?'

'Bigger. A real game-changer – five thousand acres.'

Jenny ran through her mental checklist of issues to cover in suspected suicides. 'Any financial problems that you were aware of?'

Thorn smiled. 'Hand to mouth, like we all are. No bastard chooses this life for the money.'

Jenny thought his answer odd. Small as it was, Thorn's house wouldn't have come cheap. 'You're sure he hadn't got into any kind of trouble—?'

'I'm the one who gets into trouble,' he glanced towards the kitchen, 'not Adam.'

'What about his marriage?'

'Karen's a good woman.'

Jenny detected a note of hesitancy.

'Is there a "but"?'

'Look, no one's going to pretend that a man away from home most of the year is going to live like a monk, but as they go, I'd say Adam came as close as damnit.'

'He had lovers?'

'No, not like that.'

'Then like what?'

'I don't know. Maybe he screwed the odd girl, maybe he didn't – I wasn't watching that closely. But if he did, it was no big deal. Look, you're asking me why this serious, good-hearted man I worked with jumped off a bridge – I have no goddamn idea.'

'Was he the kind who might have carried a lot of guilt if he had done something he regretted?'

'I never saw Adam get into anything he would regret. He didn't take risks. He was a planner. No . . .' Thorn seemed to search through his foggy memory, then shook his head. 'If something was weighing on his mind, I'd say it went way back. Way back, before anything I could tell you about.'

'Did he ever talk about his past?'

'I'm not the type people confide in,' Harry said. 'I don't want that shit when I'm working. Or any time,' he added, with a glance towards Gabra.

Jenny had already seen enough of Harry Thorn to agree with his self-assessment. She imagined his answer to most of life's problems would be to get stoned and feel the relief of not being dirt poor and trapped in a fly-blown African village. Her gut instinct told her that Adam Jordan would have needed more than that: he was an idealist, still hoping to leave the world a better place than he had found it.

'Do you want to see some pictures of the last project?' Thorn asked.

'Thank you. I'd like that.'

He heaved himself out of his chair and disappeared inside.

As Jenny waited, she couldn't help sneaking a glance at Gabra. Standing at the stove frying eggs, she was as content in her body as it was possible to be. Jenny found herself momentarily entranced by the curve of her neck, the tautness of her small breasts, the sheen on her flawless skin.

Gabra looked round and smiled out at her. Quietly, so that only the two of them could hear, she said, 'Something you should know about Harry – he's not as tough as he makes out.'

Jenny said, 'I guessed that.'

The naked woman returned calmly to her cooking.

When Thorn reappeared with a handful of photographs,

he didn't seem to want to talk any more. He sat in silence rolling another joint, leaving Jenny to make of them what she would. The pictures were of him and Adam in a Sudanese village in which large, family-sized huts really were made of mud and thatched with straw. In two of them Adam was surrounded by laughing, skinny children, grinning broadly. His eyes seemed to shine out at her like points of light. She noticed the villagers wore a mix of traditional dress and Western clothes; many of the adults had ceremonial scars on their foreheads. Some of the men had picks and spades; others carried hunting bows. It seemed a place in flux, caught between two worlds, like the men who had come to help them.

Jenny said, 'Has Karen Jordan seen these?'

Harry Thorn shook his head. 'Take them. And tell her I'm sorry. I truly am.'

Jenny hardly recognized the smiling, confident young man who greeted her outside the student halls. During his two years at university Ross seemed to have gained all the confidence she associated with his father, while managing to avoid acquiring his arrogance.

'Hey – you're looking well.' Ross leaned down and hugged her, then kissed her cheek.

'Wow, I'm privileged,' Jenny said. She couldn't remember the last time he had been so affectionate.

'It's the end of term – I'm feeling good. Go with it.'

That was fine with her. After six years during which she had feared their relationship had broken irretrievably, there were finally signs that the damage was being mended.

Loading his luggage into the boot of her car, Ross said, 'Where are all the bags? I thought you were hitting the shops.'

'Change of plan.'

'Working too hard?'

'Don't worry – I'm learning.'

She smiled and won one back from him. It was warm and trusting, the smile he had given her as a little boy.

As they pulled away and headed west through the hectic traffic, Ross said, 'You're sure you don't mind putting me up? I know you're busy.'

'You can stay as long as you like – it'll be fun. How's the new girlfriend – Sarah?'

'Not that new – six weeks. She's fine, and her name's Sally. She's gone to stay with her dad in Brighton for a bit – it's complicated.'

'Aren't all families?'

'Not like hers. He left her mum for another guy.'

'All right, I concede. That beats even us.'

'I couldn't tell Dad. God knows what he'd say to her.'

Jenny felt a guilty satisfaction at the thought that for the first time since she and David had separated, Ross might be seeing her as the closer ally.

'I'd like to meet her. She's welcome to stay any time.'

'Cool. She'd like that.'

Jenny waited for his mood to dip, as it so often did when they were alone together, but against her expectations Ross remained upbeat, giving her a full unprompted rundown of his term's activities, his spell as an intern in a City bank and the complex love lives of his flatmates. As they made their way across St James's Park and Hyde Park Corner towards Knightsbridge, Jenny allowed herself to believe that he was letting her back into the life he had excluded her from since the day she'd left the family home. They felt like friends again.

London's green western fringes were finally dissolving into

the Berkshire countryside when Jenny found the courage to edge the conversation around to the subject of her own faltering love life. 'Did I tell you I'm still seeing Michael?'

'I think so,' Ross said vaguely. 'He's the pilot, right?'

'He used to be in the Air Force.' She was a little hurt by his evident lack of interest. 'I know you've only met him once, so I thought it might be nice if he came over this evening and said hello.' She braced herself for a negative reaction, but again he surprised her.

'Sure. No problem.'

'Really? I can put him off to another day.'

'What do I have to say? It's fine.' He touched her arm as if to reinforce the point, and Jenny couldn't believe her luck.

It was one of the few precious summer evenings when the air was perfectly still and warm. Waiting for Michael to arrive, Jenny and Ross sat outside at the weather-worn pine table, drinking wine and talking about his plans for the future. His tutor had suggested business school, and hinted that if he studied hard enough he might even win a scholarship. It seemed so recently that he had been a surly sixteen-year-old on the brink of throwing away his education, but having struck out on his own, he seemed to have found a passion. His innocent hunger for life was infectious.

Michael's car pulled up in the cart track at the side of the house only a few minutes after eight. He appeared clutching a bottle of wine and dressed in a clean white shirt and the navy linen jacket Jenny had bought him for Christmas. She felt proud of him as he approached. He was dark and slim and carried his masculinity easily, with no attempt to posture. He glanced at Ross and Jenny could see that he was self-conscious as he stepped forward to greet him.

'Hi. Good to meet you again,' Michael said.

'And you.'

They shook hands, Ross looking him squarely in the eye just as his father had taught him to since he was a small boy.

'How was the trip to France?' Jenny asked.

'No problem. Perfect day for it.'

She gestured him to a chair and poured drinks, feeling suddenly and irrationally nervous.

'What kind of planes do you fly?' Ross asked.

'Props. Light aircraft.'

'His company has a contract to fly jockeys between race courses,' Jenny said.

'Kind of an upmarket chauffeur,' Michael added apologetically.

'Mum said you flew fighter jets,' Ross said. 'You must have seen a lot of action.'

'Here and there.' Michael glanced at Jenny and took a large mouthful of wine.

'You would have been in Afghanistan?'

'Yes. I was,' Michael answered quietly.

Jenny shot Michael an apologetic glance, regretting having raised the subject.

'What about Iraq?'

Michael nodded.

Jenny tried to change the subject. 'Ross is studying economics—'

His usual sensitivity blunted by the wine, Ross failed to take the hint. 'That must have been intense.'

Michael said, 'That's one word for it.' He stared into his glass, then stood up from the table and glanced at Jenny. 'Won't be a moment.' He went inside, closing the outside door that led to the kitchen behind him.

Too late, Ross realized his clumsiness. 'He doesn't like to talk about it. You didn't tell me.'

'I should have done. I'm sorry. He'll be fine.'

'Bad experiences?'

59

'A few.' She touched his hand. 'We'll talk about something else, shall we?'

'He could have just told me he didn't want to talk about it.'

'It's all fine. No big deal.'

She smiled, hoping to smooth things over, but like his father, Ross was quick to suffer wounded pride when he'd been made to feel foolish. He reached for the bottle and refilled his glass.

Following the bumpy start, conversation between the three of them failed to find a natural flow. During dinner, Jenny found herself having to make all the running. Michael was quiet, nervous that he was being presented for Ross's approval. Ross made gallant efforts at small talk, but the more he groped for subjects on neutral ground, the more artificial the atmosphere between the three of them became. Jenny was relieved when it was time to clear the plates and retreat briefly to the sanctuary of the kitchen.

Michael came in behind her with the dirty glasses and set them down on the counter. Sensing her tension, he placed a hand tentatively on her shoulder, half expecting her to slap it away. 'Sorry I've not been better company tonight. Tired, I guess.'

'Can't you just have a few drinks and relax?'

'I've tried—'

'What's the problem?'

'Nothing, it's just . . .'

She waited.

'I feel like I'm on show.'

'He's not judging you, Michael,' Jenny whispered. 'This was meant to be fun.'

'I know. I'm sorry. Look, I've got another early flight tomorrow. I don't think I should stay tonight.'

'Why not? Ross doesn't mind. He knows we're together.'

'We've only just met.'

'So?'

Michael was saved from explaining himself by the telephone ringing in the sitting room. Jenny glanced at the clock above the old cast-iron range – it was nearly 10.30.

'Aren't you going to answer it?' Michael said.

'I'm not sure I want to.'

Ross burst through the back door from the garden. 'It might be Sally.' He ran through to pick it up. 'Hello? . . . Oh, hi, Dad.'

Jenny grasped Michael's hand. 'Please stay. He'll be fine. I've missed you.'

Yielding, he kissed her lightly on the lips, and in their brief moment of connection the awkwardness between them dissolved. His hands held her waist; she felt their warmth through the fabric of her shirt and longed to feel them on her skin.

'If you're sure it's all right.'

'I told you it is.' She held his gaze.

He reached for her hand and delicately stroked her palm with his fingertips in a promise of what was to come.

Ross came to the door. His expression was serious. 'Mum—?'

Jenny kept hold of Michael's hand even as he tried to tug it away.

'Yes?'

'Dad wants to talk to you.'

'Your father? What about?' She steeled herself. A call from David could only ever mean he was angry, usually about something she had done.

'It's about a colleague of his – Ed someone?'

'Ed Freeman?'

Ross nodded. 'His daughter's died.'

Jenny hurried through to the sitting room and grabbed the receiver.

'David? Ross said Ed Freeman's—'

'Yes,' he interrupted, in the clipped, urgent tone he used in a crisis. 'Sophie fell ill this morning and died at five o'clock this afternoon. I only just heard.'

'I'm so sorry.' Jenny pictured David's one and only god-daughter as a pretty, black-haired girl of eight, but knew she must be a teenager by now. 'What happened?'

'Some sort of infection. That's all I know.'

'Should I call them?'

David said, 'I would be careful about that. She died in the Vale. You're going to be the coroner and Ed's going to want some answers . . .'

'What is it, David?'

'I need to talk to you properly. Can you get into town for six?'

'In the morning?'

'My list starts at seven. Shall we meet in my office?'

And just as she had during fifteen years of marriage, Jenny agreed to do as he asked.

SIX

THEY HAD SLEPT TOGETHER like married couples did, avoiding rather than seeking out each other's touch. Jenny wasn't so much grieving for the bright, pretty girl she remembered from the family parties of her former existence, as shocked by the thought of a vibrant life so suddenly extinguished. Her mood had rubbed off on Michael, who was shifting and turning in a restless, nightmare-haunted sleep. She could tell he was back in the cockpit, raining fire on dusty villages, tormented by images of broken bodies and bloody sand. Feeling for him, she reached over and stroked his arm, but he'd jerked away from her, leaving her feeling more isolated lying next to him than she would have done alone. Ross had reacted to the news of Sophie Freeman's death with a concerned formality that hid whatever lay beneath. She had never understood why men found it so hard to express perfectly normal emotions. Did they feel more or less acutely than she did? Where, she wondered, did all those tears go?

She left the house before either of them woke, leaving them, she hoped, to make more of a success communicating with each other over breakfast than they had at dinner. She trusted Michael to make an attempt, but Ross remained a partial mystery to her; just as she thought she was learning to predict his reactions, he wrong-footed her again. She had tried. If they loved her, they would, too.

She approached David's consulting room on the third floor of the Severn Vale District Hospital with a sharpening sensation of dread. A consultant cardio-thoracic surgeon, his working life had been spent exclusively with patients confronted with their mortality. Approving of those who went under the knife without a word of complaint, and dismissive of those who 'whimpered and blubbed', he had treated Jenny's 'episode' (he had refused ever to call it a breakdown) as if it were something akin to an embarrassing skin complaint. During the numb, lifeless months after she had been rendered helpless, he would look at her uncomprehendingly, as if frightened that if he drew too close he might catch the contagion, too. She knocked, feeling all the old history rushing back to meet her.

He answered the door with an abruptness that made her start.

'Jenny. I didn't think you'd make it. Come in.'

David's room was as functional and forbidding as she remembered it; a place to feel the cold press of a stethoscope and bleak words of diagnosis from a man as enviably fit as a fifty-year-old could hope to be. It was as if his tall, lean squash-player's frame radiated judgement against the weak-willed and sick.

Jenny purposefully avoided sitting in the patient's chair and instead stood by the desk, a gesture intended to show him she was here as an equal, not as someone to be managed.

'Ed must be devastated,' Jenny said.

'He and his wife both. I've seen quite a lot of him lately on the consultants' committee. He was a devoted father.' Frightened of appearing too emotional, David changed the subject. 'I'm afraid I've no coffee to offer you.'

'That's all right.'

David stood uncomfortably in the middle of the room, unsure where to place himself, then stepped over to the window and propped himself against the sill, his arms folded beneath defined chest muscles that pressed hard against his shirt. Even discussing his colleague's dead daughter, it seemed, he felt the need to impress her.

Jenny said, 'You said it was an infection.'

'It appears so.'

'Do we know what kind?'

'A strain of meningitis, I'm told. It happened so quickly I doubt the lab will have detailed results until later this morning.' David avoided her gaze and stared down at his shoes, a tic he'd had ever since they first met aged twenty-two. It usually meant he had something difficult to say.

Jenny knew she would have to coax him along. 'What did you want to talk to me about?'

'The infection ... It was an odd one. She went off to school perfectly well, complained of dizziness and temperature at lunchtime and collapsed shortly afterwards. Never regained consciousness. As far as I can tell, they pumped her full of broad-spectrum antibiotics but they didn't make a dent. Ed didn't tell me all the symptoms but I get the impression it was pretty rough – fitting, generalized oedema. I think she was haemorrhaging badly towards the end.'

'Aren't those the symptoms of meningitis?'

'I'm told you would usually expect the antibiotics to make some inroads. It's odd.'

He looked away again, wrestling with unspoken thoughts.

'I presume you asked me here in my capacity as coroner?'

'Naturally.'

'Is that all you wanted to tell me?'

She had already made the assumption that Ed or his wife, a clinical psychologist, had overlooked warning signs or

ignored early symptoms. She was expecting David to make
excuses for them and to ask her to overlook the fact to save
their feelings. She was ready with an answer – that she
would be as understanding as she always was of parents
with busy lives – but she was beginning to suspect there was
something else. The reason he'd asked to see her.

'Can I talk to you in absolute confidence, Jenny?'

She thought carefully before answering. Curious as she
was, she had to resist the risk of being compromised. 'In a
personal capacity, yes, as a coroner, well – you know the
rules as well as I do.'

'We'll make it personal, then.' He glanced at the door,
as if fearing someone on the far side might be eaves-
dropping. 'The number of deaths from hospital infection is
going up all the time – you'll be more aware of that than
anyone.'

'*Hospital?*' You think Sophie caught this from her
father?'

'It's possible. I know he's thinking along those lines. The
thing is, even if that's the case, there's very little he or I can
do about it, not if we value our careers. None of us is
considered indispensable. The moment a consultant dares
raise his head above the parapet it gets shot off.'

'Are you telling me there's a problem here that no one's
admitting to?'

David checked his watch. It was ticking round to the time
he'd have to start scrubbing up for a long day in theatre.
Sometimes he'd perform as many as a dozen heart bypass
procedures back to back, shuttling between neighbouring
theatres to do the delicate work while subordinates opened
and closed the patients for him.

'You did ask me here,' Jenny said. 'If you've nothing more
to say, I'll be going.' She moved towards the door.

'I'll tell you what the problem is, Jenny. It's not politically correct, I know you won't like it, but it's the truth, and something has to be done about it.'

'It sounds as if we've drifted beyond the personal.'

'Oh, I don't care,' he said, with a dismissive wave of the hand. 'Look – we've got C. diff, streptococcus, haemorrhagic E. coli, you name it. These are rapidly mutating, highly infectious, antibiotic-resistant strains and they're killing people – usually the sick, and now the healthy. What's more, they didn't develop here, they came from outside.'

'Outside?' Jenny tried to disguise her scepticism.

'We're inundated with patients from countries where they either don't choose to or can't afford to treat infection properly. Instead of hitting C. diff with a broad spectrum of drugs they'll use only one or two – not enough to kill the bacteria, just enough for it to develop antibiotic resistance. So another patient brings it here and we've nothing left in our armoury that'll knock it out.'

'And you can't raise this issue because . . . ?'

'For God's sake, Jenny – you can't blame an infection on *foreigners*, no matter how true it is.'

'You want to stop treating foreign patients? Is that what you're trying to tell me?'

'Someone's got to take an honest look at the situation.'

'And you're nominating me?'

'You're the coroner,' he said accusingly. 'I have to go. I'll be late for theatre.'

'Are there any documents I can look at? Would anyone be prepared to give me a statement?' Jenny pressed.

'I'm just giving you a steer, that's all.' He looked levelly at her. 'And if my name is ever mentioned in this context I stand to lose my job – you do understand that?'

'You needn't worry, David. I shan't embarrass you.'

'Thank you.' He seemed briefly grateful. 'I'd appreciate that.'

*

Jenny pressed the buzzer at the mortuary door at 7 a.m., more in hope than expectation. To her surprise, the intercom was answered by a junior technician who said that Dr Kerr was already at work. He let her in, but as she sidestepped the gurneys cluttering the corridor and made for the door of the autopsy room, he appeared through the swing doors to the refrigeration unit and called after her. 'You won't want to go in there, Mrs Cooper.'

Jenny glanced through the observation pane and saw that a negative-pressure isolation tent constructed of several skins of clear polythene sheeting had been placed over the dissection table. Its electrically powered filters were designed to clean the air inside and ensure that no dangerous micro-organisms harboured by the body could escape. Dr Kerr was at work inside it, wearing an all-in-one biohazard suit.

'He won't be long,' the technician said. 'He did the p-m last night but the lab came back asking for some more samples. You can wait in his office if you like.'

'Thanks.'

He nodded, as if reassuring himself that she could be trusted, and returned to his task.

Jenny glanced back through the observation pane and saw Dr Kerr emerging from the tent with a number of steel flasks, which he placed into a refrigerated transport box. It was a procedure she hadn't observed before and she found it unsettling. He looked up and saw her face. He waved a gloved hand then pointed, a gesture she took to mean that she should retreat to his office. She followed his advice.

More than usually aware of the warmth of the sickly sweet mortuary air, Jenny went to the office window and tried to open it. A safety catch had been fitted that allowed it to open outwards only a few inches from the frame. She pressed her face to the narrow gap and took in a deep breath. She had blithely wandered the hospital's corridors for the past four years without ever questioning whether it was an altogether safe place to be, but now it felt alive with hidden dangers. For all his many failings, David was the most unflappable person she had ever known; for him to express concern there had to be a serious problem.

It was some minutes before Dr Kerr came through the door, carrying the strong chemical smell of the antiseptic with which he would have doused himself after the procedure.

'Sorry about that. Takes a while to climb out of all the kit.'

'Those were some serious precautions,' Jenny said.

'Very necessary, I'm afraid.' His voice had lost its usual wry edge. 'I was just going to call you. I wasn't sure you'd been notified.'

'I got word last night. The girl's father is a colleague of my ex-husband's.'

'Mr Freeman. Of course. You knew Sophie?'

'No, not really.' It was partly true: they hadn't spoken since her divorce. 'Have you established a cause of death?'

'It was meningitis.'

She felt oddly relieved. 'My ex-husband implied there was concern it was something more sinister.'

Dr Kerr walked past her to his chair on the far side of the desk. Jenny noticed his eyes were bloodshot with fatigue. She could tell he had hardly slept.

'That's not an unreasonable word to use. According to her notes, from the onset of symptoms to death was only a little over eight hours. That's remarkably quick in an otherwise healthy child. And one would certainly expect bacterial meningitis to respond to antibiotic treatment in some degree, but it seems that the drugs had no effect at all. The physicians certainly threw everything at it.'

'I'm no expert, but I do know that meningitis is often fatal,' Jenny said, hoping for some words of reassurance.

'The lab started work yesterday afternoon, while Sophie was still alive,' Dr Kerr said. 'The aim was to identify the precise strain and work out the most effective drug regime. You may not know this, but the meningitis bacterium coats itself with a protein that prevents immune cells from attacking it. It's very clever: a Trojan Horse, if you like. I've even heard an immunologist call it beautiful.'

'Not a word I'd use.'

'Nor me.' He reached for his computer mouse and opened an email from colleagues in the path' lab. It confirmed his suspicion. 'They're telling me none of the samples cultured have responded to any drug combinations. Cephalosporin, vancomycin, ampicillin – nothing's worked. Of course it's too early to say with certainty, but the concern is we're dealing with an aggressive, drug-resistant strain.'

' "Aggressive" meaning what, precisely?'

'One of the major symptoms of this strain is disseminated intravascular coagulation – it means the blood clots excessively, which perversely causes multiple haemorrhages. All the girl's major organs were affected – liver, kidneys, brain. She had also developed grotesque swelling and gangrene in her limbs. It means either that the bacteria multiplied at an unprecedented rate, or that she remained asymptomatic until the disease was already far advanced. Neither possibility is particularly reassuring.'

'But we've only seen this one case?'

'So far.'

Jenny thought about what David had told her – his fear of drug-resistant organisms finding their way into the hospital through foreign patients.

'Do you have any idea where she might have caught it? Wouldn't you expect to see a cluster?'

'Every outbreak has to start somewhere, Mrs Cooper. One of the mysteries of infectious disease is why we see a sudden flare-up then a die-off for no apparent reason. Many of us carry meningitis bacteria in our bodies benignly. The process of activation and mutation is little understood.'

'But Sophie might have caught it from someone else.'

'It would be foolish not to expect more cases.'

'And the body – is it safe?'

'As much as it can be. It's stored in a biohazard body bag. My concern is far more for those who have been in immediate contact with her. I'm sure the Health Protection Agency is taking the appropriate steps.' He gave an apologetic smile that said he had nothing more to give her.

Jenny pressed him on one final point. 'Antibiotic resistance – that means this strain must have evolved defences, perhaps through not being properly treated in the past?'

'Quite possibly.'

'I need you to be honest with me – whatever your answer, I'll treat it as off the record. Are we sure that all deaths caused by hospital infection are being recorded as such? There's no management pressure to downplay a problem?'

'If there's an infection, I record it – you know that,' Dr Kerr answered carefully. 'Whether it's drug-resistant is another matter. I'm not usually required to conduct a full-scale genetic analysis.'

Jenny nodded. 'I understand.'

He had given a non-response, but she couldn't have expected him to go further. Were he to have told her that deaths were being caused by potentially avoidable infection, he could find himself a witness in multiple civil actions against his employers. A few unguarded words could cost him his career.

Courteous as always, he showed her to the door, but as she started out, he said, 'You won't say anything to put me in an awkward situation, will you?'

She couldn't recall a time when she had seen him appear so nervous. He was always the embodiment of calm.

'You know me better than that.'

He gave a slow, considered nod. There was something else weighing on his mind. 'Can you keep a confidence?'

'Certainly.'

'One of the senior managers called me last night – I shan't give the name – and let it be known that rumours would be flying around this case. I was told in no uncertain terms not to contribute to them.'

Jenny made the customary call to the Freeman household from her office at a little after 9 a.m. Ed answered. She hadn't heard his voice in over five years, yet it might have been five days. She remembered him as a naturally athletic man who had infuriated David by routinely beating him at squash. He had also shone as a neurosurgeon specializing in the treatment of brain tumours, while maintaining a sense of humour and a happy marriage to Fiona. Jenny had looked on their family as unfairly charmed.

'Ed, it's Jenny. Jenny Cooper. I'm so sorry about Sophie.'

'Yes.' He answered in the familiar monotone of the recently bereaved. 'It doesn't seem real.'

There were no words adequate for dealing with the sudden and unexpected loss of a child, and Jenny didn't attempt to find any.

'I'm only calling to say that I'll be handling matters, if you've no objection.'

'No, we're glad it's you. David called me this morning—' The phrase seemed to hang, as if he had stopped himself from completing it.

Jenny said, 'I know you won't feel like talking now, but you know where to call.'

'There is one thing . . .'

'Go on.'

He hesitated. 'You won't let David take any heat, will you? It's different for me – I've got Fiona to fall back on.'

'I understand.'

'Thank you,' Ed said. 'I'll be in touch.'

Jenny had barely set down the phone and begun to gather her thoughts when it rang again.

'Jenny Cooper.'

'Jenny, it's Simon.' The voice, which seemed to be coming from a moving car, belonged to Simon Moreton, an ever-more-senior civil servant at the Ministry of Justice who, since the day of her appointment as coroner, had always made it his business to keep a watching brief on her affairs. Jenny's mistake had been to flirt with him when they first crossed swords; and ever since he had convinced himself that they enjoyed slightly more than a merely professional relationship. 'I'm making a few house calls in your neck of the woods today – mind if I pop round?'

She didn't feel she was being offered any choice.

'When should I expect you?'

She heard him exchange words with his driver.

'I can be with you in ten minutes.'

'That soon?'

'Leaves you the rest of the day clear.'

'I'll be here.'

'Excellent. Shall I bring coffee? I know – even better, why don't I take you for breakfast? I insist. My treat, Jenny. My treat.'

She put down the phone with a sense of foreboding. Moreton was a man whose preferred way of doing business was over several leisurely glasses of wine at the table of an expensive restaurant. For him to have left London at dawn could only mean that he was sensing trouble.

SEVEN

Simon had insisted on having them chauffeured the half-mile down the hill to the harbourside. Since his promotion to Director the previous year, he had use of a government Jaguar and was eager to show it off. Jenny had learned that it paid to humour him, so she pretended to admire the limousine and tolerated his gentle flirting. It was quiet at the docks on a weekday morning, and sitting at an outside table watching the seagulls lazily circle in the warm air, it was hard to remember that beyond the pleasant introductory chit-chat, lay a conversation about a young girl who had died horribly only hours before.

A civil servant who had been brought up in the old school, Moreton delayed revealing the true purpose of his visit while he sipped his coffee and complimented Jenny on how well she looked. It couldn't have been true – after her early start she felt every one of her forty-six years – but his gentle flattery was hard to resist, and she began to feel herself relax. He had taken the trouble to study her recent cases and was full of praise for her sensitive handling of the death of a young mother killed by a police car in pursuit of an armed criminal. She didn't tell him that she had felt furious with the jury for returning a verdict of accidental death rather than unlawful killing, but today, at least, she sensed that it was to her advantage to pretend to be the woman he had always hoped she would become: 'one of us'.

He had ordered more coffee for them before he finally approached the point. 'I thought you might be interested to hear that I had a call yesterday evening – from one of my colleagues in the Department of Health. She was rather exercised about a case on your patch.'

'Sophie Freeman?'

'That's the one.'

'That was quick. She wasn't dead until eight o'clock.'

'Anything infectious and deadly and the whole machine seems to swing into operation with alarming speed – about the only time it ever does.'

'I'm impressed.'

He answered her with the questioning sideways look he often used to hint that he knew something that she might have presumed a secret.

Jenny remained inscrutable, telling herself not to let him get behind her guard.

'The last thing anybody wants is an outbreak of meningitis,' Moreton continued, 'especially as it's invariably the young who die. Curious. I'm told no one seems to know why that is.'

'There are theories, I'm sure. Presumably the Health Protection Agency will be closing down her school and monitoring everyone who's had contact with her?'

Moreton nodded. 'And in this case, very discreetly. The media have been asked to stay away, and thankfully they seem to be complying.'

'You don't want the public to know?'

'Hysterical reporting would hardly be in anyone's interests. We want our people getting on with the job, not wasting precious time batting away journalists. I'm assured we'll have some answers in a day or two.'

'And that's why you're here – you want me to keep the lid on things?'

'If you wouldn't mind, Jenny. I felt you'd understand.'

'I'm interested to know what answers you might be expecting to find.' She feigned ignorance. 'I was under the impression this was a disease that could erupt anywhere and for no particular reason.'

'That's often the case.' He was briefly distracted by a passing pleasure boat carrying a boisterous party of young foreign students, most of them pretty girls. 'But sometimes, I'm told, there's a carrier. An originating source.'

He threw the comment away in an attempt, she suspected, to prompt her into an unguarded admission.

'All I know is what Dr Kerr, the Vale's pathologist, has told me,' Jenny stalled. 'Suspected meningitis; seemingly an aggressive strain. The path' lab's findings point to it being drug-resistant and they're conducting more tests.'

'That's all he said?'

Jenny shrugged. 'I've no reason to assume he's withholding anything from me.'

'Jenny, Jenny . . .' He gave her a knowing smile. 'You're such an awful liar, you really shouldn't try, especially not to me, who knows you so well. If even I have heard that the Vale is alive with rumour, it can't have escaped your notice.'

'I'm meant to be impartial. I try not to listen.'

'Even to your ex-husband?'

Jenny met his gaze. 'Especially to him.'

'The thing is,' he continued, dismissing her denial, 'the rumours are all complete nonsense. Absolute rubbish – and that comes from the top, from the people who have no axe to grind.'

'In the Department of Health?'

'You see? Such cynicism – and you've barely opened a file.

An open mind, Jenny, that's all I'm asking of you. Doctors are very clever people, but as prone to irrational responses as the rest of us. You know, there is a very good reason why we don't let them run hospitals by themselves.'

She nodded, pretending that she had taken his wise counsel on board. 'So you'd like me to do what, precisely?'

'Respond to the facts and not the speculation, and please, no journalists. Whipping up a storm will only cost lives. We're very good at containing outbreaks, we really are.'

She got the message: if word got out, she would be receiving more than her fair share of the blame.

'Is that all?' she asked, beginning to feel stirrings of guilt at being away from her desk.

'Yes. For now.' Moreton waved to the waitress to summon the bill, relieved to have the main business concluded. 'Busy day ahead?'

'Frantic. I don't suppose you could ask people to stop dying for a week or two.'

'I have many powers, Jenny, but that, I'm afraid, is not yet one of them.' Moreton smiled. 'I heard about the aid worker who jumped from the bridge – Jordan, was that the name?'

Jenny was instantly suspicious. 'How did that reach you already?'

'It's not so much the dead man as his associate – Harry Thorn. He has one of those names that make our computers excited.'

The waitress appeared with the bill. Ever the cautious civil servant, Moreton counted out the precise change.

'Yes, an old friend of mine from the Foreign Office tipped me off – Gordon Jefferies. We were at school together. He'd had a request for intel from the Department of International Development. Apparently Thorn's outfit had been bidding for their funds, some African irrigation project or other. ID were doing the usual due diligence when it emerged Mr Thorn had a past.'

'Should I know about it?'

'It's the usual sort of stuff these types get involved in – selling information, spreading rumours among the natives.'

'Information? That sounds like a euphemism for spying. I can't say I know much about that world.'

'Everyone wants a piece of Africa, it seems; blessed with natural resources but cursed with violent tribalism. You don't do any sort of business there without men on the inside. That, I'm told, is what your Mr Thorn is. Available for hire to the highest bidder.'

'He's *my* Mr Thorn now, is he?'

Simon smiled. 'You were seen, Jenny – paying him a visit.'

She felt her cheeks glow with embarrassment. 'I was going to collect my son from college. He called when I was en route. I took a statement, that's all. He told me hardly anything.'

'Shouldn't your officer be doing that sort of legwork?'

'You know how I like to do things, Simon. Besides, I was passing his front door.'

He gave her a searching look. 'Gordon tells me he's an incorrigible liar, Jenny. And as we both know, there is no cure for that particular chronic condition. I'm just warning you to tread carefully, that's all.'

'So he's being watched? Is there some sort of parallel investigation going on?'

'To yours? Not so far as I know. But of course anything you turn up will be of interest, let us say.' He stood up from his chair. 'I really ought to be getting back on the road – I've a one o'clock with the Secretary of State. Can I give you a lift back to the office?'

'It's out of your way. Go on – you'd better hurry.'

Moreton smiled, but Jenny sensed that beneath the veneer he was anything but relaxed. He was holding something back. He touched her lightly at the elbow. 'Good to see you, Jenny. Keep me posted.'

Jenny made her way past the cathedral and across the lawns of College Green, preoccupied with unravelling Simon Moreton's coded messages over Adam Jordan and Harry Thorn. However much he had tried to reassure her that there was no cause for alarm over a single case of meningitis, the fact of the news blackout was proof beyond doubt that in the halls of government alarm had been overtaken by full-blown fear.

Rounding the corner into Jamaica Street, Jenny resolved to get a line directly into the path' lab. She recalled that Alison had once had a contact amongst its small team of haematologists – a technician she had got to know during her former career as a detective sergeant in CID. Jenny's few short years as coroner had taught her one inviolable fact about large organizations: the truth seldom emerged from the top, but often did leak out of the bottom.

Jenny heard Alison hastily ending a phone call as she approached along the hallway. She entered to an uneasy atmosphere, but Alison gave her a brittle smile and handed her a thick wedge of mail before she could ask any questions.

'Was that Mr Moreton's car I saw you climbing into earlier?' Alison asked.

'Yes.' Jenny sorted through the pile of envelopes, tossing the junk and Ministry circulars unopened into the bin. 'He wanted to talk about the Sophie Freeman case.' Jenny looked up, remembering how quickly events had unfolded. 'Oh. You may not have heard.'

'I had a call first thing, from a woman at the Health

Protection Agency. She's requested we don't talk to the media or anyone outside the investigation.' Alison plucked a note containing a phone number from the side of her monitor. 'She'd like to speak to you.'

She waited for Jenny to explain the reason for Moreton's visit.

'Government's nervous about causing a panic,' Jenny said. 'Simon's anxious we keep our inquiry low-key.' Jenny slipped the number into her pocket. 'I don't suppose you could do me a favour – that contact of yours in the Vale path' lab, what was his name?'

'Jim Connings? What about him?'

'Perhaps you could ask him if there's a story other than the official one. We won't have heard it from him, of course.'

'Story about what?' Alison asked guardedly.

'Drug-resistant infections. Staff coming under pressure to disguise them. There are a lot of well-paid people on the fifth floor who might want to keep a lid on that sort of information.'

'I can ask him,' Alison said, 'but things aren't what they were. No one's safe.'

'We have to try.'

'There's an email from DI Watling you might want to look at,' Alison called after her. 'He doesn't know what happened to the figurine in Jordan's car, but they found another couple of receipts in the junk under the seat. I've forwarded it to you.'

Jenny sat at her desk and ran her eye down the fifty emails that had arrived since she'd left the office. It never ended. Watling's was near the bottom. In the kind of terse message that only a man would write, he reported no sign of the figurine and said scans of the last traces of evidence discovered in Jordan's car were enclosed. She opened the two attachments. The first was a scan of a till receipt. The print was faded and patchy, but Jenny could just make out that it was from Blackwell's bookshop in Broad Street, Oxford. It was dated two days before Jordan's death: Saturday, 21 July. He had purchased a single item costing thirteen pounds, at 11.15 a.m. The second contained a scan of another receipt, this one from a cafe in New Street, Oxford, for a purchase made forty minutes later: two cups of Americano coffee and a bottle of water.

Jordan had evidently been to Oxford and met with someone. Jenny thought back to her last conversation with his widow, and couldn't recall her having mentioned it.

Curious, she reached for her phone and looked up Karen Jordan's number. Karen answered against the clatter of a busy hospital corridor.

'Mrs Jordan, it's Jenny Cooper.'

'I know.'

'How's your son?' Jenny asked, trying to let her feel she was on her side.

'He's fine.' She sounded unsure. 'Much better.'

'The police found a few receipts in your husband's car.'

'You mean *our* car.'

'Of course. May I ask you about them?'

'You can try.'

Jenny scrolled down through her inbox and found the previous email Watling had sent her.

'The day your husband died – Monday – he'd filled the car with petrol at somewhere called Great Shefford at a quarter to six in the evening. He also bought a sandwich and a couple of drinks.'

'Great Shefford? Where's that?'

'Berkshire. It's about ten minutes off the M4 motorway – an hour's drive from your home.'

'I've never heard of it.' She sounded confused. 'Berkshire? He told me he was going to visit his father's grave, with Sam – that's the opposite direction. Are you sure?'

'It was paid for by card – I'll send it to you if you like. You can check it yourself.'

'I will.'

'Just one other thing. Two other receipts from last Saturday, the 21st. One from Blackwell's bookshop in Oxford, one from a cafe along the road forty minutes later. Both cash, I think.'

Karen Jordan was silent for a moment. 'Last Saturday? He was never in Oxford. He went to London last Saturday. He went to visit the office. He was going to talk with Harry Thorn and the others about their new project. He even called me from there.'

'On a weekend?'

'That's not unusual.'

'When I spoke to the girl at the charity – Eda, is it? – she said he'd been in last week, not two days before.'

'Yes, he'd been there on Wednesday as well. He called me from London on Saturday at about one. He told me he was just around the corner in Oxford Street. I could hear the traffic.'

'If these receipts did belong to him, it seems he was more likely to have been in a street in Oxford, fifty miles away.' Jenny paused. 'Would you like me to check with Mr Thorn or the London office?'

Karen Jordan didn't answer.

'Mrs Jordan?'

'Do what you like. I don't care.'

She rang off.

Jenny started to call her back, then stopped herself. Nothing she could say would undo the damage of letting a widow know her husband had been lying to her. She continued her search instead by calling AFAD's London office. Eda Hincks answered, wary when she heard Jenny's voice.

'I'm attempting to clarify Mr Jordan's movements in the days before his death,' Jenny explained. 'Last time we spoke, you said he was in the office last week. Would that have been on Wednesday?'

'That's correct.'

'And did he come to your offices again last week?'

'Not that I am aware.'

'Mrs Jordan seems to think he may have been there on Saturday, the 21st.'

'No. There was no meeting scheduled for that day. Hold on, I'll double-check. Jenny heard her turning through the pages of a diary. 'Yes, he had scheduled another meeting for this Friday, with Mr Thorn and Helena Anders – she is a consultant assisting us with a funding matter.'

Jenny said, 'Do you know of any reason he might have been in Oxford last Saturday? Did he have friends or professional associates there?'

'I have no idea.'

'Do you know anyone who might?'

'I'm sorry. I can't help you.'

Can't or won't? Jenny wondered.

'One more thing – he was in Berkshire late on Monday afternoon. He bought petrol at a village called Great Shefford. Does that mean anything to you?'

'No. I'm afraid not.'

Jenny thanked her and hoped for better luck with Harry Thorn.

His phone was answered by his girlfriend, Gabra, who said he was out. Where, and at what time he might be back, she couldn't say. She sounded dreamy, as if she were high. Jenny tried asking her whether she was aware of Adam

Jordan having come to London the previous Saturday, but Gabra was equally vague. Giving up, Jenny promised to call back later.

She stared at the two receipts opened side by side on the screen in front of her, impatient for an explanation for Adam Jordan's secrecy. Oxford was only an hour's drive away. A short trip might even put the case to bed. She made up her mind to go there. Right away.

As she moved the cursor across the screen to shut down her email, the faded, illegible text on the Blackwell's receipt suddenly sharpened in her peripheral vision. For the blink of an eye she registered the title and author of the book Adam Jordan had purchased: *Warrior in White*, by Professor Roman Slavsky.

EIGHT

JENNY'S MEMORY OF OXFORD – MORE than fifteen years
out of date – only partially matched the city now. The
university term was over and tourists had moved in. They
swarmed the narrow pavements, hoping, she suspected, to
find the promised magical vista of lawns and spires around
each corner. But they would be frustrated. Apart from the
panoramic view of Christ Church from the meadows, it was
a medieval warren of a city whose beauty coexisted alongside
the charmlessness of a modern shopping precinct that cut
through its heart. It was a living place, beautiful in parts but
not the spectacle she remembered.

Cafe 1070 was inside the yard of Oxford Castle, whose
precincts had been developed into a mini-quarter all of its
own, with cafes and restaurants, and an upmarket hotel in
what had once been Oxford jail. Pushing through its glass
doors, Jenny became aware that Adam Jordan had trodden
the same ground less than a week before. She was conscious,
somehow, of his presence, his sense of purpose, as she
reached into her bag and approached a counter with one of
the photographs Harry Thorn had given her.

She introduced herself to the young waitress at the till,
informing her that she was a coroner inquiring into the
death of one of their recent customers. Alarmed, the waitress
said she hadn't been on duty on Saturday morning, and went

to fetch a colleague who had. Jenny guessed Rena was Polish; she spoke excellent English and even in their brief exchange Jenny discerned that she was an intelligent woman trapped by background in a menial job.

'Two cups of coffee and a bottle of water, all paid for in cash. I'm assuming he was with one other person,' Jenny said.

Rena stared at the photograph and frowned. 'We were so busy. The other person was a man or a woman?'

'I couldn't say,' Jenny said. 'All I know is that he had a book with him that he had just bought.'

A light seemed to dawn in Rena's eyes. 'A book . . . Yes.' She pointed to a table by the window. 'I remember, there was a man, sitting alone reading. I asked him for his order and he said he was waiting for someone.' She paused, trying to bring his companion to mind. 'It was a woman. She comes here often.' She turned to her colleague. 'You know the lady – short black hair, glasses, always working on a computer. She comes early in the morning – 8.30.'

'I know.' The other waitress looked at Jenny and shrugged. 'But I don't know her name.'

Rena said, 'She's sometimes with that guy. Is he called Alex?'

The first waitress looked blank.

'*Alex* – the blond guy,' Rena said insistently, 'the one who asked for Linda's number. He tells her he's important, teaches economics at the university.'

'Oh, *him*.'

Jenny brought out her phone and called up the web browser. 'Economics?'

Rena nodded. 'That's right. He thinks he's a good-looking guy.' She rolled her shoulders from side to side, imitating his swagger.

Jenny tapped *Oxford University Department of Economics*

into the search bar on her phone and found the departmental website. She clicked on *Academics* and up came a list of economics tutors. She scrolled through the names until at the very bottom she found *Alex Forster*. Another tap and she was looking at his CV and photograph. He had a PhD from the University of Wellington, was thirty-two years old and was a research fellow at Worcester College.

She showed his picture to Rena. 'Is this the man?'

Rena nodded, impressed with the speed of her detective work. 'The picture's a little old, though.'

It took only two phone calls, one to the Department of Economics and one to the receptionist at Worcester College, to be connected to Alex Forster's extension.

He answered briskly in the manner of a man who had been interrupted at his work. 'Dr Forster.' He spoke with a pronounced New Zealand accent.

Jenny introduced herself with her formal title – Coroner for the Severn Vale District – and got his attention. 'My inquiry doesn't directly concern you, Dr Forster,' she explained, 'rather someone you may know. This may sound rather odd, but I'm told you sometimes share a table at a cafe in Oxford Castle with a woman with short black hair. She wears glasses and often carries a laptop with her.'

'I'm conducting a tutorial at the moment, Ms Cooper. May I call you back?'

She detected a tightness in his voice, as if he'd been caught out.

She pressed him. 'I'm here in Oxford. I could speak to you in person if you wish. Or if you'd prefer to check my identity, I suggest you call my office and ask my officer to patch you through.'

'That might be wise. I'll call you back.'

Jenny ordered a coffee while she waited the few minutes

it would take for Forster to perform the same exercise as the one she had just conducted on him. Unlike a police officer, she was in no position to intimidate witnesses into speaking. She had instead to rely on their willingness to help, and her instinct was that Forster would.

He returned her call five minutes later.

'I'm sorry to have kept you waiting, Ms Cooper – you understand my caution.'

'Of course. I ought to explain – the woman I'm attempting to trace was seen talking to a man who apparently committed suicide earlier this week. I'm conducting an inquiry into the surrounding circumstances and would like to speak to her.'

'I see.' He sounded relieved. Perhaps he had feared the incident with Linda the waitress had somehow come back to bite him. 'The description you gave sounds like Sonia Blake. She's a politics tutor here in college. I tried her number but she's not answering. She's usually back in her room by about 4.30.'

'Are you and she close colleagues?'

'Like all good Oxford dons, we often have tea,' he joked.

'I'd like to reach her before then if I can. Perhaps you'd be kind enough to give me her mobile?'

Thanking him for his help and ending the call, Jenny took stock. She decided a phone call to Sonia Blake wouldn't be enough. She wanted to talk to her in person.

It was only a ten-minute walk – guided haphazardly by the tourist map she had picked up at the cafe – to Worcester College. It stood at the bottom of Beaumont Street, a short walk from the Randolph Hotel, and had the feeling of being set slightly apart from the centre of town. Its Georgian facade lacked the grandeur of the colleges in the city centre, but having passed through its unpromising entrance, she found herself in a cloister that opened onto a large and beautiful sunken quad with buildings on three sides. To the left stood a row of medieval cottages, to the right a four-storey Regency terrace, and at the far end an ancient stone wall beyond which lay a formal garden. She stood and admired the vista for a moment: an age-old secret hidden from the world outside.

'Can I help you, ma'am?'

She turned to see a college porter emerging from the lodge, a small office set just inside the entrance.

'I'm here to visit Sonia Blake.'

'Is she expecting you?'

'No,' Jenny answered truthfully.

He shook his head. 'The college isn't open to visitors this afternoon. You can't come in without an appointment.'

'I'm not a visitor,' Jenny said, pointedly ignoring his rudeness. 'I'm the Severn Vale District Coroner. I'm here on business.'

'Oh.' He drew back his shoulders, but offered no apology. 'I'll call up for you, then.'

Jenny followed him into the lodge, a room which could hardly have changed in a hundred years. As the porter went behind his desk, she cast her eyes over the rows of pigeon-holes, the foot-worn flagstones and the thick distemper paint peeling from the walls.

'Ah . . .' the porter said, setting down the phone. He was looking past her to someone who had appeared in the doorway behind her. 'There's Mrs Blake now.'

Jenny turned to see a bespectacled, dark-haired woman in her late thirties, with the serious, intense look of one with much on her mind.

'Sonia Blake?'

'Yes,' she answered, the single word enough for Jenny to detect her American accent.

'Jenny Cooper. Severn Vale District Coroner.' She hesitated. 'I believe you knew Adam Jordan.'

A look of dismay crossed Sonia Blake's face. 'What about him?'

Jenny glanced over at the porter, who had tactfully absorbed himself in his computer. 'I'm afraid he's dead, Mrs Blake – last Monday night.'

Sonia Blake spun sharply and stepped out into the cloister. Jenny followed her, uncertain how to proceed.

After a few paces Sonia wheeled round, her eyes welling with tears.

'How?'

'It seems he jumped from a motorway bridge, at least that's what the police have concluded. His wife has no idea why. It seems you were one of the last people to see him. I thought you might be able to cast some light.'

An involuntary sob escaped from Sonia's lips. She pressed a fist to her mouth. 'Come to my room.'

Jenny followed her out from under the cloister and along the length of the Regency terrace. Each of its evenly spaced doorways was numbered, and they entered at staircase six. According to a hand-painted sign inside the entrance, Sonia Blake's room was on the second floor. They climbed four creaking flights of stairs in silence and arrived outside a heavy outer oak door painted black. Sonia fumbled for keys, and unlocked it to reveal a smaller, inner door that led into a spacious study.

She gestured Jenny to an armchair, one of the few pieces of furniture not smothered with books and papers. Too agitated to sit, she stood at one of the two elegantly proportioned sash windows that overlooked the quad.

'I'm sorry, Mrs Blake. I had no idea if you knew or not.'

'It's all right. There's never an easy way.'

'No.' Jenny allowed her a moment to collect herself. 'I

don't mean to be intrusive, but can I ask what the nature of your association with Adam Jordan was?'

'Purely professional.' The answer came out a little too defensively to be entirely convincing. 'We'd only met a couple of times. I write about international development. I was doing some research on Africa and needed to talk to someone with recent first-hand experience.'

'I see,' Jenny said. 'I understand he was working on irrigation projects.'

'Yes. That's how I found him. I'd learned that his charity was doing pioneering work.'

'You approached him?'

'I did. But I really don't know anything about his personal life. He seemed perfectly happy last weekend.'

'He didn't tell his wife he was here,' Jenny answered. 'In fact, he told her he was going to London last Saturday. She had no idea he had been to Oxford.'

'Perhaps he was going on to London? We only talked for half an hour or so.'

'He telephoned her at one o'clock and told her he was around the corner from his charity's London offices. I presume that can't be right.'

'I really have no idea why he would do that. You must understand – it wasn't a personal relationship. It wasn't really a *relationship* at all.'

Sonia's attempt to distance herself seemed to Jenny at odds with the reaction she had witnessed outside the porter's lodge.

'How long had you known one another?' Jenny ventured.

'We started corresponding several months ago, while he was still in South Sudan. We met twice in person, both times here in Oxford.'

'Do you mind if I ask what you discussed?'

'We mostly talked politics. I'm researching the impact of

post-partition democracy on traditional tribal loyalties. Adam had been living amongst the people I was interested in – close to the border with the north, right in the middle of what for years has been disputed territory.'

'The Dinka people?'

'That's right.' Sonia seemed surprised by Jenny's knowledge.

'And he was in good spirits?'

'Very. Enthusiastic about his work, though a bit frustrated he had to leave his last project before it was fully completed.'

'Did he say why he had to leave?'

'The area became unsafe – tribal hostilities. Foreigners are always the first target.'

Jenny cast her mind back to her conversation with Harry Thorn, picturing him smoking his joint and talking like a weary old soldier: *'That's Africa. Tribal factions slitting each other's throats since the dawn of time. It's like a bad habit.'*

'You say Mr Jordan remained enthusiastic about his work?' Jenny said. 'I got the impression from a colleague of his that it could be pretty thankless at times.'

Sonia answered with a directness that took Jenny by surprise. 'Adam had every faith in the ordinary people. He was entirely confident he could make a real difference.'

'What about the politics of the aid business? Did he talk about that?'

The question gave Sonia pause. 'That wasn't the nature of our conversation.'

Jenny sensed she was obfuscating, but rather than press her, flashed a disarming smile.

It worked. Whether prompted by guilt or an instinct for self-preservation, Sonia said, 'Look, I'm a rational person, not a psychoanalyst, and I'm still rather shocked by the news, but if you were twisting my arm for an opinion I'd say that most people in his line of work run deep. He struck me as an idealist, but maybe a little haunted. I don't know . . .' She drew her clenched fists into her lap, as if grasping words from the air around her. 'There was probably some guilt there. A lot of us have it – some strange sense that we don't deserve what we've got and should be devoting ourselves to those without.'

'You make it sound like an affliction.'

'Perhaps it is,' Sonia said. 'Would any wholly sane person give up their home for a tent in South Sudan?'

'You don't think he was altogether sane?'

'I didn't say that. He was just . . . exceptionally driven.'

She was a difficult woman to read. One moment she was claiming to know Jordan hardly at all, the next she was analysing his every motive.

'I am curious to know why Mr Jordan travelled here to talk to you when it's so easy to communicate by other means. If it was just research . . .' She left the question half-formed, as interested in what Sonia would read into it as her answer.

'I asked him for a personal meeting,' she answered without hesitation. 'All sorts of information can arise in conversation that wouldn't occur in an email exchange or phone call.'

'But why would he lie to his wife? Did you discuss things he might have kept from her?'

'Not that I can recall.' She gave an exaggerated shrug. 'I'm sorry.'

Jenny pretended to be satisfied with Sonia's answer and found a card to leave with her. 'If anything else occurs to you, I'd be most grateful.'

Just then there was a knock at the door and Jenny took advantage of the moments Sonia had her back to her as she went to answer it: she stole a guilty glance at the papers on her desk. Among the loose pages of handwritten notes and open books, she noticed an identity tag of the sort worn by conference delegates. Attached to a length of blue ribbon and partially hidden under a journal, Jenny glimpsed the printed words *Diamond Light*.

Sonia opened the door to a young woman.

'Sorry, Katya. Would you mind waiting a moment?'

The visitor glanced across at Jenny with penetrating grey eyes set above high, Slavic cheekbones.

'It's all right. I think we've finished,' Jenny said. 'Do get in touch if you think of anything.'

'I shall.'

Sonia seemed relieved that their meeting was over, and as Jenny exited onto the landing, she closed the door hurriedly after her. Jenny started down the steps, then stopped and listened. Faintly, she heard Sonia say, 'I'm sorry, Katya. I've just had some terrible news.'

The encounter had left Jenny with more questions than answers. She didn't believe that Sonia's meeting with Jordan in the cafe had been a romantic one, but nor could she be sure that it was entirely innocent. If Adam hadn't wanted his wife to know he was in Oxford, it stood to reason he had something to hide. A lover perhaps? Pretending to have gone all the way to London would have bought him extra hours for a liaison, but it also appeared that he'd been less than truthful about his movements the following Monday. Jenny decided she would have to speak to Karen Jordan again. Whenever there was a lover, a wife nearly always suspected.

As Jenny entered the cloister and turned towards the exit, she passed two men standing in conversation. One was in his fifties and carried an air of seniority, the other in his thirties, tall, blond, and with a pronounced New Zealand accent.

She overheard the younger man say, 'Yes, the coroner called me, looking for her.'

'You've no idea who it could be?' the older man asked. 'She scarcely has any family as far I know.'

They both glanced at her at once as if detecting her interest.

Jenny stopped. 'I'm sorry. I couldn't help overhearing. I'm the coroner who telephoned you. Alex Forster, I presume?'

'Yes.' He glanced uneasily at his colleague.

'I can set your minds at rest – it's not a family bereavement. The case I'm dealing with concerns someone Mrs Blake met professionally.'

'That's good to hear,' Forster said.

The older man added, 'Yes indeed,' with a faintly embarrassed nod.

Jenny gave them her well-practised smile and walked on, feeling their eyes following her. Leaving the college and emerging into the harsher world outside its sheltered precincts, she got out her phone and dialled Karen Jordan's number.

Jenny arrived, tired after her drive, to find Karen was already pacing in the empty day room opposite the paediatric ward. Her haunted eyes stared out, dark circles as black as bruises.

'Who is she?' Karen demanded.

'A university tutor,' Jenny said. 'Sonia Blake. She specializes in contemporary African politics. But she claims their discussions were entirely professional.'

'They had more than one?'

'They met twice, apparently.' Jenny gestured to some chairs at the adults' end of the room, away from the area strewn with children's toys.

'Is Sam still making good progress?' Jenny asked, as she drew up a chair.

'I'm taking him home in the morning.'

'You'll be exhausted. Is there anyone to help you?'

'My mother's coming,' Karen answered distractedly. She sat on the corner of a chair angled to Jenny's right. Jenny could almost hear the chaotic, tormented thoughts screaming inside her head.

'I didn't learn anything that would alarm you,' Jenny said, attempting to offer some reassurance. 'She's researching the situation in South Sudan. She said she first communicated with Adam a few months ago, while he was still abroad. He was feeding her information about the situation on the ground.' She studied Karen's face for signs of a reaction, but saw only more confusion. 'You're sure he didn't tell you about her?'

'Is she attractive?'

'If it's any comfort, Mrs Jordan, I really didn't get the impression there was anything between them.' Jenny felt compelled to repeat every detail she had learned about Adam Jordan's trip to Oxford, starting with his visit to the book-shop and ending with Sonia Blake's impression of him as a man motivated by both guilt and compassion.

Jenny then asked the obvious question: did she have any idea why Adam had misled her about where he had been?

No, she answered, protesting that she and Adam had never kept secrets from one another.

'Mrs Blake did mention he was keen to get involved with a new project,' Jenny said. 'Perhaps there was something he didn't want to tell you yet?'

'I doubt it.'

Jenny studied her face. She had to have some clue: wives always did.

'Maybe you have a theory?' Jenny ventured. 'What time did he get home on Saturday?'

'Four o'clock-ish.'

'So there was time for him to have gone somewhere else.'

Karen's face twisted in anguish. 'The police never found his phone. What happened to it? He always had it with him.'

'It could easily have been thrown from his pocket. I'll have my officer summon the records – it might cast some light.'

She leaped at the suggestion. 'When you can get them?'

'It can take a while.' Jenny hesitated, but saw no harm in vocalizing thoughts Karen was already having. 'Do you think that's it? Do you think he might have been seeing someone else?'

Karen fell silent and seemed to stare into her dark inner space for a long moment. 'Adam could never lie to me. He was hopeless at it. I'd have known if there was someone else. I'm sure I would.'

Jenny saw that she was fighting hard to convince herself that her husband hadn't been hiding something hurtful from her, but also that she could think of no other explanation.

'You said he was somewhere in Berkshire on Monday,' Karen said.

'Yes. Have you any thoughts about that?'

'He had Sam with him, all day. That's all I can think about.'

'Is Sam talking yet?'

'Not really. He only has a few words anyway. He's like his father – more of a thinker than a talker.' She shuddered, as if suddenly very cold.

'Look, there's really no hurry,' Jenny said. 'Why don't I give you a few more days to see what you might remember? If there was someone else, they might even contact you – it happens.'

Jenny stood up from her chair and gently touched Karen's shoulder. 'You've still got Sam.'

It was past eight o'clock when Jenny drove up the twisting lane to Melin Bach, and the sun was slowly disappearing behind Barbadoes Hill, casting the valley in long shadows. Thankfully she had at least remembered to stop at the supermarket and restock with supplies – the last time Ross came to stay she'd learned that he was capable of eating in a single day more than she would in a week. After last night's interruption she was keen for them to have a relaxed dinner alone together to talk about nothing in particular, just to be in each other's company. It now seemed obvious that it had been a mistake to invite Michael the first night of Ross's stay – another of her many maternal misjudgements – but this evening she was determined to make things right.

She drew into the parking space at the side of the house and lugged the heavy bags of groceries up the uneven path, their stretching handles digging painfully into her fingers. Shouldering open the heavy front door, she braced herself for the smell of burned toast, thumping pop music and dirty dishes scattered over the furniture. But the house was silent, and passing through to the living room it seemed to her even tidier than she had left it.

'Ross? Ross, it's Mum.'

She dumped the bags on the kitchen floor and saw that the back door was bolted from the inside. Outside on the lawn, the six chairs were tilted neatly against the table.

'Ross!'

There was no reply.

She turned to see a note propped up the kitchen counter. A sense of dread stole over her. She forced herself to pick it up and read.

Mum, I was going to call but didn't want you to take this the wrong way. I'd like to spend some time with you – honestly! – but maybe weekends would be best when you're around more. Mates in Bristol are bugging me to meet up, so I'm going to stay at Dad's for a couple of days. Would you mind dropping my stuff off? – couldn't manage it all on the bus. See you tomorrow??

    R ☺

PS. Michael seems like a great guy. I think he likes you a lot.

She left the note on the counter and unlocked the door to the garden. Kicking off her shoes on the step, she drifted across the grass and down to the edge of the stream. It couldn't have been a more perfect evening, except that once again she had no one to share it with; and no one to blame except herself.

NINE

THE NEXT MORNING JENNY MOVED about the silent cottage and carried Ross's luggage to the car with an aching loneliness that refused to leave her. As she closed the door to the empty spare room, her eyes welled with tears, forcing her back to the mirror to fix her make-up.

On a patchy line from somewhere deep in County Cork, Michael had told her not to take it to heart: a young man needs to be out on the town with his friends, not marooned in the country. She knew it made sense, but it did nothing to right the injustice of it all. Some women were cursed in love; she had been cursed as a mother. A fractious marriage, frantic career, burn-out and divorce: life had thrown up every possible obstacle to her being the mother Ross deserved. And it was David who had reaped the reward: David, who when she had become pregnant aged twenty-five suggested she terminate and leave motherhood to when she was more established in her work.

Mist hung over the forest canopy in the valley's basin like a pall of smoke. As Jenny descended the hill, she felt a chapter of her life close. She was still a mother, but a kind she didn't yet know how to be: a mother to an adult who no longer needed her, who would never seek her out for comfort and affection again.

*

'Hello? Hello?'

Jenny came into the office to find Alison with the phone pressed hard to her ear.

'Damn. Number withheld.' She dropped the receiver back on the cradle.

'Who was it?'

'A man – he didn't say who – calling to find out what had happened to Adam Jordan.'

'Was he a friend?'

'He didn't say. He had a foreign accent.'

'What kind? African?'

'No. He didn't sound African.'

'What did you tell him?'

'Only as much as he could read in the newspaper – he jumped off a bridge.'

Alison turned to her computer and started banging the keys in a way that told Jenny she was put out.

'Is everything all right?' Jenny asked innocently. It was the question she had avoided asking for days.

Alison pretended to be surprised at her inquiry. 'Sorry. Am I being short?' She kept her eyes on the screen. 'Maybe it's because I'm expecting some results this morning. I'm sure I'll be fine later.'

'Right.' There was little more Jenny could say. Results usually meant the medical kind. Jenny assumed from Alison's lack of embellishment that it must be connected with the breast-cancer scare she had had the previous autumn. A tiny lump had been removed – caught well in time, the oncologist had reassured her – and she had been given the all-clear.

Alison briskly changed the subject. 'There's a message from the Health Protection Agency. They're asking if you can go for a meeting today.'

'Go where?'

'They're over in Gloucester.'

'They can come here if they want to talk – I'm far too busy.' Jenny headed into her office. 'Let me know if you have any luck with that number.'

'I managed to speak with Jim Connings by the way,' Alison said.

Jenny had a momentary blank.

'My contact in the path' lab. You wanted to know if they've seen a lot of drug-resistant infection.'

'What did he say?'

'Off the record, they're coming down with infections resistant to most of the drugs they can throw at them. TB, C. diff, strep, the lot. It's like you thought, patients are bringing strains in from countries where things only get partially treated. At the moment it's the very sick and the old who are dying, but they're seeing more and more healthy adults with infection. On the record, it's nothing out of the ordinary.'

'Do you think he might give a statement?'

'Oh, I expect so – for about half a million.' Alison pointed a warning finger at her. 'Don't even think about a subpoena, Mrs Cooper. I promised him it was strictly confidential. He's a friend.'

In the space of two intense hours, Jenny blotted out the world beyond her office door and made decisions in sixteen separate marginal cases, deciding she had sufficient medical evidence to issue death certificates in thirteen – the usual run of deaths on the operating table, old people found dead in their homes, and middle-aged men who had dropped from heart attacks – and three that required further exploration. When she had first taken up her post, a coroner from a neighbouring district had assured her that she would become inured to tragedy, and the day would soon arrive when even the most disturbing set of post-mortem photographs would fail to make her flinch. It hadn't happened yet. The casual randomness with which death could strike shocked her every bit as much as it always had. The remaining three cases on her desk were all of the kind that made her fear for the fragility of life. A healthy twenty-year-old woman had suffered a fatal brain aneurism on a train. A forty-year-old father of four had been crushed by a truck reversing into the supermarket warehouse where he worked. A three-year-old girl had choked to death on the lid of a marker pen in a crowded day nursery.

Jenny was struggling to end a harrowing phone call to the dead child's mother, who was demanding to know why no one had faced criminal charges – she refused to understand that the coroner had no connection with the police – when Alison appeared in the doorway with an impatient visitor.

'Dr Verma, from the HPA,' Alison said with the slight tilt of the head she used to indicate that they were dealing with what she called an awkward customer.

Dr Verma made no attempt to cover her irritation at being made to travel thirty miles for a meeting she had expected to host. She helped herself to a chair while Jenny continued to placate a mother who was now accusing her of being part of a conspiracy to protect a junior nursery nurse she held responsible for her child's death.

Ending the call on a sour note, Jenny offered her visitor a weary smile. 'It would be nice to give good news sometimes.'

Dr Verma responded with the bemused expression of one who didn't let personal feelings interfere with the serious business of work. Her short black hair and severe suit suggested that her life didn't consist of much else.

She introduced herself as the specialist microbiologist on the team handling the Freeman case. She was, she implied, an expert with knowledge far in excess of anything Jenny could hope to match, although she didn't appear to be much over thirty. Dipping into her briefcase, she pulled out a copy of the *Western Mail*.

'Have you seen this, Ms Cooper?'

Jenny admitted that she hadn't.

Dr Verma handed it across the desk. At the foot of the front page was an article headed *Mystery Superbug Kills Girl, 13*. Sophie Freeman was named as the victim of an infection said to be of unknown origin, which had caused officials to close down her school and quarantine her class-mates. An anonymous hospital source was quoted as saying that her death had caused near-panic among medical staff already uneasy about the increasing incidence of fatal, drug-resistant infections at the Severn Vale District Hospital.

'I've just received word that the story has been picked up by the national press. It's already springing up on their websites – suitably embellished of course.'

'That's unfortunate,' Jenny said, handing the newspaper back to her. 'I was told they had agreed not to mention the case.'

'We assume it's the misinformation from their inside source which made it irresistible. I don't suppose you have any idea who that source might be?'

'Not a clue,' Jenny said. 'Though I'm not sure it is misinformation. I get every impression that there is some-thing close to panic breaking out at the Vale.'

'Really?' Dr Verma feigned surprise. 'From whom?'

Jenny parried the question. 'Don't worry. I've no interest in spreading alarm, only in conducting an orderly inquiry. I presume your team will have some definitive lab results fairly quickly.'

'We already do, Ms Cooper. Meningococcal meningitis. A virulent strain, but nothing unprecedented. All those who have had contact with Sophie Freeman in recent weeks have been put on notice to report any symptoms, but no new cases have been identified. If we were dealing with an outbreak we would have expected to see several more by now.'

She reached into her case a second time and handed Jenny a document that ran to several pages. 'My preliminary report. There is more detailed analysis to be done, but we're satisfied it's more than sufficient for you to issue a death certificate.'

Jenny glanced over the dense technical text that appeared to compare the sudden onset of Sophie Freeman's symptoms with similar patterns in other recorded cases. 'What does this have to say about the issue of drug resistance?' Jenny asked.

'That's a subject for more detailed study,' Dr Verma said. 'But as I understand the law, if it's beyond doubt that death was caused by a specific and identifiable disease, you needn't concern yourself any further.'

'That would depend,' Jenny said. 'I can't limit my concern to a specific case if there's a possibility the originating cause is something else entirely. If a patient dies from an infected wound on a filthy ward, it can't simply be treated as a death from septicaemia. I have to explore the surrounding circumstances.'

'That's precisely what we do at the HPA, Ms Cooper,' Dr Verma said. 'And without wishing to be disrespectful, I should remind you that we operate some of the country's most sophisticated laboratories.'

'Perhaps you're not familiar with coroners' inquiries, Dr Verma. I don't contract my work out to other agencies.'

'Our lawyers have assured us that an inquest isn't necessary.'

'The problem with lawyers is that you can always find one who'll tell you what you want to hear,' Jenny said. 'And for the record, I don't write death certificates according to the wishes of interested parties. That would be a denial of due process.'

Dr Verma looked at her in dumb astonishment, as if it had never occurred to her that she wouldn't be unquestioningly obeyed. 'You're intent on holding this inquest?'

'I have no option.'

'When?'

'As soon as possible. I was thinking next Monday.'

'I don't know what you're expecting to hear.'

'Nor do I,' Jenny said. 'That's why it's called an inquest. Is that all? I've got a lot to do.'

Dr Verma felt compelled to have the last word. 'I'm sure our lawyers will be in touch.'

Jenny refused to be bullied. 'That's what you pay them for,' she said and smiled.

Dr Verma snapped her briefcase shut and rose sharply to her feet. 'Thank you, Ms Cooper. You've been most unhelpful.'

It's not my job to help you, Jenny said to herself as the young doctor left. It's to find out whatever the hell it is your people don't want me to know. There would be something, she felt sure. The optimistically named Health Protection Agency had the unenviable job of stopping the spread of notifiable diseases as soon as they were detected. Any failure on its part wasn't just a potential embarrassment, it could cost lives. A case of meningitis ignored by officials that proved the spark for an outbreak would most probably end someone's career. If there had been negligence at the HPA, Jenny doubted that an employee as earnest as Dr Verma was responsible, but Verma was just the sort who might be lined up to take the drop if uncomfortable truths came to light. She was young and ambitious enough to see being sent on a mission to bully the coroner as a professional compliment, and inexperienced enough not to see what she was being dragged into. Despite her rudeness, Jenny hoped it wouldn't be too painful a lesson for her.

Other cases intruded on Jenny's thoughts. She had a married mother of five to telephone, whose husband, a thirty-five-year-old construction worker, had fallen to his death the previous afternoon. The post-mortem conducted overnight had revealed that he suffered a massive coronary as a result of an undiagnosed congenital defect: a time-bomb with which he had been born had exploded at random that particular afternoon. There would be no compensation for the widow, only the small comfort that he had been fortunate to have lived as long as he had.

She was bracing herself to deliver the news, when she heard Alison answer the phone from her desk in reception.

'Yes, that's me,' Alison said. She listened to the caller in silence, then offered a muted 'I understand', before asking them to hold for a moment. She set down the receiver and came to the door of Jenny's office. The colour had washed from her face. 'Can you do without me this afternoon, Mrs Cooper?'

'Of course. Is something wrong?'

'Just a medical appointment.'

Jenny nodded, knowing not to ask any more. 'I'll see you tomorrow.'

'Thank you, Mrs Cooper. I'll be sure to make up the hours.'

Closing the door behind her, Alison gathered her things and dashed from the office. The news couldn't have been good. Jenny suspected that a mammogram had shown up a fresh irregularity her oncologist wanted to investigate immediately. It seemed so unfair. Within months of Alison leaving her ungrateful husband for the lover she should have married twenty-five years before, a tiny dark spot on an X-ray had cast the shadow that tainted her happiness and dug at her conscience. It was only natural to look for justice, or at least some shape and predictability to the chaotic chain of events that derailed and ended lives, but Jenny had long ago concluded that if they existed at all, the fates operated by laws far removed from human understanding.

She took a deep breath and lifted the phone. She would deal with the construction worker's widow, then set the wheels in motion for Sophie Freeman's inquest. The best she could do for Alison right now was to pretend that everything was normal.

Jenny pulled into the spotless driveway of David's house a little before eight o'clock. She had left it late enough that the baby, Scarlett, would be in bed. Visiting the house that had been her home for nearly fifteen years was always an ordeal, but the prospect of David and his pretty young partner, Debbie, showing off their ten-month-old girl was intolerable. Whenever she crossed their threshold, Jenny felt like a stain on their perfect domesticity.

It was Ross who came to the door. 'Hi, Mum.' He was wearing a shirt she'd bought as a birthday present, though doubted he remembered that it was her who had given it to him. 'Are you going to come in?' He glanced guiltily over his shoulder. 'Debbie's still upstairs with Scarlett – teething or something.'

'Why don't we fetch your things first?' She didn't want to turn him down, but wanted to be sure that if Debbie appeared she could make a quick getaway without having to endure a stilted conversation.

Ross fetched his bags from her car, managing to avoid the subject of his change of heart, and told her instead about his plans to fetch Sally up from Brighton the following week. She had already managed to fall out with her father and was desperate to escape to 'normality'. Jenny was tempted to ask in what way he considered David more normal than her – would it be normal for her to have a lover twenty years her junior? – but kept the petulant thought to herself. There was as little fairness within families as elsewhere. He'd learn that soon enough.

As Ross dumped the last of the bags in the hallway, David strode downstairs, quickly slipping his reading glasses into his shirt pocket. 'Jenny. Come in. Glass of wine?'

'Sure.' She didn't feel able to refuse.

'Pop out to the garage and fetch a bottle of red, would you, Ross?' David said.

Ross took his cue to give them a moment by themselves and disappeared along the hall. David steered Jenny to the spacious kitchen–diner that was fast becoming a shrine to baby Scarlett: framed photographs of her dotted the walls; finger paintings were neatly pinned to a cork board alongside Debbie's shopping list written in a neat, girlish hand.

David fetched glasses from a cupboard. 'Ed emailed to say you're opening an inquest on Monday.'

'Yes,' Jenny answered. 'Though I probably shouldn't discuss it.'

David persisted. 'I've heard the HPA have been sniffing around all over the hospital. Any idea what they've found?'

'No. I really shouldn't—'

'What about the path' lab – they must know what's going on? Any of them breaking ranks yet? They can't all be collaborators.'

'It's all about confidence, isn't it?' Jenny said. 'Someone has to step forward first. If a senior consultant were to offer himself . . .'

'Nice try.'

David leaned against the counter and folded his muscular arms. She could tell from their snaking veins that he'd been putting in the hours at the gym. When they were married, he would stand naked in front of the mirror and tell her there was nothing more pitiful than a fat middle-aged man who expected his wife to find him attractive. It was meant to be an invitation to leap on him, but she seldom did. Having sex with David had always felt like a competition she could never win: whatever she gave, he always wanted more.

'The hospital has microbiologists employed specifically to deal with this sort of thing,' he said. 'You must be able to haul them over the coals.'

'The good news is that there haven't been any more cases.'

'Yet.' She could see that he was shaping up for one of his lectures. 'Do you have any idea what it's like for those of us who live with the threat of infection every day? Frankly, every night I come home, I'm nervous of touching my own child. And that's not to mention the implications for my private practice if the hospital gets a reputation—'

'You're worried about your practice?'

'It is the reason we all have the life we do, Jenny – your home, mine, Ross's university place.'

Jenny struggled to hold her temper and took a deep breath. She tried to change the subject. 'Ross tells me his girlfriend's coming next week.'

'Listen to me, Jenny – there'll be reports tucked away on management's computers, briefing notes, emails from the path' lab – a whole host of concrete information. It just needs you to dig for it.'

'I've told you – it takes a witness to come forward. I can't go on fishing trips.'

'This is Ed Freeman's daughter we're talking about. One of my oldest friends.'

She looked at him open-mouthed, not quite believing what he had just said. 'I hope you haven't made him any promises.'

'Of course not.'

He was a bad liar.

A door slammed at the back of the hallway. Ross was returning from the garage. Jenny answered David quietly: 'You've always been very good at telling other people to be brave; maybe it's time to take your own advice?'

Ross arrived carrying a bottle of wine, and looked from one of them to the other, sensing the atmosphere between them.

'Who are you seeing tonight?' Jenny asked, trying to sound breezy.

'Just some friends.' He set the bottle on the counter. 'I've got to get ready. I'll call you about coming over.'

He vanished again, retreating to his room at the top of the house. The sound of his hurried footsteps on the stairs brought back memories of countless nights throughout his childhood when he had fled as she and David traded insults. And even though they had known they were hurting him, they hadn't been able to stop themselves.

David snatched a corkscrew from the drawer. 'Well done, Jenny.'

'Me?'

'You hardly went out of your way to make him feel welcome. He told me you didn't even have food in the fridge.'

'Oh, really? What else has he been saying?'

He dodged the question. 'I don't think he knows where he stands with you. You seem to give him mixed messages.'

'You mean I'm not at home tending to his every need?'

'Don't say it.' David snapped the cork out of the bottle. 'Do you still want this drink, or what?'

Jenny shook her head. 'I'll go and talk to him.'

'I don't think that's a good idea – Debbie's trying to settle the baby.' He filled his glass. 'She likes to keep things calm.'

'She'd rather I wasn't here.'

David sighed. 'Do we have *anything* useful to say to each other?'

He took a large mouthful of wine and gave her the look that said the conversation was over.

Jenny was more than happy to go. 'Goodbye, David.'

Stepping around David's car on the way back to her own, it was as much as she could do not to reach for her keys and scrape them along the glistening paintwork.

Hunched at her desk in her small, cluttered study tucked away at the foot of the stairs, Jenny pored over the scientific papers she had downloaded from the Internet on the subject of bacterial meningitis. Wading through the jargon, she managed to establish that the micro-organism that had killed Sophie Freeman was present in dormant form in the throats of between 5 and 15 per cent of the population. What made it particularly aggressive was the fact that it had a double skin, the outer layer of which secreted endotoxins: poisons that attacked the host's red blood cells, causing fever, hae-morrhage and toxic shock. It was also coated with a chemi-cal – a polysaccharide – which, by devious imitation, tricked the host's immune system into believing it was a friendly cell and not a deadly invader. It was, in short, one of the most cruelly efficient killing machines that nature had ever invented.

She learned that there was a lively debate over precisely how such a sophisticated bacterium had come to exist, and even why it existed at all. During the course of its evolution-ary history, it had clearly developed alongside healthy and productive cells, learning to pick the locks as swiftly as the human organism fitted new ones. But it had no purpose beyond its continued existence, no positive benefit to any other life form. It seemed to exist only in order to destroy.

The more Jenny read, the more obvious it became to her that anyone who believed in such a thing as a 'life force' had also to believe in its opposite. Every human body was, at the microscopic level, a permanent battleground in which life was winning the day only by a fraction.

She glanced up from her desk at the sound of footsteps on the path leading to the front door. It was nearly midnight and she wasn't expecting visitors. Jenny froze as the steps stopped outside her window.

'It's only me,' a voice said. Michael.

She went to the door with heart still pounding, ready to be angry with him, but opened it to find him holding flowers.

'All the way from Cork.'

He handed her what six hours earlier would have been a stunning bouquet of summer blooms, but which hours out of water had caused to wilt beyond the point of revival.

'Thank you.' She hid her disappointment, touched by the gesture. 'Any particular reason?'

'I saw them and thought of you.'

She couldn't recall him ever having given her flowers before. There was something different about him as he stepped inside. He was tired and unshaven, but his eyes were shining like they had in the first months they had been together, when each encounter was as fresh and thrilling as a teenage date.

'You know what happened to me today?' Michael said.

'No idea.'

'Near-miss landing at Cork. First time in years. Some clown of a businessman piloting his own helicopter nearly took my wing off. You know what picture I had in my mind all day after that?'

Jenny shook her head.

'You,' Michael said. 'I kept seeing you.'

'Was that a good or a bad thing?'

'What do you think?'

He smiled and kissed her on the lips, and Jenny found herself responding. And as their kiss became deeper, he pulled her to him with an urgency that he couldn't control. His hands sought out her skin, every point of contact an electric charge that shot straight to her core. Work, David, Ross, all her anxieties melted away as they abandoned themselves to the pure, delicious rush of life.

Jenny had never felt as close to him. They lay exquisitely exhausted with the smell of night-scented stocks drifting through the open window. For the first time since she had known him and for reasons completely beyond her understanding, Michael seemed truly at peace. She could feel it in the heaviness of his arm lying perfectly relaxed beneath her breasts, and in the deep, slow, steady rhythm of his breath. He had wanted her so badly, and she him, but their lovemaking hadn't been rough or urgent; they had passed a threshold and found themselves in limitless space. It had been ecstatic. There was no other word.

'Don't worry about Ross,' he murmured from somewhere in the hazy realm between wakefulness and sleep. 'He's finding his feet. I was in the Air Force at his age. He's a good kid. He loves you.'

'You really think so?'

'We both do.' His breathing grew even slower, and he sank into unconsciousness.

Jenny's mind was buzzing. Michael had never told her that he loved her before. Why now? What had changed? Had he spoken to Ross when she left them together? Is that why he said Ross loved her too? Her excitement gave way to worry. Was whatever Michael had said the reason Ross had gone? Had he felt he was intruding on them? She needed to talk, she wanted to know everything. She gently shook Michael's shoulder, but he was deeply and irretrievably asleep.

Restless, she slid out of bed and, wrapped in her robe, padded downstairs to her study. She needed to think, to find some words to explain to Ross that her relationship with Michael needn't trespass on theirs; that more than anything she wanted them all to be friends. She decided to write him an old-fashioned letter.

Rummaging amidst the semi-ordered mess, she searched for something to write with amongst the heap on her desk. A word in a footnote on one of the scientific papers she'd been reading caught her eye: *Slavsky*. She found a pen and a notebook and started to write, but the name had lodged in her mind like a thorn in a finger. She glanced back at the footnote. It referred to an article authored by Professor Roman Slavsky entitled 'Techniques in Site-Directed Mutagenesis'. Slavsky: he was the author of the book that Adam Jordan had bought in Oxford

Jenny roused her sleeping laptop and ran a search on the author's name. There were few results: a handful of mentions as a conference delegate, several highly technical published papers, one of which had a brief accompanying biography that read simply, *Professor Roman Slavsky, born 1951, was a leading Soviet biologist who defected to the West in 1989. He continued his work in the UK until his death in 2010.* She entered the title of his book, *Warrior in White*, and found that it had been out of print for over five years. Adam Jordan had bought a used, out-of-print title written by an obscure Russian scientist. It was just the sort of thing she might have done while killing time in a city filled with bookshops. Curious to know what it contained, she searched in vain for a second-hand copy for sale online, and had to content herself with placing a request with a book-search service.

Closing her laptop, Jenny told herself it was one less thing to worry about. She put it from her mind and tried to work out how she would win back her son.

TEN

JENNY ARRIVED AT THE SMALL STREET courts on Monday morning still feeling as if she were moving in and out of the weekend's light and shadow. Her sadness that Ross had only managed a cursory phone call, and made only the vaguest promise to introduce her to Sally the following weekend, alternated with the residual glow of a weekend spent making love with Michael. She was happy and astonished, she had felt things she thought she would never experience again, but entering the cool solemnity of the Victorian court building, she began to feel the stirrings of guilt at having let her thoughts drift so far from the families who were desperately waiting for her to give them answers. Passing through the security door, the familiar words of the funeral service slipped into her head – 'in the midst of life, we are in death' – and then turned themselves on their heads: in the midst of death, we are in life.

Alison was already busying herself in the small, windowless courtroom, setting out glasses and decanters of water.

'Good morning, Mrs Cooper.' She could have been addressing a virtual stranger.

Jenny hadn't spoken to her since her hospital appointment. Another person she had neglected.

She tried to repair the damage. 'How are things?'

'We've got the court for a full day and tomorrow as well

117

if we need it,' Alison answered officiously. 'Dr Kerr has asked if he can be away before this afternoon.'

'And your appointment?' Jenny asked hesitantly.

'Oh, that.' Alison turned away and sorted through the oath cards on the clerk's desk. 'Pretty much as expected.'

'Anything to worry about?'

'Nothing that will affect my work, if all goes to plan.'

She set the cards on the edge of the witness box. Jenny waited, knowing her well enough to anticipate the ebb and flow of her emotions. Alison glanced around the court, looking for another distraction, but there was nothing left to be done.

'A small secondary on the other breast,' she said dismissively. 'A few blasts of radiotherapy should see it off. Nothing out of the ordinary, apparently. Just one of those things. Best just to forget about it and get on.'

'Is there anything I can do?' Jenny said. 'Do you need time off?'

'The best thing you can do for me is not to mention it, Mrs Cooper. I'll let you know when there's something to tell.'

'How's Paul?'

'He's fine. Very matter-of-fact. But Terry doesn't know, and he mustn't.' Terry was her estranged husband, and having escaped their tired marriage, was now deeply jealous of Alison having moved in with Paul – an old friend and colleague of his – who had come back into her life after more than twenty-five years.

'You know I wouldn't say anything,' Jenny said.

'It's who he might tell that worries me. I know what people are like – they hear the c-word and they write you off. I've done it myself.' Alison drew in a sharp breath. 'I'm fine, Mrs Cooper, I really am. I've set out coffee in your

room. Would you like to talk to Mr and Mrs Freeman
before we sit?'

'If they'd like to.'

'I'll see if they're here.'

She walked quickly away.

Ed Freeman seemed to have aged more than a decade in the
five years since Jenny had last seen him. His once-black hair
was steel grey and he had put on weight. He was the tired,
shapeless middle-aged man David was determined never to
be. Fiona, his wife, had worn far better – if anything, she was
slimmer than Jenny remembered, her skin taut against her
cheekbones and smooth all the way down the front of her
neck. Clinical psychology evidently took less of a toll than
neurosurgery. The three of them were seated in the small,
functional office behind the courtroom that was misleadingly
called the 'judge's chambers': a desk and three chairs took up
most of the floor space. Ed declined Jenny's offer of coffee,
but Fiona accepted, able to lift her cup to her lips with a
steady hand. In only a few brief exchanges Jenny had picked
up the fact that while Ed couldn't see beyond his oldest
daughter being snatched away, Fiona had moved her attention to protecting Sophie's younger sister, Emily. There was
something primal about her focused determination: a forty-
eight-year-old mother, she had only this one chance of continuing the family line. Her husband had no such restriction,
and something in her manner towards him told Jenny that
consciously or subconsciously she had set up defences against
him. She hardly seemed to spare him a glance, as if ashamed,
or afraid, of his weakness; Jenny couldn't decide which.

Jenny explained that in the normal course of events, a
death from a recognized disease wouldn't merit an inquest,
but that the suddenness of Sophie's death coupled with the

fact that the meningitis was of an unusual strain made it worthy of inquiry.

Fiona Freeman interrupted her. 'What exactly do you hope to achieve? Surely the only people with anything to learn from Sophie's case are the immunologists?'

Jenny replied sympathetically. 'I understand it's an ordeal, but I won't be empanelling a jury. I anticipate a very low-key hearing.'

'That's hardly answering my question.'

Ed Freeman gestured to his wife as if to silence her. Fiona ignored him and awaited Jenny's reply.

'I'd like to explore the areas of diagnosis and treatment, whether there have been any other cases, what the lab tests have revealed, whether all necessary measures are being taken to prevent a recurrence—'

'The hospital have treated us extremely well. There's nothing more anyone could have done.'

Jenny found herself exchanging a glance with Ed. His worn-down expression told her Fiona had coped by convincing herself that Sophie's death was inevitable, and she wouldn't hear anything to the contrary. He was no longer the man she had spoken to on the phone; his desire for the truth had been consumed by Fiona's need to draw a line and concentrate her energy on safeguarding the daughter she still had. Jenny had known many grieving men and women like Fiona Freeman pass through her office: natural survivors who valued certainty over truth. Jenny sensed Ed Freeman was a late arrival in the opposing camp. It didn't bode well for the future of their marriage.

Jenny ended their conversation as reassuringly as she could. 'I'm sure we all want this over as quickly and painlessly as possible.'

*

Alison knocked at precisely ten o'clock.

'I'm afraid it's not as quiet as you might have expected, Mrs Cooper. I think people must have been talking online. It's standing room only. Mrs Freeman's going spare. She's asking her solicitor to apply for proceedings to be held in camera.'

'There are no grounds.'

'That's what I tried to tell her.'

Jenny got up from her desk and followed Alison through to the compact courtroom – the smallest in the building – which was full to capacity. Jenny recognized familiar faces on the two benches set aside for the press, but there were thirty or more people occupying the seats reserved for the public. Squeezed into the two front rows were Ed and Fiona Freeman, representatives from the Severn Vale District Hospital and the Health Protection Agency, along with their teams of lawyers.

Anthony Radstock, a local solicitor who dabbled in inquest work only to break the monotony of his probate-and-property practice, was first to address her.

'Good morning, Mrs Cooper,' Radstock said, in a gentle Somerset burr. 'I represent Mr and Mrs Freeman.'

Jenny said, 'We've met before, Mr Radstock.'

'Indeed, ma'am, and you may be as surprised as my clients to see so many members of the public attending what is essentially a private, family inquest.'

'Inquests are public hearings. Members of the public are perfectly entitled to attend.'

'Ma'am, the fact is we have evidence that this case has attracted attention through the spread of misinformation.' He produced a handful of papers. 'If you'd care to look at this.'

As Alison brought them to the bench, Jenny glanced at

the other two lawyers sitting alongside Radstock. Her note told her that the tall, quietly observant man dressed in a hand-tailored suit was Alistair Martlett, a London-based barrister representing the Health Protection Agency. The third lawyer was Catherine Dyer, a deceptively attractive woman with shoulder-length auburn hair, whom Jenny knew to have a lucrative practice defending top consultants accused of negligence. She had also been brought up from London, and represented the Severn Vale District Health Trust. The two big-city lawyers sat quietly and inscrutably, content for the local man to fight this opening skirmish.

The papers Alison handed to her were printouts of screen-grabs from social-networking sites and discussion forums. Word seemed to have spread that Sophie Freeman's death was the latest in a string at the Severn Vale District Hospital rumoured to have been caused by a mysterious superbug. It was idle misinformed chatter, but had clearly taken flight. She glanced through a discussion thread which had already attracted more than four hundred contributions.

Jenny spoke to the whole courtroom. 'I can see from what Mr Radstock has handed me that there has been a lot of groundless speculation about this case. I would like to remind everyone present that the function of this court is of course to use its powers of inquiry to isolate the facts and to find out the truth. I have no reason to exclude the public from this hearing, but I must warn anyone who may be tempted that there are strict rules governing the reporting of court proceedings. It doesn't matter if you're writing for a newspaper or commenting online – anything less than an accurate portrayal of the evidence is a serious contempt.' She addressed the press and members of the public. 'I hope I make myself clear.'

Radstock nodded, conceding defeat. The two lawyers to

his left remained silent. Fiona Freeman scowled and turned a few degrees further away from her husband.

There were three witnesses scheduled to give evidence: Dr Morley, the physician who had supervised Sophie's treatment, Dr Kerr the pathologist, and Jenny's recent visitor from the Health Protection Agency, Dr Anita Verma. Before calling Dr Morley to the witness box, Jenny first read aloud a short statement Alison had obtained from the nurse at the private girls' school Sophie had attended. Sophie had gone to her during the morning break complaining of a headache and rash. Alerted by the combination of symptoms, the nurse had tried and failed to reach her parents, both of whom were busy at work. In the meantime she had called for an ambulance, which delivered Sophie to hospital before noon. The thread of the story was then picked up in a brief statement from Mark Ashton, a junior registrar, who had diagnosed Sophie with meningitis within ten minutes of her arrival. He immediately called in Dr Morley, a consultant physician specializing in the treatment of infectious diseases.

Dr Andrew Morley looked as wrung-out by his work as any hospital consultant Jenny had known. He was forty-three years old but could have been sixty. Long hours spent working in artificial light had left him too tired to smile, with grey, pallid skin and gaunt features. Having read the oath, he apologized if he seemed a little weary – he had been on call two nights in a row.

Jenny established at the outset that Dr Morley was a colleague of Ed Freeman's, but not a personal friend. He was at pains to emphasize that he had never met Sophie before her admission; he had treated her just as he would any other acute patient. Immediately on examining her in Accident and Emergency, he had performed a lumbar puncture to collect a sample of cerebrospinal fluid. With little doubt of what the lab would find, he had her immediately transferred to the hospital's isolation unit. There, she was placed in a negative-pressure tent and attended to by specialist staff.

Sophie had exhibited all three of the classic symptoms of bacterial meningitis: extreme headache, fever with delirium and stiffness of the neck muscles. Dr Morley treated her with a broad spectrum of antibiotics as well as drugs to relieve her pain and to sedate her. There was no way of sweetening the pill: despite the cocktail of drugs, Sophie's condition had deteriorated with shocking speed and she had suffered horribly. As the bacteria multiplied, she had started to haemorrhage in all her major organs. Ed Freeman had arrived in the ward an hour or so after her admission, and Fiona shortly afterwards. Both had witnessed the convulsions that had preceded the final descent into coma and death. The only positive to be drawn, Dr Morley said, was that it was over so quickly.

When Jenny asked if the antibiotics had had any noticeable effect on the disease, Dr Morley said they had not, confessing that it was unusual, but not unprecedented.

The lawyers asked only a few questions. Radstock inquired whether there was any other course of treatment that might possibly have had an effect. Dr Morley answered no, there was not. He had tried everything. Seeking to underline this point, Martlett broke his silence to ask the doctor if he had encountered other cases where meningitis had killed so quickly.

'Not personally, I have to admit,' Dr Morley answered, 'but there are plenty of similar cases in the literature. Sometimes a patient will go to bed suffering flu-like symptoms and be dead by morning. It's a terrifying disease.'

Catherine Dyer was anxious to cement the rapidly forming impression that they were simply dealing with a tragic, but unremarkable case. 'Dr Morley, it's true, isn't it, that many people carry these bacteria in their noses and throats, and that the reasons for them suddenly springing into life, as it were, are little understood?'

'That's correct.'

'And is it also correct that sometimes there is a natural mutation in the bacteria which can cause a sudden outbreak among people with insufficient immunity?'

'It happens. Thankfully not often. We have only a handful of deaths in the UK each year.'

'Have there been other cases at this time?'

'None of which I am aware.'

'And are you able to draw any conclusions from this fact?'

'If we were dealing with a cluster we would be concerned that a new variant had developed with potential to spread rapidly into the wider population. But where all we have is an isolated case, it's more a question of determining why that particular patient was vulnerable.'

'In your view, is there any need for alarm as a result of this one case?'

'None whatever,' Dr Morley replied.

Jenny noticed Fiona Freeman nod in approval at his answer. Ed Freeman saw her, too, and looked away in apparent disgust.

'Thank you, Dr Morley,' Jenny said. 'I think that's all we need from you.'

He stepped gratefully from the witness box and Jenny called Dr Kerr to take his place.

Exposed to a courtroom filled with critical and expectant faces, Dr Kerr had none of the confidence he possessed in the mortuary. His hand shook as he held the oath card; droplets of sweat formed on his brow.

Jenny allowed him a moment to compose himself, then led him step by step through his post-mortem findings.

According to her medical notes, Dr Kerr said, Sophie Freeman was an otherwise healthy thirteen-year-old girl who had suffered only the usual childhood illnesses. But in the course of eight hours the disease had so ravaged her body that it would scarcely have been recognizable. Meningitis bacteria secreted toxins that caused systemic inflammation, haemorrhage and cell death. The body responded with an increasing cascade of immune responses, one of which was the dilation of the capillaries, which allowed the bacteria to penetrate even further and more easily, all the while tricking the body into believing they were friend not foe. As the bacteria multiplied, they crossed the blood–brain barrier, causing inflammation of the delicate tissues – the meninges – surrounding the brain. Faced with this elemental threat, the body slowly started to shut itself down in a last-ditch bid at self-defence. Through a complex sequence of biochemical reactions, blood flow was diverted from non-vital organs – skin, lungs, kidneys, digestive tract – to the two organs most essential for life: the heart and brain. But the bacteria continued to multiply and secrete ever-higher doses of toxin, and as secondary organs faded, cardiac output and blood pressure steadily lowered until Sophie suffered an inevitable and fatal multiple-organ collapse.

It wasn't so much the bacteria that had killed her, as her body's attempts to stop their progress. Or viewed another way, Dr Kerr explained, the bacteria had learned to exploit the body's responses to lethal effect. And unlike other bacteria that would colonize and coexist with a host indefinitely, once spurred into action, *Neisseria meningitidis* embarked on a rapid fight to the death. Its swiftness was perhaps its greatest weapon.

'Did you send samples of infected tissue for analysis?' Jenny asked.

'Yes,' Dr Kerr replied, but made no attempt to enlarge.

'And what did the results show?'

Jenny saw his eyes flit to the hospital's legal team in the uncertain pause before he gave his answer. 'It seems the cultures grown in the lab proved resistant to the usual suite of antibiotics that would be used against them.'

'Are you able to explain that in language we can understand?'

'These are notoriously difficult organisms to treat. Like all bacteria, they're constantly evolving and selecting for strains that resist anything that threatens them. When we take antibiotics for minor infections or consume them in our foods, they come into contact with bacteria in our bodies. Those that prove resistant are those that survive to reproduce. It's just a part of the natural evolutionary process.'

Jenny was troubled by his neutral tone. When they last spoke he had seemed deeply concerned by what the results had revealed.

She pushed him harder. 'Are you telling the court that Sophie Freeman was killed by a strain of bacteria that had evolved to become resistant to current antibiotic treatment?'

He shot another glance at the lawyers. 'So it would seem.'

'I'm no expert on these matters, Dr Kerr, but the little background reading I've done tells me that the vast majority of the world's cases of *Neisseria meningitidis* occur in tropical countries.'

'That's correct.'

'So does it then follow that any new strains of the bacteria are likely to have come from such countries?'

For the third time, Dr Kerr seemed to seek the approval of the hospital's lawyers before he answered. He opened his mouth to speak, then paused, as if thinking again. 'Statistically perhaps, but I have no knowledge whatever of the provenance of this particular strain.'

'How is this infection passed from one person to another?'

'Through saliva and throat secretions. The most usual methods are kissing, coughing, sneezing or touching infected fluids.'

'So Sophie was most likely to have been infected by someone with whom she had been in close proximity – a school friend or family member?'

Martlett rose abruptly to his feet before Dr Kerr could answer. 'Ma'am, Dr Verma will deal with this point. As you know, my clients have conducted tests on all those who have been in recent contact with Miss Freeman and found no evidence of infection.'

'Thank you, Mr Martlett.' She turned to Dr Kerr. 'I would nevertheless like to hear your answer.'

'Friends and family are clearly the most likely sources,' Dr Kerr conceded, 'but to assume that she was infected by someone in this group would be wrong, and,' he added for certainty, 'unscientific.'

'I understand.' There was no use pushing him any further. She addressed the lawyers. 'Does anyone have any questions for this witness?'

Radstock and Martlett both shook their heads, leaving Catherine Dyer, who announced that she had only one point that she wished to clarify.

'You are not a trained microbiologist, are you, Dr Kerr?'

'No, I'm not.'

'Do you possess a working knowledge of this organism's genetic make-up?'

'No.'

'So you would agree, then, that you are not in any way qualified to comment on the reasons why this particular strain may have proved particularly stubborn in the face of appropriate medical treatment.'

'You are correct in saying that is not my area of expertise.'

He hesitated. Jenny saw him glance over at Ed and Fiona Freeman. He was struggling.

'Yes, Dr Kerr?' Jenny coaxed.

'Ma'am,' Catherine Dyer pronounced, 'I think we have established beyond all doubt that Dr Kerr has no knowledge worthy of being admitted as evidence in this area.'

Dr Kerr looked from Dyer to Jenny and back again.

'Have we dispensed with this witness now?' Catherine Dyer was determined to close the issue down. 'I'm sure he has many pressing commitments awaiting him back at the hospital.'

'Is there anything you wish to add to your evidence, Dr Kerr?' Jenny said. 'This is your final opportunity.'

'Yes, ma'am . . .'

The lawyer's cheeks hollowed in disapproval. Jenny gestured her to sit.

'I may not be an immunologist, but I can't say that I'm entirely happy with treating this case as an anomalous event.'

Martlett began to rise in objection but Jenny was having no interruptions. 'Counsel will please let the witness finish. Go on, Dr Kerr.'

'As a matter of principle, I'm afraid I don't think the body should be released for burial until we are entirely satisfied that every conceivable test has been done. I do know enough microbiology to be aware that bacteria can undergo significant mutation within one incubating host. *Neisseria meningitidis* only incubates in human beings – there are no animal hosts. It's a long shot, but there is a chance that this strain of bacteria evolved in this young woman's body. If that is the case, subtly different strains may also be found within her tissue and we may learn something about the mechanisms involved.'

Martlett was now leaning back on his chair, receiving

whispered instructions from Dr Verma and another of her colleagues from the Health Protection Agency. He nodded and rose swiftly, giving Jenny no opportunity to deflect him.

'Ma'am, I am instructed this is simply nonsense. Numerous samples have been taken from the body, more than sufficient for my client's exhaustive investigations. May we please receive your assurance that such uninformed speculation will form no part of the evidence?'

'Dr Kerr's misgivings are part of the evidence, Mr Martlett. I see no reason for them not to be.'

Martlett raised his rhetoric. 'Ma'am, there is absolutely no evidence to support what Dr Kerr has just said. To suggest otherwise would be frankly irresponsible and, to use his word, unscientific.'

'And I'm sure Dr Verma will explain why your clients hold that view.' Jenny couldn't resist landing a blow herself: 'You really can't hope to restrict the evidence to that which supports your client's version of events, Mr Martlett.'

'With respect, ma'am, restricting experts' testimony to their fields of competence is a rudimentary rule of evidence.'

He was right, of course, and Jenny was more than aware that she had already nudged Dr Kerr far further than he had intended to go. She was also acutely aware that shrewd lawyers like Martlett knew how to push a coroner into outbursts which could be presented to the High Court as evidence of bias. Much as she would have liked to have given him a very public dressing-down, she had to be smarter.

'Thank you for your observation, Mr Martlett. Subject to any of you having any further questions, I am prepared to end the witness's evidence there.'

She was met with silence.

'Thank you, Dr Kerr. You may go.'

*

Dr Verma was every bit as bumptious in the witness box as she had been during their meeting in Jenny's office. Insisting that she could lay all of Dr Kerr's lingering doubts to rest, she announced that none of Sophie Freeman's family had been found to be carriers of the bacteria which had infected her, and neither had any of her school friends. Amongst the four hundred pupils tested they had found only two swabs positive for meningitis bacteria, and the positive samples were not a match for the strain that had infected Sophie. There was more good news: the fact that Sophie had been in close contact with so many young people, none of whom had developed the illness, meant they were dealing with a strain which wasn't proving particularly contagious.

'Are you able to speculate with any accuracy on where she might have picked up this infection?' Jenny asked.

'No, ma'am. Having ruled out known contacts, we have to assume she was infected by a stranger – perhaps by something as commonplace as a sneeze on a bus or in a railway carriage. Your guess would be as good as mine.'

She went on to explain that the samples that had been cultured in the Health Protection Agency's laboratories would in due course undergo detailed DNA analysis. The genetic code would then be compared with all other known strains, whose entire genomes were held on an international database. In all likelihood, in a matter of weeks, her colleagues would be able to identify the precise segments of DNA which had mutated to lend this strain its particular resilience to drug therapy. In the meantime, laboratory tests were being conducted to determine which combination of antibiotics might be most effective against it.

It was a polished and comprehensive performance, no doubt designed with the help of the lawyers to leave Jenny little room for manoeuvre, but she felt sure it fell a long way short of the whole truth. Dr Verma's entire emphasis had been on Sophie Freeman's particular case. There had been no mention that it might have been part of a wider pattern of exotic, untreatable infections that had been claiming lives at the Vale. But again, Jenny had to tread carefully. To raise issues that might be considered technically irrelevant would provide more ammunition against her. She had no choice but to stick to the case in hand.

'Dr Verma, can you say with certainty that prior to Sophie Freeman falling ill, your agency has not encountered any infection or death from this particular strain?'

'Absolutely.'

'And you would know, because meningitis is a reportable disease?'

'That's correct. All cases are made known to us and kept on a register.'

'Forgive me if there is an obvious flaw in my logic, but doesn't that mean Dr Kerr may have had a point? If Sophie Freeman were the first to manifest this strain, doesn't that mean the mutation may indeed have taken place in her body?'

'It's possible,' Dr Verma said confidently, 'but as has already been said, we have all the samples we need. We are quite happy for the body to be released for burial.'

At that, Radstock, the Freemans' solicitor, intervened. 'If I may, ma'am, my clients are most anxious to be able to bury their child as soon as possible. I'm sure you understand.'

'Of course, Mr Radstock.'

Jenny saw Ed Freeman reach for his wife's hand, and for the first time that morning she did not rebuff his affection. Jenny's gaze lingered on them for a moment, and she asked herself if she truly had any reason to prolong their agony.

'Does anyone have any questions for the witness?'

The legal teams consulted with their clients and decided that they had heard enough.

'You may step down, Dr Verma.'

She left the witness box with an air of quiet triumph.

'Is there any additional evidence to which any of the parties wish to draw my attention?' Jenny asked.

The lawyers again responded in the negative. They were anxious for proceedings to end, and behind their immutable expressions, Jenny could tell they were relieved to have had such an easy passage. But behind them in the public seats, Jenny sensed the atmosphere was growing restive. Looks were being exchanged and comments whispered as those who had sucked up conspiracy theories on the Internet sensed another official cover-up in the making. Having heard nothing revelatory, Jenny could simply have declared that Sophie Freeman had died of natural causes and brought proceedings to an end, but her conscience told her she owed her family and the wider world a fuller explanation.

'I'll adjourn briefly to consider my verdict,' she announced.

All stood in unison, and feeling the hostile gazes of the spectators like a hail of arrows, Jenny exited the courtroom.

Behind the door of her stuffy, claustrophobic office, she attempted to compose the few paragraphs that would stand for all time as the last word on the cause of Sophie Freeman's death. But as she started to write, she became increasingly unsure. Something wasn't sitting right. She cast her mind back over the evidence. None of the witnesses had entirely convinced. Dr Morley had looked harried and exhausted. Dr Kerr had been intimidated by his bosses into withholding his real concerns. Dr Verma had given a pre-prepared presentation, not testimony.

It was no good. She couldn't deliver a verdict without an answer to a question Dr Kerr would never have answered directly in court. Breaking every rule of procedure, she dialled his mobile number.

'Mrs Cooper?' He sounded alarmed to hear her voice.

'I'm about to give my verdict,' Jenny said. 'I just have one question.'

'Is this permitted?'

'No. But nor is not telling the whole truth. I need to know why don't you want the body disposed of?'

He paused, then answered in a hurried whisper. 'It just doesn't seem like good practice, that's all. While investigations are continuing it should be available for further samples.'

'The HPA say they have all they need.'

'They would, wouldn't they? Sorry, I have to go now.'

No further forward than before she made the call, Jenny was switching off her phone again when it buzzed in her hand, indicating she had an unread message. She checked her texts and saw that David had sent one thirty minutes earlier: *Call me*.

'Mr Tarlton's in theatre all afternoon,' the secretary to the cardiac team barked at her. 'I can only page him if it's an emergency.'

'Can you get him a message that I called?'

'I can't guarantee when he'll get it.'

Thanks for nothing, is what Jenny would like to have said, but was interrupted by a knock at the door.

She looked up to see Alison enter.

'Sorry to disturb you, Mrs Cooper.' She looked as if she had brought bad news.

'What is it?'

Alison took out her own phone and handed it to Jenny.

'I thought you might want to see this. I think it might be from Jim Connings at the path' lab.'

On the screen was an email sent a little over an hour earlier from an address that gave no clue as to its sender. It read: *Another neiss. men. this a.m. Female 23. Bristol. Dead.*

The anger in the public benches was palpable. Reading the mood, and with an eye to avoiding the online slander that might be coming his way, Radstock had put some distance between himself and the two barristers, who sat as still and expressionless as sentries, waiting for their verdict and the large fees they would doubtless be receiving for a successful and painless morning's work.

'Before we conclude, I've one small matter to clear up with Dr Verma,' Jenny said. She picked her out in the second row. 'If you wouldn't mind coming back to the witness box.'

Dr Verma seemed surprised, affronted even, by the request.

'It won't take a moment.'

She edged out from among her colleagues and returned to the witness box.

'You are still on oath, Dr Verma – you do understand that?'

'Yes.' Caught unawares, she was suddenly less sure of herself.

'And you do also understand that you have sworn on pain of prosecution to tell the *whole* truth?'

Her eyes travelled anxiously to Martlett, who had turned to consult with the other members of Dr Verma's team, leaving her momentarily adrift. 'I do,' she answered un-certainly.

'Then please take this opportunity to tell the court the whole truth.'

'I don't know what you mean, ma'am,' she ventured cautiously.

Martlett cut short his conversation and shot to his feet. 'Ma'am, may I request a brief adjournment?'

'No, Mr Martlett, you may not.' She turned to Dr Verma. 'I want to know why you didn't tell me that another patient was admitted to the Vale in the early hours of this morning also suffering from meningitis, and from which she has died.'

Martlett played the only card he had left. 'Ma'am, may I remind Dr Verma that she does not have to answer any question which may incriminate her.'

Competing with the sudden excited eruption on the public benches, Jenny said, 'I'm adjourning these proceedings until further notice. And when they resume, I expect answers.'

Fiona Freeman was already out of her chair and challenging Martlett and the grey-suited officials behind him, demanding to know what they were hiding from her. United in outrage, Ed Freeman followed her into the fray.

Jenny slipped out of the courtroom unnoticed. She knew now that this was only the beginning.

ELEVEN

Jenny shared a cab back to the office with Alison, expecting at any moment to receive another call from Simon Moreton imploring her not to cause any further embarrassment. She could only imagine the panic that would now have gripped the Vale Hospital management and which would rapidly be spreading like a contagion into the corridors of Whitehall.

'What amazes me is that Dr Morley must have known about this other patient,' Alison said, 'but he didn't say a word.'

'He'd been sat on. It explains why he looked so dreadful – he must have been tearing himself apart.'

'I just don't understand what they're trying to achieve.' For a former detective, Alison could be touchingly naive.

'Hospitals are incubators for superbugs. International airports for bacteria. They swap DNA, mutate, encounter antibiotics and learn to outsmart them. Who's going to agree to treatment in a hospital at the centre of an outbreak? If the management are caught out in a lie, the whole place could be shut down in days. The big bosses lose their six-figure salaries, lawsuits pile up, the Trust goes bust and eventually people start going to jail.'

'But surely they can nip all this in the bud? It's only two cases.'

Jenny stopped herself from making the cynical remark she was tempted to make. 'Let's hope there are no more, but you ought to get over there and start collecting details.'

Alison gave her an anxious glance. 'I hope it's safe.'

'Ask your friend in the path' lab – see what he thinks.'

'The doctors aren't scared, are they?' She tried to reassure herself. 'They deal with this sort of thing every day.'

The cab turned off Whiteladies Road into Jamaica Street. As it drew up to their office, Jenny noticed a woman pressing repeatedly on the doorbell. It was Karen Jordan. Jenny and Alison exchanged a glance. She looked distressed.

'I'll talk to her,' Jenny said.

Leaving Alison to pay the driver, she made her way across the pavement. Karen hadn't seemed to notice the cab pull up.

'Mrs Jordan?' She wheeled round. 'Sorry. I was at court.'

'What's happening? Why isn't my husband's case being dealt with? He's been dead a week. People keep asking me when the funeral is and I can't tell them.' Her eyes brimmed with tears of frustration. 'They think it must be something to do with me, I know they do. Have you any idea what that's like? . . . I don't know why he did it, I don't *know*.'

Alison hovered at the kerb. 'I'll be getting on, Mrs Cooper –' she glanced uncertainly at Karen Jordan – 'unless you need me.'

'It's all right.'

She crossed the road to her car, preferring the unseen dangers at the Vale to the all-too-raw emotions of a grieving widow.

'Why don't you come inside?' Jenny said.

Karen's tears had subsided by the time Jenny returned from the kitchenette with cups of coffee for them both.

'Only instant, I'm afraid. Best I could do.'

She drew her chair around to the same side of the desk so that there was no barrier between them. If she were to get truthful answers, she would first need Karen's absolute trust.

'I'm sorry I shouted,' Karen said. 'After your last phone call, I thought you must be hiding something.'

'Forget about it,' Jenny said. 'And no, I can promise you, I'm not hiding anything.' She trod carefully. 'When a death seems to have been the result of suicide, it's important that every effort's made to find the motive. Sometimes there is none, but that's rare. You told me your husband seemed perfectly happy – do you still think that's the case?'

Jenny hoped Karen had come to see her because there was something she was finally ready to say.

'Perhaps we'd spent so much time apart that I'd stopped knowing him. We'd talk a lot about Sam, about work, ideas, but there was always a private side to him, a part I could never quite reach.'

'I got hold of his medical records,' Jenny said. 'It seems he'd hardly been to a doctor in his adult life, certainly not with any emotional problems.'

'It was me who was the emotional one. Adam was always very balanced. He wasn't even a difficult teenager – his father told me that. I know he was very upset when his mother died – he was still at college – but he hardly ever spoke about it. He was so independent. Determined. He seemed to channel everything into his work.'

Jenny said, 'I'm interested to know how he got involved in AFAD. Did he always want to work in that field?'

'He studied economics at Manchester, then did a Master's here at Bristol. He specialized in economic development – what it takes for Third World countries to be able to run themselves without aid. He spent three years with UN programmes in Uganda and Congo, then about four years ago he met Harry Thorn. It was at a conference in London. That's where I met him, too.'

'Through Mr Thorn?'

Karen shook her head. 'I already knew Harry. I'd spent a year after university volunteering in Ethiopia. Harry was running an AFAD operation in the next village – trying to teach peasant farmers how to rig up solar panels.' She smiled faintly at the memory. 'I got talking to Adam in the lunch break. He started telling me how much he hated the idea of simply doling out aid parcels and so I told him about AFAD – how their philosophy was to establish basic infrastructure, giving local people the means to be self-sufficient. Ten minutes later I was introducing him to Harry. It was like watching someone who'd just got religion. Adam said his whole life changed that weekend. He left the conference with a new job and a new girlfriend.'

Jenny looked for more pieces in the story. 'So did you and Adam work together for a time?'

'Nearly two years in Ethiopia. Adam loved the practical side but I got more interested in the politics. It seemed to me we were doing a lot of projects in the face of official resistance. There's a breed of African politician that doesn't like communities supporting themselves. If people are depending on you for the food in their mouths, you're virtually guaranteed their loyalty. I wanted to get into policymaking, so decided to study for a doctorate. It meant a lot of time apart, but we figured if we could stick living together in a tent with a bucket for a latrine, we could cope with a bit of separation.'

'And then you must have had Sam?'

She nodded, a wistful expression lightening her face. 'It was a bit of an unintended surprise, but if anything, being a father made Adam even more responsible. He was suddenly thinking about the future, making plans. He saw me working for the Department of International Development, or even the UN; in a year of two, he was going to end up running a charity like AFAD and train other people up to take over the fieldwork. A marriage of the practical and political, he called it. Oh, and we were going to write a book together, no, lots of books.' She closed her eyes as if trying to ride a spasm of pain. 'Is that what you wanted to know?'

Jenny nodded. 'It helps.'

'I don't see how. It doesn't help me.'

Jenny said, 'Tell me about Harry Thorn.'

'What do you want to know?' She seemed suddenly defensive.

'Look, I won't be anything less than truthful, Mrs Jordan. I've been told that, officially at least, he's viewed with some suspicion.'

'Who told you? What have you heard?'

Jenny was candid. 'A colleague at the Ministry of Justice was told by a friend in the Department of International Development that he's someone they keep an eye on. I wasn't given specifics, only that he's thought to have got embroiled in politics on the ground. You'll know more about what that means than me.'

'You can't drive down the road in Africa without paying someone off,' Karen said. 'And you certainly can't run a project or help set up a business without getting caught up in the local way of doing things. Harry's been in Africa most of his life, and the only reason he's survived is because he knows how to handle people. Trotting out the Foreign Office line isn't going to help when you're at a roadblock with a Kalashnikov pointing at your chest.'

'Have you got any particular instance in mind?'

'Not really.'

She was an unconvincing liar. Jenny looked at her, sensing she was getting somewhere close to the truth.

'You must be thinking of something.'

'Africa's awash with rumours, most of them baseless.'

'But . . . ?'

'I don't know . . .' She sighed. 'A couple of years ago people were saying arms were being smuggled around Sudan in aid cargoes, but even if it did happen, it had nothing whatever to do with Harry or AFAD.'

There was something desperate in her denial, Jenny thought. She was trying to convince herself that it couldn't be true, that her idealist husband couldn't have become caught up with something as distasteful as movements of illegal weapons.

'I think you know what my next question's going to be,' Jenny said.

'There's no truth in any of it,' Karen protested. 'Adam would sooner have died than get involved in that sort of thing.' It took her a moment to register the Freudian slip. 'Look, Harry's an old friend. I trust him. Yes, he's an operator, but he's an honest one. Honest to what he's trying to achieve.'

'Is that why you came here today, to tell me that?'

Karen stared at her, then lapsed into a conflicted silence.

Jenny patiently sipped her coffee, sensing she was about to cross a divide.

A long, pregnant moment passed before Karen found her voice. 'Something happens when you take government money for a foreign project. You think it's given on the terms you've agreed, but it never is – there's a whole lot of other strings attached that you don't even know about until you're so far committed there's no way back.'

'Such as?'

'It all depends what the British interest happens to be. It might be that we're supposed to be supporting one faction against another, or trying to smooth the way for a mining company, or encouraging the locals to vote against the government. Whatever it is, we're expected to play our part. But Harry's always had his own agenda. If he thinks the local population need a uranium mine like a hole in the head, he'll tell them so. He doesn't do political bullshit. Nor did Adam.'

'Is that what happened in Sudan?'

'If it did, I didn't hear about it. But Adam would have told me.'

'I understand they had to leave early.'

'That was tribal stuff, not politics.'

'I can't pretend to know how Africa works, but I do know something about how government operates. It strikes me that if Harry Thorn was considered uncooperative, attention might have shifted to your husband.'

'I told you before – we didn't have secrets from each other.' Once more, she seemed to be trying to convince herself that the truth and what she wanted to believe were the same thing.

'I could be wrong, Mrs Jordan,' Jenny said, 'but I think what you might be telling me is that I should speak to Harry Thorn again – if only to make sure.'

'When? I can't go on like this much longer. The thought of Adam stuck in some—' She couldn't bring herself to finish the sentence. 'All Adam ever wanted was to be surrounded by nature. It's what he loved, what he lived for.'

'Tell me,' Jenny said. 'I'd like to hear.'

'He wasn't scared of dying. He was perfectly happy with the thought that we all return to dust and begin over again. He used to say that he didn't believe in God, he believed in life. He didn't mean *being* alive, he meant the whole of life, the entire vast, intricate, interconnected system. He thought that it was so complete that you didn't need a God, except as a way of trying to make yourself feel that you counted for something more than just a grain of sand in the desert . . . But I remember him saying that if you could accept that, if you could just come to terms with your tiny role in creation, it was all you needed to find peace.'

'Do you think he managed that?'

'Yes.' She nodded. 'I think I do.' There was a stillness about her, now that she had finally shared something of the truth about the man she loved. She managed to smile. 'I've taken enough of your time.'

'Oh, while I remember,' Jenny said. 'Someone telephoned here last Friday. My officer took the call. It was a man asking what had happened to your husband. He had a foreign accent – I'm afraid my officer couldn't place it except to say that it didn't sound African – if that means anything.'

Karen shook her head.

'And do you still have no idea what he was doing in Berkshire, or why he didn't tell you about his visit to Oxford?'

The respite was over. Karen's face hardened in anger. 'Nothing I can say is going to stop you, is it? You don't care who you hurt or how much.'

'Mrs Jordan, please—'

'Go ahead. Do what the hell you like. I don't care!'

She crashed out of the office, slamming the door so hard behind her the sound struck Jenny like a fist.

Alison's inquiries at the hospital proved as difficult as Jenny had feared. The mortuary had been locked down, Dr Morley had made himself scarce, and the director of the path' lab claimed to be too busy to talk until at least the end of the day. She had managed to pick up only the barest details from the receptionist who had booked the deceased woman into Accident and Emergency. She had been brought in by two female friends, both in their early twenties, who claimed not to speak English. One of them wrote down the girl's name – Elena Lujan – and managed to communicate the fact that she was Spanish. As far as Alison could ascertain, nothing else was known about her.

A phone call to CID established that they were none the wiser. The hospital's security video showed the woman being helped into the building by her two friends, one of whom was white, the other Asian. Efforts were being made to trace them. The Spanish consul had been informed. None of the local colleges or language schools had a student by that name, and a search of the social networks had drawn a blank. They were still awaiting word from the Border Agency as to when and where Elena Lujan had entered the country.

Alison could only think of a couple of good reasons why a Spanish girl would be dumped at a hospital without details, and called a former colleague, a detective sergeant in the vice team. He confirmed that hundreds of unemployed young Spanish had arrived in Bristol in the last year. Most struggled to find work and some were ending up in the sex trade. Thirty minutes later, he called back to say a contact had confirmed that a girl named Elena had been working at the Recife Sauna in Western Street, St Paul's.

'You're not planning on going there yourself,' Alison said, as Jenny grabbed her bag.

'I'd prefer the actual truth to Dr Verma's version of it,' Jenny said.

'If you're going to catch something, you'll certainly catch it there.'

'I'll be careful who I touch.'

'You're not going by yourself!'

Alison fetched her jacket and chased after her.

The Recife was set at the end of a run-down arcade of shops in what was still the poorest of Bristol's inner-city districts. Walking from Alison's car, they passed a gossiping crowd of Pakistani women dressed in brightly coloured saris, and a smiling, toothless Rastafarian sitting drinking a can of Red Stripe on the steps of a launderette.

'Hey, pretty lady,' he called out to Alison, patting the step at his side, 'come and sit down.'

'Sorry,' Alison said, 'we've got a better offer at the sauna.'

He let out a joyous whoop and threw up his hands, laughing uproariously.

'I'm glad I've made someone happy,' Alison said.

They arrived outside a blacked-out shop window bearing the words *Exotic Sauna and Video Lounge*.

'Prepare to be turned on,' Alison said, and led the way inside.

They entered a reception area decorated with fading posters of tropical beaches. It had the locker-room smell of steam, mildew and cheap deodorant. A girl with peroxide-blonde hair, dressed in tight, low-slung jeans and a top that stopped short of her sparkling navel stud, came through a doorway behind the desk.

She froze, as if nothing had prepared her for being confronted with two suited women at the front of house.

Alison produced her identity card, introducing herself as the Severn Vale District's Coroner's Officer. 'We're not police. Do you understand? You're not in any trouble.'

'Police?' The girl spoke in a heavy Eastern European accent.

'No. Not police. All we want to know is if you had a girl who worked here called Elena – Elena Lujan?'

The girl's eyes moved suspiciously from Alison to Jenny, then flicked downwards to the rim of the desk.

'We are not police,' Jenny said. 'It's OK. Elena Lujan died in hospital this morning. We just need to know if she worked here. We want to trace her family.'

The girl shot out a hand, pressed what Jenny guessed was a silent panic button beneath the desk, and turned to the door.

Alison ran forward and caught her. 'Elena. Was she here?'

The girl rounded like a cornered animal and spat into Alison's eyes. Startled, Alison loosened her grip and the girl fled into the dingy corridor beyond.

'The little bitch!' Alison wiped her eyes on her sleeve and chased after her.

Jenny followed, but was immediately met with the sight of Alison being manhandled back towards her by a large, heavily muscled and tattooed young man who was unimpressed by her threats to have him arrested. Beyond them, Jenny caught glimpses of several semi-dressed young women and middle-aged men flying in panic from behind the flimsy doors of massage cubicles.

'You can't do that,' Jenny protested.

He flung Alison towards her and bundled them both out through the door. 'Get the fuck out of here!'

'What did you think you were doing, Mrs Cooper?' Dr Verma strode self-importantly towards the cordon that the police had strung up around the Recife, dressed in head-to-toe disposable white overalls.

'Trying to contact the relatives of Elena Lujan; it's fairly standard procedure.'

'The police tell me you've managed to scatter all the occupants of this building to God knows where.'

Jenny was unrepentant. 'If your agency had informed me of Miss Lujan's death instead of trying to conceal it from me, perhaps it wouldn't have happened this way.'

'Has it occurred to you that we might have delayed precisely to prevent this sort of dispersal? You could have sent infected people all over the city.'

'You told my court Sophie Freeman was an isolated case.'

'If you would leave us to do our job we might stand a chance of containing this outbreak.'

'So you're admitting it's an outbreak now? Are there any other cases I should know about, or have you decided that the coroner should be the last to know?'

Dr Verma showed no sign of backing down. 'I suggest you follow your officer to our mobile clinic, Mrs Cooper – it might be best to take some precautionary medication.' She nodded to the navy-blue van double-parked further along the road, lifted the police tape and stepped underneath.

Jenny could have reminded her that lying to her court was a serious act of perjury that could land her in prison, but trading words with a junior official would be futile. For Verma to have had the confidence to behave so brazenly, she must have received assurances from the highest level. Whoever it was who was deciding that the law could be trampled over, Jenny was sure of one thing: they had to be frightened they were dealing with something far out of the ordinary.

Her phone rang for what felt like the hundredth time that day.

'Hello?'

'Mrs Cooper? It's Andy Kerr.' He sounded agitated.

'Hi.' She moved away from the cordon and anyone who might be tempted to listen in. 'What's up?'

'I heard you tracked down the last victim's address.'

'Not her home – the place where she worked. A massage parlour.'

'I heard she lived in a bedsit upstairs, with a lot of other girls.'

'Then you know more than me.' Jenny glanced up at the three floors above the shop front. Shabby curtains were drawn across the windows. 'Who told you that?'

'A guy from the path' lab.'

'How did they get hold of the information?'

'He didn't say.' He hesitated. 'I don't suppose you've got time to meet? I think we should.'

The place Andy Kerr had suggested was the Beaufort Arms, a tiny pub untouched by the previous three decades, tucked away in a narrow street off Blackboy Hill. It was an occasional weekend haunt of his, he said, somewhere you'd come to hide away with no danger of bumping into friends or colleagues. Sure enough, apart from the two old men at the bar, they were the only customers. Jenny's throat was still sore from the antibacterial spray an HPA medic had insisted on pumping into everyone who'd been near the Recife. Andy cheered her up with the news that she'd still be tasting it in three days' time – it was designed to stick there, and it did what it promised.

They sat at a corner table away from the ubiquitous flatscreen playing non-stop sport and exchanged apprehensive glances, each waiting for the other's bad news.

Andy reached into his rucksack and brought out a folder containing a dozen or more photographs of a female body badly disfigured by disease.

'Miss Lujan,' Andy said. 'I did the p-m straight after I came back from court. The HPA sent a Home Office pathologist called Glazier up from London to join me.'

'Did you know about her case when you came to give evidence?' Jenny asked.

'No. Her time of death was recorded as 8.30 this morning, but I wasn't aware of her until midday. I may have been asked to soft-pedal in court, but not that much.'

Jenny believed him. A Presbyterian upbringing in Belfast had forged him into an often frustratingly cautious, but unswervingly honest, man. She didn't believe he could lie to her even if he wanted to.

He turned through the pictures that showed the body from various angles inside an identical negative-pressure tent to the one in which Sophie Freeman's body had been autopsied. The limbs were swollen to almost twice their natural width and the tissue of the cheeks so filled with fluid that the eyes were barely visible. The entire surface of the skin was covered with a blotchy rash, which in places had started to become black with necrosis. Andy explained that, as with Sophie Freeman, the cause of death was multiple organ failure caused by the body's extreme reaction to the invading bacteria. Being older, Elena was a little stronger and her vital organs had kept her alive when circulation to much of her body had already ceased – hence the large areas of dead tissue. It was a horrific sight, on a par with the worst road accidents. It made Jenny feel nauseous. She had to look away.

'Do we know for certain if it's the same strain that killed Sophie Freeman?' she asked.

'We won't have a confirmed match until tomorrow, but the lab did say the cultures they've got are resisting antibiotics in exactly the same way.'

'What did Glazier have to say?'

'Not much. He observed, took his samples and left as soon as we were done. I got the feeling he'd been told not to talk to me if he could help it.'

Jenny said, 'If we've got two unconnected cases already, I'm assuming we should expect more.'

'That's the interesting thing,' Andy replied. 'This girl was working in a sauna, which I presume involves having sex with lots of different men. You couldn't have a more efficient incubator than a steamy, enclosed space.'

Jenny shuddered as she recalled the warm, damp air inside the Recife and wondered what she might have drawn down into her lungs.

'It's no accident that the meningitis belt stretches across the tropical regions of sub-Saharan Africa,' Andy continued. 'No one knows for sure why Africa is where most of the world's cases occur, but the temperature and close-packed populations are significant factors, I'd say.'

'I had no idea it was an African disease.'

'It's not exclusively, but they have the lion's share of cases. There are regular epidemics across the middle of the continent. They mostly occur within a 500-mile-wide belt from Senegal and Gambia in the west across to Sudan and Ethiopia in the east. Just like the flu, new variants appear every year. The World Health Organization is working like crazy to develop a vaccine. I'd hate to have been the one to break the news about this strain.'

Jenny tried to ignore the connection her mind had made between Adam Jordan's work in Sudan and what Andy had just told her, but it lodged there, a malignant presence, as they continued to talk.

'Is that where you think this strain came from?' Jenny asked.

'Possibly. African hospitals are likely to treat with only a limited range of drugs, simply through lack of resources. There's no surer way of breeding resistance – the bacteria that survive the effects of one or two drugs then form the base pool from which the next generations evolve. A few years down the line you've got a strain with a whole range of defences.'

'Like this one.'

Andy nodded. 'Precisely.'

Jenny said, 'Why all the secrecy, do you think? If this was flu we'd have nothing but public health warnings. There'd be no question of hushing it up.'

'That's what I've been asking myself. And I can only think of two possible explanations.' He paused to swig from his bottle of beer. Jenny recognized his expression: he was testing himself, making doubly sure he was justified in what he intended to say. 'Unless we're talking state secrets,' he continued, 'people tend to hide things when they're frightened of their errors being exposed. So we're dealing either with a disease that has been overlooked, or with cases which have been mishandled in some way, or —' He paused once again, checking himself.

'I appreciate this is just conjecture, Andy. I'm not going to quote you.'

He moved a little closer towards her, dropping his eyes down to the table, as if he were slightly ashamed. He was a pathologist who prided himself on dealing only in provable facts, not in guesswork. 'My contact in the path' lab has a line in to the commercial laboratory where they're carrying out a full DNA analysis of the bacterium. He thinks they're looking for signs that it's a recombinant strain.'

'Meaning . . . ?'

'That the DNA has been artificially recombined by geneticists – in a lab.'

Jenny looked at him disbelievingly.

Andy was deadly serious. 'It could happen with the best of intentions. For example, if you're working on a vaccine, you'll need to create one that kills as many iterations of the disease as possible. If you're tackling meningitis, you'll probably have cultures of several drug-resistant strains. These days it's no great technical feat to splice the antibiotic-resistant cassettes of DNA from each of those strains, and insert them all into a new, recombined variant of your bacterium. You deliberately create a monster in order to learn how to kill it.'

'And this happens?'

'All the time. It's standard practice. But in the UK you need a government licence to modify DNA. My contact checked the registers and couldn't find any applications relating to this organism.'

'Could it have come from abroad?'

'It could have come from anywhere.'

'You said the secrecy could be to disguise an error. What kind?'

'I genuinely have no idea,' Andy said, 'and I might not have troubled you with any of this, if it wasn't for one thing.'

'There's more?'

Andy nodded, his expression saying he scarcely believed it himself. 'After Elena Lujan's post-mortem, Glazier wanted to collect some samples of cerebrospinal fluid and brain tissue from Sophie Freeman's body. I had the technicians bring it into another tent and open it up. You know how the brain tissue is stored along with—'

Jenny nodded, not wanting to dwell on this unpleasant detail. One of the many indignities of post-mortem was that the dissected brain couldn't be crammed back into the opened skull. Post-autopsy, the individual sections were placed in a plastic bag along with the other major organs and stitched into the abdomen, while the skull was stuffed with cotton wool to prevent it sounding hollow to the touch.

Andy continued. 'When they opened her, the brain tissue was gone. All of it. And the spinal fluid had been tapped out, too.'

'When? Who by?' Jenny was stunned.

'If it was anything to do with the HPA they're pretty convincing liars. But the thing is, her body was stored in a locked drawer. My mortuary is staffed twenty-four hours a day and I can tell you now, no second autopsy took place. That body must have been taken, opened elsewhere, and returned later, all without my staff's knowledge.'

Jenny's mind filled with bizarre and outlandish possibilities, none of which made logical sense.

'How did Glazier react?'

'He was as spooked as I was. Scrubbed up and got away as fast as he could.'

'Have you reported it?'

'When I told my line manager she told me that if I said anything to anyone – including you and the Freeman family – I couldn't expect to have a job in the morning. I was left in no doubt she meant it.'

Jenny tried to think calmly and rationally. 'OK, let's not worry about how the body was accessed. Let's just try to think who might have had an interest in examining infected tissue.'

Andy Kerr shook his head. 'Outside of the HPA I can't think of anyone. It's the weirdest thing I've ever known.'

Jenny left Andy Kerr with instructions to keep his head down, to communicate with her only via her private email account and to make a detailed note of any conversations with superiors who tried to silence him. It would all come out in the end, she assured him, but walking back to her car through the narrow Clifton backstreets, she felt less than confident. What had happened to Sophie Freeman's body had unnerved her. At best it indicated a serious degree of panic and infighting at levels far higher than the hospital management and the local office of the Health Protection Agency. But how high? And who had the sophistication and resources to remove and then return a hazardous body?

Her deep feeling of disquiet intensified as she climbed behind the wheel of the Land Rover. She had intended to stop off briefly at the office before driving home, but something was holding her back. It was Adam Jordan. The seemingly illogical connection she had made while talking to Andy Kerr was gnawing at her. The mention of Sudan was an uncomfortable coincidence, but it felt like more than that. Then she remembered: the book. The book Adam Jordan had bought in Oxford was written by a Russian biologist.

She dialled Karen Jordan's home number. The phone rang several times. A gruff, male voice answered in a pronounced Wiltshire accent.

'I'm calling for Karen Jordan,' Jenny said uncertainly. 'It's Jenny Cooper.'

'Mrs Cooper the coroner?'

'Yes—'

'Oh. Detective Sergeant Cawardine, Avon and Somerset CID. It seems Mrs Jordan disturbed some intruders. I'm afraid she was hurt.'

TWELVE

KAREN JORDAN WAS SITTING PROPPED up in a bed at the end of the busy ward in Bath Royal United Hospital. Her right arm was in a sling, the right side of her face black with bruises. She was dressed in a green, hospital-issue surgical gown.

She turned her neck stiffly as Jenny approached, her face too swollen for any expression to register.

'Hi,' Jenny said, shocked at the sight of her battered body. 'I hope you don't mind—'

'No,' Karen answered in a hoarse whisper.

Despite the drugs that would have been pumped into her, the single word was still an effort. It had been a vicious and sustained assault. Another livid bruise at the V of her gown suggested she'd been kicked in the chest, an injury that only occurred when someone was lying defenceless on the ground.

'Who told you?' Karen croaked.

'I called your home yesterday evening. A detective answered the phone. He said you disturbed burglars.'

'So they tell me.'

'You don't remember?'

'They came at me from me behind. I didn't see them.' She flinched in pain.

Jenny sat on the visitors' chair at the side of the bed,

wondering how much, if anything, she should tell her of what she had learned from Dr Kerr.

Karen forced the issue. 'Well? You didn't come here to commiserate.'

'You're sure you're all right to talk?'

'Just tell me what you want.'

Jenny took her at her word. 'When he was in Oxford, your husband bought a book. It was called *Warrior in White*. Did he mention it?'

'No. He was always buying books.'

'It was written by a Russian biologist called Slavsky. I think he might have worked for the Soviet military.'

'And?'

'I thought it might still be at your home.'

'You want to know if they took a *book*?'

She was too bright to be fobbed off, even while sedated. Jenny had to give her more. 'Secretly meeting a university tutor, buying books by obscure scientists, driving down to Berkshire without telling you. It's not too far-fetched to want to see if there's a connection.'

'They took my jewellery, computer and television.'

'I didn't mean with what happened to you,' Jenny lied.

Karen Jordan managed a hint of a smile. 'Do you know what I think?' she said, resting her head painfully back against the pillow. 'You've got an imagination as crazy as his.'

Jenny left the hospital without answers, but with Karen Jordan's permission to call at her house, where her mother was looking after her son, and to see if the book was anywhere to be found. Jenny hadn't yet formed a mental image of Karen and Adam Jordan's marital home, but if she had done, she wouldn't have pictured an end-of-terrace in a well-to-do street at the west end of Bath. The houses were early Victorian and built solidly of dressed stone with wide bay windows; the kind that Jenny would have assumed were the homes of lawyers, doctors and business people, not an African aid worker and his mature-student wife.

Jenny was met at the front door by a far younger and more businesslike woman than she had expected. There was nothing grandmotherly about Claire King. Within seconds of meeting, she let Jenny know that she had taken a day away from the office to look after her grandson. They passed through a tiled hallway to a tastefully decorated sitting room. Aside from a square dark shadow on the wall where the flatscreen had hung, there were few signs of a recent burglary. After spending the entire night screaming, Sam had finally gone to sleep, Claire King said. Thank God he had been at day nursery and not with his mother when she was attacked.

She gestured Jenny to one of the leather armchairs.

'How is she?' Claire King asked. 'She called to say you were coming, but she sounded dreadful.'

'There's nothing that won't mend, but I'd say she was lucky.'

Claire King shook her head, as if to expel unwanted thoughts.

'I've looked for the book she mentioned, but I can't find anything.' She nodded towards the shelves that covered most of one wall. 'Is there any significance to it? I thought you'd be more interested in anything Adam had written down.'

'He bought it a few days before he died. There was a receipt in his car.'

'I see. So it has some relevance?'

'Perhaps.' Jenny trod gently. 'The hours and days preceding a suicide often hold a clue. I get the impression that he might have been a more complex man than he appeared on the surface.'

Mrs King looked at her critically. Jenny noticed that her clothes, though unfussy, were of the most expensive kind: Bond Street, not Bath. Her perfect hair and age-defying complexion would also have come with a hefty price tag. She wasn't the kind of woman, Jenny imagined, who would have readily chosen a man in Adam Jordan's line of business for a son-in-law.

'Is that a polite way of suggesting he had some sort of mental condition?' Mrs King asked. 'Have you found something in his medical records? Karen must have a right to know.'

'There's no evidence of any illness,' Jenny said. 'Your daughter would be the first to hear if there were.'

Claire King glanced over at some photographs lined up on a shelf. There were several of Adam and Karen together in a small African village, and one of him holding a newborn Sam to his naked chest. He had an untamed beard and narrow, bony shoulders, like a figure blown in from a previous age.

'Did you know Adam well?' Jenny asked.

'Well?' She seemed embarrassed by the question. 'I couldn't say I understood him, particularly.'

'Something of a free spirit?'

'He was certainly that.'

Jenny gave her a look to show her that she understood her mixed feelings perfectly.

'He came from a good family, well-educated, money, but I'll admit there was something . . .' She looked again at the photograph. 'He just didn't seem to engage with reality the same way as other people do.'

'How do you mean?'

'I suppose it was hard to understand what drove him. I'm not even sure Karen truly did. But do you know who he reminded me of?' Over the hurdle now, she was warming to her theme. 'He was like one of those people you meet growing up that you knew were never going to make it past thirty. He wasn't a drinker or a drug-taker – quite the reverse – but he'd take stupid risks as if he couldn't see the consequences. Bringing a six-month-old child to an African village with no doctor, for example. It's almost as if he felt a need to tempt fate.'

Jenny was intrigued. She had thought of him as an idealist, but not as reckless. And now the word was in her mind, she saw a death wish behind the smile, a buried grief subconsciously pulling him back to its source, keeping him balanced precariously on the edge.

'I understand that he lost his mother when he was at university. And of course, he'd gone to visit his father's grave—'

'Are you suggesting he was more attached to them than to his own wife and child?' Mrs King said. 'I find that hard to believe.'

'Because . . . ?'

'My daughter couldn't have done any more for him. She was devoted. Frankly, I don't know how she put up with all his travelling, coming and going as he pleased.'

She folded her hands on her lap: a vision of the respectable bourgeois life Adam Jordan had been determined not to have. And yet the tension between the two worlds must have tugged at every fibre of his being. He returned from his African adventures to this solid, respectable house. Nowhere could have been more comfortably middle class and insulated from the horrors of the world than suburban Bath. And only yesterday Karen had told her about his plans for the future: he *had* been thinking responsibly; he was planning to come home to work behind a desk.

'Do you have any idea why he might have killed himself, Mrs King – if that is indeed what he did?'

'There's some doubt about that?'

'Until there's a verdict, there's always doubt.'

Mrs King nodded, considered the earlier question for a moment, then surprised Jenny with the insightfulness of her answer. 'I can only think that the mind of an alternative type like Adam must be a very confused place. If you define yourself by all the things you reject, but yet you're still attached to many of them, I'd call that a recipe for self-hatred, wouldn't you?' She saw the contradiction in his make-up as clearly as Jenny did. 'There was a mischievous side to him, but I didn't often see him having good, honest fun. Yes . . .' She appeared to cast her mind back over the many occasions on which he had disappointed her. 'You know, I think deep down he was haunted by the fact that the people he was trying to help didn't . . .' She struggled to find the right words. 'He was too bright not to see the futility of a situation. He must have known he was on a hiding to nothing.'

Jenny thought of what Karen had told her in her office about Adam's image of grains of sand in the desert: he had found his place in eternity, perhaps, but not in life. Failing to fit the mould in his own country, he had gone in search of self among the unfortunates of the world, only to find another kind of rejection.

'None of this excuses suicide, of course,' Claire King said. A note of bitterness entered her voice for the first time. 'I'm afraid that for all the pious talk he was far too caught up in his own wants. Karen won't have it, but if a man's being unfaithful, what more proof do you need?'

'Unfaithful?'

'Yes.' She seemed surprised. 'Hasn't Karen mentioned it to you? He'd been taking cash out of their savings account every week since he came back from Africa. I told her –

there's no other rational explanation. He was obviously seeing someone.'

Jenny left the Jordans' house without having found the book, and with even more questions about Adam Jordan's final days. Typing Claire King's name into her smartphone, she learned that she and her husband were the joint directors of a company that owned and managed a large portfolio of property in and around the city of Bath. A string of mentions in the local press confirmed that they were pillars of the community: patrons of several charities and active in the local Conservative Association. Her suspicions were correct. Adam couldn't have married into a family less likely to appreciate his efforts. Returning from an aborted project in South Sudan, he might have been feeling particularly judged. But depressed enough to leave his two-year-old son and jump from a bridge? It didn't add up. And nor, Jenny felt, did taking cash from their account to conduct an affair.

She returned to the office to find Alison brimming with manic efficiency, and a small mountain of death reports that had accumulated in her in-tray.

'Someone from Dr Verma's office called,' Alison said busily. 'They've established that Elena Lujan lived above the Recife with about eight other girls and a junior manager. So far they've managed to trace six of them. None of them is showing symptoms, and they're all being tested. They've also confirmed she had the same strain as Sophie Freeman, but haven't been able to establish any common link between them. Apparently they asked Mr Freeman the obvious question, but he's denied visiting the Recife or knowing Miss Lujan. They're widening the search, hoping to find someone who might have overlapped with them both. CID told me they kept a hidden camera in reception – I expect they're having fun with that.'

'The HPA's being very cooperative all of a sudden.'

'I expect they've decided to keep their enemy close,' Alison said. 'But they are the experts. I don't see why you shouldn't trust them.'

Jenny toyed with the idea of letting Alison in on what Dr Kerr had told her the previous afternoon, but decided against it: her former colleagues in CID never missed an opportunity to fish for information, and when it came to keeping secrets from them, Alison had a poor record.

'How did you get on with Mrs Jordan?' Alison asked. 'I heard about the break-in. No arrests yet, I suppose?'

'No.' Jenny decided to keep the darker theories that were forming in her mind to herself. 'Nice house, middle of the afternoon – it was just her bad luck she arrived home when she did.'

Alison nodded, though her expression said she detected that Jenny wasn't telling the whole story.

'I spoke with Adam Jordan's mother-in-law. She thinks he may have been quite troubled underneath.'

'That hardly counts as a revelation.'

'She also told me that he'd been sneaking cash out of a joint account every week since he came home. She thinks he was up to something.'

'Sex, you mean?'

'That's what she thinks. Though she's no real evidence of it, as far as I know.'

'He was a man. What more do you need?'

'I've asked her to get Mrs Jordan to forward the details when she's able. Maybe you could chase up his phone records while we're waiting?'

'You seem to be going to an awful lot of trouble for a suicide, Mrs Cooper. Do you think this is wise?'

Jenny stared at the unforgiving heap of paperwork on her desk. Six new deaths – mostly routine, but those were always the ones that caught you out – screamed for attention. She tried to switch her focus from Adam Jordan, Sophie Freeman and the dead Spanish girl, but a new thought had crept in to haunt her. What if there was a connection between Adam Jordan and Elena Lujan? He had spent months in the meningitis belt of Africa. It wasn't beyond the bounds of possibility that he had become a carrier and passed the disease on. Perhaps he had somehow become aware of the fact? And if he had visited Elena at the Recife, might it explain the phone call from the man with the unplaceable accent? Could there be other cases as yet unreported? Had Jordan become an unwitting angel of death? And the more she thought about the burglary at the Jordans' home, the more likely it seemed that it was related to Jordan's secretive activities.

She fired off an email requesting Dr Kerr to take samples from Jordan's body. She wanted every conceivable test. Then from the thin file of papers forwarded from the police, she extracted the list of effects found in Jordan's pockets. Among them had been a bank card. She had intended to wait for Mrs Jordan to forward his statements herself, but Jenny doubted she would be in any hurry to have her mother's suspicions confirmed. She called up the pro-forma she kept on her hard drive, filled in a request for production of evidence, and sent it off to the legal section at the bank's head office.

Adam Jordan didn't strike Jenny as the sort of man who would have been visiting a prostitute, but if that was the case, it naturally followed that he would have sought to hide the fact. But it still left Jenny with no clue why he had lied about his trip to Oxford. She gave herself ten minutes to indulge her curiosity before turning to her other neglected cases. She ran several searches on Sonia Blake, playing with different keywords, and began to form the impression from comments made about her in the press that she was a controversial figure in her field.

Most of her work, it seemed, had been on the subject of covert, proxy wars in various developing parts of the world, principally Africa and Central America. But far from following the usual academic line that it was immoral for Western governments to pursue their interests through mercenaries and militias, at a London conference the previous summer Sonia Blake had proposed that there were times when playing dirty was entirely necessary to pursue just ends. What was moral about standing by while competing factions slaughtered each other in pursuit of mineral wealth in the Congo, she argued. In her view it was far better to pay a private army to put the violent factions down. 'To be squeamish about the means of achieving just ends is to pretend that it's possible to live on a high moral plane separate from the parts and aspects of humanity you happen to despise,' she was quoted as saying. 'It is not. We are all part of the same species, the same mechanism; what threatens a part, threatens the whole.'

She had discussed the case of aid workers who had been complicit in the shipment of arms hidden in consignments of grain to democratic factions in Somalia. 'Their crime was to support a just outcome rather than to be principled spectators to a massacre,' she had said. 'Sometimes it's impossible to be a decent human being and not have blood on your hands. History shows us that the forces of evil are always present, always probing for every weakness like a virus invading the body. On this earth there can never be any such thing as peace, only temporary victory in a relentless, never-ending sequence of conflicts.'

It struck Jenny as odd that Adam Jordan had chosen to correspond with Sonia Blake, unless it had been to take her to task. What little she knew of his philosophy seemed entirely at odds with the woman's vision of perpetual war. Perhaps it was a reflection of just how negative his state of mind had become; he had after all been forced to abandon an irrigation project for fear of being caught up in tribal conflict.

Jenny typed Sonia Blake's name into a search engine and selected the 'images' option, just as Adam Jordan must have done from his tent in South Sudan, curious to see what image of her he would have first encountered. Scattered amongst the host of people around the world sharing the same name were photographs of her from various academic publications and conference bulletins. Most often she was photographed speaking from a platform, gesturing imploringly as she spoke, but down towards the foot of the page Jenny's eye was caught by a very different picture. It was a headshot of a slightly younger Sonia Blake next to a man, which looked as if it had been taken in the late 1970s. Jenny clicked on it and found that it was attached to a report from an Arizona newspaper, the *East Valley Tribune*, published some six years ago. The headline read: *Wilderness Remains Were Murdered Scientist. Daughter Demands Police Inquiry*.

Jenny read on. Sonia Blake's father, Roy Emmett Hudson, was a pioneering geneticist who had gone missing in March 1982 from Scottsdale, Arizona. He was last seen watching a baseball game at his daughter's elementary school. Many theories had been advanced during the intervening years to explain his disappearance, including the allegation that he had defected to the Soviet bloc. But a quarter of a century later, hikers had discovered his skeletal remains in mountains some thirty miles from his home. He had been shot once through the base of the skull. His daughter and several former colleagues at Genix Inc., the major global company whose fortunes had been made on the back of his research, had called on the Arizona State Police to launch a murder inquiry. The local police chief, Mr Jackson Slater, was quoted as saying that 'with no witnesses or DNA it would be easier finding bear tracks in a dust storm'. Sonia Blake maintained that the most likely explanation was that her father had been murdered by rivals in a cut-throat race for patents in the early years of the biotech industry. 'Most of those people are still around,' Sonia had told the newspaper. 'Someone knows who ordered my father's killing and I urge the State to offer immunity to any witness who'll testify.'

Jenny keyed in 'Roy Emmett Hudson' and beyond the article she had just read, found nothing. Not one single mention.

THIRTEEN

IT WAS LATE IN THE AFTERNOON when Alison appeared in the doorway and made the surprising announcement that Jenny's ex-husband was in reception asking if he could see her. As far as Jenny could recall, David had never once set foot inside her office, preferring to meet on neutral ground. For a man whose territorial instinct and sense of pride were deeply bound together, entering her professional domain meant a large step down. She had to assume he was desperate.

'Jenny. Sorry to intrude.'

He closed the door behind him, checked it was firmly shut, and cast a furtive glance around the room as he edged into a seat. She had seldom seen him so jumpy.

'It's not Ross—?'

'No. He's fine. Well, I assume he is. He seems to be out most of the time. Wouldn't that be nice—' He stopped himself extemporizing on the theme. Jenny allowed herself an inward smile: his four short words told her that Debbie's oppressive domesticity was at last beginning to grate.

'This is an early finish for you, isn't it?' Jenny ventured.

'I had to reschedule some of the list – there's a team of microbiologists going over the theatres. That's why I'm here.' He ran a nervous hand over his temple. 'These people aren't HPA – I know all their staff – but no one seems prepared to tell us who they are or what the hell it is they're looking for. Word's got out of course – I'm already getting panicked calls from the cardiologists who refer my private patients.'

'Sounds like a sensible precaution,' Jenny said.

'By whom?' David demanded. 'And why the secrecy?'

'I've no idea,' Jenny answered truthfully.

'Ed Freeman tells me there's been another meningitis death – a prostitute.'

'That's right. So far it's the only other case I'm aware of.'

'Had she been in the hospital? Is that what this is about? Are they looking for a carrier in the Vale?'

Jenny said, 'I'd like to know as much as you would.'

'Come on, Jenny – you must have some idea. I have patients whose lives are at risk from the slightest infection. What am I meant to tell them?'

Jenny thought of what Dr Kerr had told her during their most recent meeting. It was tempting to feed the rumour in amongst the senior medical staff, but she had given him her word.

'I adjourned my inquest because I was only getting half the truth. It sounds to me as if your bosses have brought in an expensive private company to sweep the hospital. They want to be able to look squarely into the news cameras and say hand-on-heart they did everything they could. It's the only way they can appear competent.'

'And pass the blame on to Ed.'

'He's tested negative.'

'Maybe, but is that conclusive? And even if it is, do you honestly think that's the story they're going to tell? The man's already at breaking point. And his wife's hardly the most understanding when it comes to that sort of thing.'

'What do you mean?' Jenny asked.

David agonized for a moment, perhaps fearing that he

had already said too much. 'Between ourselves, he has been known to stray. But from what he's confided in me, Fiona more or less abandoned interest in that side of things after their youngest was born, so she can hardly lay all the blame at his door.'

Jenny interrupted him. 'You think he might have visited this girl?'

'It's not impossible. But I'd hate to see him blamed . . .'

Jenny tried to unscramble David's confused messages. 'Who are you here for, David – you or Ed?'

'I can't deny a degree of self-interest, but mostly for Ed of course. I'm frightened for him, Jenny. He's too good a man to be able to live with the thought that . . . You know what I'm saying.'

'He's suicidal?'

'Getting there. But for God's sake, don't repeat that. He'll never work again.'

'David, I think I trust you, and hard as it might be, you're going to have to trust me. If there's something to be found, I'll find it.'

David said, 'You'll be lied to, Jenny. Remember – no one knows how to bend the truth like a doctor.'

It was Fiona Freeman who answered the phone. She was quiet, but able to talk, unlike her husband, evidently. It took only a brief exchange to detect that all was not well between them. Jenny told her the adjournment would continue for a few more days while Elena Lujan's case and possible sources of infection were being investigated.

Feeling the need to offer some small words of comfort, Jenny said, 'I know Miss Lujan's case must have alarmed you, but all the tests so far show no obvious connections between her and your daughter.'

'Well, we'll see, won't we?' She was clearly not about to find her husband innocent any time soon.

Adam Jordan's bank statements arrived by email late in the afternoon, bringing another story of suspected marital infidelity into sharp focus. Amidst the routine household payments were weekly cash withdrawals, nine in total, each of £120. All had taken place at cashpoints in central Bristol on Wednesday mornings between 10 and 11 a.m. The preciseness of the amount certainly suggested a regular habit of some sort. Jenny recalled glimpsing a tariff in the reception of the Recife: a thirty minute 'massage' was £50. The other fact that caught Jenny's attention was that there was £28,000 in the account. There was a monthly transfer from Adam Jordan's employers of a little over £2,000, but sums of several thousand pounds were being transferred in at odd intervals from another account in Adam's name. Of all the problems they might have had, money wasn't one of them.

Deciding against disturbing Karen Jordan in her hospital bed, Jenny called her home number and got through to her mother. Dealing with her crying grandson, Claire King was in no mood to talk, but Jenny pressed for an answer to one question: had Karen ever asked Adam to explain why he was withdrawing cash from their account.

'Several times,' she responded tersely. 'He said it was getting-by money. He was lying. It's as simple as that. And please don't trouble Karen until she's out of hospital. I don't think she could take much more.'

She put down the phone.

Jenny's final act before leaving the office for the evening was to call Sonia Blake in the hope that, having absorbed the reality of Jordan's death, she might have remembered some small but telling detail that would unlock the reason for Adam Jordan's secrecy, but she was met with an answer-phone message saying Sonia was away in Brussels until the following day. Jenny asked herself whether now wasn't the moment to let him rest. All she could offer his family, it seemed, was shame heaped on top of grief.

The humid air that had sat oppressively over the city throughout the afternoon had been banished by an Atlantic breeze that swept in a clear and balmy evening. Jenny drove north over the Severn Bridge beneath an unbroken blue sky. Leaving the sweeping panorama of the estuary behind, she headed into the deep green of the valley and experienced a different kind of elation: the forest seemed to absorb her into its heart, a single, vast, living, breathing entity. Making the final switchback turns into the village of Tintern, the signal returned to her phone and a message alert sounded. She had voicemail. Michael had called to say he had arrived early from a round-trip to Cornwall and was on his way over. The news was like an unexpected gift.

It was too beautiful an evening to stay at home. As soon as Michael arrived, Jenny insisted they go for a walk. She took him along a narrow footpath that skirted the oak woods on the hill behind her cottage then struck out across sloping, sheep-dotted meadows. After a steep climb they arrived on a ridge above a small raised valley untouched by the passing centuries. Stone walls, some a thousand years old, were the only human marks on the landscape. This was the place, Jenny said, to which she would often come to remind herself where she lay in the grand scheme of things. You could feel small here, but also part of something: the continuum of life.

'Like flying,' Michael said. 'Leaving the world behind.'

'No, it's not about escaping,' Jenny said. 'It's about find-ing where you fit in.'

'You think I'm trying to escape?' Michael said.

'When I met you, you were.' Jenny looked at him. 'Not any more.'

He smiled and reached for her hand. They touched finger-tips. 'I think you're right,' was all he said, and kissed her.

They tumbled through the door of Melin Bach, laughing and breathless from running down the hill, and, as naturally as breathing, made love. Then, spent and drowsy, they sat outside to eat, the air still enough for candles to stay alight. Having drawn so close together, their conversation drifted naturally back to their young lives as they filled in the many spaces in the incomplete stories they had constructed for each other. Jenny had heard almost nothing of the brutal boarding school to which Michael had been abandoned while his father was moved from country to country working for an oil company. Nor did she know that he had joined the RAF along with his oldest and closest friend, who was killed when his training jet malfunctioned and exploded in a fireball: Michael had landed the same plane only thirty minutes before. Michael knew about the dark incident in Jenny's young childhood, but she had never told him what it had felt like when she was older to watch her mother fall out of love with her father and leave them both for life with another man, or how for every day of the six years in which she and her father had lived alone together, she had felt his loss far more keenly than her own.

'Between us I think we've covered every shade of guilt,' Michael joked.

'Do you think we could ever let it go?' Jenny said. 'Move on, be free?'

'Mmm.' He sipped his wine and looked at her in the flickering light, giving it some serious thought. 'I always used to think not – if I thought about it at all. But now I think there might be a chance.'

'Because of me?' Jenny said with mock surprise.

'You've come through more than I have and survived pretty well.'

Jenny was strangely touched and felt herself blush.

'Why are you embarrassed?' Michael asked.

'I don't know. I suppose I'd got so used to always being the one with problems.'

Michael said, 'Is that how you see me?'

'No—'

'Hey, I'm kidding.' He reached for her hand and squeezed it. 'We've both caught a lot of flak along the way. That's fine – we understand each other. Why don't we talk about something else. Why don't you tell me what you're working on? Your life's so much more interesting than mine.'

She wanted more from him, but he had opened up to her more in the past week than he had in the previous year; to expect anything further tonight would be greedy. So she told him about the strange death of Adam Jordan, and how she suspected he had gone in search of answers in Africa only to find even deeper dilemmas, and damaged souls like Harry Thorn. Michael's expression grew serious as she described the dope-smoking aid worker whose stunningly beautiful girlfriend cooked naked in front of strangers with no hint of embarrassment.

'That's what happened,' Jenny said. 'I don't think she was stoned, she just seemed perfectly matter-of-fact, as if it's what everyone does.'

'Perhaps she's with him for the money, wherever it comes from. Houses in Notting Hill aren't cheap.'

'He could have inherited.'

'He certainly won't have earned it honestly, not in his profession.'

'You don't know that.'

'He might have found himself a sideline. A Red Cross guy

I met in Afghanistan said after ten years in the field an aid worker was either certifiable, on the make, or a genuine saint, and there aren't many of those.'

'Maybe you only met the cynics?'

'There's a lot to be cynical about in that business. Even if all you're trying to do is give stuff away, you've still got to trade your way in, then find a means of keeping useful. Even starving people know how to work an angle, perhaps better than most.'

'What kind?'

'Contraband, weapons, money. Your man Thorn would know all about it.'

Even though Jenny hadn't much trusted Harry Thorn, she found herself resenting the casual way in which Michael assumed he was a crook, and that by implication she was naive for not having marked him down as one.

'He may be genuine, he may not. I don't know until he's put to the test.'

'He'll be a good liar, good enough to fool a jury. He'll tell them about all the skinny little children he's saved and they'll lap it up. I would have done until I'd seen the reality with my own eyes.'

'Or maybe he'll tell the truth,' Jenny said.

'I'm telling you the truth. If he's come from a war zone he'll be a creature of war – you can't avoid it.' He tipped more wine into his glass. Their conversation was making him tense. Talking about war had stirred up unwanted memories at a moment when his defences were weakest. She could see the battle raging inside him as he fought to push them away.

'How was Cornwall?' Jenny said, trying to steer the conversation onto less uncomfortable ground.

Michael stared into the candle flame with unblinking eyes, as if he hadn't heard her.

'Michael?'

He didn't answer.

'Michael, I'm sorry – it was the wrong thing to talk about.' She reached for his hand. 'Don't go quiet on me. Tell me what you're thinking.'

'Honestly?'

'Of course.'

'I was thinking that when we made love tonight it was the first time I've ever connected it with having children.'

Jenny smiled, a little bemused. 'You'll be glad to know there's no danger of my getting pregnant.'

'I'm not so sure I am glad.'

Jenny found herself lost for words.

'Don't you ever think about it?' Michael asked.

'No. I can honestly say I don't.'

He looked disappointed.

'Michael, I'm forty-six and worked off my feet. Even if it were physically possible, the last thing on God's earth I need is a baby.'

'No . . . You're right.' He sounded unconvinced.

They lapsed into silence again, Jenny struggling to deal with all the possible implications of what he had just announced: he wanted to be a father, to have a child with her. It was out of the question. What was he thinking?

Before she had even recovered herself, he made another announcement: 'You know, I think you should make more time for your son.'

'What?'

'I think he'd give you a chance if he thought there was room in your life. I think he feels your attention's always been tied up with work.' He raised his eyes and met her gaze.

'He told you that?'

'More or less. But hearing about your parents, I can see

how it happened. Your mum left home when you were twelve and that was about the age Ross was when you split from David.'

Jenny was speechless.

'We're always acting out our pasts. We can't seem to help it. Look at me now.' He shook his head. 'Get so close to you, bare my soul, then feel a need to drop a bomb.'

'Do you have any idea how hurtful that was? I never left Ross. David and I separated, and not before time.'

'You did leave, Jenny, consciously or subconsciously, you chose the moment. Someone's got to tell you or you'll never fix it. Better it's this asshole than some other one.'

Jenny stared at him in disbelief. 'I did not leave my son. You have no idea what I went through in that marriage.'

'I think he wants you to fix it, Jenny, but he doesn't know how to ask. And this has nothing to do with David – just you and Ross.'

Jenny shoved the table hard towards him, upending glasses and sending plates clattering onto the ground.

'Go home, Michael! And don't even think about trying to call me. I don't want to know.'

She marched into the kitchen, slammed the door hard and locked it, suddenly not caring if she ever saw him again.

FOURTEEN

JENNY LEFT THE HOUSE EARLY in the morning without checking to see if Michael had left a message or sent an email. Screw him. She felt violated, as if he had tricked her into lowering her defences to the point that when he struck he could wound her most deeply. She had trusted him completely, and all the while he was biding his time, waiting for the moment to deliver his judgement on her inadequacies as a mother. And on top of that he had had the gall to suggest she have his baby, which doubtless he would expect her to neglect. He was having a crisis. He was confused. He had to be, there was no other explanation. Well, if he expected her to act as his emotional dumping ground, he had another think coming.

Her fury turned to steel in her blood; she was ready to knock down anyone who dared stand in her way. It brought a strange sense of freedom: the guilt at all her unattended cases fell away. Today belonged to Adam Jordan: she was going to London to interview his colleagues at the AFAD offices. No one ever wanted to admit their small part in events leading to an untimely death, but she would offer them no choice: they would answer her honestly or have the truth dragged out of them in court.

All along the motorway her angry thoughts jumped between the answers she was going to demand from Jordan's colleagues, and the unwelcome memories stirred by Michael's accusation. Like images from a nightmare, she was assailed by half-forgotten details of the weeks and months leading up to the moment when she left David. Again and again her mind replayed her lowest and cruellest moments; she was haunted by an image of Ross's uncomprehending face as he came to the car window as she prepared to drive away from the house for the last time. Her leaving home had been like her death to him, a taunting voice told her Michael was right; you knew full well what it was that you would have to kill in order to survive.

Only the rush and confusion of London streets forced the accusing ghosts from her mind. She parked underground near Marble Arch and made her way on foot across the West End towards D'Arblay Street in Soho. The people she passed were freaks, weirdos, thieves; there was no compassion in her today; every face belonged to an enemy. She arrived at her destination: a doorway sandwiched between a cafe and a shop selling leather gear and instruments of bedroom torture. *Calm down, Jenny. It's just work. Breathe.*

The voice of a young African man came over the intercom. Jenny heard him consult with Eda Hincks before he admitted her and told her to make her way to the third floor.

She climbed six steep flights of stairs and arrived on a narrow landing at the top of the unloved building. A tall, serious woman in her late twenties with scraped-back blonde hair came out to meet her.

'Mrs Cooper. I am Eda Hincks. How may I help you?'

'I'd like to come in and talk, if you wouldn't mind.'

'Now is not convenient.'

'I was being polite,' Jenny said, heading off further explanation. 'I need to ask some questions about Adam Jordan.'

'We have a meeting shortly—' Eda began, in another attempt to head her off.

'We'll be quick, then. Shall we get started?'

Refused a choice, Eda reluctantly led Jenny into the small but tidy open-plan offices beneath the sloping mansard roof. There were four desks, only two of which were occupied – one by Eda, the other by a slim young African man with trusting brown eyes. Eda introduced him as Toby Ormondi.

'Toby arrived from Nairobi two days ago,' she explained. 'He never knew Adam.'

Toby looked up from his computer and gave a cautious smile.

'Is this all of you?' Jenny asked.

'There's Mr Thorn, his partner, Gabra Giorgis, and now and then we're joined by staff from our African offices.'

'Do you have many?'

'Two – Nairobi and Addis Ababa. But you have to understand, it's a very lean operation. When we need staff, we hire them in.' Eda gestured Jenny to a chair and carefully flicked off her monitor as she sat.

Jenny had imagined the aid agency's offices would be larger, busier, and filled with purpose. The room in which she found herself felt like a lonely outpost with little connection to the people it served.

'Have you ever worked out in the field?' Jenny asked.

'Yes,' Eda answered without embellishment. 'But I prefer to run the office.'

Jenny imagined the Africans preferred it that way, too. Eda didn't possess a personality that promised to bring joy to the needy. She took a notebook from her bag. 'I'm trying to build a picture of Mr Jordan's state of mind at the end of his life. I'd like to know precisely what he was doing in South Sudan.'

Eda reached across her desk and picked up a file. 'The

project portfolio. Take a look for yourself.' She handed it to her.

Jenny turned through the pages. There was technical information describing how water from a single well could be rationed to grow acres of crops using buried pipes to bring life back to arid soil, then a selection of before-and-after photographs of the site, together with pictures showing Adam Jordan and Harry Thorn hard at work with a team of locals, digging trenches with hand tools. Sure enough, dried-up scrub was transformed into an oasis. The final pictures showed Adam and several smiling, bone-thin men in sweat-stained T-shirts standing amidst neck-high maize plants.

'How long did this all take?' Jenny asked.

'A little over six months,' Eda replied. 'Unfortunately we were forced to suspend the education and maintenance programme when fighting broke out. This village, Anaku-bouri, was close to the border with the north. Even post-partition, there's still violence. Have you heard of the Janjaweed?'

'Vaguely.'

'They're Arab fighters, mostly nomadic. They've a long history of conflict with the settled population over land use. There's also a religious element. Just another of Africa's problems,' she added with a trace of sarcasm that Jenny assumed was the closest she came to humour.

'Was Adam Jordan depressed by that?' Jenny asked.

'We all were disappointed. We heard reports our system was destroyed.'

'What about the people? He must have made a lot of friends. Were many hurt or killed?'

'Of course he made friends. And more than likely some became casualties in the fighting. Until we have our own reports, we don't yet know who.'

Jenny tried for more detail, but Eda persisted with her

studiedly bland answers that delivered no new insight into Adam Jordan. And all the while Toby appeared to take no notice of their conversation as he tapped quietly on his computer. Jenny decided to up the pressure.

'Do you know the two main reasons people kill themselves, Miss Hincks?'

She seemed thrown by the question. 'Depression, and . . .' She shrugged.

'Shame,' Jenny said. 'Was Mr Jordan depressed, to your knowledge?'

She shook her head.

'Did he have anything to be ashamed of?'

Eda's eyes darted involuntarily to Toby.

'He completed his project precisely as planned. He had no reason for regret.'

Her answer rang as hollow as a pebble hitting the floor of a dry well.

'Somehow I struggle to believe that. It wouldn't be human.'

'What wouldn't be human?' A voice bellowed from across the room.

Jenny swung round to see Harry Thorn stepping through the door, thrusting his phone into the pocket of his threadbare jeans. He glanced at Toby, who started up from his desk and headed out. Harry clapped him on the shoulder as he passed, as if in thanks. The penny dropped – the gesture was for tipping him off. Toby had been transcribing their conversation and relaying it straight to Harry's phone by email.

'Turning up unannounced is your signature, isn't it, Mrs Cooper?' Harry looked ruffled and hung-over, and even from several paces smelt sourly of stale smoke. 'You think we've got something to hide? Do your worst, turn the place over. See if I fucking care.'

Jolted by the violence of his outburst, Jenny tried to remain composed. 'If you prefer, we can leave all this to court.'

He was standing close by now, looking down at her in a way that suggested he might just grab her by the lapels and toss her out of the door. 'Why don't you piss off, Mrs Cooper, and leave us to get on with our work?'

'I would have liked to spare Mrs Jordan the ordeal of a lengthy inquest.'

'I've spoken to Karen. She's heard all there is to know.'

Jenny felt her frustration turn to anger. 'There are aspects of Mr Jordan's work in Africa I would appreciate your help in understanding,' she said coolly.

'How's this? Don't listen to the cock-sucking spooks who think we must be terrorists because we refuse to work for them.' He smiled at her surprise. 'You think they haven't knocked on my door, too?' He laughed, a short dismissive burst like gunfire. 'You know squat about Africa. Take some good advice and leave it to those that do.'

'Why did Adam Jordan take his life, Mr Thorn?'

Harry looked at her with narrow, reptilian eyes. 'The problem with Adam was he took it all to heart. Me, I've learned to keep the sluices open. In it comes, then washes right out again. That's the only way to survive in this business – keep the sluices open.' He looked at Eda Hincks, who since his arrival had displayed neither shock nor embarrassment. She seemed to admire his bravado. 'Show Mrs Cooper out, Eda.'

'I'll see you at court, Mr Thorn,' Jenny said, and made her own way to the door.

Harry gave a dismissive grunt, and as Jenny crossed the room, he said, 'Some can take it, some can't. That's just how it fucking is.'

*

Jenny stepped out onto the hot pavement with the feeling that she had panicked Harry Thorn, not so much by her unannounced arrival – he had been anticipating that – but by her insistence. He was used to playing rough, to bargaining and twisting his path out of awkward corners the African way, but it couldn't work with her. Behind the bluster, she had seen fear. There had been something else, too: someone who had truly learned to keep the sluices open would have kept his cool. Harry had shown all the signs of a man whose grip was loosening, a man whose past was rushing up to meet him. Push him a little harder and he might just crack open.

Turning left onto Great Marlborough Street, Jenny saw Toby emerge from the coffee shop across the street. And as by some sixth sense, he sensed her presence, glanced her way, then guiltily averted his eyes. She started towards the kerb, hoping to intercept him as he turned right towards the office, but anticipating her, he went left and melted in amongst the pedestrians heading towards Oxford Street.

Crawling through the west London traffic, Jenny tried her best to convince Alison that she was as good as in the office. In an extended phone call that lasted nearly the entire hour it took to progress as far as Heathrow, she answered queries, dictated emails and made decisions to issue death certificates in three separate cases. Alison remained stoical in the face of her abandonment, but her silent disapproval held up a mirror to Jenny's impulsiveness. Again, she questioned whether it was pride, pig-headedness or neurosis that was driving her to pursue the Adam Jordan investigation beyond all reasonable limits. It was Alison who unwittingly provided part of the answer when, at the end of their extended call, she was silent for a long moment, then asked, 'I'm not being rude, Mrs Cooper, but are you sure this case hasn't stirred

something –' she hesitated, groping for the appropriate word
– '*unhealthy* in you?'

'What do you mean?' Jenny asked.

'I don't like to be personal, but I've seen you react this
way before. It's because he left his child like that, isn't it?
You don't like to accept that someone can behave so cal-
lously without a good reason. But sometimes there just isn't
one. People who have been good fathers and husbands can
suddenly be selfish and cruel. Don't you think you should
try to accept that?'

Her plea was as heartfelt as it was unprompted, and
delivered with such concern that it was impossible for Jenny
not to take it to heart.

'Thank you,' she found herself saying. 'I'll give it some
thought.'

Little thought was required. Alison had simply put into
words what was obvious to both of them: unable to mend
her own broken family, she spent her whole working life
trying to fix other people's. But was that unhealthy? Did
accepting this truth make her choices any easier? The one
that faced her now was whether to continue on to Bristol
and devote herself to all the other bereaved families awaiting
her answers, or to turn off the motorway to retrace Adam
Jordan's steps on the day he died. As she approached the
exit road, the sensation in the pit of her stomach made the
decision for her.

Great Shefford was a small, mostly modern-built village a
little over two miles from the motorway. She approached
through a patchwork of fields, many of which were planted
with hybrid rapeseed that made carpets of brilliant, unnatural yellow too dazzling to look at directly. She turned at a
crossroads where the Swan pub stood, and headed out of
the village centre to its margins. After a short distance she

arrived at Brookside filling station. Behind it, a grassy meadow rose up in a gentle slope. Jenny pulled in and found hers to be the only vehicle on the forecourt. Feeling a little foolish, she fetched the picture of Adam Jordan she had taken to carrying with her and took it into the small garage shop.

Jenny approached the counter. A large woman in her early twenties was seated on a high stool, turning through the pages of a gossip magazine.

'I wonder if you could help me.' Jenny handed her the photograph. 'I'm Coroner for the Severn Vale District. Unfortunately this man died a little over a week ago.'

The girl looked at the picture, then up at Jenny, with vacant eyes. 'You what?'

'I'm a coroner. I have to determine the cause of death . . .' Jenny could tell she wasn't following. 'He was here on Monday the 23rd at a quarter to six in the evening. He bought petrol, drinks and a sandwich. He had a young child with him in the car, he may have brought him in.'

The blank face behind the counter failed to animate.

'Do you remember if you were working then, or if not, who was?'

The girl said, 'I work Mondays till six.' She looked down at the photograph and frowned. 'I might have seen him.'

'He was driving an estate car. An old black Saab.'

'I remember a man with a black girl.'

'A girl? What was she like?'

'I say girl, she was a woman. Small, thin . . . And there was a kid. A little white boy. And she was holding him.' She nodded. 'That's it, that's what made me look – she was black but holding a white kid.'

Jenny felt her heart quickening. Now she had someone to look for. A living witness to Jordan's final hours. 'Do you remember anything more? What did they do? How did they seem together?'

The girl shook her head. 'That's all I remember, really, except . . .' She hesitated for a moment as an image floated back to the surface of her mind. 'There was another guy, that's right . . .'

'With them?'

'No. They were here in the shop. He was standing here paying, and the girl came and tapped him on the shoulder and said something, maybe his name.'

'Adam?'

'Yeah, that's it. She said, "Adam?" And he looked round and another car, a small one, had pulled up alongside his and there was a bloke getting out of it. Then the man you're asking about went outside, and I think shook hands with him. And then they went around there. There's a little place you can park out the back of the building. I think that's where they went.'

'Both cars?'

'I think so.'

'And this other man? What did he look like?'

'Thirtyish, thirty-five. Kind of . . . ordinary. Glasses. Yeah, he was wearing glasses.'

'Have you seen him before?'

'Maybe. I couldn't say for certain.'

Jenny glanced up behind the counter and saw a security camera.

'You don't have any of this on tape, do you?'

'Not that far back, no.'

Jenny continued to interrogate the cashier for several more minutes, hoping to pick up any small detail that might lead her closer to the girl or the nondescript man they met with, but all she could offer was her impression that Adam Jordan and the girl hadn't been intimate. 'It was more like she was working for him or something,' she said, 'when she tapped his shoulder, she seemed nervous, as if she didn't like to touch him.'

Jenny left the shop and drove her car around to the side of the building, where she found the entrance to an unmade track leading to a farm. A galvanized five-bar gate stood open, and just inside it was space enough to park three or four cars side by side. Jenny stared through the windscreen at the empty field beyond and tried to imagine what on earth would have brought Adam Jordan to this spot only a few hours before his death. Puzzling over who the second man might have been, she recalled Harry Thorn's outburst: *'Don't listen to the cock-sucking spooks who think we must be terrorists because we refuse to work for them.'* His weary, mocking smile. *'You think they haven't knocked on my door, too?'* And the girl. Who was she? Jenny's initial thought had been that it might have been Harry Thorn's girlfriend, Gabra, but she was over six feet tall. The girl with Adam had been small and slight.

Jenny turned the Land Rover around and started back to the motorway, wondering where to look next, and even if she dared. She had driven less than half a mile when her phone rang.

'Mrs Cooper – it's Andy Kerr.' He was speaking from beside a busy road, his voice partially obscured by traffic.

'What's happening? Any more news on Elena Lujan? Please don't tell me we've more cases.'

'No.' Jenny heard him swallow nervously. 'It's nothing so obvious.'

'Oh?'

'After what happened to Sophie Freeman's body I had the technicians run an audit on the forty or so we've got here at present. I don't know if you've heard that the hospital's being swept by a team who are refusing to talk to anyone. They won't even say who they work for.'

'I had heard something along those lines.'

'I thought it might be them. I assume they're some sort of private company hired in by the management. That's the only way I could think that someone would have got access to the locked refrigerator. The thing is . . .' He paused, as if questioning his own soundness of mind. 'None of the other bodies had been touched, except one. Your road-bridge suicide – Adam Jordan.'

Jenny felt as if she had just wandered into a darkened room to hear the door click shut behind her.

'Precisely the same procedure,' Dr Kerr said. 'Cerebro-spinal fluid drained and brain tissue removed. Have you any idea what the hell's going on?'

FIFTEEN

JENNY ARRIVED IN THE MORTUARY to see Adam Jordan's body lying on one of the two tables. Dr Kerr had emptied the contents of the clear plastic bag containing the previously dissected major organs onto the stainless-steel counter and was now meticulously sorting through the pieces. Jenny tugged a paper mask from a dispenser and pulled it over her mouth and nose.

'My God.' The smell of the reopened body was overpowering.

'Someone's had it out of the fridge, that's why,' Dr Kerr said, engrossed in his task. 'You can see the decomposition in the tissues. It must have been gone twelve hours or more.'

Jenny glanced behind her. There was a technician wheeling a gurney past the door in the corridor, but otherwise they were alone.

'It's all right, he knows,' Dr Kerr said. 'It was him who spotted it.'

Jenny could see sections of heart, lungs, kidneys and liver, but no sign of brain tissue.

'Same MO?' she asked.

'Exactly. The top of the bag was even folded the same way. Someone had taken a lot of care to cover their tracks – they'd re-stitched using the same holes. Must have taken hours.'

'Have you told anyone?'

'No. Thought I'd keep this one quiet. My manager might already know, of course.'

'What are you checking for?'

'Any other signs of interference. I think they may have taken biopsies, but there's nothing else missing, as far as I can see.' He stopped work for a moment and looked at her over his mask. 'This man did not have meningitis, and there is no evidence of the bacteria in the back of his throat.'

'Someone must think there's a link. Perhaps because he'd been in Africa?'

'Who would know that?' Dr Kerr said. 'It doesn't make any sense. Why choose a body that has no connection?' He let out a sigh that seemed to say the incident caused him a profound loss of faith. He was a man who lived on procedure; the sacred rules had been violated.

Jenny said, 'All I can think of is something that sounds too elaborate – whoever it is, whoever *they* are, might be trying to concoct a link where none exists, fabricating evidence that Adam Jordan brought the bacteria into the hospital.'

'They'd still have to know Jordan's history. Not even I would know that, unless someone like you told me.'

Jenny said, 'Are you sure it's safe to talk in here?'

'After this, I don't think I care either way. Last time I checked my contract, complicity in the theft of body parts wasn't a requirement.'

Jenny said, 'I admire the sentiment, but I'd rather we didn't take the chance.'

They stepped out of the back door of the mortuary and sheltered from the rain under the loading-bay canopy. Huddled in a corner where they couldn't be seen from the hospital building opposite, Jenny gave Andy Kerr the highlights of Adam Jordan's recent history. She told him about

Harry Thorn and his uneasy relationship with British officials in Africa, about Karen Jordan and the break-in at her home, and ended with Sonia Blake and the newspaper article she'd found about her murdered father.

Far from being surprised, each element fed into a picture he had already partially formed.

'I thought you'd be more sceptical,' Jenny said, when she came to the end of her story, 'or at least think I was being paranoid imagining that anything could connect it all together.'

'Not at all,' he said. 'It's starting to make some sort of sense.'

'It is?'

'The team sweeping the hospital are going through this place like they really mean business. I'd put money on them being from the Defence Science Lab at Porton Down – they're the only outfit I can think of with the manpower and expertise. They'd also have people capable of borrowing bodies from my mortuary – whoever it was needed keys.'

'Porton Down is the military's research laboratory in Wiltshire?'

'Government and military. It's also where the HPA have their Centre for Emergency Preparedness and Response.'

'That would explain the secrecy. I still don't see why they singled out Adam Jordan's body. There must have been hundreds, if not thousands of people who had travelled to Britain from central Africa in recent months.'

'What about the girl he was with?' Andy Kerr said. 'Do you think she was African? What do you know about her?'

'Nothing,' Jenny admitted.

'Maybe someone else does? She could be the connection.'

'What sort of connection? Do you mean she might have been carrying the infection?'

He shrugged. 'It's all shooting in the dark. I don't like to speculate.'

'I'm asking you to. I need to make some decisions. Do you think I should be looking further, or should I just sign Sophie Freeman and Elena Lujan's deaths off as due to natural causes?'

He looked uncomfortable being challenged so directly.

'Natural causes would mean that there had been no human act or omission that contributed, of course,' Jenny added. 'But last time we met you seemed to think that might not be the case. You were talking about recombinant strains.'

'All right.' He couldn't have sounded more reluctant. 'I'm going to stick to logic, OK? We've got a drug-resistant strain of a highly dangerous organism. It either evolved naturally in a human host or, less likely, it's leaked out from a vaccine-research project, possibly through someone who works in a lab becoming infected. If it's entirely human in origin, your initial suspicion would be an African source. If there's a connection with a lab, you'd turn to the Public Register of Genetically Modified Organisms to see who in the UK has a licence to work with these bacteria. As I mentioned to you, I've checked it – there are currently three university labs working with meningitis, all on standard strains, none of them modifying to create anything like what we've seen here. But if government or military scientists have a project running it might not be on the register – there's an exemption from publication on grounds of national security.'

'So there's a possibility this strain might have escaped from a government laboratory?'

'It's one possibility among many,' Andy said. 'No more than that.'

'How could that happen? They must have every precaution imaginable.'

'You'd be surprised. All it takes is one act of carelessness. One of the lab staff gets infected, goes to a shopping mall or cinema and sneezes, or leaves a trace of infected mucus on a door handle or rail. It's not particularly likely, but it's not impossible, either.'

'It sounds plausible,' Jenny said, 'but if that's the case, I can see even less reason why Adam Jordan's body would be of any interest.'

Andy Kerr's glance told her he had a suspicion.

'You've already speculated once,' Jenny said, 'so don't try to convince me you've got a rule against it.'

'I could make a wild guess, but that's all it would be.'

'Go on.'

'He could have acted as a courier, bringing samples from Africa. If you're importing a new strain, someone has to bring it in. It's the kind of job you would only give to someone entirely trustworthy.'

'Why would a courier jump off a bridge?'

'If he thought he was doing one thing, but found out he was really doing another?'

They exchanged a look, both suddenly suspecting they were dealing with something far darker than they had feared.

Andy stepped back out of sight as a car crept past. The driver, a woman, appeared to glance in their direction.

'Relax,' Jenny said, 'it's just someone looking for a space.'

'Yeah,' Andy said, turning sharply, 'nothing to worry about.' He pushed through the door and disappeared inside.

Jenny had never seen Andy Kerr frightened, and the ominous feeling that there was more going on in his mind than he had felt able to share grew stronger during her short journey back to the office. She knew him well enough to appreciate that he wouldn't have mentioned the highly secretive government laboratories at Porton Down unless he was convinced of their involvement, but it was the implications of that prospect that he hadn't felt able to discuss. Was he frightened for himself or for her, she wondered. Now, as she thought of Jordan standing on the motorway bridge, she pictured him filled with an irredeemable guilt at his part in something that had gone far beyond whatever he had intended. But she still had no clear insight into the inner man. Had he remained an idealist or had he been corrupted? Was it conceivable that he'd been turned and was doing the bidding of the 'spooks' Harry Thorn so loathed?

'Mr Moreton just called,' Alison said, the moment Jenny stepped through the office door. 'He wanted to know when you're planning to resume the Sophie Freeman inquest. He seemed a little impatient.'

'He'll have to put up with it. I'm still gathering evidence.' Her spirits sank at the sight of yet another fresh pile of reports waiting for her attention.

'Dr Verma phoned earlier.' She handed Jenny a note. 'They've found the other two girls from the Recife and they seem to be clear. I think she's hoping you'll see your way to writing Elena Lujan's death certificate without an inquest.'

'There's a short answer to that,' Jenny said, and dropped the memo into the bin.

'As long as you think you've time.' Alison got up from her desk and pulled on her jacket.

'You're going?'

'I haven't left my desk since 8.30 this morning, Mrs Cooper. Some of us do have lives.'

It was a comment intended to both wound and inspire guilt. It succeeded on both counts.

'Of course,' Jenny said.

'Good night, Mrs Cooper.' Alison picked up her briefcase and left.

Jenny lifted the heavy heap of papers and moved into the quiet cool of her office. Often this solid Georgian room, closed off from the world by its heavy oak door, served as a place of respite and sanctuary, but in the stillness of a late-summer afternoon its quietness soon became oppressive. The harder she tried to push Adam, Sophie and Elena from her mind and concentrate on the mundane tasks before her, the more she imagined their ghosts moving through the slanting light and their whispered voices in the empty rooms beyond. She looked up from her desk, frustrated at being impeded by such irrational thoughts, but there it was: a force as irresist-ible as it was confounding, leaving her no choice but to push all else aside and dig deeper. Immediately.

She began with the Freemans, and was grateful to reach Ed on his mobile phone. He was unusually quiet – he hinted at a row with Fiona – and Jenny almost thought better of troubling him with more unsettling information. But he had anticipated the promise of another insight and was eager for Jenny to tell him what she had found. She couched the connection with Porton Down as the remotest possibility, but it was one he seized on.

'That's who those sly bastards are, sneaking around the hospital.'

'We don't know that,' Jenny insisted.

Ed was dismissive. He had made up his mind. 'What are you going to do? They'll be the last people to tell you the truth.'

'I'll start by looking for a connection. You don't know anyone who works there who might have come into contact with Sophie?'

'No.'

'Had she been anywhere she wouldn't normally go in the last few weeks – a friend's house?'

'I've been through all this with Verma's people – it was still term time, just the normal routine of home and school.'

'She must have been somewhere else besides.'

'She went into town a few times with Fiona. That's all. There's no point to this, it's hopeless.' He seemed overcome with despair. 'Don't you have powers to demand answers? We're not looking for a public apology; we just want to know where it came from.'

Jenny persisted, 'Maybe she had a boyfriend you didn't know about – is that possible? Have you checked all her online activity?'

'There was no boyfriend.'

'What about the cinema – or anywhere she might have been close to other people? Just think . . .'

He fell silent.

'Ed? Are you still there?'

'I just thought of something,' he said quietly. 'I belong to Hampton's—'

'I know it. St Edward's Road.' Hampton's, in affluent Clifton, wasn't so much a gym as a fully fledged country club. David had been a member before he declared that it had become too effeminate for his manly tastes. As Jenny remembered it, there were tennis and squash courts, a gym, and a large and elegant kidney-shaped pool.

'I dropped in one Sunday morning – about a month ago. Fiona had to go to her mother's. The girls came with me and went swimming.'

'You'd forgotten this?'

'No—'

'What are you saying?'

He gave a despairing sigh. 'There's someone I sometimes have coffee with.'

'Who?'

'No one you know. We're just friends. But Fiona read a couple of texts one time and made assumptions.'

'She doesn't know you were there?'

'The girls had promised her they'd be doing their music practice, so it was all a bit of a secret . . . Oh God. What have I done?'

'I won't mention this to anyone, I promise. I'm just ruling out a possibility.'

Ed Freeman fell into another unreadable silence.

'Whatever I find out, I'll speak to you before doing anything,' Jenny said. 'You have my word.'

'Sure,' he grunted.

Hoping that this particular lead would lead nowhere, Jenny called the anxious manager of Hampton's and, after first assuring him that her inquiry remained strictly confidential, asked him to forward the contact details of all club members who had visited during the twenty-four hours before Ed and his daughters. Alarmed, he tried to play for time, asking to consult with his company's solicitors. Jenny gave him a straight choice: comply immediately, or find himself a witness at her inquest. She left the decision with him.

Switching her attention back to Adam Jordan, Jenny tried to plot her next moves. She needed to trace the girl he had been with at Great Shefford, but felt it was still too soon to share this information with Karen Jordan. There was no point going back to Harry Thorn or his employees – they wouldn't break ranks this side of the witness box – which left her with only one possibility: Sonia Blake.

Jenny paused to marshal the rush of thoughts her name prompted. Stay rational, she told herself, reason it through, one step at a time. She knew only three things about her for certain. She was a respected academic with an expertise in

African conflicts. She was a pragmatist who didn't shy from advocating violent means to achieve just ends. And her father had been a geneticist who was murdered thirty years ago in Arizona. Her father's profession was an odd but resonant detail that Jenny found vaguely disturbing. It was made all the more so by the fact that Adam Jordan went to meet her having just bought a rare, out-of-print book by a Russian microbiologist. Even viewed through the prism of pure logic, there was a theme emerging.

Sonia Blake was, Jenny imagined, just the kind of person who, alongside her academic career, might have become involved with governments or other shadier interested parties in the conflict-ridden areas she researched. But Jenny had no handle on that world and no means of understanding it. For all she knew, Adam Jordan and Sonia Blake might have had a professional relationship that extended far beyond anything she had admitted during their brief interview. To talk to her again felt like a step into the unknown, perhaps even a dangerous risk, though what was at stake Jenny couldn't say. She paced her office and prevaricated, wrestling with how she should approach her, what she should give away and what she should hold back, until she had argued herself to a standstill. Deciding finally to play it by ear, she searched out her number.

Sonia Blake answered her phone in a distracted voice, as if she had been deep in thought.

Jenny felt a pressure behind her ribs as she opened her mouth to speak; she was inexplicably nervous. Stumbling slightly, she apologized for disturbing her yet again, but explained that certain facts had come to light which she would like to discuss.

'Oh. I'll do what I can.' Sonia Blake sounded mildly irritated by the request.

Attempting to seize the upper hand, Jenny said, 'May I ask if you work for anyone outside the university, Mrs Blake?'

'No.' She was affronted. 'What does this have to do with Adam Jordan?'

Again, Jenny wanted to prove that she wasn't afraid of being direct: 'His employers were under pressure to work for British interests. I wondered if you might have anything to do with that world.'

'It's my area of study. That's why I made contact with him.'

'And that's as far as your interest extends?'

'Yes . . . But I'm intrigued to know what you're getting at, Mrs Cooper. I don't know if I can help you, but if you'd like to meet, I'll happily give you the benefit of what little relevant knowledge I might have.'

Her tone had shifted yet again. Jenny's instinct was not to trust her, but the offer of a meeting was too enticing to turn down.

'That would be very helpful. Are you available tomorrow?'

'I'm going to Oslo – academic conference season, I'm afraid. I return next Tuesday.'

'What about tonight?' Jenny said impulsively.

She hesitated. 'I suppose that would be all right. As long as we're not too late – I've an early start.'

'I can be with you by eight.'

'Well, you know where to find me.'

Ninety minutes later, Jenny finally found a parking space in a city that seemed determined to repel all outsiders who arrived by car, and made her way on foot through the narrow streets of Jericho to Worcester College. Several shots of filthy service-station espresso had done little to banish the exhaustion of having spent eight hours on the road in a single day. This was the last trip she would make on this case, she promised herself, no more running around the country chasing shadows.

'Mrs Cooper?'

The porter had spotted her from the window alongside his desk and come out of his lodge to greet her.

'Mrs Blake will be back shortly. She's gone for her evening run.' He smiled, as if the notion were slightly mad. 'Nice evening for a turn round the gardens. Down the steps to your left, and through the passage.'

Feeling that she had been offered no option, and in no mood for crossing swords with a busybody, Jenny did as he suggested. At the foot of a flight of stone steps, she passed through a narrow stone passageway that connected the quad to the gardens beyond.

She turned right, following a cinder path that led behind the terrace of medieval cottages to a large and gracefully curving lake. Willows swept the surface of the water, providing shelter for a contented colony of ducks. She wandered on around the lake's perimeter, admiring the shifting views of the ancient college buildings, and paused to sit for a while on an ornamental stone bench dappled with lichen. How strange it must be, she thought, for a woman like Sonia Blake to live in such rarefied surroundings yet to have her mind filled with the dirty politics of troubled, faraway countries.

Stirred by the first hints of a chill evening breeze, she continued on her way. The path took her past the college playing fields and through some tasteful modern accommodation blocks, before leading her into a courtyard behind the far side of the quad. A long flight of creaking wooden stairs delivered her back almost at her destination, on the ground floor of Sonia Blake's staircase.

It was ten minutes past the time they had agreed to meet, so Jenny carried on up the stairs to the second floor. She found Sonia Blake's oak door slightly ajar.

'Mrs Blake?'

Silence.

Pushing the inner door open, she peered inside. The room was much as she remembered it, strewn with books and files. Then something caught her eye: liquid was dripping from the edge of the desk; a cup had been recently knocked over and the contents spilled over loose pages and items of mail scattered about the computer monitor.

'Mrs Blake, are you there?'

Jenny stepped through the door and called again. The dead quiet was interrupted only by the slow drip-drip of coffee onto the carpet. Approaching the desk, she dipped her finger into the small pool of brown liquid and felt that it was cold. She noticed, too, that the toppled cup had a brown ring halfway down its interior surface, as if it had been standing, half-full, for some time.

'Mrs Blake?'

The silence remained unbroken.

She crossed the room and approached the one internal door. Her heart beat hard against the wall of her chest as she twisted the brass knob and pushed it open. It gave onto a small bedroom. The single bed was made, the wardrobe closed. To the right of the chest of drawers was another door. Jenny knocked on it and, receiving no reply, opened it to find a small passageway no more than ten feet long. At the far end was another door. She approached it, turned the handle and found that it was locked.

Retracing her steps, she became aware of the sound of a wailing siren that grew louder as it approached, then came to a stop not far away. She went to one of the windows overlooking the quad, and moments later saw police uniforms and the porter walking briskly through the cloisters in her direction. She turned away with a rising sense of dread. Something was badly wrong; she had felt it from the moment she saw the toppled cup. Acting by instinct rather than reason, she took out her phone, and switched on its camera, and took as many photographs of the room as she could before the sound of heavy boots reached the final flight of stairs.

She met the two constables on the landing. 'Both doors were open,' she said. 'I came to meet Mrs Blake. Has something happened?'

They pushed past without answering her.

It was the porter who spoke, doubled over from the effort of running up the stairs. 'A woman's body's been found on Port Meadow,' he gasped. 'They think it's her.'

'She's *dead*?'

'She always ran with her phone strapped to her arm. They checked. It was hers.'

The news sucked the breath from Jenny.

'How?' she whispered.

The porter shook his head. 'That's all they've told me.'

Another set of footsteps was racing up the stairwell, faster and more agile than the ones that had preceded it. Alex Forster appeared, calling out to the porter as he scaled the final flight two steps at a time.

'What's happened?'

One of the police officers stepped out of the room and barked at the porter. 'Who else has got keys to this door?'

'Just me,' he answered.

'Will somebody tell me what's going on?' Forster demanded.

The constable pulled out his radio. 'Everyone stay over here. We're treating this as a crime scene.'

SIXTEEN

IN THE FIFTEEN MINUTES IT HAD taken Detective Inspector Gregson and his team to arrive, Jenny had managed to be excused to visit the bathroom, moments she used to email the dozen photographs she had taken of the inside of Sonia Blake's room to Alison's account and delete all trace from her phone. She had no idea what, if anything, the pictures might contain; her only thought had been to secure the proof of what she had found. She no longer felt able to trust anyone.

Alex Forster had sat silently on the stairs, making no attempt to question the police once he had heard of the body's discovery, or to ask Jenny what had brought her back. The porter, however, whose name was Davies, had maintained a non-stop monologue. He hadn't seen anyone suspicious come or go, he kept repeating to the two constables, 'The only person I let into the college was Mrs Cooper, and she went round the garden, I saw her.'

Nearly two hours later Jenny found herself dog-tired, hungry and alone in a stark office on the second floor of St Aldate's police station. She had heard nothing more about the circumstances of Sonia Blake's death, or even if it had been confirmed. A detective constable scarcely older than her son had taken her statement before asking her to 'wait a moment' while he consulted his boss over whether he could let her go home. A moment had stretched to an hour and Jenny was at the end of her tether. DI Gregson hadn't even done her the courtesy of putting his head around the door.

She was on the verge of making a unilateral decision to walk out when Gregson finally deigned to appear. No older than thirty-five, he was one of the polished, well-spoken new breed of officer whom Jenny suspected had come up through the graduate fast track. But what he possessed in intelligence, he lacked in grace. In the few minutes she had spent in his company at the college she had got his measure as a man who went about his work with a belligerent neutrality that treated everyone with equal disdain. Alongside him was a woman no older than he was, but from the quality of her suit and the lightness of her bearing, Jenny could tell that she wasn't a police officer.

'Sorry to keep you waiting, Mrs Cooper,' Gregson said without feeling. 'You'll appreciate we had to verify a few of the facts in your statement.'

'No,' Jenny said, 'I don't.' She glanced at the woman taking a seat next to him behind the desk. 'Jenny Cooper, Severn Vale District Coroner.'

'Ruth Webley,' the woman said politely. 'I work for the intelligence service – anti-terrorism.'

Jenny tried to appear unfazed.

'You'll probably know that our two services work closely together,' Gregson explained. 'Miss Blake's death prompted an alert.'

Ruth Webley cast Gregson a glance that said she would prefer to speak for herself. 'Obviously there are thousands of people who come to our attention in various ways,' she explained. 'Mrs Blake was simply someone who, in her professional career, had associated with various persons of interest to us. The fact that she appeared on our database doesn't necessarily carry any sinister significance, but we would like to rule out the possibility that anything untoward occurred.'

'Of course,' Jenny said, resolving not to say a word more than she had to.

Ruth Webley waited, and when Jenny offered her nothing, smiled in a patient way that said she had suspected Jenny would be less than forthcoming. 'I ought to begin by saying that initial indications are that Mrs Blake died from natural causes. She seems to have collapsed while out jogging. We've not had post-mortem results yet, but we've no reason to think her death itself was suspicious.'

Jenny waited for the 'but'.

'The situation with her room was a little odd, however,' Webley said. 'We've spoken to an occupant upstairs who passed by her door approximately thirty minutes before you say you arrived. He's sure the outer door to her rooms was shut fast.'

'I've told you how I found it.'

She referred to a copy of Jenny's statement. 'You also say you went inside. Why did you do that?'

'As I said, I called her name, looked through the open door, then noticed the upended cup on her desk. It seemed odd – suspicious, I suppose.'

'An upended cup prompted you to trespass into the room of a woman you had met only once before?'

'Not trespass, I was concerned.'

'Because . . . ?'

'I assumed you would have read my statement.'

'I have, several times. But I'd appreciate hearing it in your own words, Mrs Cooper.'

Jenny had told the detective constable only what she thought the police needed to know. She had no intention of giving Ruth Webley any more. While the coroner's job was to root out the truth and publish it to the world, she had learned from her two previous encounters with the security services that Webley's concern would be to make sure that any inconvenient facts remained well hidden.

Choosing her words carefully, Jenny repeated the story she had told earlier. She was inquiring into the death of an aid worker named Adam Jordan, and Sonia Blake was one of the few people he had spoken to in his final days. One of Jenny's lines of investigation was into whether his apparent suicide was linked to his work in South Sudan. During her first meeting with Sonia Blake she had established that Sonia had sought Jordan out during her research into the political situation in that country, but she had seemed too shocked by the news of his death to give all the answers Jenny would have liked. She had arranged today's meeting to fill in the gaps. It was as straightforward as that.

Ruth Webley took careful notes throughout.

'Mr Forster tells me that you initially made contact with Mrs Blake through him. How was that?'

Jenny had slipped. She must be more tired than she thought. Now her explanation would sound as if she had been concealing something. As casually as she could, she explained how a receipt found in Jordan's car had led her to the nearby cafe where the waitresses helped her discover Sonia Blake's identity through her frequent companion – Alex Forster.

Ruth Webley swept her hair back from her forehead, which Jenny saw was furrowed with frown lines. 'You must have read a lot of significance into this meeting to go to such lengths.' She was no fool. Far sharper than the detective.

'I'm sure you've read your files, Ms Webley. It's not the first time.'

'What was the significance, in your mind?'

'I had no idea.'

'Really? You weren't influenced by the fact his wife had no knowledge of his visit to Oxford?'

Jenny met Webley's gaze and decided it was time to go on the offensive. 'You've spoken with Mrs Jordan?'

'Her husband worked in a sensitive field. Surely you would be more surprised if we hadn't, Mrs Cooper?'

'If you have information relevant to my inquiry, I'd be grateful if you would disclose it immediately, Ms Webley.'

'Mrs Cooper, I hardly need remind you, of all people, that certain information remains privileged in the interests of national security. If there is anything that can lawfully be released to you, I assure you it will be.'

'You've approached his former colleague, Harry Thorn, too. What do you suspect him of? I'm entitled to know.'

'I've already answered you, Mrs Cooper.'

'Then we have nothing more to say to each other.' Jenny rose from her chair. She addressed DI Gregson, who remained seated. 'I'll see myself out, shall I?'

'We haven't completed our interview.' He remained the impassive bureaucrat. Jenny would have preferred a straightforward bully.

'Are you going to arrest me?'

He looked impatiently down at his notes.

'Then good night.'

She walked to the door and let herself out.

'Busy night, Mrs Cooper?'

Jenny had arrived late in the office the next morning and had yet to shake off the effects of two sleeping pills swallowed deep in the night to switch off her racing thoughts.

'I had a call from a woman named Webley,' Alison said, 'at about midnight. Apparently you made a quick exit from St Aldate's police station in Oxford.'

'What did she want?'

'What business you had with a woman called Sonia Blake, and what did she have to do with Adam Jordan.'

Jenny rubbed her aching temples. 'What did you tell her?'

'The truth. I've never heard of her.'

'Did she believe you?'

'I got the impression she was rather frustrated.'

'Good. Did you get my email?'

'Yes,' Alison said cagily. 'The printouts are on your desk.' Jenny saw Alison look at her with concern. 'Are you sure there's nothing you want to tell me? It does sound as if you've got yourself mixed up in something. Just because I'm under the doctor doesn't mean you have to carry it all on your shoulders.'

'I appreciate the thought,' Jenny said, and changed the subject. 'I don't suppose we've had an answer from the manager of Hampton's Health Club?'

'That's on your desk, too.'

'Thanks.' Jenny headed for her office. 'I could do with some coffee. As strong as you can make it.'

She threw her bag and jacket over a chair, her impatience to see the message from Hampton's bringing her back to life. A list of names and their contact details stretched over three sides of paper. She scanned through them, noting the proliferation of expensive addresses. No wonder the manager had sounded anxious. Every top-rate taxpayer in Bristol seemed to be a member. Halfway through the third page an entry leaped out at her: *Fielding, Christopher, Major (Salisbury member)*. The address next to his name was a military one: Bulford Camp, Salisbury, Wiltshire. A quick check on her computer confirmed that Bulford, home to several regiments, was only ten miles from Porton Down. Containing her excitement, she reminded herself that the small cathedral city of Salisbury was home to hundreds, if not thousands, of military personnel. It was the Army's principal centre in the south of England. It was hardly surprising that the only Army officer on the list should live within commuting distance of the government and military laboratories. Still, it was a lead.

Alison arrived with coffee. 'What have you found? It's Jordan, isn't it? I knew there was something more going on with him.'

'Actually, it's Sophie Freeman.'

Without naming Dr Kerr as the source of her theory, Jenny told Alison that one of the laboratories where rarefied strains of the most dangerous diseases were to be found was at Porton Down, and that she had just discovered a potential connection with the dead girl.

'Then why don't I deal with that for you?' Alison said, reaching for the list.

Jenny placed her hand on top of hers. 'Not yet. I haven't been through it properly.'

'This is what I'm worried about, Mrs Cooper – you've really got to trust people. You mustn't let yourself get paranoid.'

'Is that what you think I am?' Jenny said defensively.

'Why don't you try to take it easier today?' Alison said, avoiding the question. 'Now, what can I help you with?'

'I'll let you know.'

Alison gave her the kind of look a mother would give a wilful teenager. 'You won't be able to keep this up, you know.' And having uttered her warning, she left Jenny alone.

Jenny didn't need Alison to tell her she was slowly coming apart at the seams. After many months of keeping her anxiety contained, she felt it stirring again. She could trace its arrival back to the moment Alison had shown her the photographs of Adam Jordan's car, when she realized that the Dinka doll was missing. A childish, superstitious part of her had read it as a portent.

She studied the slightly indistinct colour printouts of the photographs she had hurriedly taken in Sonia Blake's study room. Apart from the spilled coffee they were wholly unremarkable. There was no sign of disturbance, no drawers left open, no books pulled from the shelves. If there had been a deliberate break-in while Sonia was out on her regular evening run, the intruder had come for something specific. But what? She pored over the images, trying to isolate some small clue, some object out of place, but found nothing. It was just an untidy academic's room.

Resigned, she was pushing the pictures aside when she registered a detail she had entirely forgotten: during her initial visit several days before, she had spotted an identity tag on the desk. She looked again at the close-up shot of Sonia's desk; there was no tag. She remembered the two words she had seen printed on it: Diamond Light.

Switching on her computer monitor, she entered the words into a search engine and came up with an immediate result: *The Diamond Light Source.* She clicked the link and found herself looking at an image of a large circular building in the Oxfordshire countryside at Harwell which, she learned from the accompanying text, was home to the UK's national synchrotron. She read on, picking her way through the jargon and learning that the synchrotron was a particle accelerator, a 561-metre-long circular tube through which electrons were accelerated close to the speed of light. But unlike its famous cousin at CERN, the Diamond synchrotron didn't collide particles together. Its function was to collect the energy they shed in the form of light to use for scientific experiments.

But this was no ordinary light. The kind the synchrotron generated was at the far end of spectrum between X-ray and

infrared and invisible to the human eye. Having been collected, it was channelled into twenty-two separate 'beamlines'. The light was many millions of times more powerful
than any that could be produced from a conventional source,
and in the X-ray spectrum was at such minute wavelengths
that a beam could be focused to create an image of something as small as a molecule. It was, in short, one of the
most powerful microscopes in existence.

What had Sonia Blake been doing there? Her field was
international relations, not science. Jenny scouted further
through the website and learned that it was a publicly
funded facility available free of charge to scientists who
intended to release their research to the public domain, and
for a fee to commercial companies or researchers whose
results were to remain confidential. The beamlines were
used by scientists from a host of different disciplines to
examine samples down almost to the atomic level. Life scientists used them to analyse the chemical make-up of the
most fundamental parts of the human organism.

Jenny tried to think of a reason why Sonia Blake would
be visiting such a facility. Could it have been entirely innocent? Perhaps, but two facts told her she had to look further:
Blake's late father had been just the sort of scientist who
would now be using the Light Source to peer at the building
blocks of life; and according to the map on the website, the
facility was fourteen miles from Great Shefford and almost
exactly the same distance from Oxford.

Jenny was considering her next move when her mobile
phone rang. Another unknown caller. Anticipating Webley,
she answered frostily, 'Jenny Cooper.' It was even worse.

'Detective Inspector Ian Gregson. Thames Valley Police.'

'What can I do for you, Inspector?'

'I thought you might like to know the result of Mrs
Blake's post-mortem examination.'

'I'd be grateful.'

'As we hoped, it's nothing sinister – cardiac arrest caused by something called endocarditis. Apparently it's an infection in the lining of the heart. Feels like a head cold, but physical exercise is about the worst thing you can do for it, I'm told. Just one of those things, the pathologist says. Plain bad luck.' He delivered the news with the same deadpan tone she had grown to loathe the night before. 'I don't suppose you've thought of anything overnight that might be of interest to us.'

'I thought Mrs Blake's death wasn't being treated as suspicious.'

'It isn't.'

'Then I'm afraid I don't follow.'

'I'll leave it with you, Mrs Cooper. I'm sure we'll be in touch.'

The conversation was over in less than a minute. No apology for holding her like a prisoner for most of the evening, just a vague hint of a threat. If she had been tempted to share anything with him, he had ensured she never would now.

Jenny had recorded endocarditis as a cause of death several times in her career. From memory, the infection clustered in the heart valves and caused the surrounding tissue to swell. Its victims were usually old, infirm or run-down. Sonia Blake could easily have fallen into the latter category. A driven professional woman was just the sort to deal with a niggling symptom by trying to jog it off.

There it was. The exit sign was lit. Sonia Blake was dead and would never be able to testify to what had passed between her and Adam Jordan. Jenny was free to forget about her. Except that she couldn't. Gregson's call had been a crude attempt to trade one piece of information for another. Webley's involvement was proof that Sonia Blake and Adam Jordan were suspected of being part of something far bigger. She wasn't being paranoid: she was in a simple race to get to the truth before it was buried.

Jenny grabbed her bag and pushed through into reception, where Alison was gathering yet another pile of papers to burden her with.

'I'm going out to fetch some coffee,' Jenny said.

'You just had some—'

'Won't be a minute. See if you can get hold of Major Fielding. You'll find him on the list from Hampton's.'

'Mrs Cooper—'

Jenny slipped out through the door and dashed down the corridor.

SEVENTEEN

SIMON MORETON'S VOICE BARKED OUT of all six speakers as Jenny once again headed east on the motorway.

'What the hell's going on, Jenny? I've got the top brass at the HPA on my back saying you're refusing to conclude a perfectly straightforward inquest.'

' "Straightforward" is not a word I would use.'

'It's a death from meningitis.'

'That's part of the story.'

'There's only so much of this I can tolerate. It's not just the HPA. I'm told the parents of the dead girl are deeply distressed by the delay.'

'Believe me, Simon, if you had half the facts you wouldn't be saying any of this.'

'Such as?' he challenged.

'Nice try.'

'Jenny, unless the Freeman case is resolved by the end of the week we are going to have to carry out an urgent review of how you conduct your business.'

'Is that a threat to remove me from the case? On what grounds – being too conscientious?'

'Jenny, please—'

'Who's been talking to you, Simon?'

His momentary pause was enough to confirm her suspicions.

'Let me guess – a rather attractive young woman named Ruth Webley.'

'I've no idea who you're talking about,' he answered.

'I'll make you a deal,' Jenny said. 'I'll move as quickly as I can on the Freeman inquest, and you remind Ms Webley and her colleagues that they've no business interfering with a coroner's inquiries, no matter how uncomfortable it is for them.'

He answered with an ominous silence.

'So the law no longer applies?' Jenny said. 'The Coroners Act has been repealed, has it?'

'Jenny,' he said pleadingly, 'I like to think we're friends.'

'They've really got you on the hook, haven't they? Why don't you just show these people the door and tell them they can't interfere with justice?'

'There are limits. You know that as well as I do.'

'No one respects boundaries, Simon. It's one of the laws of nature – boundaries are battlegrounds. Someone or something is always trying to move them.'

'I really can't protect you this time, Jenny.'

'Then see if you can manage not to do me any harm.'

'You don't make it easy.'

'Think how dull your life would be without me.'

Another sigh. This one more wistful.

'Where are you, by the way? Your officer sounded at the end of her tether.'

'Never mind. Goodbye, Simon.'

She ended the call and was about to switch off her phone when she noticed that she had a voicemail. She checked it, expecting to hear a grudging apology from Michael – it was about time – but it was from Ross, asking if she was free to have dinner with him and Sally. Jenny called straight back. She'd love to. She'd pick them up from David's at eight. The deal sealed, she rang off, feeling her worries about him dispersing like smoke in the wind.

It wasn't the porter she had encountered on the two previous occasions behind the desk in the lodge at Worcester College, but a junior deputy with a thin frame and a cautious, helpful smile. Jenny introduced herself and informed him she was here to look over Sonia Blake's rooms. In a dilemma, he explained that his boss, Mr Davies, had told him that the police had left instructions that no one was to be allowed in without their express permission. Jenny patiently informed him that the police had no power to obstruct her inquiry, and if it was any comfort, all she wanted to do was look. She wouldn't be disturbing a thing.

A warm smile won him round. Asking her if she could keep her visit quick, he fetched the keys and led her across the cloister. Jenny learned that his name was Will, and that the police had been back earlier that morning asking if any unauthorized visitors had been spotted in recent weeks. They had been up to Sonia's rooms but hadn't appeared to take anything.

They emerged from the vaulted stone roof of the cloister into bright sunlight. A large group of boisterous Chinese students spilled out of a doorway ahead of them.

'Summer school,' Will explained. 'The Chinese don't seem to do holidays.'

Coming up behind them was Alex Forster. His eyes widened in surprise, as if Jenny were the last person he was expecting to see.

'Mrs Cooper.'

'Good morning.'

'Is there anything I can help you with?'

'I don't think so. Not at present.'

Forster glanced to the deputy porter as if for an explanation, but Jenny headed him off. 'Sorry, Mr Forster. I'm in rather a hurry.'

She stepped past him and continued on to the far staircase, Will following at her heels.

'Do you know if he and Mrs Blake were close?' Jenny asked, as they started up towards the second floor.

'You'd see them together now and again, but she always seemed quite a loner to me.'

'Do you know if she got on with her students?'

'They seemed to like her.'

Jenny remembered Katya, the girl who had come to the door the first time she had visited the college. She tried to describe her, but Will couldn't place her. There were so many students coming and going, it was hard to remember faces.

The full glare of the sun was streaming through the landing window, making stage-light beams of circling dust. While Will unlocked the oak door, Jenny gazed out over the quad and felt herself slip back in time. She pictured young men in frock coats dreaming of making fortunes in far-off continents, with all the weight and confidence of an empire behind them.

'Mrs Cooper?' Will held open the door. 'I'll stay out here if you don't mind.'

The office was more or less as she had seen it the previous afternoon, except that the cup had been tidied away and the papers on the desk had gone, along with the computer. The expanse of wall opposite the windows overlooking the quad was lined floor to ceiling with a fitted, heavy bookcase, and against the wall opposite the door, a set of cheap bookshelves of the kind you might slot together yourself was loaded with disorderly files.

Jenny began her search – for what, she had no idea –

with the stack of three drawers in Sonia's desk. They were as chaotic as Jenny's, filled with dead pens, assorted stationery, and in the middle drawer, several birthday cards from students and some photographs taken on a punting trip. Jenny pulled them out for a closer look. Sonia was the oldest in the group, wearing a wide-brimmed straw hat and drinking champagne. She looked a little drunk, abandoned even. The top drawer seemed to serve as a way-station for items that went in and out of pockets and handbags: keys, loose change, a wristwatch, a deodorant stick, a couple of bracelets and what looked like a pendant – a rectangle of silver metal an inch wide, with a ring attached to its bottom edge, hanging from a chain that seemed a little too heavy-duty for a woman's necklace. Curious, Jenny picked it up, hooking her finger through the ring. But as she lifted it from the drawer, the chain snagged and the ring separated from the body of the pendant. To Jenny's surprise, she saw that this was no mere piece of jewellery. The ring was attached to a triangular, razor-sharp blade that had been sheathed in the pendant. Keeping her back to Will, she studied it more closely and noticed that the ring was fashioned to spread the weight of impact across the knuckle. It was a carefully engineered weapon: hook your middle finger through the ring and you could strike out with a blade that would slice effortlessly through flesh. Still unseen by Will, she returned it to its sheath, then slipped it into her jacket pocket.

With her blood pumping a little harder, Jenny turned to the shelves laden with files. The subjects were scrawled on the spines in Sonia's semi-legible hand: *Egypt – Revolution* stood alongside *French C19th Colonialism* and *Somalian War*. On another shelf were files that appeared to be more directly connected with her teaching: exam papers, copies of student essays and papers relating to the university's Politics department. The haphazardness of it all told Jenny that Webley and her people would already have been through and taken anything of interest to them. Ready to give up and accept that she was unlikely to find anything more she spotted a small file buried amongst others with a single word, *Slavsky*, written on the spine. She pulled it from the shelf, but opened it to find it empty. All that remained were a few traces of torn paper pinched between the spring clips; the contents had been hastily removed.

She put the empty file back, knowing now that Professor Slavsky was a man of interest not just to Adam Jordan.

'Will you be long, Mrs Cooper?' Will said, hovering nervously in the doorway.

'Just a moment.'

'I think there's someone coming.'

Sure enough there were footsteps and voices approaching up the stairwell.

'That's all right,' Jenny said, pretending indifference.

She hurriedly scanned each one of the bookshelves. There was a large selection of novels, mostly by literary writers, as well as many thick academic tomes. The footsteps drew closer.

She heard a voice she recognized as the porter's, thick and hoarse as if he'd been roused from sleep, call out, 'Is she in there? I told you not to let anyone in.'

'Leave him to me,' Jenny said, continuing to study the shelves.

She alighted on a section filled not with political books, but scientific texts. She saw titles including 'Brock, *Biology of Microorganisms*' and 'Primrose, *Principles of Genomics*'. She searched the spines for Slavsky's name, but failed to find it. She turned back to face the desk as the porter's voice berated Will, 'What do you think you're doing? What did I tell you?'

'Sorry, Mr Davies. But Mrs Cooper—'

The porter pushed past Will and shoved his way into the room as Jenny leaned down to pick up a scrap of folded paper that had fallen beneath the desk.

'What do you think you're doing?' he demanded, red-faced and perspiring. 'The police said no one was to be allowed in.'

'As I explained to your colleague, the police have no right, and certainly no power, to obstruct a coroner's investigation.' Jenny spoke calmly. She glanced at the piece of paper she had picked up. It looked as if it had been torn from a message pad. It was thick with phone numbers, names and doodles. In the bottom corner Sonia had written *Gina*, and absentmindedly illuminated it with intertwining flowers.

'Give me that!'

Davies shot out a thick hand and seized her wrist in a powerful grip that cut off the blood.

'Out.'

She dropped the note. 'Let go. You've no right—'

'You can call the police, then.'

He hauled her onto the landing, kicked the outer door shut and let her go.

Will stood mute, avoiding her gaze.

'Go on, call them,' Davies taunted.

'You could do with learning some manners, Mr Davies,' Jenny said, refusing to rise.

'You shouldn't have done that,' Will whispered to his boss, as Jenny started down the stairs.

'You can shut your mouth,' Davies hissed back at him.

Slavsky. The name bounced tirelessly around her brain as she made the twenty-minute drive from Oxford to Harwell. Sonia Blake had kept an entire file on him. Why? Adam

Jordan had bought his book. He connected the two of them, but all Jenny knew was that he had been a Soviet biologist who defected to the West. There had been mention of the Soviets in the article reporting the discovery of Roy Emmett Hudson's remains, but he clearly hadn't defected. Slavsky might conceivably have been working in a similar field to Hudson, a fact which might have been of interest to Sonia Blake, but it was hard to find a reason that would tie in Adam Jordan.

The questions continued to mount as she turned into the Harwell Science and Innovation Campus. She found herself driving along a dead-straight road named Fermi Avenue, approaching a large, circular construction that sat incongruously amidst the surrounding fields. The other buildings nearby were as anonymous as those in an out-of-town business park. But there was nothing unremarkable about the worlds behind the bland exteriors. Aside from the synchrotron, Jenny had learned that the campus was also home to the Rutherford Appleton laboratory, which, among other things, was an international hub for cutting-edge research in particle physics. More than ten thousand scientists and engineers were based here, working to solve the secrets of dark matter and probing the atmospheres of distant planets.

All their collective brainpower, however, had failed to conjure names for the campus's grid of internal thoroughfares any more charming than Road One, Road Two and Road Three. Jenny had wanted to be awed, but the entrance to the Diamond Light Source reminded her of an airport terminal. A glass and steel atrium, sterile and air-conditioned, all function, nothing beautiful to catch the eye.

She arrived at a reception desk separated from the rest of the building by a panoply of barriers, cameras and high-grade security guards. The corporate smile of the man behind the desk faded as Jenny explained that she was a coroner inquiring after a recent visitor who had died less than twenty-four hours before.

Jenny waited while he called through to a superior and watched the occupants of the building come and go. She was struck by how young they were. Most were in their twenties, nearly all were male, and not one suit and tie between them. Anywhere else, she would have mistaken them for students on their way to a bar.

The security manager was named Dawn Leyton. Jenny guessed she was ex-military: superficially polite, squarely built and without warmth. She handed Jenny a visitor pass and took her through the security barrier. Then she led her across the atrium and along a small enclosed corridor, accessed by a separate card-swipe, off which she had a small, impersonal, paperless office.

'Do you have any identification?' Leyton asked.

Jenny gave her several. Leyton studied each of them in turn before typing her name into a computer. Jenny glanced at the monitor's reflection in the window behind her and saw that she had searched under 'images', which had thrown up a number of photographs from the rash of newspaper reports that had so inaccurately reported her life story two years before. If she had chosen to, Leyton could have read all about the troublesome coroner who as a child was implicated in the suspicious death of her five-year-old cousin; her run-ins with the police and, of course, her arrests.

'It's a simple query,' Jenny said, growing impatient. 'All I need to know is who it was Sonia Blake was visiting when she came here.'

'For what purpose?' Leyton inquired.

'It may be of relevance to an inquest I'm conducting.'

Leyton said, 'This concerns a death? Is it a criminal matter?'

'It's a coroner's inquest,' Jenny said, straining to remain

civil. 'Depending on what emerges, criminal charges can sometimes ensue. There's no suggestion of any crime at this stage.'

'Whose death does this inquiry concern?'

Jenny considered the consequence of Leyton consulting with superiors, who within minutes would be in touch with government departments, whose security protocols would see her request finding its way to Ruth Webley and her colleagues before it was ever answered. A flash of inspiration sent her on a different tack.

'A Spanish prostitute called Elena.'

'Surname?' Leyton said, glancing back at her computer, doubtless ready to search the Internet again.

It was time to pull rank. 'I get the impression you're not eager to assist,' Jenny said. 'That's fine. I can either come back with the police or summon you to give evidence to my inquest. Which would you prefer?'

'What happened to this prostitute?' Leyton hedged.

'Would it make it easier if you had an official order? I can have one emailed to you right away.'

'Is this person implicated in the death?' Leyton said, ignoring Jenny's offer.

Jenny met her gaze. The show of politeness was over. Leyton, she sensed, was a real brute. The kind that would need a punch between the eyes to realize who it was she was dealing with.

'There have been four deaths, Ms Leyton. Three of them within my jurisdiction. Either you cooperate, or I'll consider you to have obstructed my investigation. I'm sure you are bright enough to understand the implications of that.'

Leyton checked her screen one last time. 'Email me the order. I'll get you the name.'

*

Half an hour later, Jenny followed Leyton along a corridor that led into the heart of the building. She began to feel the pervading sense of excitement in the air: the anticipation of scientific secrets that had remained stubbornly hidden being unlocked. The small amount she had read online had given her only a basic understanding of what happened here, but she had learned that each of the beamlines – the sources of light channelled from inside the circular particle accelerator – had its own experimental station divided into three compartments. The raw light entered an optics hutch, where it was tuned to the correct wavelength before passing through to the experimental hutch, where it was aimed at the sample being analysed. The process emitted X-rays, so the scientists observed from a separate insulated room.

They arrived at a numbered door that might have been the entrance to a supplies cupboard, but which in fact led to a beamline control cabin. Leyton's knock was answered by an edgy, slender-limbed man in his early thirties whose name Jenny had already been told was Dr Jason Kwan. According to Leyton's records, it was he who had requested Sonia Blake's visitor pass.

Leyton made cursory introductions and waited, as if expecting Jenny to hold her conversation in the corridor.

'We'll need to have a moment alone,' Jenny said.

Leyton glanced at Kwan, then nodded – satisfied, Jenny assumed, that she would get full particulars of the conversation one way or the other.

'You'll see Mrs Cooper out of the building when you're finished?'

Kwan gave a nod and Leyton turned and walked away, with solid jailer's footsteps.

The control room was cramped and stuffy, and cluttered with computer equipment. A bin overflowed with empty coffee cups and food wrappers, and to pass the dull moments its occupants had built a pyramid of soft-drinks cans in a corner of the floor.

'You're part of a team?' Jenny asked, trying to put him at his ease.

'My colleagues are at lunch,' Kwan replied. 'What would you like to know?'

Jenny helped herself to one of the three swivel chairs while Kwan perched nervously against a desk.

'The reason I'm here, Dr Kwan, is to ask you what you know about Mrs Sonia Blake. I believe she visited you here.'

He nodded.

'Unfortunately she died yesterday.'

'I heard.'

'Oh?' Jenny tried to conceal her surprise. 'How did you find out?'

'I saw it online. One of her colleagues I'm friends with must have posted it.'

'*Friends?* You mean someone on a social network, not an actual friend?'

'Yes.' He seemed to tolerate her old-fashioned distinction.

'Do you mind telling me what she was doing here?'

'She contacted me. She said she was interested to see how the beamline worked. I said sure, and arranged for her to come over.'

'Do you remember when that was?'

He drummed his fingers on the table as he tried to recall. 'She emailed me in about May and came here at the beginning of June. A Friday, I expect – that's my maintenance day. You can check the visitor log.'

'I will,' Jenny said. 'What did she want to see, exactly?'

'How the equipment works. She told me her father was a geneticist – back in the seventies and eighties – she said she wanted to understand how the applied science worked now.'

'Did she talk about her own work at all?'

'Not much. She mentioned she was writing about Africa. She said there's a lot of politics around disease prevention there. I think maybe that's what she was interested in – how researchers try, say, to develop a vaccine.'

'Any particular kind?'

He shook his head.

'She didn't mention meningitis?'

He thought for a moment – or at least, gave the impression of doing so. 'No. I don't remember meningitis.'

'What did you show her?'

'Just some regular crystallography work.'

'Crystallography? I'm sorry. I'm afraid this is all new to me.'

Now on more comfortable territory, Kwan gave her a potted explanation of how he spent his days. He was a full-time beamline scientist whose job was to assist the various research teams who came to use the equipment. His particular beamline was tuned to the highest possible X-ray frequency and used to examine biological molecules. For the purposes of the experiment, these were arranged in a crystalline array using a number of sophisticated, but standard, laboratory techniques. In a typical project, he might be assisting a team developing a vaccine to study the chemical make-up of a protein molecule. If, for example, they could determine the make-up of a protein that acted as a receptor on the surface of a bacterium, they could engineer a corresponding chemical bond that could be incorporated into a drug designed to attack it.

This form of microbiology, it seemed, was like peering inside a lock in order to build a key to fit it. The secrets revealed by the beamlines were starting to turn the raw data of the human genome into the medicine of the future. Smart drugs engineered to attack or rebuild only specific cells would all owe a debt to the synchrotron.

Jenny did her best to follow. It was fascinating, but none of it answered her question: why had Sonia Blake wanted to see the technology in operation?

'Why wouldn't she?' Dr Kwan said. 'She was an academic. She was curious.'

'Did you see her or speak to her again?'

Kwan shook his head. 'It was just the one time.'

'Have you ever heard of a man named Adam Jordan?'

'No.'

Jenny decided she found him more convincing when he was being vague. She tried him with one more. 'What about Professor Roman Slavsky?'

Kwan shuffled his weight from one foot to another. 'Sure. I've heard of him. He's a famous microbiologist.'

'Famous for what? Excuse my ignorance.'

'It's a long time since I read about him, but as far as I remember, he'd got a long way with recombinant techniques during the eighties. He came from Russia with a large section of the human genome already decoded. He'd been made to work on a biological weapons programme, but when he was here he turned his skills as a geneticist to therapeutic medicine.'

Jenny said, 'Did Sonia Blake mention him?'

Kwan said no, she hadn't. She had been too busy asking him questions to talk about anything else. She was a bright lady. She picked things up quickly.

Jenny glanced up and ran her eyes across the pristine tiles on the suspended ceiling.

'Is there any recording equipment in here?'

'No way,' Kwan answered hurriedly. 'No cameras.

Nothing. We often do commercially sensitive work here – not today, this project is public domain – but some of our data could be worth millions, billions even.'

The perfect place to speak in confidence, Jenny thought, as long as you trusted whoever you were talking to. 'Thank you, Dr Kwan. I'll take your contact details, if I may.'

Kwan walked her back to reception at a brisk pace, eager not to continue their conversation in public. Everybody they passed seemed to nod or say hello, and they all noticed Jenny. She got an impression of a tight-knit community in which rumour would spread fast. Kwan would probably spend much of his afternoon explaining her visit to inquisitive colleagues. This was just what Leyton intended, Jenny suspected: Kwan's punishment for bringing her here was to be cast under a cloud of suspicion.

Jenny found herself feeling a pang of sympathy for him. The strain of conjuring half-answers to her questions had taken a visible toll. Whatever he had failed to tell her seemed to weigh heavily.

Before he left her, Jenny said quietly, 'I suspect you haven't been entirely truthful, Dr Kwan, but if I'm honest, nor have I. Why don't we talk again – somewhere you'll feel more comfortable, and when you've had time to think?'

He looked at her for a moment with eyes wide open in astonishment, as if she had given voice to his most intimate secrets.

'I'll be in touch,' Jenny said, and handed him her business card.

He stuttered a goodbye and hurried away across the atrium.

Passing through the security barrier, Jenny fleetingly caught the eye of a man waiting at the reception desk. He wore a well-cut suit with an open-necked shirt, and had a square military jaw. He didn't look like a scientist. As she exited the building, she thought she could feel his eyes following her. From beyond the door she shot a glance back through the plate glass, but he was now looking the other way. If she had studied him for a moment longer, she would have seen him reach into his pocket and retrieve his phone.

EIGHTEEN

'I've been wondering when you'd be back,' Karen
Jordan said. She lowered herself onto the sofa in her sitting
room, holding her body stiffly, any sudden movement causing her to screw up her eyes in pain.

'I thought you might like to know what I've found,' Jenny
said. She sat on a straight-backed wooden chair made from
dark, rich-smelling African teak.

'I'm sure you'll tell me, whether I like it or not.'

'I went to visit Harry Thorn at his offices,' Jenny said. 'He
wasn't exactly helpful.'

'He never is,' Karen said. 'He's a misanthrope.'

'He did say two things that interested me. He mentioned
that people he called "spooks" imagine his organization to
be criminal because he refuses to work for them.'

Karen Jordan gazed off into space, seeming to distance
herself even further from their conversation. 'That sounds
like Harry.'

'When you came to see me in my office you mentioned
that there had been rumours of arms shipments hidden in
aid cargoes. Is that what he's suspected of being involved
with?'

'Probably. I wouldn't know. He would have kept that sort
of thing from Adam. Harry's got broad shoulders.'

'I get the impression part of you admires this misanthrope,'

Jenny said, curious to understand Karen's evident mixed feelings towards him.

'He's a survivor. That's got to be worthy of some respect.'

Jenny detected judgement of her late husband in Karen's remark. She had seen it often in the partner of a man who had taken his own life. Disbelief turned to anger, then rapidly to condemnation before emotions finally resolved to a level of acceptance. Primal laws dictated that a man was meant to fight to his last breath in defence of wife and children. Desertion through suicide was one of the worst forms of violation.

'He also said that your husband's trouble was that he took things to heart.'

'Evidently.'

'He didn't tell me what precisely.'

The corners of Karen's mouth curled into an ironic smile. 'If I knew, don't you think I would have told you?'

'Have you spoken with Harry Thorn recently?'

'Of course I have,' she snapped. 'He doesn't know why Adam killed himself any more than I do. Anyone can specu- late, but that's all it can be. None of us can know what was in his mind.' The effort of her outburst had caused a sharp pain in her bruised ribs. She sat for a moment with her eyes shut tight against it.

'I didn't mean to go over old ground,' Jenny said. 'I was just anxious to know if you had any insights into what your husband might have become involved with?'

'What do you mean – *involved* with? He wasn't involved with anything.'

Jenny trod carefully. 'I told you about his visit to Great Shefford earlier in the evening before he died. I went there – to the filling station he visited. The girl behind the till remembered a man with a young child at about that time, but he had a young African woman with him, too, who she wasn't sure spoke English. And then another car drew up alongside Adam's driven by a man in his thirties. The African girl noticed him, and then apparently alerted Adam to his presence. He went out to meet him, shook hands, and then it seems they both drove their cars around to a lay-by at the back of the garage. For what purpose, I don't know.'

Karen looked at Jenny, her mask slipping to reveal her shock. 'A girl? Who is she?'

'I thought you might have an idea.'

'No. What happened to her – did she go with Adam or the other man?'

'I don't know. But the cashier did say she behaved more like an employee than a girlfriend. It seems she was carrying your son.'

Karen blinked, as if trying to banish the disturbing image from her mind: her child clinging to a woman she had never met.

'I shouldn't jump to the obvious conclusion,' Jenny said quickly. 'There's a lot more. Would you like to hear?'

She nodded.

Her look of disbelief gradually turned to one of bewilderment as Jenny explained that the filling station was only a short drive from the Diamond Light Source, a facility used by the country's leading scientists, not least by microbiologists. This could have been dismissed as a coincidence, except that Adam's other secret meeting had been with Sonia Blake, who had visited the building only weeks before. Although she was an academic whose expertise was in African politics, she also happened to be the daughter of a pioneering geneticist who had been mysteriously murdered in 1982. Adam had clearly been interested in the Soviet biologist, Slavsky, but the coincidences didn't end there. Sonia Blake had died, seemingly of natural causes, but papers relating to Slavsky had been taken from her university room.

Jenny paused, giving Karen an opportunity to assimilate what she had heard.

'There's more?' Karen said.

'I'm afraid so.'

Finding it hard to countenance the facts herself, Jenny explained as gently as she could that her husband's brain tissue and cerebral fluid had been removed, and that the same thing had happened to the body of Sophie Freeman, a thirteen-year-old girl who had died of drug-resistant meningitis.

'Does any of this make any sense to you?'

'No,' Karen whispered. 'Nothing.'

'Was he the kind of man who normally shared things?'

'Yes.' Jenny saw something stir in her. A twitch in the muscles of her face. 'There had been outbreaks of meningitis in areas he'd been working.'

'He told you that?'

'It came and went most years. I remember him saying there's no vaccine – you can only treat the disease with drugs, lots of them. They were too expensive for a lot of districts. It was always a source of tension.'

'You mean political tension?'

'Medicine's always political in Africa.' They seemed to be sharing the same thought. 'They become a kind of weapon.' Pieces appeared to be falling into place for her. 'Perhaps that's what he witnessed – drugs being withheld? Nothing would have made him more angry.'

'Where would drugs come from, typically?' Jenny asked.

'Charities and governments. Britain spends a lot in East African countries – they're all our former colonies.'

Seconds passed in silence as they both struggled to form a narrative that would have led to Adam's death. Jenny realized it was the first time that she had laid out the facts end to end, and it was leading to the most disturbing possible conclusion.

'Sonia Blake was well connected,' Jenny said. 'If something was happening – if drugs were being held up for political reasons – she's an obvious person to have been told. She might have sought Adam out as her informer in the field. What do you think?'

'It's possible. But why wouldn't he have told me?'

'Too dangerous?'

'Oh God.' The words fell from Karen's mouth in desperation. 'What the hell did he do?' Her eyes travelled the room in incomprehension, as if the answer might lie in the hand-stitched African rug, or the framed photographs of grazing antelope that hung on the wall. 'The burglars that came here – do you think that's what they were?'

Jenny said, 'Did Adam keep papers at home? Has anything belonging to him gone?'

'Only his computer. They took that, and mine.'

'Did he back it up?'

'I doubt it.' Karen's eyes flashed with anger. 'They knocked me out cold. It was clinical. This is government, isn't it? He didn't kill himself – they murdered him, didn't they?'

'It seems unlikely,' Jenny said, but without conviction. In Adam's line of work, it seemed to her anything was possible.

Tears spilled over Karen's cheeks.

Jenny's instinct was to try to comfort her, but hard as it was she resisted and checked herself: professional boundaries had to be maintained. She decided instead to give her a moment alone.

'I'll be out in the garden,' Jenny said.

She found her way along the hallway to the back door, leaving Karen sobbing fitfully. The garden extended no more than fifty feet from the house, but had been laid out to create an African oasis. The deep borders that ran around its circumference were densely planted with tall savannah grasses, some over eight feet high, that stirred and crackled with every subtle movement of the air. She took a seat at the rough-hewn wooden table and from it could see only sorghum, pampas and sky.

She weighed the wisdom of tackling Harry Thorn with Karen's theory and decided it would be a waste of breath. She would leave him to Karen and the courtroom. But she would have to speak to DI Watling, the detective who handed Adam Jordan's case to her so abruptly after he was found. The speed with which he had discounted the possibility of foul play wasn't unprecedented, but if the worst of her suspicions proved true, the decision might not have been his. It wouldn't have surprised her to learn that he had had a call from Ruth Webley. And then there was the issue of Adam's phone. Had it been crushed under the wheels of a truck and conveniently swept away, or had someone retrieved it? She could only wonder at what secrets it might have held. Then there was the African girl, and the man who came to the filling station – he had already taken on the guise of spy in her imagination – she had to find them. But where to begin?

'Adam planted all this.'

Jenny turned to see Karen Jordan stepping through the back door.

'Even when he wasn't in Africa he was trying to recreate it.' She limped onto the small patch of lawn and kicked off her sandals. 'He said going there was like going back to the source, where it all began. Where life and death slug it out most keenly. He liked to say there was an honesty in Africa – no pretence that human beings are above it all.' The grasses leaned in a gust of wind, their dry, tough stems clicking together like a shower of falling twigs hitting stony ground. Karen pushed stray wisps hair back away from her eyes, and Jenny saw the face that Adam would have fallen in love with: soulful and dignified, but with a longing in her for a purer world than the one in which she found herself. 'I wish I could just let him go, let him fly away on the breeze.'

'There'll be a time for that,' Jenny said. 'But it's not yet.'

Il Carretto hadn't changed in the dozen years since Jenny had first come here with David. The same dusty gourds hung in bunches from the mock beams and the waiters, though a little older and fatter, still moved between the tables singing along to the same Dean Martin songs that played on a continuous loop. But while the restaurant was just as Jenny expected, Sally was a revelation. She had pictured a dark, delicate, introverted girl looking to her son for solid, masculine reassurance, but the young woman sitting across the table was red-haired, forthright, and had unselfconsciously dominated the conversation. There wasn't much Jenny didn't know about her life history by the time they had ordered coffee, or about her wayward father and his twenty-five-year-old male lover.

'I can understand Dad falling for a *man*,' she said. 'Why not? But Franky's so neurotic and petty – you'll just have wiped the kitchen counter and he'll come along and do it *again* – and that's what he's always accused Mum of being.' She spoke as if Jenny were intimately familiar with all the personalities involved. 'I don't know why he can't see it.' She grinned suggestively. 'I guess there must be other compensations.'

Ross shot Jenny an apprehensive glance that anticipated her disapproval, but her mind had drifted away from Sally's story to what awaited her in the morning. She had returned to the office late in the afternoon to learn that Simon

Moreton had issued an ultimatum: resume the Sophie Freeman inquest tomorrow, or be removed from the case. He had also 'strongly requested' that Elena Lujan's death be dealt with in the same hearing. The press had started to renege on their promise to keep reporting to a minimum, and the delay was stoking fears of a cover-up. It had been a close decision whether to call Simon's bluff, but in the end Jenny had agreed to do as he asked. A hurried court hearing would bring her no closer to the truth about Sophie's death, of course, but it did present the opportunity to pose some difficult questions that might pave the way to a later resolution. But the conundrum, as ever, was how far was it safe to go?

Sally nudged Ross with her elbow. 'Don't be so uptight. You told me you were cool with all that. Don't tell me you're a secret homophobe.'

'No,' Ross said, with an appeasing smile learned from his father.

'Well, don't act like you are.' She leaned forward into Jenny's space. 'Has he always behaved like an old man?'

'Not at all,' Jenny said, resenting the girl's attempted put-down of her son. 'He's always been very open-minded.' Unlike his father, she might have added, but if Sally had an ounce of insight, she would soon glean that for herself.

'Another thing I keep telling him is he's lucky to have divorced parents who can both look after themselves. My mum can't handle being on her own at all. She's at my sister's house every day. She won't even begin to think about dating anyone. It's crazy – she's really quite good-looking.'

'Give her time.'

'It's been nearly a year. It's not like he's in any danger of coming back. How long did it take you to start seeing other men?'

Jenny's mouthful of coffee lodged part-way down her

throat. She swallowed hard. 'It takes a lot of readjustment when you've been married a long time.'

Ross looked away, embarrassed at the turn the conversation had taken.

Sally kept her eyes on Jenny but her hand firmly on top of Ross's. 'You see, she doesn't say that. She claims she's glad not be fighting with him the whole time. She claims she *prefers* being on her own, but she's obviously lonely as hell.'

Jenny glanced at Ross, sensing his discomfort. 'Has she got any close friends?'

'Not really. You know, I think she might still be trying to compensate for what's happened. I think she feels she has to keep reassuring my sister that everything's still all right – even though she's twenty-six.'

'It's always complicated.' Jenny glanced down into her cup, hoping Sally would take the hint and change the subject.

Sally traced a finger along the back of Ross's hand. 'What do you think?' she asked him.

'I don't know. I haven't met her.'

'You've heard me talk about her enough.'

Jenny suppressed a smile.

'Mum's got to be in court tomorrow. I should get the bill.' He slipped away from her and went in search of Mario, the pot-bellied proprietor.

Sally gazed after him, wearing an expression of concern.

'I don't have to go just yet,' Jenny said. 'Is he all right, do you think?'

'I guess,' she answered, ambiguously.

'Is there a problem?'

'He's really the one who ought to be having this conversation.'

Jenny glanced over to where Ross was waiting patiently for Mario to finish relating a lengthy and dramatic anecdote to customers at the till. 'What conversation?'

'I shouldn't really—'

'I'd be grateful if you did.'

Sally's eyes tracked from Ross back to Jenny. 'Has he told you he's been seeing a counsellor at college?'

'No.' Jenny felt a spasm of anxiety. 'What about?'

'I think he might have something he wants to say to you.'

'Like what?'

Sally tilted her head, indicating that Ross was returning to the table.

'He said we can pay on the way out. Are we ready?'

Jenny and Sally exchanged a glance.

'I won't be a moment,' Sally said. She slid out of her seat and headed to the Ladies.

'She seems very nice,' Jenny said, trying her very best to sound sincere. 'How long is she staying?'

'A few days, maybe longer. Depends on Dad and Debbie, I guess.'

'You're both welcome at my place.'

'Thanks,' Ross said. 'Maybe at the weekend.'

The conversation lapsed into awkward silence. Jenny let it stretch on as he picked at the drips of candle wax that had fallen onto the tablecloth.

She tried to coax him. 'Sally mentioned you've been seeing a—'

'How's Michael?' Ross said, cutting across her.

'We haven't spoken for a couple of days.'

'Oh. Is everything all right?'

'We had a few words.' Jenny downplayed their argument.

'I liked him. You won't push him away, will you?'

'Why would I do that?' Jenny said, shocked at his sudden directness.

'I think sometimes you can do it without even realizing.'

'What do you mean?'

'I don't know. I just think he's good news, that's all.'

Seeing Sally reappear, he stood up from the table, relieved to have avoided the issue, whatever the *issue* was. 'Can we split the bill?'

'No. My treat.'

'If you're sure. Thanks.' He slid his arm around Sally's waist and, using her as a shield, steered her through the tables to the exit.

Jenny made her way to the counter alone to pay the bill, a tremor in her fingers as she slotted her credit card into the machine. Sally's revelation had shaken her. She had always tried to convince herself that Ross had remained insulated from her problems, but if he had been seeing a counsellor, it could only be her fault. She feared she had shaken his faith in life itself. His comment about her pushing Michael away had tapped into her deepest fears. Ross understood instinctively. He didn't have to articulate the words, he *felt* it in her: that she was frightened to live, because deep down she didn't believe she deserved it, didn't believe that she could love and be loved as other people could. And somehow along the way, she feared she had passed him the same disease.

She folded the receipt into her purse, deliberately delaying the moment of goodbye. If she failed to hold back the onrush of emotions, she feared she might embarrass herself. Be strong, she told herself. For God's sake.

'Would you like a lift home?' Jenny asked pleasantly.

'No need. We'll walk. But thanks,' Ross said. 'It was a lovely dinner.' He spoke graciously, but from an unreachable distance.

Jenny said, 'You'll think about the weekend?'

'Sure,' Ross said. 'That sounds great. I'll call.'

'Bye,' Sally chimed in, and hand in hand they turned and walked away.

Jenny watched them for a moment, Sally leaning her head

into his shoulder, closer to him than she would ever be. Perhaps he'd call, perhaps he wouldn't. He was getting as hard to read as David. Starting back towards her car, Jenny was seized by a dread that he would only ever drift further away, that he'd shut the door on her for good. She could deal with anything else, but not that. Please not that.

In the midst of her anxious thoughts, a male face, dark and soft-featured, was briefly illuminated by a phone's light in a stationary Range Rover idling on the opposite side of the road. A glimpse of profile was enough to make her turn around – he had been looking at her, *watching* her – but the light had gone out and the man's face was once again hidden in the darkness. The car pulled slowly away and moved off up the hill.

'Pull yourself together, Jenny,' she whispered to herself. 'Now you really are becoming paranoid.'

NINETEEN

CALL ME. WE SHOULD TALK. THEN A PAUSE. *You know how much I care about you, Jenny*. She had lain awake agonizing until 2 a.m. before her pride finally gave way, but when Michael had answered the phone he had groaned that she must be out of her mind to call in the middle of the night. Go back to bed.

So much for being in love. Steve would have trekked through a blizzard to be with her. Even David, when they were first seeing each other, had once hitchhiked all the way to southern Spain to where she had been working in a cheap bar. He had slept rough at the roadside and fought off muggers in Barcelona, just to share a few sleepless nights in her mosquito-infested bedsit. The difference between her and Michael, she had decided in the depths of the night, was that she was still in the fight, while he was looking for a way out of it.

Jenny couldn't comprehend life without a struggle, without something to kick against. Every tree, every blade of grass, every bird and insect was radiant only in the face of what it had overcome in order to exist. Life was a constant, defiant celebration in the face of death. Driving through the Wye Valley early in the morning as it shrugged off its mantle of mist, she felt like a kind of animist. She absorbed the energy of the forest and marvelled at the alchemy that had created it from dust. Passing under its arcing canopy more intricate than any cathedral ceiling, she wondered if Michael could ever understand how she fitted with the world. Adam Jordan would have done. He had shared her need to go back to the source; to move in time to the raw pulse. She had a picture of him in her mind: in a mud-stained T-shirt, drinking water from a hand-pump at the end of a day's work, children playing nearby in the dust. She had a feeling she would have liked him; in fact, if he was anything like the man she imagined, she probably would have fallen a little in love with him, too.

Alison spoke only to tell Jenny that the lawyers had arrived and were anxious to begin. It was a Friday morning and they all wanted the inquest dealt with in time for them to be safely back in London by evening. Jenny tried to embark on a long-overdue apology for her neglect in recent days, but Alison was impregnable. Jenny had left her in the lurch one too many times to be forgiven. The bond of trust between them had been broken, and nothing Jenny could say at this moment would rebuild it.

'Is Dr Kerr here?' Jenny asked.

'He is,' Alison answered abruptly. 'You'll be glad to know Major Fielding's answered his summons, though I can't say he looks happy about it. Shall I tell them you're ready?'

'Yes, please.'

Alison turned to the door.

Jenny said, 'I haven't told you all that I found out yesterday, but when I do, I think you'll understand.'

'You and I have always had different priorities, Mrs Cooper. I think we can safely say there can be no argument about that now.'

The scent of her perfume hung in the airless office as a reminder of her disapproval, but also, Jenny sensed, of the desperation it masked. Beneath the manicured exterior, she was in fear for her life.

The courtroom was even more crowded than it had been before Jenny had adjourned at the news of Elena Lujan's death. The rumours circulating in the hospital had spilled out into the world beyond. A dead thirteen-year-old girl had become public property. Sitting behind their lawyer and angled away from one another, Ed and Fiona Freeman might as well have had a wall between them. Fiona was inhabiting a realm of anger and recrimination; Ed was simply drowning in grief.

Hidden at the end of a row at the back of the court was Dr Kerr. Jenny could see only half his face, but it was sufficient for her to register his fear at what horrors the witness box might hold for him. He would be wondering if he would end the day with a job to return to.

Jenny took her seat on the raised dais at the head of the court, grateful that after years of relying on pills to get her through the courtroom ordeal, she was at last able face it without. Her heart beat slow and steady. She was apprehensive but strong. All that stood between her and the truth were four witnesses and three determined lawyers. Turning to address them, she reminded herself they were only human; beneath the bravado they would be as nervous and as fallible as she was.

'Thank you, everyone, for your patience over the last few days. I believe we're now in a position to proceed to the conclusion of the evidence. If we could begin with Mr Freeman, please.'

Fiona Freeman folded her arms across her chest and looked away, as if disowning her husband.

'Ma'am, if I may . . .' Alistair Martlett, counsel for the Health Protection Agency, was on his feet. 'We have received two brief, and if I may say so, obscure statements, one from Mr Freeman and one from a Major Fielding. Neither appears in any way relevant to the issue of what caused Miss Freeman's death. May I suggest we hear Dr Verma first? You may find that no further evidence is required.'

'I appreciate that you are used to civil trials, Mr Martlett, but these proceedings are not a contest. You are here to assist my inquiry into the truth. I will decide on the relevance of the evidence and in what order I call it.'

'With the greatest of respect, ma'am –' she had never heard the phrase used less sincerely – 'I am only seeking to save this witness, in particular, the distress of giving evidence.'

It was a cheap shot, but it stung nonetheless.

'I'm sure your clients would prefer to dispense with the inconvenience of an inquest altogether, Mr Martlett, but I'm afraid they're not above the process of law any more than you or I. Come forward, please, Mr Freeman.'

Martlett exchanged a look with the small team of lawyers behind him, as if to say they should have expected nothing less of a jumped-up coroner from the backwoods.

Ed Freeman mumbled the oath in a voice that barely carried to Jenny, let alone to those at the rear of the courtroom. Gently reminding him to speak up, she started to lead him through the facts of his visit, along with his daughters, to the Hampton's Health Club, although she was careful to omit reference to the still-anonymous woman friend he had met there. If necessary she would visit that detail later, but for now she would spare him – and Fiona – the embarrassment.

The two girls swam in the pool for a little under an hour while he sat in the cafe, he explained. It had been busy that day, but not excessively so. It was an expensive club, always clean, the last place you would expect to pick up a disease. Neither of his daughters seemed to suffer any ill effects. As far as he was concerned, it had been a perfectly harmless trip.

Anthony Radstock, the Freemans' solicitor, had no questions for his client, evidently relieved that Jenny had resisted straying into uncomfortable territory. He had the kindly face of a confidant, and she imagined Ed Freeman had confessed to him everything there was to know about his secret companion.

'I have no wish to trouble Mr Freeman any further,' Martlett said, 'and would like to take this opportunity to extend my client's deepest sympathies to both him and his wife.'

Ed Freeman muttered a thank you and began to step from the witness box, but Catherine Dyer, counsel for the Severn Vale District Hospital Trust, rose to her feet and stopped him.

'Just a moment, Mr Freeman. I shan't be long.' She gave a disarming smile. 'If you could tell me – were you alone in the cafe?'

Jenny saw Martlett suppress a smile. Somehow he had persuaded his younger colleague to do his dirty work. She fought the urge to intervene as Freeman stared at her, shame and astonishment temporarily halting his answer.

'No.'

'Were you with a woman?'

Fiona looked at him with a contempt beyond loathing.

'I was.'

'Can you tell us who this woman was?'

Freeman looked helplessly to Jenny. She had as good as promised him this wouldn't happen. She had to do something.

'You're not obliged to name this person, Mr Freeman, certainly not in open court. What's the point of this question, Miss Dyer?'

'I'm merely seeking to establish if he may have had contact with anyone who might have been carrying the meningitis infection.' And for added emphasis, she said, 'Exchange of saliva is one of the most common modes of transmission.'

'I have not had intimacy with any woman,' Freeman said. 'Besides which, I have tested negative for infection.'

'I'm told it's not impossible for someone to play temporary host, given the right set of circumstances. I appreciate it's an uncomfortable question, especially as the only other confirmed case in the locality was that of a young woman who worked in a city-centre massage parlour.'

'I have not engaged in any physical intimacy with any woman,' Ed Freeman repeated, then added unconvincingly, 'other than my wife.'

'Or any man.'

'Is that a joke?'

'I'm sorry, Mr Freeman. We have to cover all possibilities. Are you sure that you've never visited the Recife sauna and massage parlour, whether or not for sexual purposes?'

'I have not.' He was furious, and Jenny could see that he held her entirely responsible for his humiliation.

'I fully appreciate that it's not the sort of thing that any married man would care to admit to, but by your own admission, you have sought out female company—'

'That's enough, Miss Dyer,' Jenny interrupted.

'Ma'am, I'm afraid it isn't. If Mr Freeman is unwilling to name his companion in the Hampton's cafe voluntarily, perhaps I can ask him to confirm whether he met this woman through an Internet site called Lunchdates.com.'

'Miss Dyer, I've no idea where you're dredging this from,

and I don't need to know. It's inappropriate. You don't have to answer, Mr Freeman.'

'Ma'am, this evidence comes directly from my client's lawfully maintained records. They detail the websites visited by Mr Freeman on his hospital computer, and the contents of his emails. He has specifically granted my clients access to this information in his contract of employment. If you'd like to check, I have a copy here.' She reached for a document and held it up.

'It's all right, Miss Dyer.'

Ed Freeman clung to the edge of the witness box for support.

'I've no desire to go into specifics,' Catherine Dyer continued, 'but I would like to ask Mr Freeman once again to assure the court that he hasn't had sexual relations with anyone who might be considered promiscuous.'

'You've already had that question answered, Miss Dyer. That's enough.'

'As you wish, ma'am. My clients will gladly make their records available to you.'

Catherine Dyer sat, her job done. No denial could dispel the innuendo once it had been raised. Ed Freeman stepped down from the witness box a man suspected of being the agent of his daughter's death, and with his wife unable even to meet his eye. What's more, the offer of evidence of his computer usage had been cleverly made. To refuse to review it would lay any verdict Jenny reached open to challenge. She would now have to look at it and, to Dyer's obvious delight, she requested that any documents be handed to her before the end of the session.

Major Christopher Fielding was a younger man than Jenny had expected, only thirty-three years old and with a boyish, benign face that didn't seem to match the seriousness of his profession. He was dressed in a civilian suit, but it did little to disguise his military bearing. He read the oath briskly then looked to Jenny with a bemused expression, as if awaiting an explanation for his summons to court.

Jenny said, 'Major Fielding, I see from the statement that you kindly provided to my officer that you belong to the 4th Battalion Military Intelligence Corps, and are currently based at Bulford Camp, Salisbury.'

'That's correct.'

'And on the 16th of July this year, you paid a visit to Hampton's Health Club in Bristol.'

'I did.'

'Can I ask you why you were there?'

'I had been on overnight business in Bristol, and called in the next morning. I belong to a club in Salisbury that has reciprocal membership.'

'I appreciate that this may sound a slightly odd question, but do you mind if I ask what kind of business?'

'I can answer up to a point—'

'Please do,' Jenny said.

Fielding picked his words carefully. 'I'm on a regional liaison committee. Every few months the various law-enforcement and intelligence-gathering agencies come together to swap information on issues or individuals of interest to us. We had several sessions over the course of a weekend. It's meant to make us more efficient.' He smiled at what appeared to be his idea of a joke.

Jenny said, 'Were you at the health club alone or with colleagues?'

'Alone. But if I might say so, I question the relevance of this. Since being contacted by your officer I reported to the Medical Officer and have been confirmed completely free of any infectious diseases.' He reached into his jacket and produced a document. 'I have a letter here.'

Alison fetched it from him and handed it to Jenny. In a few short sentences it confirmed the military doctor's finding that Fielding had tested negative for meningitis and a whole tranche of other infections. Jenny could have left it there – his presence at the club was always likely to have proved coincidental – but now she had him in the witness box, she felt it wouldn't hurt to ask a few more questions.

'I appreciate you having gone to this trouble, Major Fielding. Thank you.' She handed the letter back to Alison. 'But tell me, have you had reason to visit the military research establishment at Porton Down in recent months?'

'I have been there once or twice,' he answered, as if the question was entirely expected.

'You're aware that it's a facility where research is carried out to defend against hazards presented by chemical and biological warfare.'

'I think that's common knowledge, ma'am. But if you're suggesting, as I think you may be, that I somehow transmitted this bacteria, I think the tests disprove that. I can also assure you I haven't set foot inside a laboratory.'

He smiled again, polite and assertive, and Jenny detected a strange familiarity. It wasn't his face she recognized, rather his demeanour. It was in the slight upwards tilt of his chin and the tightly cropped military haircut. He was of a type; the same type as the man who had glanced her way inside the entrance to the Diamond Light Source. It was a wholly unjustified, irrational connection to have made, certainly not one she could articulate in open court, but it stuck and refused to dislodge.

'Have you been in close contact with anyone who has been inside a laboratory?'

'Not that I am aware.'

'But you might have been?'

'It's possible, of course.'

Jenny had exhausted all questions she could reasonably have asked him. She had no choice but to thank him for his help and offer him to the lawyers for cross-examination. Not surprisingly, none of them took her up on it. After fewer than five minutes in the witness box, Major Fielding was walking smartly towards the exit.

Dr Anita Verma bristled with impatience as she stepped forward to give evidence for the second time in a week. Jenny reminded her that she was still on oath to tell the whole truth, and asked her if Elena Lujan's remained the only other reported case.

'Yes,' Dr Verma replied curtly. 'Miss Freeman and Miss Lujan's cases remain the only two in the country that we know of. We're making no assumptions, but it's good news so far.'

'Do you have any idea how long this infection takes to incubate?'

'Between two and ten days. In the normal run of events we would have expected more cases by now. To that extent we've been very fortunate.'

'Are you any closer to understanding how these two women came to be infected, Dr Verma?'

'We've yet to isolate the source. It's possible we never will. The most likely explanation is that it was an infected individual who has remained asymptomatic or who has moved on elsewhere, even abroad.'

'Or who came from abroad? From the meningitis belt of Africa, perhaps?'

'There are all manner of explanations. As you know, Miss

Lujan worked as a prostitute. It's possible she had an infected client. We may be lucky and trace him, but we may not.'

'And transmission from Miss Lujan to Miss Freeman?'

'We can't say. This disease can spread through a cough or a sneeze, rather like a cold. They could have been travelling in the same bus, passed each other in the street, or been infected by a third party entirely separately.' She looked sympathetically at Ed and Fiona Freeman. 'Other than adding to the condolences already offered to the family, I'm afraid there's not much more I can assist you with, ma'am.'

Jenny turned back through her notes, buying herself a moment to draw up her courage. She was in no doubt she would need it. 'Actually, there are several things you can help me with, Dr Verma.'

The witness responded with a look of surprise.

'I presume that by now your laboratories have carried out a detailed analysis of the strain that proved fatal to Miss Freeman and Miss Lujan.'

'That work is ongoing.'

'It is the case, isn't it, that it has proved resistant to the effects of all the usual antibiotics?'

'Yes,' she answered hesitantly.

'It is also the case that antibiotic resistance can be artificially inserted into a bacterium almost as a matter of routine. In fact, I've heard that genes that code for antibiotic resistance are often used as "markers" when carrying out complex gene manipulation.'

'Yes, but—'

'But what, Dr Verma?'

'This strain is clearly one that has *evolved* to develop antibiotic resistance. I'm afraid it's like an arms race – micro-organisms evolve to create chemical defences to drugs. When two strains, each of which has a different resistance, combine, you have a new one with double the defences. In this case, multiple defences.'

Jenny looked at her closely, wanting to read the reaction in her face. 'Have you pursued the theory that this strain was developed artificially?'

Dr Verma replied without missing a beat. 'No such organism has been created in a British laboratory. If any such work were being carried out, my agency would have been notified. It has not been.'

'You've pursued the theory and discounted it – is that your answer?'

Dr Verma glanced at Martlett, then back at Jenny. 'Yes.'

Jenny kept her in her gaze. 'Is that an entirely truthful answer, Dr Verma?'

'Of course.'

'Can you tell me who the team that have been sweeping the Vale Hospital during the last few days work for?'

'They're reporting to us.'

'Can you please answer the question?'

'They are experts in detecting and handling dangerous organisms.'

'From the military laboratory at Porton Down, in Wiltshire?'

Martlett rose to his feet. 'Ma'am, the identities of the staff my clients use to carry out their investigations is hardly relevant to the fact at issue. There really seems to me to be nothing more of significance to be gained from this witness.'

Jenny said, 'As I have already explained, that is a matter for me. Sit down, please, Mr Martlett.'

Martlett glanced back at the three lawyers seated behind him and, taking his cue from them, reluctantly gave way.

Jenny continued with her questioning. 'Is it safe to assume

that you brought in such people because you feared an outbreak?'

'It's a perfectly sensible precaution.'

'Are you able to tell me what they found?'

'So far they've found nothing. No trace of this organism other than in the two fatalities.'

'That is good news,' Jenny said. 'But can you tell me why they found it necessary to remove all brain tissue and spinal fluid from Sophie Freeman's body without even informing Dr Kerr, the hospital's chief pathologist?'

Dr Verma stared back at her, her eyes widening first in surprise, then alarm. For once, she was at a complete loss for words.

Jenny glanced at the lawyers, who had immediately started exchanging panicked whispers. Her question seemed to have caught them all unawares. Ed and Fiona Freeman looked at each other for the first time that morning.

'You are aware that Miss Freeman's brain and spinal fluid were removed? Dr Glazier, the pathologist you instructed to carry out the post-mortem on Elena Lujan, was present in the mortuary when the discovery was made.'

'No,' Dr Verma said weakly. 'This is the first I've heard—'

'The brain tissue and spinal fluid were also taken from the body of a man named Adam Jordan. He had died in a fall from a motorway bridge. Can you explain that, Dr Verma?'

'No—'

'Ma'am,' interjected Martlett, 'these allegations are entirely unknown to us—'

'They're not unknown to the hospital, Mr Martlett. Dr Kerr reported this to his manager.'

Martlett hurriedly consulted with Catherine Dyer and the team behind her. 'Ma'am, Dr Verma can't be asked to testify to something of which she had no knowledge.'

'Then I expect your clients to produce a witness who does have the knowledge.'

'That may take some time, ma'am.'

'It won't take long to summon Dr Verma's superior. I expect to see him here this afternoon.' She turned to Dr Verma. 'You may stand down for the time being, but please remain in the room. I may well want to hear from you again.'

As Verma escaped from the witness box, Jenny addressed Martlett. 'Mr Martlett, your clients should know that this inquiry will continue until they have provided answers. Clearly someone higher up the chain of command than Dr Verma has assumed that the small matter of the gross violation of a child's body was something that could be hidden from my view. I would like you to make this plain: it cannot.'

Martlett gave a disdainful nod.

Radstock, the Freemans' solicitor, rose. Behind him, Fiona Freeman was silently sobbing into a Kleenex. Her husband ventured to put a hand on her arm. She pushed him away.

'Ma'am, my clients are understandably deeply disturbed by this allegation. Can we please have your assurance that you will substantiate it?'

'We'll hear from Dr Kerr now, Mr Radstock. I apologize to your clients, but sometimes surprise is necessary.' She looked out across the rows of puzzled faces. 'Will Dr Kerr please come forward?'

No one stood.

'Is Dr Kerr in the room?' She felt a wave of anxiety rise up from deep within her. 'Dr Kerr?'

The door at the back of the court opened.

'Dr Kerr?' She heard a note of shrillness enter her voice.

Simon Moreton entered. He looked at her, and slowly and emphatically shook his head.

'Fetch the witness, please, usher,' Jenny barked at Alison. 'We'll rise until he's found.'

She stood up and left the courtroom. As she closed the door behind her, she heard Ed Freeman's angry voice above the commotion: 'What in God's name have you done to my daughter?'

The knock at the door sounded ominously.

'Come in.' Jenny didn't look up from the email she was typing to the director of the Severn Vale District Hospital Trust. 'Attempting to pervert the course of justice, Simon? I could have you thrown in the cells for contempt.'

'I believe you've already met Miss Webley.'

Jenny looked up and saw the young intelligence officer at Moreton's side. She was carrying a small tan briefcase and appeared taken aback at the modesty of the room in which she found herself.

'Good morning, Mrs Cooper. I'm sorry to disturb you.'

'I'm not sure either of you are quite grasping the seriousness of this matter,' Jenny said, barely containing her fury. 'Where's Dr Kerr? He's a witness. A lawfully summoned witness.'

'There's no call for alarm. He's quite safe,' Moreton said. 'He's just needed to answer a few questions.'

'Questions from whom? You know that obstructing proceedings is unacceptable.'

'I'm well aware of that, Jenny, but extraordinary circumstances call for extreme measures. May we?' Moreton gestured to the two chairs that Jenny had failed to offer them.

She shrugged. She could gladly have hit him, especially when she saw the unctuous, apologetic smile he gave Webley as he drew up her plastic chair. Jenny wondered if he had already booked their table for lunch at the Hotel du Vin.

'I'll leave this to you, Ruth, shall I?' Moreton said.

Webley unfastened her briefcase as she started to talk. 'Mrs Cooper, I appreciate this is irregular, to put it mildly, but there are issues of national security involved.' She glanced at Moreton. 'I'm told I can trust you.'

'Trust me to do what, precisely?'

'There were several options open to me, Jenny, but you're an experienced coroner with an impressive record. I was assured you would appreciate the delicacies of the situation.'

Jenny didn't believe a word: for Simon not to have just shut her out – as he had tried to in the past – could only mean that he was frightened of her or, more probably, of what she might know. She was tempted to challenge him simply to remove her from the case, but a wiser voice told her to make the most of her advantage.

Jenny looked him in the eye. 'All right. I'll listen.'

Moreton responded with a grateful smile. And in it, Jenny could see that he had convinced himself that he had finally converted her to his cause: expedient justice.

'I'll be honest with you, Mrs Cooper,' Webley began ominously, 'organs and spinal fluid were taken from the cadavers as part of a thoroughgoing investigation into what we have had to treat as a potential emergency. I apologize for the impression of a cover-up, but when something as potentially dangerous as a fatal epidemic threatens, you have to do what it takes. I'm told those samples are necessary for studying this organism – they provide a bank, if you like.'

'Are you intending to explain this to Mr and Mrs Freeman?'

'Yes, of course.' She glanced at the documents she held in her hand. 'And to Mrs Jordan.'

Jenny waited for her to continue.

'This is an unusual situation. There are several organizations involved. Initially the Health Protection Agency thought it was dealing with a simple outbreak, but an analysis of this strain of meningitis revealed – as I think you've worked out – that it carries the characteristics of a recombinant organism. That immediately triggered the involvement of the biological weapons team from Porton Down and my service. Our procedure is quite simple: we worked through our watch list to look for any possible connections. One of the names on our list was Sonia Blake's. We had received intelligence that she had been in contact with a man named Adam Jordan. We looked into his background, tried to find him, then discovered he was dead. I think you can appreciate our interest, especially as he'd recently returned to the country from an area where this disease is commonplace.'

'What did you think he had done?' Jenny said.

'We had no idea, but we do know this about him.'

She brought some blown-up photographs out of her brief-case and handed them over to Jenny. They were similar to pictures she had seen at AFAD's offices: a lush, green plantation standing in the midst of a parched, dry landscape. Adam Jordan could be seen in one of them, sitting shirtless behind the wheel of a stationary jeep.

'One of his organization's irrigation projects. It's marijuana. Twenty-five acres of mature crop alongside the maize. From what I hear, he and his boss, Mr Thorn, took a principled stand on the issue – growing a lucrative cash crop was the fastest way out of poverty for these people.'

Hiding her disappointment, Jenny said, 'Maybe they had a point.'

'I'm sure they did, but once you're in the drugs business you're in everything that goes with it. People will do almost anything for a share of that kind of money, particularly somewhere as war-torn and poor as South Sudan.'

'For what it's worth, I get the impression that Adam Jordan's heart was genuinely in the right place. Why else would he have been in contact with someone like Sonia Blake?'

'We're keeping an open mind about his motivations,' Webley said coldly, 'and about why he jumped off a bridge. Let's just say the picture looks increasingly complicated.'

Jenny thought back to the photographs of Jordan's car that Alison had shown her. 'Was it your people who got to his car the morning after he died?'

'What do you mean?' Webley was puzzled.

'The police took photographs – there was a wooden figurine hanging from the rear-view mirror. Someone took it before my officer arrived later that morning.'

'No,' Webley said. 'I know nothing about that.'

For a reason she couldn't pin down, Jenny believed her.

'Is there anything else we should know? Really, Mrs Cooper – you'll have to take my word when I say we have only a sketchy knowledge of what Adam Jordan had been doing.'

Again, Webley sounded sincere, but Jenny reminded herself who she was. It was her business to win trust as a means of extracting information. Human feelings existed merely to be exploited. She thought of the African girl with Adam at the filling station, of his regular withdrawals from a cashpoint in central Bristol, of Sonia Blake's visit to the Diamond Light Source, of her father's murder and her interest in the Soviet biologist Roman Slavsky. All were pieces of the puzzle that Webley and her colleagues were desperately trying to piece together, as she was. But she also recalled her last conversation with Karen Jordan, and her suspicion that Adam had seen legal drugs withheld from disease-stricken communities in South Sudan; drugs that were being used as weapons in a proxy war. A war over what, Jenny couldn't begin to speculate. Oil? Minerals? Or perhaps nothing more than political influence in the great, long-playing African game?

Karen's words rang in her head as she looked into Webley's expectant face: '*This is government, isn't it? He didn't kill himself – they murdered him . . .*'

Jenny served her the question straight. 'Did you have anything to do with the break-in at Mrs Jordan's home?'

Webley was bemused. 'Why on earth would you think that?'

'Because his colleague, Harry Thorn, says that the British government is never off his back. In fact, he gives every impression that independent aid agencies such as his are seen as tools of foreign policy, and when they refuse to play they find themselves in trouble.'

Webley smiled. 'I think you'll find that Mr Thorn is generally considered to have "gone troppo", as the Australians say, some years ago. The file I've seen suggests that he would be one of the last people our agents would attempt to deal with.'

'And Adam Jordan?'

Webley hesitated, choosing her words with care. 'He wasn't unknown to us, but neither was there a close relationship. As I said, the picture is complicated.'

It was Jenny's turn to dissemble. 'It's clear you know far more than I do, Ms Webley. Perhaps you'd be good enough to forward me all you have for the purposes of Mr Jordan's inquest.'

Ruth Webley's voice hardened. 'I'll pass your request on, certainly, but we can't allow the inquest you're currently conducting to go any further.'

'What do you mean?'

Moreton leaned forward. 'Jenny, you know as well as I do that this inquest is turning into one massive fishing trip.

Both girls died of meningitis. There's nothing more to say. If you insist on delving further I'll have no choice but to request the Secretary of State to have you removed on grounds of unfitness.'

Jenny fought her desire to fire back and forced herself to think ahead. She was now as sure as she could be that there was a connection between Jordan's death and those of Sophie and Elena. And if she were removed from one case, it would surely follow that she would be removed from the other.

'All right,' she said. 'But perhaps we can we agree on a compromise?'

Moreton looked pleasantly surprised. 'What do you suggest?'

'All rise.' Alison's voice rose above the hubbub that had continued unabated for the full twenty minutes since proceedings had been abruptly adjourned.

Jenny entered the courtroom at a brisk walk and sat at her desk without looking up. Dismissing the lawyers' attempts to register their protests, she began to read from a handwritten note she had brought in with her. 'Having heard all the evidence currently available to me, it is clear that Sophie Freeman died from a deadly antibiotic-resistant strain of meningitis. Much as I would like to inquire further into the nature of this organism and the manner and circumstances of her infection, the law places limits on the scope of a coroner's inquiry which, in this case, I judge I have reached. Normally, in the case of a person who has died as a result of an infectious disease contracted by chance, a verdict of death by natural causes would be returned. I do not feel able to make such a finding, so am therefore returning an open verdict.'

All three lawyers rose as one to voice their objections.

Jenny glanced up and saw the shock and dismay on the faces of Ed and Fiona Freeman.

'I have nothing more to add,' Jenny said. 'The inquest is closed.'

She exited as swiftly as she had entered, feeling, for the first time in her career as coroner, that she had delivered grieving parents a bitter injustice. She only hoped she could find answers before one of them decided life was no longer worth living.

TWENTY

'JESUS, JENNY. WHAT DID YOU think you were doing? I just had a call from Fiona Freeman. She said you didn't even offer an explanation. One minute the inquest was in full swing, the next you'd delivered an open verdict. Now they're both going over the edge.'

Jenny had been back behind her desk in Jamaica Street less than an hour when she answered the call from David. She was already consumed with guilt, and he was confirming her worst fears.

'I will speak to them. It's just—'

'Just what, Jenny? Have you any idea how upsetting this is? I told them they could trust you, for God's sake.'

'I know!'

'And?'

'I said I'll talk to them.'

'When?'

'When I've something to say. It may take some time. A few days.'

David sighed, infuriated. 'This is hopeless. Thanks for nothing. I hope you can live with yourself.'

She started as he slammed down the phone. A hard lump had formed in her throat: all the symptoms of anxiety clawing at her one by one. She knew the signs well enough; she was approaching the load at which she would soon no longer be able to function without resorting to the drugs she thought she had kicked for good. If only she could grow a skin as thick as her ex-husband's she could push on, confident that she had done the right thing, but she was like a child, tossed to and fro by the emotions of others. Where was her sense of herself? *You're a coroner, for pity's sake, you can't let him diminish you like that.*

The words boosted her self-esteem for a fleeting second, only for a fresh wave of anxiety to surge over her. Teetering towards a full-blown panic attack, she grabbed her handbag and searched for the Xanax she kept tucked away for emergencies.

She popped one out of the foil and swallowed, forcing it past the tight muscles of her throat. As the drug seeped into her blood and slowly began to untie the knots that had threatened to choke her, she asked herself why she couldn't be like David, Simon Moreton, Ruth Webley and the lawyers who had barracked her. They all asserted themselves as naturally as they breathed, while she, just as Dr Allen had told her, invariably found herself on the defensive. She was always the one reacting, always searching for the sense of entitlement that others seemed to claim without conscious thought.

It was a chemical calm, but a calm nonetheless. She used it to weigh her options. Part of her was desperate to give up the fight and bury herself in the hundred mundane cases mounting on her desk, but each time she tried to imagine the calls she would make to the Freemans and Karen Jordan, all she could feel was the emptiness of their despair. No, retreat wasn't an option, but the way she was feeling, neither was going it entirely alone.

Jenny went through to reception, where Alison was behind her desk, her things arranged neatly around her, a safe and secure pocket of order in which she had ensconced herself.

She continued to type on her computer, her expression registering nothing other than mild irritation as Jenny recounted all that she had found out about Jordan and her suspicion that his death somehow linked with those of Sophie Freeman and Elena Lujan.

'I need to find the African girl,' Jenny said. 'We can't know anything without her.'

Alison didn't answer.

'I thought that might be something you could help with – your contacts in the police.'

'I'm sorry, Mrs Cooper,' she answered flatly. 'I can't.'

'It shouldn't be that difficult. Someone connected with Adam Jordan must know who she is.'

'I'm not sure I know how to make myself any clearer.'

'I'm only asking you to do your job.'

'No. You know that's not right. You're asking me to get involved in something they don't want us involved with.' She shook her head. 'I can't do that any more.'

'Have Moreton and Webley spoken to you, too?'

'Mr Moreton did, yes. But it's not because of him . . . I need to give myself the best chance, Mrs Cooper. I'm not ready to say to hell with it all.'

'Oh.' Jenny tried to fathom her reaction. 'I just . . . I thought you wanted to keep on as normal.'

'I do. But this isn't normal, is it?' She met Jenny's gaze. 'You're talking about murder, and not just the ordinary kind. You know as well as I do, Adam Jordan's case is the least normal we've ever had.'

'What makes you say that?'

'You've got in so deep you can't see it for what it is.'

'What do you mean, Alison?'

'I mean you'd be foolish not to give it up now. But I know I'm wasting my breath.'

*

It wasn't yet five o'clock, but in their brief phone call Detective Superintendent Owen Williams of the Gwent police had suggested the Chepstow Castle Inn as their meeting place. Nestled at the foot of the town next to the medieval castle that stood imperiously on a cliff overlooking the Wye, the pub was far enough away from the police station for him not to risk being seen by his colleagues. Several times in recent years she had persuaded him into investigations in which his force could claim only limited interest, and the new Chief Constable – a 'frigid English bastard with both thumbs stuck up his backside' – wasn't prepared to tolerate any more of the border skirmishes Williams so relished.

She carried her orange juice out from the empty bar to the garden at the rear, and found him soaking up the late-afternoon sun, a pint glass in his hand.

'Come to disturb my tranquil waters again, Mrs Cooper?' Williams said, in the exaggeratedly sing-song Welsh accent he had cultivated to make every sentence sound like a line of poetry.

'Some might say I've made your life more interesting, Superintendent.'

'Too bloody interesting. What have those English scum-bags dealt you this time?'

Blinking against the sharp sunlight, Jenny gave him the essentials of the Adam Jordan case. He betrayed no hint of alarm or surprise as she told her story. Nothing that happened in England, it seemed, could ever shock him, not even the suggestion of an innocent aid worker being murdered by government agents working to suppress details of a dirty African war. For a man whose professional life had been mostly taken up with small-town burglaries and closing-time brawls, he had an admirable ability to absorb the un-expected.

'So in a nutshell, Mrs Cooper, you'd like me to knock on the door of MI5 and drag them all down to Chepstow police station,' he said with a wry smile. 'I can't see that being too much of a problem.'

'I was hoping you might help with tracing the girl.'

'And how would I justify that, exactly? I can't see that a crime has been committed in Wales.'

'I live in Wales—'

Williams gave a tolerant smile and took a packet of cigarettes from his shirt pocket.

'I think I may have been followed. I went to a restaurant with my son and his girlfriend. There was a man outside in a car. He was watching me.'

'After all you've told me I'd be surprised if you weren't being watched, but it still doesn't get me over the border all the way down the M4 to bloody Berkshire, does it?'

'There's nothing more to be found out there. I've a feeling she'll be in Bristol – that's where he'd been withdrawing money.'

'Last time I checked, Bristol was still in unliberated territory, Mrs Cooper. Cigarette?'

She wavered.

'Thank you.'

She shared the flame from his battered brass lighter, recalling the first time she had seen it. It had been in the interview room at the police station nearly five years before, when Williams had arrested both her and her then boyfriend, Steve, who had had the habit of growing marijuana on his farm tucked away in the woods. Williams had been wise enough to see that the tip-off had been a malicious attempt to throw Jenny off her investigation, and days later was dragging reluctant witnesses to her impromptu courtroom in Chepstow Baptist Hall. In no small part thanks to him, the death of fourteen-year-old Danny Wills in a privately run juvenile prison had been exposed as a vicious murder.

'You remember the Danny Wills case?' Jenny said.

'I remember your face when I nicked you. You were wearing a blue silk dressing gown, and not a lot else, as I recall.'

'You told me to hold the inquest here in Chepstow so you and your team could help out. What if I were to do that again? The African girl's a witness I need to trace – no one could object to that.' Jenny tried to read Williams's face.

He blew out a long, thin stream of smoke and turned to her with a look of amused resignation. 'You always find your bloody way round everything, don't you, Mrs Cooper?'

It was six o'clock. She was tired and tense, but it was too early to give up on the day, and the weekend loomed like a void. Driving back through the valley Jenny found herself glancing nervously in her rear-view mirror, checking for phantom followers. She hadn't truly allowed herself to believe that she had been watched coming out of the restaurant with Ross and Sally, but Williams's comment had unnerved her. Suddenly her rural haven didn't feel so safe any more. She had planned to drive home and call Dr Henry Blake, Sonia Blake's ex-husband, a man whom she had established was an immunologist working at Oxford's John Radcliffe Hospital, but a cautionary instinct told her that might not be wise. A few simple keystrokes on a GCHQ computer and every word of her landline and mobile calls would be relayed directly to Ruth Webley.

She descended into the village of Tintern, but rather than turn left up the hillside to Melin Bach, she continued on past the abbey ruins and around the bend in the river until she arrived at the phone box that stood a little along from the

Rose and Crown pub. Pulling off the road, she again checked
her mirrors, but the only vehicles in view were a tractor and
an old Toyota pick-up truck that belonged to a local stone-
mason. Save for a handful of tourists who had stopped to
admire the view over the Wye, there was no one in sight.

It had been years since she had pulled open the heavy,
creaking door of a red phone box. Its familiar, powerful
odour – as unpleasant as ever – evoked teenage memories of
being marooned at far-flung railway stations, rain beating
against the scratched and broken panes; and of precious ten-
pence calls to long-forgotten boyfriends, the 'I love you's
whispered in the desperate dying seconds after the warning
pips had sounded. But coins, she discovered, were no longer
necessary. The phone demanded her credit card and charged
her obscenely before allowing her the privilege of dialling a
number.

She connected to a receptionist and asked to be put
through to Dr Henry Blake. She tracked him down to an
extension in the immunology department.

'Dr Blake? It's Jenny Cooper. Coroner for the Severn
Vale.'

'Severn Vale? I thought this was an Oxford matter.'

'This isn't about your ex-wife.' She hesitated. 'Well, in a
manner of speaking it is, but I'm not the coroner dealing
with her case.' She was floundering. *Pull yourself together,
Jenny.* 'I'm dealing with another death, one that occurred in
my jurisdiction. I was talking to your wife before she —'

'Hold on. Whose death are we talking about here?'

'The name of the deceased was Adam Jordan.'

'I've never heard of him. I'm sorry. I don't think I can
help you.'

'Could we please meet, Dr Blake?' She headed off his
protest. 'It really is most urgent.'

'I'm very busy this week—'

'Tonight. I can be with you in an hour and a half. I'd be grateful.'

He made no reply. In the silence, she could hear the faint click of computer keys. She guessed Blake was doing what had become second nature to her: checking the bona fides of his caller online even as their conversation was in progress.

'My inquiry is into the death of a man who had met professionally with your wife,' she continued. 'He was an aid worker recently returned from South Sudan. This may mean more to you than it does to me: he had bought an out-of-print book by a Professor Roman Slavsky. Your ex-wife had a file on Slavsky in her college rooms, but after her death I found its contents to be missing.'

She heard the sound of Blake's breath on the receiver. Her mention of Slavsky seemed to have shocked him.

'How well do you know Oxford?' he asked her.

'Better than I did a fortnight ago.'

'I'll be at the High Street entrance to the Botanic Garden at 8.15.'

'I'll hurry.'

Blake rang off, and as Jenny set down the phone she saw from the corner of her eye a dark, expensive-looking car drive slowly past, the driver invisible behind its tinted glass. She waited, frozen, until it had turned the corner and disappeared from view, then hurried to her Land Rover.

The figure waiting outside the iron gates opposite Magdalen Bridge took her by surprise. She had pictured a precise and businesslike man in a suit; a younger version of her ex-husband. Blake could have been mistaken for a student: he wore jeans and a long-sleeved V-neck T-shirt that hugged his slim torso. Thick black hair flopped over his forehead.

'Dr Blake?' she ventured cautiously.

'Yes.'

'Jenny Cooper. Sorry I'm late. I always forget there's nowhere to park in this city.'

His eyes, dark blue, scanned her with a scholar's precision. He would be comparing her with the photographs he had seen of her online. If he had taken five minutes to read the press reports triggered by her name, he would know her whole life history, too. The Internet had made it a curse from which she would never entirely free herself.

'Hi.' He extended a hand. 'Henry Blake.'

She saw in his eyes something of the deep seriousness behind his casual appearance. He was an observer, she sensed, someone whose mind never ceased making connections.

She glanced at the locked gates. 'Oh, are we too late?'

'I've a key.' He reached into his jeans pockets. 'I'm one of the "friends", a trustee, actually.' He unfastened the padlock. 'Don't tell any of my colleagues – they'll think I've lost my edge.' He led her through the gate and carefully locked it after them. 'I was advising on the medicinal plants collection and discovered a premature interest in horticulture. It's funny how things take you.'

Jenny smiled, sensing that he was nervous of her. The anxious mention of his colleagues told her he was wary of being seen with her, too. A deserted garden was one of the few safe places to meet.

They set off along the gravel path between immaculately striped lawns planted with specimen trees and shrubs towards a circular ornamental pond.

'Are you fond of gardens?' Blake said stiffly. Small talk didn't seem to come naturally.

'I've a patch of wilderness I occasionally try to tame,' she answered, 'but it doesn't seem to like me interfering with it. I think of it that way – like it has a life of its own.'

The corners of Blake's mouth twitched into a hint of a

smile. Jenny felt him relax a little. She had been in his presence only a minute or two, and could already be sure that his marriage to Sonia would have been short on frivolity.

'Would you like me to tell you what brought me to your ex-wife?' Jenny asked.

Blake glanced across at her with an expression that told her he half-suspected the answer.

'I can't say I want to hear it, but I suppose I had better.'

For the second time in the space of a few hours, Jenny recounted the story of Adam Jordan's violent death and his secretive trip to Oxford two days beforehand. She told him how she had arrived at the cafe in Oxford Castle and been led first to Alex Forster, then to Sonia Blake, and then to a world of which she had little or no understanding. Obeying an instinct to keep some of the pieces to herself, she stopped short of telling him about the African girl and the meeting at Great Shefford, and skipped on to her second visit to Sonia's rooms. She described the events immediately after her death, the fragments of information she had collected the following day, and her visit to Jason Kwan at the Diamond Light Source.

Blake had been listening in silence as he paced evenly along the path, but mention of the Diamond Light Source brought him abruptly to attention.

'Sonia visited the synchrotron? You're sure?'

'She's on the visitor log.'

'Do you have any idea why?'

'Curiosity, Kwan said. Though I can't put my hand on my heart and say I believe he was telling the whole truth. They've got some pretty stiff security policing that place. He didn't seem altogether at ease.'

Blake shook his head. 'I thought she'd got over all that.'

'All what?' Jenny asked.

He sighed heavily, as if a great burden had been placed on his shoulders. 'Do you know about her father?'

'I know he was a geneticist who was murdered thirty years ago. I read an article about the discovery of his remains.'

'That was about the last straw for our marriage.'

They had arrived at a second small pond surrounded by large slabs of tiered rock carpeted with alpine plants. A nearby pine tree carried the scent of mountains in summer. Blake stopped and sat on one of the granite shelves. Jenny sat near, though not close, allowing him the space to be alone with his thoughts.

'One thing you have to understand about Sonia is that she was driven, completely consumed, by the obsession to find out what happened to her father. She was seven years old when he vanished. One moment he was watching her play softball, the next he'd disappeared with some guy in a suit. That's all we ever knew for certain.' Jenny could see he was having to wring the story out of himself. 'What you won't read on the Internet is that straight after he went missing, his wife was given the third degree and ended up having a breakdown. Sonia lived most of her childhood with an alcoholic grandmother in New Jersey. I guess the memory of her dead father was all she had to cling on to.'

'Who was it harassing her mother?' Jenny asked.

'First of all it was the company he'd worked for. It was the Wild West days in the biotech industry and his outfit was in a race for patents. Millions of dollars were at stake. It was natural enough to assume he'd vanished somewhere with the company secrets. And then came the intelligence agencies. As a young guy he'd worked for a few years in the US military. Apparently there was a lot of bioweaponry stuff being explored back in the late sixties. Not the most ethical work, but for three years' service the Army would pay off your student loan. His dad worked in a steel mill, so it was a hard offer to resist. Anyway, he did his time at some facility in Georgia called Cornmill Creek – I don't believe Sonia ever found out exactly what it was he was doing there – and when he vanished fifteen years later, they thought he might have been turned by the Soviets all those years ago and finally jumped ship.'

Blake picked at a loose crumb of rock and tossed it into the pond. 'I think on some level Sonia had bought into that version. She wanted to believe he was still alive. I used to think that perhaps her studying politics had just been one huge, lifelong attempt to understand how principles could lead a man to abandon his family. When his body turned up it was more than she could handle. Turns out the most likely explanation was a rival company had simply had him killed – just business. So what do you do when the mystery you've built your life around solving is effectively solved?'

'Ditch your husband?'

'That came later.' He looked at her. 'I tried to coax her back to normality, but she still wouldn't let the Soviet thing go. I told her it was crazy, but she got it into her head that her father had some knowledge, some Cold War secret they wanted that he wouldn't give them. If he hadn't joined them, he must have been killed by them – that was how she rationalized it.'

'Hence her interest in Roman Slavsky.'

'Mmm,' Blake said with resignation.

'What's his story? I can't find much about him.'

'He was in my business – immunology. Apparently he worked until his late thirties on the Soviet biological weapons programme. Anthrax, smallpox and God knows how many hybrid viruses and bacteria. He came across to the West in eighty-nine. According to the myth, he brought the results of ten years' work with him as well as a vial of recombinant bubonic plague. He ended up at Porton Down for the next ten years – the same work, but for our side. But of course, when it's us building bioweapons it's purely for defensive purposes.'

'Do you know what happened to him?'

'Not long after the turn of the century he set up his own business. He stopped publishing when he went commercial, of course, but I gather he was working on gene-specific drugs. I heard his principal interest was in post-transcriptional gene silencing.'

'I'm afraid you'll have to explain.'

'Think of a woman carrying a breast-cancer gene. If you can isolate the sequence that codes for malignant cells, your next task is finding out how to disable it. That sequence will be repeated in every strand of DNA in the nucleus of every cell in the body. DNA is like a zip – two long strips of code that join in the centre. An enzyme travels along its length *transcribing* it, literally reading the code and translating it into a single-stranded copy – RNA – that carries the data to the parts of the cell that make proteins. RNA is also involved with gene expression – in other words, a sequence in the RNA will be responsible for turning the basic DNA code into actual cancer cells.

'Slavsky's commercial work was concerned with introducing modified RNA into human cells that would silence the undesirable bits. It was the beginnings of personalized medicine. Give it another fifty years and we'll have machines that'll decode your specific gene sequences and manufacture drugs that will operate only on your individual genetics. We're already developing a lot of the theory, the big challenge is in turning highly specialized laboratory processes into something that can be done on an industrial scale. Slavksy was trying to patent the fundamental techniques that everyone who follows in the next twenty years will have to license.'

'Did he succeed?'

'His company's still running.' Blake gave a philosophical smile. 'But from what I can gather he worked himself into an early grave. He died of a pulmonary embolism in 2008. According to Sonia, of course, he was cunningly murdered by Russian agents using his own creations against him.'

'Did she have any basis for this? Did she know him?'

'From what I could work out, he did his very best to avoid her. She finally cornered him at a conference in Munich in 2007, not long after her father's body had been found. All she got out of him was the fact that he had been aware of the work going on at Cornmill Creek back in the sixties and all the way through the seventies. Apparently someone on the US side had been leaking secrets. Slavsky maintained the Americans continued their programme long after the Biological Weapons Convention which came into effect in 1975 and that his work in the USSR was largely intended to counter that. She came home depressed and disappointed, of course, but it seemed she had managed to stir something in his conscience. About three months later he sent her a copy of an article published in the *Washington Post* in November 1981. It was a full three columns written by a staff journalist claiming to have spoken to anonymous sources who'd worked on the US Army's biological weapons programme based at Cornmill Creek. It dismissed the Army's claim that their work was purely defensive and spoke about live experiments carried out in the late 1960s. Apparently the aim had been to create a bioweapon that would only affect the Vietcong. The idea was to spray anthrax from the air and to give US troops drugs to render them immune from infection. Fortunately, it seems, the tests went badly. A lot of people died and it never made it to the battlefield.'

Blake paused, and looked up at a noisy flock of starlings that twisted in a dramatic spiral against the clear sky and swooped as one to land in the branches of a large beech tree. Jenny watched the way he observed them, as curious and analytical as he was captivated.

'What was the significance of this article?' Jenny asked.

'Sonia became convinced the unnamed source was her father, and that he was killed by his own government. That's when the paranoia took over.'

'Did she find any evidence to support her theory?'

'No – and for the obvious reason. Her father was about to make his fortune, for God's sake. Why would he have done anything as stupid as talk to a journalist?'

'A guilty conscience?'

Blake shook his head. 'Most scientists aren't big-picture people. We spend our lives looking down microscopes. Sonia never got that. She was trying to create this grand conspiracy that simply didn't exist.'

They fell into silence for a long moment as Blake seemed to draw away from the painful memories. 'Do you know much about her interest in Africa?' Jenny said.

'I'm not really the man to ask. We had only spoken a handful of times in the last two years. As far as Sonia was concerned, you were either with her or against her, and I'd been placed squarely in the latter camp.'

He gazed off along the path as if keen to move on and draw the conversation to a close.

'I think she was interested in the politics of the African aid business. Adam Jordan may have been talking to her about how drugs are used, or withheld, as a political tool.'

Blake nodded. 'That was Sonia's kind of territory. The man you should talk to is Alex Forster. I gather they'd been together off and on for a while.'

'Really?' Jenny recalled Forster's reaction to the news of her death – the way he had sat silently on the stairs, showing no outward emotion – and thought how unlike a lover he had seemed.

Blake eased himself off the shelf of rock and onto his feet. 'I should be getting back.' Mention of Forster had carried unhappy associations. He set off towards the gates, forcing Jenny to follow at his heels.

'Just a couple more things, Dr Blake. Does the name "Gina" mean anything to you? It was written on a piece of paper I found under Sonia's desk.'

'No,' he answered abruptly.

'Can you think of any reason why she might have been visiting the Diamond Light Source?'

'I don't know. But it wouldn't surprise me if she was still worrying away at the Slavsky connection. What you have to understand is that she was sane enough to hold down her job, but when it came to her father, mad enough to believe anything.' He shot her a guilty, sideways glance. 'I tried to help her out of it, I really did.'

They walked on in silence, Jenny detecting that Blake's feelings towards his wife were more ambiguous and complex than he had admitted.

She pushed on into even more uncomfortable ground. 'The manner of your wife's death – endocarditis – are you satisfied with that?'

Blake quickened his pace, the sharp gravel crunching beneath his shoes.

Jenny persisted. 'I know it can be caused by stress, but she was a very fit woman.'

They were fast approaching the locked gates and Blake seemed anxious to seek the sanctuary of the busy street beyond. Jenny stepped in front of him as he reached for the keys to the padlock. She could see it rushing to the surface now: any moment his angry eyes would be filling with tears.

'Tell me, Dr Blake?' she challenged him.

He met her gaze, his face tight with the effort of holding back feelings too painful to articulate.

'There's something more, isn't there?'

'I'm a rational man, Mrs Cooper, a scientist. I don't—' He choked on his words and looked down and away, ashamed of letting the mask slip.

'You don't *believe*—?' she prompted. 'You don't believe in what? In conspiracies? That your ex-wife died from a heart infection?'

'She did. That was the immediate cause,' he answered sharply. 'I know the pathologist. We studied together.'

'But? There is more, isn't there?'

She caught another spark from the blue eyes beneath the fringe. She read disbelief in them; amazement.

'Please tell me,' Jenny insisted. 'It's important.'

She had won. She saw Blake bending to the inevitable, ready to confess what he had been holding back their entire meeting.

'I spoke to him yesterday, off the record. He said there were indications of a more extensive infection but that the police told him to "keep his findings simple". But they asked him to provide tissue samples. They didn't say what for.' He exhaled, eyes closed. Relieved at having shared his secret.

'The police asked him for tissue samples?'

'Yes. He gave them a number – blood and tissue from the major organs.'

Jenny felt needles travel up her spine.

'This infection he suspects – does he have an idea what it is?'

'There are several possibilities.' He ran his fingers agitatedly through his hair. 'He offered me some samples. I accepted. A colleague and I are going to look at them this weekend.'

Jenny said, 'Are you telling me you suspect this was something given to her deliberately?'

'I've already told you, Mrs Cooper. I don't believe in conspiracies. I'm a scientist. I form my opinions based on evidence.'

'But you'll let me know what you find.'

He nodded, and then, with all the effort of contradicting beliefs to which he had held fast for years, said, 'Do you think I'm in any danger? I have a young child.'

'I don't know how to answer that question,' Jenny said.

He glanced towards the street, then stepped back out of sight of the passing pedestrians. 'There's another way out onto Rose Lane. It's quieter. We should take that.'

TWENTY-ONE

HENRY BLAKE HAD TURNED LEFT out of the side exit of the Botanic Garden and vanished through another set of iron gates that led onto Merton Fields, leaving Jenny to make her way back along the narrow lane towards the High Street alone. During their final minutes together, he had revealed that in her more unstable moments, Sonia had instructed him that should she die an untimely death she wanted him to make sure he was satisfied of the reason. She had suffered from an acute phobia of being murdered like her father, which at times had become so intense that Blake had forced her to see a therapist. As they parted, Jenny had felt a need to answer his honesty with a confession of her own. She told him about Adam Jordan and the African girl, and her lingering suspicion that his death was connected to those of Sophie Freeman and Elena Lujan. He had listened but voiced no opinion, wondering, perhaps, if she was every bit as unhinged as Sonia had been.

'But doesn't it sound odd to you?' Jenny had asked. 'Why would only two people fall ill from such an aggressive strain? And doesn't all that you've told me suggest that Sonia was being rather more rational than you'd thought?'

'There is nothing I can say that would be in any way helpful or constructive,' Blake had said. 'If I went down the road of wild speculation, I'd no longer be a scientist.'

Jenny brushed her fingers against the privet hedge at the side of the lane; the warm air drifting across from the Botanic Garden smelt of lavender and honeysuckle. Nowhere could have felt safer, more permanent and secure, nowhere more removed from the sinister world of biological weaponry. She stopped short of the High Street and dialled Alex Forster's number. She connected to an answer message: '*I'm unable to take your call. Please leave your details and I'll get back to you.*' She sent him a text, but received no reply. He was keeping his head down, and perhaps with good reason: it occurred to her that she may have misread his reaction to Sonia's death. His silence on the stairs might have been prompted by pure terror.

Tintern Abbey stood luminescent beneath a moon brighter than a December sun. Jenny imagined the ghosts of its long-dead monks haunting its shadows, chanting their vespers to the silent valley. She shivered, her imagination running wild, conjuring malignant spirits in the hedgerows; every silhouetted tree a stooping monster. She pressed on up the lane to Melin Bach, anxious to escape the unnatural night. She swung left and right through the tight bends, the cow parsley erupting from the verges clawing at her car like outstretched hands. A rusted iron gate tied to stone posts with bailer twine signalled the final bend. She took it fast, the headlights sweeping left, but instead of picking out her cottage, they illuminated a stationary car parked outside. She stamped on the brakes, skidding to a halt inches from impact as the driver's door flew open and an angry male figure jumped out.

'Jesus Christ, Jenny!'

She caught her breath, her heart ramming hard against her ribs. It was Michael, standing in the middle of the road, hands pressed to the side of his head. She opened the car door and climbed out, trembling.

'You could have killed me.' He was pointing to the gap, less than two feet wide, between her car and his.

'What are you doing here?'

'What am *I* doing?'

'I'm sorry. I wasn't expecting you.'

'Forget it. Can we go inside? I've been sitting here for two hours.'

'That's hardly my fault.'

'Look, I need to talk to you.'

'About what a bad mother I am?'

'No. About why I was met at work by intelligence officers.'

They stood in the kitchen drinking cheap red wine. Michael drank his first glass in two mouthfuls and poured another.

'It wasn't even home base. I'd picked up clients at Biggin Hill and delivered them to Exeter. They hadn't called the office to track me down, I checked.'

'Who?' Jenny asked, her arms folded defensively across her middle. She wasn't ready to forgive him yet.

'There were two guys. Thirties. Suits. Ex-military types.'

Jenny thought of the man who had inadvertently caught her eye at the Diamond Light Source. 'Short dark hair, square jaw. Knows he's good-looking?'

'Friend of yours?' It was an accusation, not a question.

'I might have seen him. Go on.'

'No names, just a vague flash of some ID or other and mention of the intelligence service. They offered to take me to the local police station and have the conversation on tape, but to be frank, I didn't fancy getting in their car. We spoke there, next to the Cessna.'

'About what?' Jenny snapped, impatient for answers.

'About the nature of our relationship. Had you spoken to me about any of your current cases? Had you mentioned a man called Jordan? It was a bad mistake saying yes to that.' He paused for another mouthful of Merlot, wiped his lips on the back of his hand. 'What had you said? Did you believe it was suicide? If not, why not? What had you been doing in Oxford? Something about a woman called Blake. Oh, and what were you doing visiting something called the Diamond Light Source?'

'Did they believe what you told them?'

'No. And as a gesture of their goodwill they left me with this.' He lifted his shirt to reveal a vicious, fist-shaped bruise on the left side of his ribcage. 'That was the good-looking one. I got the impression he'd done it before.'

'Oh,' was all Jenny could say.

He took another long drink. His hand had started to shake.

'Sorry if I seem a little nervy. It's not every day you get roughed up by government agents. I guess I ought to thank you for the lesson – I always vaguely thought they'd be civilized.' He reached for the bottle again. 'What the hell's going on, Jenny?'

'How long have you got?'

'Try me.'

They took the bottle through to the sitting room, and once more Jenny found herself retelling the story which seemed to become more incredible with each repetition. Michael demanded every detail, from the exact nature of Adam Jordan's last project in South Sudan to Henry Blake's fear that his ex-wife's death might not have been an accident. Throughout, he maintained the focused intensity of the fighter pilot he had once been listening to a pre-sortie briefing.

'What are you thinking?' Jenny asked when she had finished. She had been expecting a reaction, but Michael just stared into the empty grate.

'Something happened in Africa,' he said eventually. 'Maybe Jordan couldn't live with it.'

'I'd guessed that much. But Slavsky, Sonia Blake, her father, all of that . . .'

'It sounds like a small world,' Michael said, 'with everyone feeding off each other's research. Sonia Blake had got herself deeply involved. From what you've told me, commercial secrets would be as dangerous to know as government ones. But the pair who paid me a visit wouldn't have been protecting commercial secrets, would they?' He was thinking aloud. 'Unless they were Intelligence Corps. Did you say you had a witness who was a major from Bulford?'

'Fielding – yes. But his connection seemed coincidental.'

'Intelligence Corps observe. That's what they do. Your man Jordan wasn't a member of Hampton's, was he?'

'I don't know. It doesn't seem likely.'

'He lived in a smart street in Bath. Wealthy in-laws, plenty of money in his account.'

'His name wasn't on the list of visitors.'

'From what you've told me about him, it wouldn't surprise me if he had an alias.'

Jenny glanced at her watch. It was nearly 1.30, but the question felt too urgent to leave unanswered until morning. She picked up the phone and dialled Karen Jordan's number. It rang interminably before Karen answered, dragged from her sleep, no doubt bracing herself for more bad news.

Jenny apologized for getting her out of bed and got a scratchy response. 'What the hell do you want?' Karen demanded.

'Did Adam belong to Hampton's Health Club in Bristol, by any chance?'

'What?'

'Hampton's. It's in Clifton.' Now Jenny felt foolish.

'I know what it is. We both belonged to the one in Bath. What's that got to do with anything?'

'Oh.' Karen's answer had thrown her. 'I think Adam may have been followed there.'

'Followed. Who by?'

'This should wait till I know more. Sorry.'

'*Who by?*' Karen insisted, fully awake now.

Jenny glanced over at Michael. He shrugged. Her call.

'Military intelligence.'

Silence.

'Mrs Jordan, I'm sorry. Does that make any sense?'

'I don't know . . . I don't know what to think.' Her flare of anger had given way to confusion. 'Something came back to me today – my memory's been shot, but I keep getting little snatches, you know . . .'

'What is it? What do you remember?'

'Coming home the day I disturbed the burglars . . . I walked along the hall past the sitting-room door towards the kitchen. They stepped out behind me. It was an instant, a split second, two moving shadows on the wall to my right. And a man's voice saying a word – it sounded like "koos" – just as the lights went out.'

'Koos?'

Jenny saw Michael's eyebrows rise in surprise. He leaned over to the small table where she kept a message pad and pen.

'Do you remember anything else?'

'No. Just that.' She sounded tired now, as if sleep was clawing her back.

'Sorry again, Mrs Jordan. I'll call you when I've got news.' Jenny rang off and glanced down at what Michael had scribbled with a stub of pencil. *Koos – Arabic – cunt.*

'Arabic? You're sure?'

'Picked it up in Iraq. They use it like we do – it's the worst.'

'Middle Easterners? Why would they have broken into Karen Jordan's house?'

'They speak Arabic in parts of North Africa, too. Listen to me, Jenny, I don't think you should get any further involved. You're dealing with dangerous people.' He pointed to his injured ribs. 'I don't want a phone call telling me you've ended up alongside your clients.'

'You're forgetting a little thing called duty. I thought you of all people would understand that.'

'Come on, Jenny—'

'Come on, what? You think I should abandon my job?'

'Have you forgotten what I told you already?'

'Oh, no. I shan't be forgetting that in a hurry.'

'You know what I mean.' He reached for her hand. 'Jenny, please. It's late. Let's go to bed. We can talk about this in the morning. I don't have to be in Bristol until midday.'

'Michael, I'm not giving up until I've found the cause of Adam Jordan's death. Given how we met, I don't think you can claim that comes as any surprise.'

'I'm helping you out of a corner. You've told me what your psychiatrist said. Carrying on like this isn't going to make you happy—'

She wrenched her fingers out from between his.

'I was married to a man who liked to give lectures on what would make me happy.'

'For God's sake, Jenny.'

'Avoid the issue, have sex, and it'll all be all right – is that your answer?'

He moved away from her and stood up. 'You can be vicious, you know that?'

'You were honest the other night, I'm being honest now.

I'm not going to change, Michael. This is who I am.' Jenny looked at him, searching for the man she hoped was still in there, the decent, fearless, level-headed one she had fallen more than a little in love with.

'I'm not going to prop up a self-destructive personality, Jenny. What would that make me?'

'Are you asking me to choose between you and my case?'

'Think about it, Jenny. You are loved. You just don't seem to want to realize it.' He paused at the door, as if hoping she'd change her mind and beg him to stay.

Jenny woke to the sound of the outdoor brass bell clanging insistently. Not content with a noise to wake the whole valley, the caller started on the knocker. Jenny glanced bleary-eyed at the clock and saw that it was not yet 8 a.m., and it was Saturday morning. Half asleep, she swung out of bed and hauled on a robe over the top of a T-shirt that served for a nightdress. She caught her reflection in the mirror: her hair was a mess, she looked dreadful. She stumbled out onto the landing, her heart pounding.

'Who is it?'

'Only me, Mrs Cooper.'

It was Williams's voice. Thank God.

'Hold on. Coming.' She walked stiff-backed down the stairs, her spine protesting at hours spent in the car over recent days.

She slid back the iron deadbolt and opened the door to find him dressed in sky-blue slacks and a short-sleeved shirt intended to match, but failing by several shades.

'I'm not stopping. Teeing off at nine sharp. The Rolls of Monmouth, if you please.'

Jenny smiled weakly. His gaudy outfit was giving her a headache.

'Had a bit of luck with your young African lady, though.'

He dipped into his pocket and handed her a USB stick. 'One of my boys got hold of this – CCTV of your Mr Jordan with a girl who looks like she's the one. Nothing fancy, just a bit of old-fashioned detective work. The nearest watering hole to the cashpoint he'd been visiting, actually – Revolution. Know it?'

Jenny shook her head.

'Can't say it looks like my kind of place, either.'

'Any idea who she is?'

'I may well do, Mrs Cooper. There's an email on there from a colleague in the Border Agency. It was sitting in my inbox first thing this morning; thought you'd like to see it soonest. We have a twenty-one-year-old female from South Sudan granted a six-month visitor's visa on June 8th this year. A Mr Adam Jordan and a Mrs Sonia Blake are listed as her sponsors. Her registered address is in Redland, Bristol.'

'You've contacted her?'

'I thought I'd wait to be guided by you on that. Better be off – the vice-captain can't be late. Gwent Constabulary versus West Mercia. I shan't be getting up tomorrow if we don't tan their English hides.'

Jenny watched him go, and smiled at his retreating back; a boy in blue who'd just delivered her a stick of dynamite.

Zetland Road was a leafy, gently sloping street of handsome semi-detached Victorian villas. But every now and then as she drove slowly downhill, Jenny noticed a property with a disorderly array of doorbells and a mismatch of curtains at unwashed windows. These would be student houses, rented out by landlords for tax-free cash in the hand. Fifteen young people at £100 a week was more than double the rent a pristine property could attract from a single tenant. Jenny had come to know such places well for their suicides and the accidental 'party deaths' that were an unlovely and recurring feature of a coroner's caseload in a university city.

The girl who had been captured in the fifteen seconds of colour footage had been tall and slender and wearing a simple cotton dress that came below her knees. She had followed Adam through the door of the bar, waited patiently while he ordered drinks, her hands clasped demurely in front of her. Then he had steered her out of frame with no sign of intimacy between them. They definitely were not lovers, Jenny had decided. Her impression was that he had been acting more as a tutor or guide. The girl had seemed a little lost standing in the bar, unsure where she was meant to place herself, waiting for Adam's instruction.

Jenny parked and made her way on foot the last few yards to the address which the Border Agency had supplied. She arrived at a chipped and scuffed front door surrounded by chained-up bicycles. She looked for the girl's name on the ten or more bells: Ayen Deng. She found it second from the bottom. 'Deng' written in smudged ballpoint. She pressed the bell. If it had rung higher up the house, no sound reached her on the front step. She pressed again and waited. A minute passed and still no response. As she tried a final time she heard the chain slide back on the inside of the door. It was opened by a slightly built, dark-haired teenage girl with large trusting eyes. She scarcely looked old enough to be a student.

'I wonder if you can help me,' Jenny said. 'My name's Jenny Cooper. I'm the local coroner.' The girl looked startled. 'No need to worry. I'm just looking for someone who lives here – her name's Ayen. Ayen Deng.'

'Ayen's not here,' the girl said uncertainly. 'She left about three days ago.'

'Left for where?' Jenny said.

'No one knows. She just took her stuff and left. You can
see her room – it's empty.'

'Would you mind?'

The girl shook her head, too frightened of a coroner to
refuse.

They climbed eight flights of steps, arriving at a mansard
level under the roof. The girl, who said her name was Lucy,
opened the single door off the landing and let Jenny into a
room barely big enough to hold the single bed and cheap
wardrobe. The mattress was bare, no case on the pillow,
blankets neatly folded.

'Did you know her at all?' Jenny asked.

'Only a little. She spent a lot of time up here by herself.'
There was something reticent in her tone, a trace of guilt
perhaps.

Jenny waited for her to offer more.

'What do you want to know?' Lucy said, looping her hair
nervously behind her ear.

'Anything you can tell me. She was seen with a man who
died. I'm inquiring into his death.'

'Oh.'

'I'm not talking about a crime. But she might be a useful
witness. I need to find her if I can.'

Lucy started to gabble. 'I didn't really talk to her that
much. She didn't seem to want to. Some of the others tried.
I know my friend Kathy spoke to her a few times, but she's
over at her boyfriend's this weekend. She didn't know if it
was all made up or what. I mean, she wasn't even studying.
Kathy said she was probably pretending to be an asylum
seeker.'

'Slow down,' Jenny said calmly. 'There's no problem, I
just need to know what she said.'

Lucy took a breath. 'She told Kathy she came from this
village in Sudan where everyone died. She said she was the

only person left alive. All her family had died, all her friends. Everyone.'

'Did she say when this happened?'

'I don't know.'

Jenny tried to appear to take the information in her stride, eager to keep the girl's confidence. 'Was there anything else? How did everyone die? Did she say the name of the place?'

'Some sort of disease, I think. You can ask Kathy, I'll give you her number. That's all I know. Honestly.'

Jenny brought out her phone. 'Why don't we give Kathy a ring?'

Jenny's call, made on speakerphone, was answered by a teenage girl who sounded as if she must still be in bed, fending off a playful boyfriend.

'Sorry. Sorry about that,' Kathy said, stifling giggles. 'Who is this again?'

'Jenny Cooper.'

'Do I know you?'

'She's the coroner,' Lucy butted in. 'It's serious, Kathy. It's about Ayen. Someone's died.'

'Died? Who?'

'A friend of Ayen's,' Jenny said. She finally had Kathy's attention. 'I need you to tell me everything you know about her.'

Kathy repeated what Lucy had told her, adding little to the narrative.

Jenny pressed for details of the deaths in the village. What had they died of? How many? But Kathy insisted that Ayen had said nothing more than she had already told her. It had been as much as she could do to get her to talk at all.

'Can I ask what prompted you to do that?' Jenny said.

'I felt sorry for her. She was always hiding away in her room. I thought she must be lonely.'

Jenny urged her to think hard and recall whether she had said anything else, however slight or irrelevant.

'Something about a man who had helped her – Alan? Adam?'

'Adam. Adam Jordan. What did she say about him?

'That he helped her get out of Sudan.' She paused. 'Yeah, that's it. I remember now – the place she came from was called Ginya.' She pronounced it with a hard 'g', the 'y' almost silent.

There it was, another missing piece. *Ginya*: the word Sonia Blake had doodled on the scrap of paper Jenny had picked up in her room.

Jenny said, 'Did she seem healthy?'

'Very. She was beautiful.'

'Frightened?'

'A little, perhaps. I thought she was just nervous of speaking to me. Is she all right?'

'I'm not sure.'

As Jenny spoke, she saw Lucy stoop down and pick something up that she had spotted jutting out from under the end of the bed. It was a small wooden figure attached to a leather thong.

'Can I see that?' Jenny said, cupping her hand over the receiver.

'Hello?' Kathy said. 'Are you still there?'

Jenny was turning the doll over in her fingers. She was in no doubt: it was identical to the one that had gone missing from Adam Jordan's car the morning after his death.

TWENTY-TWO

JENNY WAS SITTING WITH KAREN JORDAN in her garden, surrounded by the gentle, familiar sounds of a suburban weekend: cricket commentary on next door's radio, a barking terrier, children squealing and splashing in a paddling pool. Normality a universe away from where Karen found herself adrift. Sam was emptying a big red crate of assorted toys onto the grass, examining each in turn with a calm, determined seriousness. He wasn't a child who would grow up to take life lightly, Jenny thought, especially if he were forced to carry a burden like Sonia Blake's, never knowing how his father had come to leave his life so violently. Karen didn't seem to notice how intelligently her son was playing – if play was an appropriate description for such detailed observation – she seemed lost in a fog. The doctor had told her it was post-traumatic stress, she said, but the drugs he had given her were as bad as the symptoms. She felt absent. Numb. She was looking down on the world, unable to plant her feet on the ground.

Jenny asked if she felt strong enough to talk.

'You can't upset me,' Karen said. 'I'm not feeling anything.'

'Sam seems very sharp. I'm guessing there's a lot of his father in him.'

'He got my nose and mouth, that's all. Poor him. The rest is pure Adam.'

Jenny told her story gently. She began with the girl, Ayen. Karen stared at her blankly. She had never heard of her, had no idea that her husband had sponsored a young woman to come from Sudan, let alone that he'd been giving her money, *their* money, to feed and house her.

'What about the village – Ginya? Does the name mean anything to you?'

Another blank. Immediately before his return, Adam had been working at a settlement called Katum, though she understood there were many by that name scattered about the bush. And the fact that a girl called her home Ginya didn't mean that it would carry the same name on a map or in official documents. There were tribal names and official names, all of which carried a load and significance that were impossible for an outsider to appreciate, even understand.

Jenny broached the subject of Ruth Webley and the photographs of Adam next to the marijuana plantation. Karen gave an indifferent shrug.

'So what? If you don't make money you can only subsist, and not even the South Sudanese are content with that any more. If you know money can get you vehicles and clean water and drugs for your children, that's what you'll want.'

'He didn't object to that?'

'Of course he did, but we're not starving, are we? Our child doesn't have a one in four chance of not surviving to adulthood.'

'What I'm skirting around is whether he might have got involved in the business end of it. I've seen his bank records,' Jenny confessed. 'There seems to have been quite a lot of money—'

'How do you think we live like this?' Karen interrupted. 'Adam inherited money. Most people would be glad. He was eaten up with guilt. At least he acted on his conscience.' She glanced over at the row of expensive houses opposite. 'Not many do.'

'No.' Jenny felt a surge of relief. Adam as drug dealer was a disturbing and contradictory figure she had found neither likely nor convincing.

'What about Harry Thorn? Does his interest go beyond the pragmatic?'

'Adam hinted that he thought it might, but he didn't want to know about Harry's deals on the side. It would have made things too complicated.'

'I can see that,' Jenny said. 'Quite a minefield he was operating in.'

'Tell me about it.' Karen's cup slipped, spilling tea down her blouse.

'Here.' Jenny handed her a paper tissue. 'Was it the mention of Harry?'

'Probably,' Karen said, dabbing ineffectually at the stain. She made a show of pretending she cared, then let the damp tissue fall from her fingers onto the grass.

Jenny stooped to pick it up. She was losing her, pushing her too far, but she needed a little more. She waited a moment, making small talk about the exotic grasses that seemed to have grown even taller since her last visit – Adam's little piece of Africa. He would have to sleep with the window wide open so he could hear it sway in the wind, Karen said. He would have slept outside if she had let him.

'The village,' Jenny said. 'Ginya. Are you sure Adam never said anything about what happened there?'

Karen didn't answer.

'Mrs Jordan—?'

'No! He didn't tell me, all right?'

'He might have been trying to protect you,' Jenny said gently, 'and Sam, of course.'

'He was restless,' Karen said. 'Troubled. Even when he assured me he was fine I could feel it.' The truth was finally coming to the surface. 'He couldn't smile, not with his eyes; it was if he'd put on a mask.' She turned sharply to look at Jenny directly. 'Was it our people who killed him?'

'We don't know he was killed.'

Karen screwed up her eyes and tears spilled out over her cheeks. 'I can't talk any more. Please don't make me.'

Jenny glanced down at Sam. He wore a frown of deep concentration as he turned the wheels of an upturned toy car with delicate, probing fingers.

'Are you sure you'll be all right – with Sam I mean?'

'Don't worry. I shan't jump off a bridge. Even I wanted to, I can't, can I?' She flicked out a hand and gripped Jenny's wrist, her fingers clutching her tightly. 'I just need to know. I need to know who took him from me.'

'You will,' Jenny said, 'I promise – I almost forgot, I've something for you.' She dipped into her handbag and pulled out the wooden figurine. 'Ayen had left it behind in her room. If it was the same one that was in your husband's car, it might mean she was with him the night he died. And with Sam, of course.'

Karen turned her gaze to her son, but he had already spotted the doll in her hand. For a moment he was quite still, and then he got to his feet and walked very determinedly towards the open back door of the house without looking back.

'Sam, come back,' Karen called after him.' She passed the doll back to Jenny. 'Sam!'

He ignored her, and climbed the step and went inside. Jenny wished for his sake that he'd been able to cry.

Jenny drove across country on autopilot, every bend in the road between the motorway and Oxford imprinted on her subconscious. It was to be her fifth visit in a little over a week. She had taken a pill the moment she stepped out of Karen Jordan's front door, doubting she'd have the courage to confront Forster without chemical assistance. She was cross with herself for weakening, but she was tired – more than tired, *emotionally drained*. First it had been one death, then two, then three, now God knows how many. Fragments of all their stories jostled in her mind. There was no sense to it, no pattern, just a series of images that assailed her from all corners. Adam's smashed body, Sophie's bloated, swollen face, Sonia Blake stumbling and falling, clawing at the grass, and stick-thin bodies with rigor-mortis grins scattered in the dust. And a single young woman huddled in the shade of a solitary tree, wide terrified eyes staring out above hands covering her nose and mouth. Jenny could smell the corpses, the stench rising in the scalding heat of the African sun. Christ, she was dealing with butchers. Pure evil. She felt her stomach lurch, the bile rise in her throat. She jabbed a finger at the window control, desperate for air. *Deep breaths, Jenny, deep breaths.*

She started violently at the sound of the phone blasting out through all the car's speakers. She would have to learn how to operate the damn thing.

'Hello?'

'Ah, Mrs Cooper. Thought you'd be glad to know we won. Humiliated the buggers.'

'Oh, good.' Surely he hadn't called to tell her the result of his golf match.

'Find the girl, did you?'

'No. She'd gone. About three days ago. The housemates don't know where. I don't suppose you could help.'

'Where do you want me to start – Africa?'

It was meant as a joke, but Jenny wasn't in the mood.

'How about Harry Thorn?'

'Not another trip to bloody London.'

'The Portobello Road – you'd like it. He's got a girlfriend who cooks breakfast naked.'

'Now you're going to tell me it can't wait till Monday.'

'I'd like to say it could, but I'm getting a little anxious about the body count. It seems Miss Deng was the sole survivor of a village wiped out by some sort of disease – that's the story she told, anyway.'

'Couldn't you stay at home for a while, Mrs Cooper? It'd make me sleep easier.'

'I don't want you to sleep, Detective Superintendent, I want you to find Ayen.'

'Where are you now?'

'On my way to Oxford – does that meet with your approval?'

Williams sighed. 'I'm not normally a superstitious man, Mrs Cooper, but I've got a bad feeling.'

A large and excited party of summer-school students had gathered outside the porter's lodge. Taking advantage of the confusion, Jenny weaved through their midst, managed to avoid the gaze of Davies, the porter, and hurried through to the cloister and into the quad beyond. She searched for Forster's name on the hand-painted boards at the foot of each staircase. His accommodation was also on the second floor. The stairs were similarly well trodden, the paintwork similarly scuffed by a thousand student trunks. Forster's outer door, his 'oak', was ajar. Jenny pulled it open and knocked.

'Who is it?' he answered in his curt tutor's voice.

'Jenny Cooper.'

She could sense his alarm. There was a brief silence from his side, then slow, resigned footsteps. The figure who greeted her was pale and unshaven. He wore reading glasses that aged him ten years. Jenny glanced past him and saw that he'd been working at his desk, but had pulled the lid of his laptop closed shut.

'What do you want?' He made no attempt at politeness.

'I think you might prefer not to have this conversation on the stairs.'

Reluctantly, he stood aside and let her in to his conspicuously orderly room. The furniture was modern: an angular leather sofa with matching armchairs; books meticulously arranged in height order on glass shelves; no stray paper in sight. A man adept at wiping his tracks, Jenny thought.

'Well?' Forster challenged.

'I understand that you and Mrs Blake were closer than I had appreciated. You must have been aware of her complicated family history.'

'You've been talking to her ex-husband.' He grunted. 'What of it?'

'Given her interests, and her recent involvement with a man who died falling from a motorway bridge, I thought you might be wondering about the circumstances of her death.'

'We know how she died. It's a serious condition that can go undetected. Sonia was hardly one to run to a doctor over trivial symptoms, so she probably won't have had a diagnosis.'

'Were you still lovers – recently, I mean?'

'Not for months. Though what concern it is of yours, I've no idea.'

'It's a long and involved story, Mr Forster, but I'll give you the most recent instalment. The dead man was called Adam Jordan. He was a thirty-two-year-old aid worker recently returned from South Sudan. He met with Sonia and I believe they communicated online. At the beginning of June this year, they sponsored a young woman from Sudan to come to the UK on a six-month visa. It turns out she was the only survivor from a village that had been wiped out by some sort of disease.'

She studied his features for a reaction, but spotted it instead in a nervous scratching of his fingers on the lip of the desk.

'Did she tell you about the girl?'

'No,' he said dismissively.

'Jordan? Did she mention his name, tell you his story?'

'Only the vaguest details after you came here first. Look, this really isn't my territory. Sonia was Politics, I'm Economics – and not African economics, I might add. Strictly First World only. Our relationship, such as it was, was purely personal.' He pulled off the reading glasses and rubbed his eyes. 'I really have nothing to say to you. I don't know this man, Jordan. Sonia didn't trouble me with all the details of her work, any more than I did her with mine.' A sideways tic of the head. He was angry and straining to contain himself.

Jenny tried to isolate what it was that was making him so defensive. He'd shared a bed with Sonia, he would have known her intimately, heard stories of her father repeated night after night. Why the attempt to shut the conversation down?

What was so threatening? She ran her eyes along the unnaturally neat shelves designed to reveal nothing, yet saying much about their owner. *First World only.* His was a serious and applied mind, not that of some muddle-headed idealist; an outsider from the former colonies determined to stake his place at the heart of his profession. Sonia had come to him as she had to her ex-husband, looking for a man who would bring order to her chaos; a lover and a father. He must have felt worshipped for a while, at least until he realized the full depth of her obsessions, what he had got himself into: a relationship with potential to threaten his untarnished career; and a source of gossip amongst waspish colleagues searching for his Achilles heel.

Jenny chanced her arm with the theory. 'I've no wish to draw you into anything that might damage your reputation, Mr Forster. I didn't have to talk to you in person; I could merely have summoned you to my inquest to give evidence in public.'

'I've told you, Mrs Cooper, I've nothing more to say.'

In anger, his accent grew stronger, back to its New Zealand roots. She pictured a small town as neat as his room, his every achievement faithfully reported in the local paper; proud parents making a scrapbook of the clippings. No, there would have been no natural place in that narrative for a girlfriend or wife like Sonia Blake.

'Let me tell you a little of what I know and see if you still feel the same, Mr Forster.' She gave him no chance to object. 'In the late 1960s Sonia's father worked on a biological weapons programme for the US Army. In late 1981 an article in the *Washington Post* exposed the programme's work, citing anonymous sources. A few months after it was published he was murdered in Arizona. Sonia persisted in believing he was killed by Russians. She tracked down a defector, also a military biologist, named Roman Slavsky. She kept a file on him. Immediately before he came to meet her here in Oxford, Adam Jordan bought a book Slavsky had written. Straight after her death, or perhaps even before, the contents of Sonia's file on Slavksy went missing from her room.'

'How do you know that?' Forster said.

'I came here the day after she died – you saw me. I went to her room and saw an empty file with Slavsky's name on it.'

'What were you doing in her room?'

'My job. Looking for evidence.'

He shrugged. 'I tried not to involve myself with that side of her . . .' he hesitated, 'with her more unconventional activities.'

It was odd, his detachment. He had been affected by Sonia's death, Jenny could see it in the greyness of his face, the heavy shadows under his eyes, but from his words alone she wouldn't have guessed it. He seemed frightened, or *unable* to grieve.

'What exactly was the nature of your relationship, if you don't mind my asking?' Jenny said.

'I do mind,' Forster said.

There. He averted his face: the first sign of emotion.

'Her ex-husband said you were lovers. If you'll pardon me, you don't appear to be reacting as a lover might.'

Forster stepped away from the desk. 'My feelings are a private matter. Unless you've anything useful to say, I would kindly ask you to leave. I have a lot of work to do.'

'Are you angry with her? Is that it? Was her death a culmination of events? Help me, Mr Forster – I'm in the dark here, people have died.'

For a passing moment her plea seemed to have breached his defences. He seemed about to speak, when they were interrupted by the sound of Jenny's phone. She glanced at the screen and saw that it was Simon Moreton calling.

'Excuse me a moment.' She took the call. 'Simon?'

'Jenny,' he said briskly. 'Yet again, you seem to have caused something of an inter-departmental crisis. Welsh detectives charging around Bristol at your behest, I hear?'

'I'm hearing the Jordan inquest in Chepstow. There are no suitable venues on the English side of the border.'

'I see. Look, I'm afraid I don't know exactly what's going on.' A note of urgency entered his voice. 'This is just scraps of gossip from mates over in Vauxhall – but I get the impression you've strayed into some extremely sensitive territory.'

'I've not *strayed* anywhere. I'm simply doing what the law requires.'

'Don't get pompous on me, Jenny, I'm trying to help. I just had a call saying our friends from south London are going to bring you in for questioning.'

'They've no authority.'

'Moot point.'

'Simon, I'm doing nothing improper. Phone them. Tell them I'm not to be interfered with.'

'Good in theory, not in practice,' came Moreton's weasel reply. 'There are occasions when protocol is bypassed and everyone looks the other way. I sense this might be one of them. It's up to you, but I think perhaps you ought to cooperate.'

'And my inquest?'

'Jenny, I'll only say it once.' He lowered his voice, as if that simple safeguard might allow him to avoid detection by imagined listeners. 'Nothing I can do will help you on this one. Believe me. I am truly sorry.'

He ended the call.

Jenny turned to Forster. Before she could speak, he said, 'I don't know what she was involved with. I didn't want to know, and she respected that.'

'But you knew it was significant?'

He drew in a breath and exhaled, exasperated. Jenny could imagine the conversations that must have taken place in this room: Sonia excitedly wanting to share the latest link in one of her convoluted conspiracies and Forster insisting he must know nothing that might damage his precious career.

'If you tell me, I may not need to call you, Mr Forster. I have no wish to compromise you.'

He gave her a calculating look, weighing the odds of

getting her off his back if he gave her what she wanted. Or perhaps she was being too harsh? Perhaps there was an honest though conflicted man beneath the hard exterior. Sonia must have seen something endearing in him, after all.

'This is the truth, Mrs Cooper – I know nothing about your African girl, and I only heard Sonia mention Adam Jordan after his death. She was clearly being very secretive, which frankly was quite unlike her. I know about her interest in Roman Slavsky, but I never looked at the file myself. The day after you first came here, I think she may have moved some papers from her rooms. I went in there briefly and saw boxes on the floor.'

'Did she say where she took them?'

'We didn't discuss it. I can't even tell you for certain that's what she did.'

'Where might she have taken them?'

'I don't know. She has no office as such at the faculty. Her room was always such a mess. For all I know she might just have been getting rid of stuff.'

'Did she ever mention the word *Ginya*?'

Forster shook his head. Jenny judged his denial genuine.

'Who do I ask about these papers? Are there friends, colleagues?'

They were interrupted a second time, on this occasion by four loud knocks on the door. Jenny and Forster traded a glance, both reacting with alarm to the knocks' abruptness.

'Mr Forster?' It was a man's voice, impatient and businesslike. A detective, perhaps.

Then a second voice: 'Are you in, sir?'

'Coming.' He hesitated, then nodded towards the bedroom.

Jenny moved silently across the room and slipped through the internal door. She fastened the bolt securely from the inside as Forster went to admit his visitors.

'Good afternoon. How may I help you?'

She didn't linger to listen in on their conversation. She knew who they would be. She quietly opened the connecting door and found herself in the small passageway that linked Forster's rooms to Sonia's. The door to Sonia's bedroom was open. Jenny went through, locked it after her, and made her way through to the sitting room that looked to have been disturbed yet again since she had last seen it. She let herself out onto the next-door staircase.

She had started down the stairs when an instinct told her she had taken a wrong turn. She slipped off her shoes and ran noiselessly up the two flights to the landing above. Moments later she heard the sound of a door being staved in from inside Sonia Blake's rooms. Jenny pressed herself hard against the wall, managing to stay almost, but not quite, out of sight from the landing below. Her two pursuers emerged from the open door and clattered down the stairs without an upwards glance. As their footsteps faded, she glanced over the banister and caught a fleeting glimpse of the square-jawed man she had seen at the Diamond Light Source, the one who had tried to break Michael's ribs.

TWENTY-THREE

JENNY HID AT THE TOP OF THE STAIRS for a full twenty minutes before making her way cautiously down to the bottom. From here she continued down to the sub-level that she remembered led to a small courtyard and the extensive grounds beyond. It wasn't safe to return to her car, nor did she want to risk exiting onto the street at the front of the college, so she turned left towards the modern accommodation blocks and set about finding another way out. After a prolonged search, she chanced on a gate at the side of the playing fields that opened onto a Jericho side street. Without a clear map of the city in her mind, she was as good as lost. Her only thought was to move away from the centre and in so doing shave the odds of being seen. Keeping the college at her back, she started walking. Canal Street, Mount Street, then a dogleg into Juxon Street, she tried to lose herself in their ordinariness.

Emerging onto Walton Street, she turned left, and found herself approaching the Victoria pub. Drinkers sat at outside tables soaking up the milky afternoon sun. She made her way inside and ordered a glass of Chardonnay and some mineral water. Finding a seat in an unoccupied corner facing the door, she sipped her wine and tried to decide what to do next. It wouldn't be safe to return to her car, nor could she switch on her phone without the risk of it being tracked. She had turned it off after escaping through Sonia Blake's rooms and felt strangely helpless without it, as if she had suddenly lost a limb.

Carless, phoneless and with only the flimsiest of leads, she was nearly out of options. Alison was in no state to help, Moreton had abandoned her and Michael had made his feelings more than plain. The only two allies she had left were Detective Superintendent Williams and Andy Kerr. She had already pushed Williams beyond reasonable limits, which left her the pathologist. Andy was bending under pressure from his bosses, but four years of working with him told her she could trust him, at least just for a little while longer.

There was no payphone that she could see, but with a well-aimed smile Jenny persuaded the young Greek working behind the bar to lend her his phone.

Andy answered her from inside the autopsy room – she could tell from the high-pitched whine of a rotary saw carving through bone.

He sounded relieved to hear her voice. 'Hold on, I'm going to take this in my office.'

She waited while he hurried the length of the mortuary to resume their conversation in private.

'Hi.' He was short of breath when he came on the line again. 'What happened? I was told I wasn't required to give evidence.'

'Who told you?'

'Some guy called Moreton. He said he was your *superior*. I didn't know you had one.'

'Arguably I don't. Look, I have to be quick. There's more to tell than I can manage now. I just need you to think about this: Adam Jordan brought a girl back from South Sudan. I'm trying to trace her, but if what she told her housemates is right, she was the only survivor in a village that was wiped out by disease. The place was called Ginya.' She spelled it out: 'G-I-N-Y-A.'

She heard him tap the letters into his computer.

'Can't see anything,' he said.

'But it's the meningitis belt, right? That could wipe a village out.'

'Mmm.' He was unconvinced. 'You'd expect more than one to survive. But listen, I've found something. I took some more samples from Jordan's body – the full range – and had them analysed. I was looking for any sign that he'd been the vector for the meningitis bacteria. We found some—'

'Found what?'

'I got the results this morning. The lab cultured bacteria – the identical strain to the one that killed Sophie Freeman and Elena Lujan – from his *stomach contents*.'

Jenny floated the barman an even sweeter smile, indicating that she wouldn't be long now. 'That's not where you'd expect to find it, I presume?'

'It's about the last place. Bacteria wouldn't arrive in the gut until the final stages of infection. And it wasn't in the culture taken from his bowel, just the one from his stomach.'

'Is that significant?'

'He must have swallowed something. My guess is that it was shortly before he died. There was very little in his stomach – perhaps a light meal a couple of hours before-hand.'

'He bought sandwiches earlier in the evening.'

'That makes sense. But unless they happened to be laced with hybrid bacteria, my guess is he swallowed the bacteria in liquid suspension.'

Jenny thought back to the events of Jordan's last day: the trip to Great Shefford with Ayen Deng, a meeting with a man at the back of the petrol station, and then the detour to visit his father's grave.

'You know, I've been thinking he might have been some sort of courier, after all. He must have had this stuff with him.'

'Unless he didn't drink it voluntarily.'

'We can't judge that. His body was too badly damaged.'

'I have to go now,' Jenny said. 'I'm on someone else's phone. Keep this to yourself – we're on to something.'

'Sure—'

He wanted more, but Jenny couldn't give it to him. It was better that he didn't know. Just in case.

Shortly before his death, Adam Jordan had swallowed liquid containing meningitis bacteria of the kind which days later had killed a schoolgirl and a young woman, neither of whom, to Jenny's knowledge, he had ever met. Making her way through more unfamiliar streets, Jenny tried to fit Andy's bombshell into the constantly distorting picture of Adam Jordan's final hours. The single fact that leaped out at her was that the specialist team from Porton Down who had helped themselves to body parts and tissue had more than an inkling of what they might find. They had linked Jordan's death to those of Sophie and Elena, but how? The answer, she felt sure, would one way or another have to involve Sonia Blake. Webley had said Sonia Blake was on a 'watch list', which had to mean that at least some of her communications were being intercepted. Something of what she had shared with Jordan must have found its way into official hands. Sonia may well have become aware of the fact; Jordan's death may have proved it to her beyond doubt. If that had prompted her to hide her papers, they must have held something of deep significance. Jenny considered contacting Forster again, but discounted it as too risky. It left her with one last port of call: Henry Blake.

Unusually for a small British city, Jenny noticed, Oxford

had black cabs of the kind you could hail in the street. But on a sunny afternoon in mid-tourist season they were a rare commodity. She had walked another mile and arrived on the main thoroughfare of Woodstock Road before she spotted an orange light. She tumbled into the back seat, grateful for the cool of the air conditioning and asked the driver to take her to the John Radcliffe Hospital. The backs of her heels had been rubbed to blisters by her shoes, and her shirt clung uncomfortably to her body with perspiration.

'Doctor?' The cab driver made a stab at being friendly.

'No. Coroner.'

'Oh. Dead people.' He glanced at her in the mirror. 'There can't be many laughs in that.'

'One or two.'

'Still, I bet it makes you glad to be alive.'

Jenny smiled, and for a few moments the simple observation made her feel stupidly happy. 'Yes. It does.'

The massive grey six-storey building on the southern fringes of Oxford had all the outward charm of a Soviet ministry, but was one of the UK's handful of world-class hospitals. Even after nearly five years of weekly visits to the Vale, Jenny still felt an anxious tightening in her chest as she stepped through the sliding doors and took her first breath of antiseptic air. Along with the ill and the anxious, she joined the long queue at reception, all the while keeping a wary eye on the shifting sea of visitors and patients passing up and down the concourse. She scanned their faces in dread of seeing the square-jawed man, until she was finally granted her turn at the desk. The receptionist was a harried West Indian woman whose good nature had been stretched to breaking by a drunk in search of a casualty – his brother, he insisted – whose name he couldn't recall.

'Can you tell him it's urgent,' Jenny said, as the reception-ist dialled Blake's extension.

'When isn't it? Dr Blake, there's a Mrs Cooper to see you.' She glanced up. 'Yes, she's standing right in front of me. I've got a line a mile long here – what's it to be? Thank you.' She rang off with a sigh. 'Fifth floor. He'll be there to meet you.'

Jenny melted into the crowd, keeping her eyes on the floor as she made her way swiftly to the elevators.

Blake was waiting for her as the lift doors opened, dressed in a lab coat. He waited for the two other disembarking passengers to disperse before speaking in an agitated whisper.

'Did you have to come here now? I've got colleagues—' He glanced over his shoulder as if they might suddenly have materialized. 'It's not a good time, or place.'

'Ten minutes.'

'Five.' He led her along the corridor to a recessed rest area: several high tables and stools and a couple of vending machines.

'Coffee?'

'No thanks.'

He punched some buttons on the machine and collected an espresso for himself. He looked as if he had already consumed far too many. His tension was palpable.

'Are you all right?' Jenny said.

He brought his coffee to the table and pushed his long fringe back over his forehead. 'It's Q fever,' he said quietly. 'Sonia had Q fever.'

'I've never heard of it.'

'*Coxiella burnetii*. It's an acute infection that can feel like mild flu. It can cause pneumonia and endocarditis. It comes from animals – most human cases are people who work with livestock.' His eyes flicked left and right. 'The thing is, it's highly infectious. A single bacterium can be all it takes.' He gulped his espresso. 'Makes it a favourite for biological weapons. And guess what? This strain has immunity to tetracycline, doxycycline and erythromycin, and as far as I can see from the literature, that makes it pretty much a one-off outside the sort of labs our friend Professor Slavsky cut his teeth in.'

Jenny could see that he scarcely believed it himself. He was still processing the information: his pupils were dilated like those of a patient in shock.

'Do you think she was given this deliberately?'

'It's notifiable. I checked with the HPA – but there haven't been any reported cases recently. It's easily done – a few drops of infected liquid in a drink. That's how I'd do it.'

Jenny thought of Sonia's regular trips to the cafe in Oxford Castle. How easy it would have been for her killer to slip a fatal dose when she was distracted at her laptop, as simple as leaning over for the sugar bowl.

'I wish I was surprised,' Jenny said, 'but who would have done that?'

The question hung unanswered in the air between them.

'I spoke to Forster,' Jenny said. 'That's why I came here. He told me Sonia had moved several boxes of papers from her rooms in college after Jordan died, including, I suspect, her material on Slavsky. Forster doesn't know where she would have taken them. I couldn't really get a handle on their relationship. He seemed at one remove somehow.'

'No, that was Sonia. She was an expert at that. If she wanted you to know something, you wouldn't hear the end of it. But if she wanted to keep a secret, she could do that, too, and be devious with it.'

'How do you mean, devious?'

'Her research – the off-piste stuff. It's not easy to win

people's trust in that field. I overheard her on the phone many times, weaving stories, inventing personalities for herself. I used to think that if she hadn't been so paranoid, she would have made a good spy.'

'I'd seen her as emotional, not calculating.'

'She was both, but a real operator.'

'Was it just the need to find out who killed her father that was driving her, or was there something else?'

'That's how it began, but I think she picked things up along the way that reinforced it all. She would tell me bits and pieces: African governments rumoured to be developing biological and chemical weapons – you can imagine the sort of thing – but since she met Slavsky . . .' He shook his head. 'I got the feeling there was something else, too.' He tailed off, lapsing into edgy silence.

Jenny watched Blake picking distractedly at the cuff of his lab coat. Since early in their first meeting she had felt inclined to trust him – he had a sort of innocence – but yet she felt she wasn't hearing the whole story. He remained too nervy for a man who had revealed everything.

'All right, I'll tell you something,' Jenny said. 'Shortly before he died, Adam Jordan had swallowed what the pathologist thinks was a liquid containing the hybrid meningitis strain that killed the two young women in Bristol. It's shown up in cultures from his stomach contents. He had no other signs of infection.'

'Hybrid?'

'That's the word he used. Like your Q fever, it's antibiotic-resistant. I understand that's not hard to achieve in a lab.'

'It's easy.' He spoke as if from a long way off, swept away on the wave of thoughts her revelation had prompted. 'Any first-year postgrad could do it these days. You could buy the kit and do it in your kitchen.'

'I've no idea how it got there, only that your ex-wife has

to be part of the story. If I knew where she'd put the papers . . .'

'They won't be anywhere you'll ever find them. I know that much. I can't be part of this, Mrs Cooper. I've got a family, a career. This isn't my fight.'

Jenny seized her chance on his moment of weakness. 'If you give me what I need, you'll never have to hear from me again.' She touched his arm. 'I mean it. I have no interest in involving you further.'

He wanted to escape Sonia's madness once and for all. She could sense his desperation for normality to reassert itself.

Blake spoke in a rush, as if lingering on the words would give them power to do him harm. 'She called me a few months ago. She sounded wired. She said she wanted to tell me something in confidence. I didn't want to know, but she didn't give me a lot of choice. She said she'd been contacted by someone in the biotech business wanting her help in exposing something. I've no idea what this "thing" was – I didn't ask – but Sonia seemed overwhelmed by it, as if it was all too much responsibility.'

'What did she want from you?'

'God knows. I fobbed her off, to be honest. I told her she couldn't trust me now I had a daughter – my child would always come first.'

'Did she give you any clue as to who this person might have been?'

'I told you, I cut her off before she got me involved.'

Suddenly and without warning, Blake got down from his stool. 'That's all I've got. Time's up.' He tapped his wristwatch and headed off back along the corridor.

The elevator seemed forever stuck on the lower floors, so Jenny took the stairs down to the ground. As she stepped

·out into the main concourse, her mind churning with questions, she spotted a man standing with his back to her at the
reception desk. He turned his head a fraction, and a glimpse
of the side of his face was enough: it was *him*, and right
behind him a second man with the same close-cropped hair.
Jenny ducked back around the corner and caught her breath
at the foot of the stairs. She felt her legs wanting to give way
beneath her.

You're OK. He didn't see you.

A sign to her left pointed towards Accident and Emergency. She moved off, eyes fixed on the corridor ahead. Ten,
fifteen paces and still no hand on her shoulder. She glanced
back and saw the second man jogging up the stairs to the
first floor, a phone pressed to his ear, eyes registering the
faces of those coming down. She hurried on, moving as fast
as she could without drawing attention to herself. What
would happen to Blake? Would he tell them everything? Or
was it he who had alerted them to her presence?

She arrived in the hectic waiting area of Accident and
Emergency, headed for the exit and ran for the first taxi in
the rank. She didn't know who or what to trust any more.

TWENTY-FOUR

THE CAR-HIRE CONCESSION was in a quiet street behind Oxford station, but it took Jenny a tortuous half-hour to complete the rigmarole of form-filling before she finally got her hands on the keys.

It wasn't much of a plan, but having failed to secure a lead on Sonia Blake's missing papers, it was the only option she had left: she was going to track down Jason Kwan, the beamline scientist, and force him to cough up whatever he had failed to tell her in his office at the Diamond Light Source. Denied the use of her phone, she would have to use the Internet to locate his home address and number. But where to get online at 6 p.m. on a Saturday evening?

She arrived at the junction at the end of Abbey Road. It was left to the city, or right to head out of town on the Botley Road. Even in a hire car, driving back into town felt like too big a risk, but she was certain she wouldn't find an Internet cafe between Oxford and Bristol. She felt the tempting pull of the dormant phone in her pocket – surely a few seconds online wouldn't betray her? Her fingers dipped into her jacket pocket and closed around it, ready to take a chance, when it occurred to her that if she took out the SIM card and managed to hook up to a Wi-Fi signal, she could use the Internet without being traced. It was a criminal's trick she'd heard Alison talk about: clever paedophiles never used their own Wi-Fi to get online if they could help it, but hijacked someone else's. It was a ploy that had led to a number of false arrests.

She turned right, and then right again into the next residential street, pulled over to take out the SIM, then crept along at kerb-crawler's speed, waiting for an unsecured wireless signal to appear on her screen. She picked one up within two hundred yards. Pulling over, she searched Kwan's name in an online phone directory and came up with his home number in Reading within seconds. It was too easy. She flicked by reflex to her emails, cringing as they flooded into her inbox: endless reminders of cases she had neglected, pleas from relatives of the dead she had kept waiting for weeks, and in amongst them a message from Ross.

'*Mum, where are you? I thought we were coming over today. Michael's been calling asking if you've been in touch. Should we be worried??? Ross.*'

She started to type in a reply, but dried up after '*I'm fine*'. She wasn't fine, and he was right to be worried. She pressed delete and wrote simply: '*Back later. Sorry. I'll call. Mum x.*' She switched off and fought against a sensation of panic. She could have been with him, she could be at home being a proper mother, but instead she was chasing around the country being pursued like a criminal. It was time to move on.

Three miles out of the city she turned off the main road in search of a phone box and found herself in the village of Cumnor. Driving along its narrow lanes past ancient thatched cottages, it would have been easy to believe that the outside world was as peaceful and benign as this tranquil backwater. She passed the post office and found an open-sided phone kiosk next to a bus stop. There were ponies grazing in the field behind, children on a trampoline in a neighbouring garden. She dialled Kwan's number.

Any more than seven rings and you were certain to get a machine. She counted three, four, five . . . He picked up on six, wary of an unexpected caller.

'Dr Kwan, it's Jenny Cooper. We met at the Diamond Light Source.'

He didn't answer her.

'Please don't hang up. I need to talk to you.'

Still no response.

'Dr Kwan, this is very urgent. I can come to your home.'

'No, no. I'll call you back.'

The line went dead. Seconds passed and the payphone remained silent. She glanced up and down the lane, expecting to see the thugs she had escaped twice appear at any moment.

Call, damn you!

More than a minute had passed and she was ready to risk calling back when the old-fashioned bell sounded its double ring. Jenny grabbed the receiver in a palm slippery with sweat.

'Dr Kwan?'

'You're in a payphone, yes?' His voice was distorted. He had switched from a landline to a mobile phone.

'Yes.'

'Alone?'

'Completely.'

'OK.' He sounded calmer now. 'How can I help you?'

'I haven't time to be anything less than frank. Sonia Blake, the woman who visited you, has more than likely been murdered.' He made an involuntary sound, a muted exclamation of shock, or was it fear? 'Her death was somehow connected with a recombinant strain of meningitis that has just claimed two lives. There can't be any more secrets, Dr Kwan. If you know something, you either talk to me, and I'll promise to protect you as best I can, or you can take your chances with whoever gets to you first. I know I'm biased, but I think I may be the safer option.'

'I don't have anything to tell you.'

'I don't want to have to, but I could always summon you to court.'

She waited, sensing she'd pinned him down.

'You can't come here, not to my home.'

'You're being watched?'

'I have a girlfriend. She's pregnant. I don't want her involved.'

Jenny tried to come up with a meeting place in this unfamiliar stretch of the country, and could think of only one. 'There's a village called Great Shefford not far from you. I'll be in the lay-by behind the filling station in one hour.'

'Then what?'

'We talk for a while, then I leave you to get on with your life. Isn't that what you want?'

He hesitated, threatening to baulk at the last.

'You have my word, Dr Kwan.'

'All right. I'll be there.'

Jenny climbed into the car with the sense that one way or another things were about to play out. She delved into her bag for a second Xanax: she'd climb back on the wagon when this was all over.

The pill made her feel how she imagined brave people must feel most of the time. She was aware of her fear but able to step away and see it from the outside as something vaguely absurd. It was a powerful sensation. From her parking space behind the filling station at Great Shefford she scanned the passing traffic with a cool detachment. If her two pursuers from the hospital arrived before Kwan, so be it. She wouldn't go without a fight. She had found Sonia Blake's razor necklace in her jacket pocket and slipped it around her neck: an innocuous silver ring on a chain that only a woman would notice was unusually hefty.

Nine fifteen. The sun had dipped behind the hill and all she could see of the approaching traffic were headlights. Kwan was late, but she had expected that. He had a girl-friend to deal with, then, if he had any sense, a few turns around the block to make sure he wasn't being followed. Ten minutes later, a car approaching from the west slowed, then indicated left. It came to a stop in the middle of the road, the driver making sure of the ground ahead before he committed himself. Jenny flicked her lights. It was the signal Kwan needed. He turned in and silently reversed his Prius alongside her VW, making sure his front end was pointing out towards the road.

Jenny wound down her passenger window and called across. 'My car or yours?'

Kwan nodded at her to come across, too frightened to let go of his steering wheel.

Jenny strolled around the front of the Toyota, letting him see that she wasn't afraid, and climbed into the passenger seat.

'Sorry to disturb your weekend.'

Kwan shook his head as if to say he had found himself in a situation beyond his comprehension.

'Did that woman from security debrief you after I called? What was her name? Leyton.'

He nodded. 'Not just her.'

'What happened?'

'Two other guys turned up. Said they worked for mili-tary intelligence. They took me over to some Army base in Salisbury. Had me there most of the day. No lawyer, nothing.'

'Were they asking about me?'

'You, Sonia Blake, and some guy called Adam Jordan.'

Jenny could smell the sweat leaching out of his pores. He wiped his forehead with his wrist.

'What did you tell them?'

'The same as I told you.'

'Did they give you a punch in the ribs?'

He looked at her, startled. 'How do you know?'

'They did the same to a friend of mine.' She gave him a sympathetic smile. 'I'm sorry. It could have been a lot worse.'

He turned away again, his eyes scanning the road neurotically. 'I read Sonia collapsed with a heart condition.'

'She had Q fever. A recombinant strain. I'm told it's a favoured candidate for biological weapons.'

'Shit,' Kwan whispered.

'Does that make any sense to you?'

'Those guys kept asking me who killed her. I told them all I knew is what I read in the news, but they wouldn't have it. They kept on saying she was killed, who killed her, what did she know?'

'And you stuck to the line that she'd just come to see you to learn how the beamline works.'

'Yeah.' He glanced across at her, lips pressed together, facial muscles contracted, as much as he could do not to tip over the edge and start to sob.

'You know what comes next, don't you?' Jenny said. 'Tell me what was going on, Jason,' she used his Christian name for the first time, 'and we'll see what we can do.'

'I don't see what you can do.'

'Organize police protection for one thing.'

'From military intelligence?'

Jenny had only a sketchy recollection of the law of habeas corpus, but she knew that even government agents or military intelligence had no lawful right to spirit civilians away without charge. 'Have you committed any criminal offence?'

'No.' He corrected himself. 'I don't think so . . . I don't know.'

Jenny looked at him. 'Tell me, Jason.'

He had started to weep. How he had survived a lengthy interrogation Jenny couldn't begin to imagine.

'Do you need a moment?'

He shook his head.

She fished a clean but crumpled paper tissue from her pocket and handed it to him, struggling to feel sympathetic towards a crying man. She wouldn't have made much of a nurse.

'Tell me what you know.'

Drying his eyes, Kwan started to talk. He had worked as a beamline scientist for nearly five years, he said, having joined the Diamond Light Source immediately after completing his PhD at Imperial College, London. His job was to operate the machinery and assist the research teams who hired it to get the clearest possible data. He didn't usually concern himself with the end-point of his clients' research, but often picked up details from their conversations. The publicly funded teams had no problem talking about their work – free use of the synchrotron automatically placed their results in the public domain – but the commercial ones tended to be highly secretive, and with good reason. Often they were developing pharmacological products in direct competition with other companies: the first across the line secured the patent.

A little over a year ago he'd been at a meeting of the European Crystallographic Association in Potsdam, Germany. Sonia Blake approached him in a hotel lobby after a seminar in which he'd been speaking on developments in protein-imaging techniques. It wasn't a subject you'd expect to excite the attention of an attractive woman, but they had ended up having dinner and spending the night together in

her hotel room. It was to be the first of four or five such encounters with her over the course of the next twelve months.
Twice they met at conferences, and on other occasions in
Oxfordshire hotels. Sonia would initiate their meetings, call
to say she was feeling lonely and would he like to spend
the evening together? She was always relaxed, friendly, and
– unlike any other woman he had ever been involved with –
intrigued by his work. At their first meeting in Potsdam she
told him she was writing a paper on the political implications
of gene-based medicine. It wasn't so much the hard science
that interested her as what it would mean for medicine to
be tailored to the individual. Would our genomes be owned
by private companies? How would knowledge of our every
genetic flaw affect our rights?

By their third meeting she had told him about her father's
involvement in the early years of the industry and the
questions surrounding his murder. The next time they
hooked up, she talked about Professor Roman Slavsky. She
claimed to have information about work his company was
doing which pushed way beyond all established ethical barriers and which was probably illegal in the UK and most
Western jurisdictions.

'Did she say what kind of work?'

'Not directly. I just remember she started asking me
questions about my scientific ethics. Did it matter to me
whether I was working on public-domain or commercial
research? Did I think it was acceptable for knowledge about
the human genome to be exclusively owned by businessmen?
And one strange question that always stuck in my mind:
would I assist a project to create an influenza vaccine that
would only work on blond people?'

'That was her pillow talk?'

'I know. I should have guessed she wasn't after me for my
body.' He almost smiled. 'The fifth time we met – the very

last time – we went to a hotel. She told me she'd been in touch with someone working for a biotech company that was doing some deeply unethical research. She said this guy was too frightened to talk to her, but he was going to be at Diamond for a couple of weeks and could I get to know him, maybe drop her name into the conversation to see how he reacted.'

'Who was he?'

'I can give you an email, that's all.'

'Because . . . ?'

'Because I have a duty of confidentiality.' He struck the wheel with the heel of his palm in frustration at the unfairness of his predicament.

'What about the name of the company?'

'Confidential.'

'No problem,' Jenny said calmly. 'What happened then?'

'Nothing. I told her I wasn't going to spy for her. It was too dangerous for me.'

'Let me guess – she wasn't content with that?'

'Emails, phone calls, she wouldn't let it go. I told her I wanted nothing more to do with her. But the next thing I knew, she turned up at Diamond. She called me in my office and said if I didn't let her in, there was going to be trouble. I didn't have a choice. As soon as I closed the door she started threatening me – either I handed over the company's research data or she'd phone my girlfriend and tell her about our affair. I told her I didn't have access to it, but she wouldn't believe me. She was like a mad person. Obsessed.'

'What did you do?'

'I got a USB and saved some public-domain stuff onto it. There was no way she was going to understand it, and one protein molecule looks pretty much like any other.'

'Did you hear from her again?'

'No. Nothing till I read she'd died.'

Jenny said, 'Did you get the feeling that she'd spent a whole year working up to that one moment?'

'I slept with Sonia Blake five times and I still don't know who or what she was. I guess that was the idea.' Kwan slowly shook his head. The confession had exhausted him.

Jenny watched as Kwan's tail lights disappeared around the bend. It was getting late. The traffic had all but vanished from the road. The lights on the filling-station forecourt flickered and went out, leaving her staring into darkness. All she had left was the anonymous email address Kwan had left her – *agcto997@hotmail.com* – and a decision to make: whether to trust him. She turned the key in the ignition and headed out onto the road, not sure where she was going or what to do next. A mile or so passed in a blur of indecision, her thoughts ricocheting between the equally forbidding prospects of appealing to Simon Moreton for help and protection, and continuing to act alone. Her courage was beginning to fail when the dim light of a phone box in a lay-by up ahead seemed to summon her. *Williams.* She needed to speak to Williams.

Performing the same trick she had in Oxford, Jenny took the SIM card from her phone and checked Williams's number in the contacts file. The air had turned cold under a cloudless sky, and she stood shivering in the roadside booth as she waited for what felt like minutes for her call to connect.

Williams answered from inside a noisy pub. 'Who's this?'

'It's Jenny. Jenny Cooper.'

'Bloody hell! I've been trying to get hold of you all evening. I thought we'd lost you.'

'Sorry to disappoint. Where are you?'

'In sodding London – what does it sound like? Hold on . . .'

Jenny waited as he picked his way bad-temperedly across a crowded bar before making it to the relative peace of the street.

'Thank God for that. You'd die here sooner than find a place to have a quiet pint—'

Jenny cut him short. 'Any luck with the girl?'

'I'm not sure—'

'What does that mean?'

'We got to your Mr Thorn's place and found the door kicked in, the whole place turned over. No sign of him or his lady friend. Same at his office – door in, papers everywhere, not a soul in sight. I'm afraid I had to call in the local Old Bill.'

'There's a girl who worked there. Eda. Eda Hincks – c-k-s. See if you can find her.'

'I know—'

'You've spoken to her?'

'Mrs Cooper! Listen!'

She fell silent. He had never shouted at her before.

'Tell me where you are,' Williams insisted.

'I'd prefer not to say.'

'You're not to go home tonight. There was an incident at Thorn's office – a violent incident. A woman was nearly killed. Look, how about if I arrange for someone to pick you up? . . . Mrs Cooper? Are you there?'

Jenny dropped the receiver onto the cradle and ran to her car.

TWENTY-FIVE

SHE HAD DRIVEN FOR AN HOUR across country, winding through back roads heading vaguely west until, overtaken by tiredness, Jenny had pulled into a shabby hotel somewhere in the Wiltshire countryside near Marlborough. There was a shower, a bed and, most importantly, Wi-Fi. Aside from that, the room was typical of a cheap English hotel: rickety mismatched furniture and a tasteless patterned carpet no longer able to disguise several decades' worth of stains. Hanging her jacket on the wardrobe rail, she wished she'd been brave enough to have had a stiff drink before coming up, but there was another of life's ironies: she could take on half a dozen hostile lawyers in a crowded courtroom and play cat and mouse with military intelligence officers, but couldn't face the embarrassment of stepping between a handful of leering men at a bar.

Kicking off her shoes, she picked up the phone – a grubby relic of the 1980s – and dialled into her voicemail. There were three messages in a row from Williams left earlier in the evening, each one a little more desperate than the last, two ring-offs from a caller too impatient to speak, then a brief and enigmatic communication from Alison: '*I'm trying to reach you, Mrs Cooper. Please call me immediately you receive this.*' Jenny recognized her measured tone: it was the voice she used to break bad news to relatives. She assumed that Alison must have some of her own. More than likely she had buckled under the stress of Jenny's neglect and decided she couldn't cope with work any longer. She steeled herself to call her back, but chose the cowardly path of listening to the next message first.

'Jenny, it's David. I need to speak to you urgently. I'm at a weekend conference in Glasgow. Call me on the mobile.'

It was left just before nine. He had called again thirty minutes later:

'Jenny, I really need to speak to you. Ross is down with some sort of fever with headache and chest pains. He argued with Sally, she's gone home to York, and Debbie's climbing the walls thinking it's something infectious. I told her to call an ambulance. I can't get home tonight – there's no plane. Where the hell are you? No one knows where you are!'

Jenny struggled to recall David's number and wasted precious seconds retrieving it from the contact list on her SIM-less mobile. She punched it into the room phone. David answered at the first ring.

'Jenny? Where are you? Didn't you get my messages?' His panic was making him shout.

'Wiltshire. I just got them—'

'He's at the Vale, in the isolation unit. They don't know what it is.'

'It's not meningitis?' Jenny struggled to push the word past her lips, which along with her hands had become numb. Paraesthesia – one of the first symptoms of acute anxiety.

'Doesn't seem so, but culture tests take a while. They've pumped him full of antibiotics, but as far as I can tell . . .' He struggled to remain calm. 'I don't even know why I'm asking this, but I don't suppose you have any idea what it might be? It's not just him I'm concerned for – he was with Debbie and the baby all day, all week in fact.'

'Q fever.'

'*What? I can't hear you!*'

The numbness had become tingling, sharp pins and needles spreading through her limbs and deep into her viscera. Her diaphragm tightened, every breath an effort.

'Tell them to test for Q fever.'

David lapsed into astonished silence. 'Q fever? That's an animal disease.'

'I'll call you back in ten minutes.'

As she put down the phone she heard him yell, 'Jenny! What's your number? Where the bloody hell are you?'

Grabbing her smartphone, Jenny fumbled to log on to the hotel Wi-Fi and ran a search: *Q fever symptoms*. A slew of results appeared. She chose the most respectable source she could find – the HPA's Centre for Infection – and was confronted with a list: sudden onset, high fever, nausea, fatigue, myalgia, sweats, chest pains and, further down, endocarditis.

She stared at the screen. All she could hear was David's unfinished sentence: 'They've pumped him full of antibiotics, but . . .' *They were doing nothing*, is what he hadn't been able to bring himself to say.

She needed to speak to Henry Blake, but only had the hospital number. She stabbed at the phone with clumsy fingers and got through to the John Radcliffe switchboard, but just as she had feared, the home numbers of staff were strictly off-limits, even for coroners. Changing tack she tried the Radcliffe's pathology department, roused a technician, and finally extracted a mobile number for Chris Randall, the pathologist who had carried out the autopsy on Sonia Blake.

Dr Randall was at a dinner party and in no mood to be disturbed by a coroner. Only when Jenny had raised her voice loud enough for the whole floor of the hotel to hear that Sonia Blake died from a recombinant strain of Q fever did he offer a bemused apology and let her have Blake's personal number.

Waiting for Blake to pick up his phone, Jenny was aware that she had broken through to a sudden clarity. The sensation of panic had given way to anger and a ferocious desire to act. She was no longer *feeling* anything. Her only thoughts were of what she might *do*. Her world had become binary: her son's life or death.

'Hello,' Blake answered groggily. He was in a room with a television playing.

'It's Jenny Cooper. I think my son may have Q fever.'

'Right.' He didn't believe her. 'You know how late it is?' It felt like a routine he had acted out before with Sonia.

'He's in the isolation unit at the Severn Vale District Hospital, Bristol. His name is Ross Tarlton – I keep my maiden name. His father is a consultant cardiac surgeon there. Please do not question what I'm telling you.' She heard her voice as if it were a stranger's: clipped and mechanical. 'I am calling you because frankly I could think of no one else who might have a clue what to do with an antibiotic-resistant strain that has been engineered to kill. Can you help me?'

'Jesus . . .' was all he could say.

'I'm not interested in bringing your name into this, Dr Blake, I just need some insight. I need to *do* something.'

Jenny heard a woman's voice from another room, demanding to know who was calling this late.

He gave an evasive answer, but the woman grew more insistent as she drew closer.

'Please,' Jenny insisted.

'All I can tell you is that ideally any agent used as a BW would be developed alongside an effective antidote, especially if there was any risk of infection to the administering party.'

The woman's voice was in the room now: 'For Christ's sake. It's not about *her*, is it? I thought we'd agreed.'

Blake ended the call.

BW. Biological Weapon. An image of Ross in a plastic tent passed before her eyes. Medical staff in biohazard suits; drips, wires, monitors and the crushing sense of life slipping away through delirium into darkness.

Jenny forced her mind back to the problem. She needed to know who had killed Sonia Blake. Without that knowledge she had nothing. She could call Ruth Webley and pray that she wasn't complicit in murdering innocent civilians, or she could hold that option in reserve until she had exhausted all others. She had very few left.

A list formed in her mind. Three steps. She worked through them.

Step one. She would check the Public Register of Genetically Modified Organisms. There was an outside chance it would list any application to alter the genetic make-up of Q fever. Her search engine brought up the government website on which the register was hosted. Her fingers worked the screen at lightning speed, adrenalin pumping now, but within seconds she had the answer she feared: *Your search returned 0 results.*

Step two. She reached for the landline and dialled Kwan's number, planning to threaten him with immediate arrest for obstructing the course of justice unless he gave her the name of the company Sonia Blake had been pursuing. Kwan was screening his calls. She was starting to leave a message when the phone was answered and a woman's voice came on the line.

'Who is this?'

'I'm a coroner. Jenny Cooper. I need to speak to Dr Kwan immediately.'

'Coroner?'

'Please pass me to Dr Kwan if he's there.'

'He isn't. You said you're a coroner – is he all right?'

'I assume so.' Jenny stumbled. 'When did you last see him?'

'He went out earlier this evening. He had to fetch something from work. He hasn't called. I don't know where he is. You don't know anything?'

'No.' Jenny hesitated, but her conscience pricked. 'Listen. Call the police and tell them he was recently detained by officers from military intelligence. It was in connection with his work.'

'His work?'

'Yes. That's all I can tell you.'

This time it was Jenny who put down the phone; she had given her all she could.

Step three. Her final option. Jenny took up her phone and keyed in the email address Kwan had given her earlier that evening. What the hell, she had nothing to lose by telling the truth. She gave the full story:

I am the Severn Vale District Coroner, Jenny Cooper. I believe you knew Sonia Blake. You may know she died last week. Her death was caused by a recombinant strain of Q fever. I came into contact with Mrs Blake while investigating three other deaths, this time caused by a recombinant strain of meningitis. My son, too, may now have been infected with Q fever. If you have any information to assist me in this crisis, you may answer in confidence, but I would, of course, prefer to talk to you in person. Lives have been lost. Please don't allow a young man to die if you can possibly avoid it.

As she sent the message, water dripped on to the screen. Jenny had glanced up at the ceiling, looking for the source, before she realized it was a tear from her own eye. She felt no connection with it; it belonged to someone else.

The landline rang. Jenny stared at the receiver as a player of Russian roulette might at the cocked pistol. Was it the front desk? Did she have visitors waiting for her in reception? She answered, ready to jump from the window if she had to.

'Are you there, Jenny?'

'Yes.' It was David. 'Sorry—'

'Sorry? What are you doing in a hotel in fucking Marlborough when our son may be dying, or is the answer too tragically obvious for words?'

'I'm alone, David! I'm trying to get information.'

'Jenny, listen to me. I don't know what the hell it is you're playing at, but I do know that no one with an ounce of maternal feeling would be sitting where you are with a dangerously ill son only half an hour's drive away.'

'If you'd hear me out—'

He wouldn't. 'Debbie's the only mother he's had today, and frankly, it sickens me.'

'Go to hell, David.'

She slammed down the receiver and in a fit of fury ripped the cable from the socket. The bare phone wires whipped back and struck her face. *Shit!* She snatched the cheap vase from the desk and flung it at the television mounted on the wall. Glass exploded and scattered to the four corners of the room, leaving the flat screen shattered. Jenny stood barefoot and paralysed, nowhere to tread without cutting her feet on splintered glass. *Stupid. Stupid. Stupid.* It was over. There was nothing more to say or do. She would drive to the hospital, be a mother for the last minutes she had left, give David the satisfaction of seeing her destroyed along with their son, because it was, after all, exactly what she deserved.

Jenny left the door of the room swinging open and headed down to the lobby. She elbowed her way past the group of overweight men in suits all reeking of beer, who grinned and nudged one another as they spilled out of the bar, and pushed out into the night. The car park was at the rear of the rambling Victorian building and largely unlit. She found her hire car squashed in tightly between two others. She had started to edge in to try to open the driver's door when she heard the sound of tyres crunching over gravel. A car made its way towards her and came to a stop pointing directly at her, blinding her in the full glare of its headlights.

The driver climbed out. Jenny felt her fingers clenching into a fist.

'Mrs Cooper!'

The voice from behind the lights belonged to a woman.

'Alison? How did you get here?'

'Your husband called. He had this number. You have spoken to him?'

'Yes.'

She was walking towards her, a strange shambolic figure silhouetted against the headlights, wearing an anorak over her cotton pyjamas.

'I'm glad I wasn't arrested dressed like this,' Alison said drily. 'I was doing over a hundred on the motorway. I'm sure Ross would like to see you. Would you like me to drive?'

'No.'

'You really don't look in any fit state—'

Jenny felt a faint vibration in her pocket.

'Come on.' Alison reached out a hand.

Jenny dodged away from her and fetched out the phone. A red dot had appeared on the mail icon. The symbol in the top left corner indicated that she still had a sliver of Wi-Fi signal.

'Let's go,' Alison insisted.

'Wait.'

It was a reply to the email she had sent to the address Kwan had given her. She opened it.

If you are genuine, I can help. Your number?

'Do you have a phone? I need your phone,' Jenny said urgently.

'Mrs Cooper, we've no time for this.' There was a catch in her voice. 'He really is very ill—'

'I've got someone who can help. Give me your bloody phone.'

Taken aback, Alison did as she asked.

'What's your number?'

'You know it.'

'I've forgotten.'

Alison recited her number through clenched teeth as Jenny tapped out a reply and marched back towards the building to make sure that the email was sent.

Alison called after her. 'Are you going to tell me why we're still standing here while your son—'

'While he's dying? Yes, I know that. I'm aware of that.'

'You can't let this happen, Mrs Cooper. I promised your husband he wouldn't be by himself. Now get in the car. We'll talk on the way.'

Alison grabbed Jenny's shirt. Jenny twisted away, running between the cars, disappearing into the shadows.

'Mrs *Cooper*!' Alison was beside herself. '*Please*.'

It came. Alison's phone lit up and rang.

Jenny fumbled with unfamiliar controls. 'Jenny Cooper. Hello?'

'Hello.' The voice was male, thirties, quiet, ordinary. He made no attempt to introduce himself.

It was left to Jenny to make the running. 'Did you know Sonia Blake?' The question seemed the only one to ask.

'Not personally. But yes, we had contact.'

'About your work? You were at Diamond, weren't you? You're working for a company—'

'Please be careful.'

Jenny couldn't help herself. 'You were the man who met with Adam Jordan at the filling station. That was you, wasn't it?'

'Do you want me to end this call, Mrs Cooper? It would be very easy for me.'

Jenny glanced left at the sound of Alison's approaching footsteps.

'My son – I think he's got Q fever.'

'You said.' He fell silent, as if reaching a momentous decision.

Alison was standing right behind her now. Jenny could hear her angry breath.

'Four people dead,' Jenny said, gently coaxing him. 'Ayen Deng is missing, so are Adam Jordan's colleagues, and now Jason Kwan. And that's all on top of what happened in Africa. This has to end. I think you know that. I think that's why you've called me.'

Still he didn't answer.

'You've something to say, I know you have. You can trust me. I can protect you.' It was only a half-truth, and he sensed it.

'We have to meet – face to face.'

'But my son—'

'I might be able to help. How sick is he?'

Jenny turned to Alison, asked the question she hadn't dared ask before. 'How long do they say he's got?'

'He needs you tonight.'

'I heard,' the caller said. 'You've given me a big problem.'

'No,' Jenny said, 'I didn't start this. Now how are you going to end it?'

Seconds passed. Jenny let him think, weigh the odds. She offered a silent prayer.

'Make a note of this postcode.' He spelled it out. 'You'll see the forest entrance. Turn in and go along the track to the right. There's a pull-in on the left after a hundred yards. I'll try to be there in fifty minutes.'

'Where is this place? You don't know where I'm starting from.'

'The Cottesloe Hotel, Marlborough – I traced your IP address. There are very few secrets in this world, but I do have some of them. Now hurry.'

TWENTY-SIX

ALISON HAD PLEADED WITH JENNY to go to Ross and leave it to her to meet with the caller, but Jenny knew it couldn't have worked. He would already have looked her up, memorized her face, taken pains to decide whether she was a woman he could trust, possibly with his life. She couldn't have lived with herself if he'd seen Alison and turned tail. She had made one concession and had phoned the hospital. The nurse in the isolation unit handed her to the registrar who had care of Ross during the night, and just to make him feel better, Jenny told him that she was on her way. He confirmed to her that Ross had become infected with Q fever and tried his best to reassure her, promising that a new combination of drugs would reverse the pneumonia that had set in. Jenny hadn't the heart to tell him his efforts would more than likely be in vain.

As she drove the hire car out of the hotel with Alison following, she had asked herself again whether, if she arrived too late to see her son alive, she would be able to live with her decision. The answer was no. But nor could she live with not having done all in her power to save him. She had no choice: her life – or all that she counted as her life – ended with his. And having accepted the fact, she felt as eerily peaceful as the night.

The satnav led her fifteen meandering miles along country

roads and single-track lanes that twisted along ancient boundaries and over chalk downs before descending into the ink-black Savernake Forest. Centuries-old oaks and spreading beeches reached out to each other from opposite sides of the road, forming a shadowy tunnel that seemed to close in more tightly with every passing yard. The road dipped and the canopy grew denser, blocking out every speck of sky. The outer darkness was complete.

A disembodied voice quietly instructed her that she had arrived at her destination. Jenny slowed, searching the unbroken line of trees at the roadside in search of the forest entrance the caller had described. She caught sight of it up ahead – a rough forest track wide enough only for a single vehicle. She slowed and turned in, Alison's Ford tailing her all the way. The VW's underside scraped noisily over the thick ridge of grass growing down the track's middle, forcing her to creep along at walking pace. She followed a slow right-hand bend and arrived at a fork. To the left she could make out the outline of a stationary trailer partially loaded with timber. She followed the instruction to continue round to the right, following the track through several more steep bends until she arrived at what he had described as a pull-in: a semi-circle gouged out of the bank big enough only for a forestry tractor to make a three-point turn.

Jenny pulled over and drew to a halt. Alison came alongside and wound down her window.

She pointed to the track up ahead. 'I'm going to turn around and reverse up there. You should turn around, too – best to face him head-on. Sound the horn if you need help. And don't whatever you do get out. Let him come to you.'

'Fine.' Jenny let Alison feel she was in control, a detective again.

Alison shifted into reverse, turned her car in the tight space and reversed twenty yards further up the narrow track.

When she killed her lights she became invisible. Jenny followed suit, jerkily turning the VW around so it pointed back the way she had come. She dipped her lights, let the engine idle, and waited.

Only a few minutes had passed when the first flickers of light probed through the trees, rising and dipping as the approaching vehicle bounced through the deep ruts. Jenny readied herself, feeling her fingers tighten around the rim of the steering wheel. The lights drew closer and finally appeared around the nearest bend. The oncoming car, a silver saloon, slowed and came to a stop some twenty feet ahead of her. After a few seconds' pause, the phone on her passenger seat rang.

It was him, the voice she had heard less than an hour earlier. 'I presume that's you, Mrs Cooper.'

'It is.'

'Who's that behind you?'

'My officer. Don't worry – she's fifty-seven and wearing her pyjamas. Would you like her to step out of her car so you can see her?'

'That's all right.'

'Then why don't you come and join me?'

He considered the offer. 'OK.'

He dimmed his lights, allowing Jenny to see him as he climbed out. He was tall, though stooped at the shoulders. Early thirties. Jeans and a lightweight hiking coat, a small rucksack over one shoulder. He walked towards her; short brown hair, glasses, as anonymous as a bank teller. She leaned over and popped open the passenger door. With one more nervous glance to Alison's car, he climbed in next to her. She sensed his discomfort; it was more gaucheness than fear.

'Jenny Cooper. Pleased to meet you.' She offered her hand.

His handshake was limp and non-committal.

'Am I allowed to know your name?' Jenny asked.

'Guy,' he said awkwardly.

He started to unzip the rucksack. 'I've got the antibiotics for Q fever – the intravenous version. I didn't think he'd be able to swallow. I don't know the exact dosage.' He brought out a clear plastic bag containing a number of small glass vials.

Jenny hurriedly stashed them in the stow-box in the side of the driver's door, out of his reach.

'I don't know if you want this—'

He was holding a small steel flask about the size of a coffee cup with a screw-down top.

'What is it?'

'Meningitis,' he said, as casually as if it had contained coffee. 'It's not particularly dangerous, not to most people, at least.'

Jenny looked at it, too frightened to touch.

'Put it in the glove box,' she said.

He did as she asked.

'Are you in any danger?' Jenny asked.

'Probably. But I had nothing to do with what happened. I'm just a lab technician. We weren't even sure what we were doing. This isn't what Professor Slavsky wanted.' He turned to her. 'I need you to know that.'

'You work for Slavsky's company?'

'Yes. Combined Life Systems.' He seemed surprised. 'I thought Kwan would have told you—'

He stopped in mid-sentence, startled by the sound of an approaching engine. They both stared out of the windscreen as an array of four headlights headed in their direction. They belonged to a large four-wheel-drive vehicle that was tearing up the track, showing no sign of slowing. Alison switched on her headlights, leaving Jenny and her passenger caught in the cross-beams, light from both directions bouncing off the mirrors and reflecting off the windows.

It all seemed to happen inside the space of a single second: Alison shot forward, slewing around the outside of the stationary VW and angling straight into the path of what Jenny could now see was a black Range Rover. It didn't slow, but rather seemed to accelerate as it ploughed headlong into the front nearside of Alison's Ford. The impact of metal on metal and exploding glass made a sound like a dull explosion. The Ford's bodywork crumpled like tinfoil, and the whole concertinaed wreck was shunted at high speed across the loose dirt, before tipping on its side and slamming hard into the foot of the bank. Continuing in its trajectory, the Range Rover skimmed Jenny's wing and pitched violently, front first, into a drainage ditch to her right. All its massive momentum translated into a half-somersault that brought its roof down hard onto a tree stump. It came to rest nearly upside down, its four wheels spinning noiselessly.

'Alison!' Jenny threw open her door.

'Don't!'

Guy snatched at her, but she slipped away and ran towards the wreckage. It was lying on its right-hand side. Alison would be jammed in against the ground, trapped by twisted metal. The front end was so staved-in, the only way out for her would be through the rear windscreen.

'Alison!' Jenny pounded on the underside of the car.

There was no answer.

'Alison!'

She turned sharply at a sound coming from the Range Rover. The driver's door had fallen open. In the near-darkness, Jenny saw a dark, heavy-set, balding figure clamber to the ground and stagger out of the ditch.

'Mrs Cooper!'

Guy was climbing out of the VW, frantically waving at her to come back.

'Give it to me. You give it to me,' the approaching figure said, in a low, threatening growl.

Jenny stood her ground. 'Who the hell are you?' She was fearless; there was liquid fire in her veins.

'*Koos.*' He spat the word at her and kept coming, now only feet away.

Jenny heard Guy shout out again, '*Stop!*' but his voice seemed distant, muffled. She was staring at the man as if through a tunnel, as he reached his right hand inside his jacket, his small eyes fixed on hers, then her fingers found the coldness of the metal ring at her neck, and as he brought out the gun, she pulled the knife from its sheath and her fist was already travelling in a back-handed arc towards him. He looked up in surprise as the tiny blade glinted, a speck of diamond in the night, then sliced downwards, meeting his skull at the right temple and cutting hard and deep in a diagonal across his forehead. It tore through his right eye, nose, lips, jarred over his teeth and finished its journey in the hard bone of his chin. He screamed – an ugly, piercing wail – and dropped the gun, pressing his hands to his face as blood fountained out between his stubby fingers. Suddenly Guy was at her side, picking up the gun and pushing her back towards the VW.

'We've got to go! We've got to go!'

She climbed into the driver's seat, then thrust Alison's phone into Guy's hands.

'Call an ambulance.'

Without looking back, she took off along the track under the overarching trees, as if in a different tunnel: one that led straight to her son, knowing it was what Alison would have wanted.

Still using Alison's mobile, Jenny made a single call to Williams, waking him from a drunken sleep in a west

London hotel room, to ask him to make arrangements for Guy. His full name was Guy Harrison and he was a senior lab technician at Combined Life Systems. That was all she knew, and all for the moment that he wished to tell. They made the rest of the journey in silence. Jenny didn't dare call the hospital, knowing that if she heard it was already too late she might jerk the wheel and send them barrelling into the concrete barrier separating the motorway carriageways. She felt herself skating along the edge, the forces of life and death pulling at her with equal ferocity.

Williams's three uniforms jumped out of an unmarked car and were opening the passenger door the moment she pulled up outside the hospital. A quiet 'Come with us, sir', and Guy was gone. She took the drugs he had given her, left the steel flask in the glove box, and made her way into the building alone.

The isolation unit was on the sixth floor at the far end of the east wing, as far away from the hospital's vulnerable heart as it was possible to be. She rode up in an empty elevator, her hand closed around the plastic bag containing the vials in her jacket pocket. It was nearly 3 a.m., and the long white corridor was deserted, the only sound a geriatric moan from behind one of the swing doors to the wards known affectionately to the staff as death row. It was no place to be ill, let alone to die.

Jenny turned the corner at the far end and was confronted with a welcoming committee. Three figures stood up from the seats in the bay outside the secure, air-locked entrance: Simon Moreton, Ruth Webley and her square-jawed friend. She strode past, ignoring them.

Moreton stepped into her path. 'Jenny, we're going to have to talk.'

'I need to see my son.' She pressed the buzzer requesting admittance.

'I'm afraid you won't be allowed in,' Moreton said. 'They're taking extreme precautions.' He glanced nervously at Webley and her companion. 'There are special procedures for suspected BWs. Contact with dedicated medical staff only.'

'There are no longer any civilian doctors with your son,' Ruth Webley said dispassionately. 'He's being cared for by a team of military specialists.'

Jenny looked through the observation pane to the vestibule and a further set of double doors beyond. No one came. She pressed the buzzer a second time and held it down.

'I'm sorry, Jenny,' Moreton said. 'You can't go in.'

'I have to,' Jenny protested. 'I have drugs for him.'

She watched the three of them exchange uncomfortable glances.

'The medics think he has Q fever,' the square-jawed man said. He spoke like an NCO, not the officer she had assumed him to be. 'A recombinant strain –' he pushed back his shoulders – 'possibly administered deliberately.'

'Do you think I don't know that?' Jenny said. 'Will someone please get me through this door? I have drugs.' She pulled the small clear plastic bag from her pocket. 'Please.'

She saw the look of incredulity on his face as he exchanged glances with Webley.

'*How* do you know?' Webley said.

Her colleague was turning away, reaching for his phone. Moreton was struggling to keep up, already out of his depth.

Jenny became aware that her mind was leaping beyond this conversation to consequences far further down the line. Her response to Webley came not from any conscious calculation, but as if by instinct: 'Hasn't Jason Kwan told you?'

The officer shot another glance at Webley, bewilderment turning to alarm.

'You picked him up this evening, didn't you?' Jenny challenged.

'Jason Kwan's body was identified thirty minutes ago. He'd been shot through the head. He was in his car, just along the street from his home.'

Jenny felt the muscles of her diaphragm tense. She had smelt his fear as they had sat in his car at Great Shefford. *Poor man*, she silently repeated to herself, *poor, poor man.* Instinctively she said, 'I don't know how he knew – he wouldn't say – but he got me these.'

It was a semi-truth, but one that seemed to slot into Webley's understanding of events, which Jenny was beginning to suspect was more limited than she had previously thought. Webley nodded to her colleague – his name was Carson – and told him to go ahead. He called through to the ward. A short while later the outer door buzzed and Jenny was directed over the intercom to deposit the drugs on the floor of the vestibule and leave directly. As the outer door closed, a female medic dressed in a white biohazard suit came through the far set of doors and collected them. After a few moments, another military doctor called through and asked to speak to Jenny. He told her that there was no time to check the contents of the vials she had provided, but that without effective antibiotic treatment the advanced pneumonia that had taken hold would invariably prove fatal. Did she wish to take the risk of injecting an unknown substance into her son's body? She answered that she did.

As she handed the phone back to Webley, she felt Moreton, who had remained silent during the last several minutes, place his hand on her shoulder.

'I think Mrs Cooper should have some time to herself now. It's very late.'

Webley ignored the request. She had seen the holes in Jenny's story and wanted answers. 'How did Kwan come to have these drugs? He was just a beamline scientist. Did he know who manufactured this strain of Q fever? There must have been other parties involved.'

'I really think this should wait until tomorrow,' Moreton protested.

'It's in all our interests we share this information,' Webley insisted. There was a note of desperation in her voice. 'Mrs Cooper, I'm appealing to you – please. If you have any information about the origins of this organism we need to have it now.'

She turned to Webley. 'What was your interest in Sonia Blake?'

'You know I'm not at liberty to answer that.'

'Then we've nothing further to discuss.'

She pushed between Webley and Carson and collapsed onto one of the vinyl hospital seats.

Webley scraped her nails through her short, practical hair. This was her decision alone, Jenny inferred. Despite the impression he would like to have given, Carson was clearly the underling.

'Might I suggest a breakfast meeting?' Moreton said hopefully.

Webley cut him down with a glare. 'All right, Mrs Cooper. Sonia Blake occasionally supplied us with information in the field of recombinant technology and biological weapons. She had built up an enviable network of connections through her academic work. People in the field seemed to trust her, perhaps because her subject was politics and not science.'

'But you didn't trust her. I presume her interests extended to our weapons programme?'

'There isn't one,' Carson interjected. 'We develop defensive capability only.'

Jenny smiled. 'I read that on your website.' She aimed another question at Webley. 'How did Adam Jordan die?'

'I have no idea,' Webley answered.

'Why take his organs? What were you looking for?'

'I believe I've already explained. He was associating with Sonia Blake. She was on a watch list—'

'No.' Jenny wasn't satisfied. 'You were watching Adam Jordan before he died.' She glanced at Carson, who was standing like a policeman at Webley's side, hands clasped in front of his crotch. 'Your colleague Major Fielding was following him.'

Webley glanced at Carson as if to grant him permission to speak.

'Jordan made several attempts to make contact with British intelligence agents in South Sudan,' he said, 'but failed to attend either of the meetings he had arranged. We made a number of informal approaches on his return, but he claimed he had nothing to tell us.' He shrugged. 'Africa's a rough place, especially his patch. I got the feeling Jordan wasn't cut out for it.'

They waited impatiently for Jenny's response. She wanted to trust them, to believe that they had had no part in Jordan's death, but if she handed them everything, if she gave them Guy Harrison, she would lose both him and the truth. She hadn't come this far to let that happen.

Jenny looked at Moreton, then at Webley. 'I'll offer you a fair exchange: I can give you the source of both organisms in return for an unimpeded public inquest into Adam Jordan's death.'

Webley shot Moreton a glance, expecting him to stamp down hard on the suggestion, but he said nothing.

'Any inquest would have to be held in camera,' Webley said, with a note of concern. 'We couldn't have the media reporting the evidence. That would be out of the question.'

Jenny said, 'Take it or leave it.'

'Mrs Cooper, if you don't cooperate fully—'

Moreton, who had remained tight-lipped, snapped. 'With respect, Miss Webley, this issue will be settled far beyond your pay grade. Jenny, you'll have to trust me, but for God's sake give her what she needs – you've got far more pressing concerns.'

She felt the sting of his judgement like a sharp, sobering slap in the face. He was right, of course, there was only one thing that mattered, but submission would mean the fight was over, reality would come crashing in.

'Jenny?' Moreton coaxed.

'The company's name is Combined Life Systems,' she said flatly. 'It was founded by the late Professor Roman Slavsky.'

She hadn't finished speaking when her eyes filled with tears, and the sides of the tunnel caved in and buried her.

'Mrs Cooper? . . . Mrs Cooper?'

Jenny woke as if from the depths of a coma, to find herself lying on a sofa in an unfamiliar, brightly lit room. A middle-aged nurse was looking down at her.

'You can see your son now, if you like. They've lifted the restrictions.'

The words travelled to her through the fog. She moved stiffly into a sitting position, images from the events of the previous evening ghosting behind her eyes like scenes from a half-remembered film. A clock on the wall opposite swam into focus. It was 9 a.m. She'd been asleep since six.

'Just buzz at the door,' the nurse said. 'They'll be expecting you.' She turned to go.

'He's all right?' Jenny asked.

'Turning the corner.' She bustled out, leaving Jenny alone.

Turning the corner. What did that mean? She pushed up to her feet, desperate to get to him, and caught her dishevelled reflection in the windowpane. Her hair was wild, her crumpled shirt was hanging open to her navel. As she fumbled for the buttons she noticed the fabric was spotted with blood. *Alison.* Jenny relived the moment of impact, the brutal sledgehammer collision that had tossed Alison's car aside like a toy. She saw the squat, bald-headed man reaching into his pocket, felt the sharp pain in her knuckle as she had sliced into his skull. She glanced down at her hand and saw the bruise across her middle finger: a neat black line. She reached up to her neck and felt the chain, complete with the ring. She lifted it over her head and dropped it into the plastic bin marked *Sharps.*

The sister gave her a mask, gown and gloves and led her along the ward to the sealed negative-pressure cubicle at the far end. She was allowed to view Ross through the perspex window but not permitted to step through the door and touch him – not yet – that would have to wait at least another twelve hours. A medic in a biohazard suit was at his bedside recording his vital signs and keying them into a hand-held computer. He would be in the care of the military medics until they were satisfied they had beaten the infection, the sister explained, and thus far the indications were positive.

He was lying still, sedated and unconscious, breathing steadily through a mask, stripped to the waist. Jenny's eyes traced the contours of his unclothed body, thinking how unrecognizable he was from the skinny boy she had seen off to university. The figure lying on the bed was a fully formed man, tall like David, but with the deep, broad chest and heavily defined muscles of her father and his stock. Yes, the Cooper genes had won the day. Her blood was running through his veins.

'His girlfriend's on the way,' the sister said. 'She called a few minutes ago. She'll be here in half an hour. Poor girl spent the night on a train from York.'

'What about his father?'

'He called earlier. He sounded very relieved to hear he was doing well.'

'Not on his way?'

'He said he'll be here later this morning.'

'Can I stay with him for a while?'

'Only a few minutes, I'm afraid. However small the chance, we can't risk you getting infected.'

Looking at her son lying helpless, her own survival had never felt less important. If she could have traded places with him, Jenny would have done so in a heartbeat.

TWENTY-SEVEN

FOR FORTY-EIGHT HOURS, JENNY had scarcely seen the outside of a hospital or police station. Ross had made slow progress; the infection had been neutralized by Guy Harrison's antibiotics, but his depleted body had been pushed to the very margins of life, and the journey back would be slow, with inevitable setbacks on the way. Thankfully he was conscious now and could speak a little, he had even held her hand and squeezed it, but at every visit she had competed for his attention with Sally, who had assumed the role of nursemaid with an easy cheerfulness that Jenny had never been able to equal. Jenny hadn't told him that he had been deliberately infected by someone who had thought that killing him as they had Sonia Blake would stop her from digging down to the truth. Whether she ever could was a question for another day. For now, she just wanted to see him strong again.

David had been at the bedside during several of her visits, kidding and joking with Ross and Sally, but had hardly spoken a word to her. She had begun to explain the chain of events which had led to her arriving at the hospital with life-saving drugs, but he hadn't wanted to hear. David inhabited a reality that didn't allow outlandish facts to intrude. She knew he would simply blot out what didn't suit him and hold her morally responsible for what had happened to their son. How ironic, Jenny thought, that it had always been him who accused her of not squaring up to reality.

Michael had removed himself from the scene entirely. Jenny could hear his 'I told you so' in his brooding silence. He had warned her what would happen, and it had. No mother worthy of the name would have done what she had, his absence seemed to shout, and neither would any lover of his. She had hoped he would make his point and reappear, but as days passed she had a fearful sense that she was losing him, that he had chosen the moment of his vindication to slip away. She had left him messages, pleading like a lovesick teenager for another chance, but he hadn't answered her, and deep in the seat of her being, Jenny started to believe that perhaps he never would.

On top of everything else, she had endured three inconclusive sessions with the Wiltshire detectives who had accompanied the ambulance to the Savernake Forest. Webley had been a lurking presence in each of these encounters, silently making notes and guiding the police officers with nods and glances along a prescribed line of questioning. The occupants of the Range Rover had vanished into the night. The absence of footprints suggested another vehicle may have arrived to collect them. Their identities remained unknown. All that could be said for certain was that the man Jenny had struck in self-defence had spilled several pints of blood onto the forest floor and he hadn't been admitted to any hospitals. There were few doctors in the country qualified to repair a slashed eyeball, but none that had been contacted had reported having done so. The Range Rover was registered to a shell company with untraceable directors, and none of the fingerprints recovered matched any on the national database. By their third session, the country detectives were running out of ideas and Webley had tactfully suggested that their time might be better spent elsewhere.

The file, it seemed, was being shelved until the arrival of further evidence.

Shortly before dawn on Wednesday morning, Harry Thorn, Gabra Giorgis and Ayen Deng had been apprehended at the port of Swansea while attempting to board a ferry to Cork. Williams's men arrived at the Border Agency's offices less than three hours later to find that Webley's people had already spirited them away by helicopter. Jenny suspected it was a move designed to crush the remnants of her morale and dissuade her from pressing ahead with an inquest into Jordan's death, and for a long, bleak morning she had been tempted to do just that. But help arrived unexpectedly in the unlikely form of Simon Moreton.

The deal had been struck in Moreton's office in Petty France the following afternoon. Webley had been replaced by her superior, a lean and unsmiling man named Fitzpatrick, whose expressionless grey eyes reacted to nothing. Across the polished mahogany desk, Moreton eloquently argued Jenny's case for holding an inquest, causing her to wonder what was motivating him. Had the near loss of her son pricked his conscience? Was he telling her his affection for her ran far deeper than he had ever dared to admit? It was a little of both, she concluded, and perhaps – she tried to convince herself – recent events had so shocked him that he was finally putting self-interest aside to strike a rare blow for justice.

Fitzpatrick had no interest in issues of legal principle, less still in the ancient right of the coroner to hold a free and open inquest. His only concern was what Guy Harrison might spring on an unsuspecting world from the witness box. His officers' initial visits to Combined Life Systems had, it seemed, proved unfruitful. The company's employees had denied working on either meningitis or Q fever, and no incriminating evidence could be found at their laboratories, housed in an anonymous business park near the Berkshire town of Hungerford. The company had another facility in the small Gulf state of Qatar, but jurisdictional issues prevented it from being searched. The problem with microorganisms, Fitzpatrick said without irony, was their size. The UK plant had an incinerator in which the evidence could have been disposed of in minutes. The real asset resided in the knowledge, which could have been hidden electronically anywhere in the world.

Fitzpatrick had studied the written statement Harrison had produced from his safe house somewhere in the South Wales countryside, but wasn't satisfied. He demanded to have exclusive custody of him for several days before he set foot anywhere near a coroner's court, and he certainly wasn't prepared to allow his evidence to be reported. Moreton refused on both counts, placing no faith whatever in Fitzpatrick's assurances that Harrison would be returned, unharmed, to give evidence.

They reached stalemate.

The silence stretched to the point where the first to speak would have conceded defeat. Fitpatrick stared unblinking out of the eighth-floor window across the rooftops towards the spires of Westminster Abbey and Parliament beyond. Moreton sat forward on his throne-like chair, elbows on the table, fingers steepled in front of his face. Jenny looked from one silverback to the other and, ignored by both, felt compelled to break the impasse.

She addressed Fitzpatrick. 'I think what you're looking for is something to prise Combined Life Systems open – physical evidence linking them directly to these organisms. Would it help our cause if I could give you that?'

For the first time that morning, the perfect neutrality of Fitzpatrick's expression gave way to something approximating a smile. He thought she was joking.

Jenny reached into her bag and brought out the small steel flask Harrison had handed to her the previous Saturday night and placed it on the corner of Moreton's desk.

'Guy Harrison gave me this. Apparently it contains live, recombinant meningitis bacteria that he took from the lab. You'll more than likely find they contain an antibiotic-resistant cassette unique to Combined Life Systems, for which they hold the patent. It carries resistance to all commercially available drugs and several that have yet to make it to market. I'd bet my house on the same cassette showing up in the Q fever and meningitis cultures the HPA already have. It's the company signature.'

The Adam's apple in Fitzpatrick's slender neck rose and fell, his eyes fixed on the flask. 'Is this safe?'

'Apparently.'

'No reporting of Harrison's evidence.'

Moreton, eyes wide in alarm, agreed. 'Now what the hell do we do with this thing, Jenny?'

In line with their agreement, the inquest was a low-key affair. It was held far away from the public gaze in a community hall on the fringes of Chepstow, where the suburbs of the small market town bled into the lush green fields and woodlands of the Wye Valley. As it was unannounced to the outside world, the only journalist who had got wind of the hearing was an ageing reporter from a local newspaper, whose chin was nodding towards his chest even as nine puzzled jurors swore their oaths and settled into their uncomfortable schoolroom chairs. The few seats set aside for the public remained unoccupied. Apart from the handful of witnesses, a junior sent from Ruth Webley's office to take a note, and two police constables sitting either side of the door, the only others present were Karen Jordan and her mother, Ed and Fiona Freeman, and a slight, middle-aged Spanish woman named Pepita Lujan, Elena Lujan's aunt and representative of the family. A solitary solicitor, Martin Brightland, represented Karen Jordan. Far removed from the realm of his usual small-town practice, he sat alone and exposed in the front row, determined if at all possible to keep his contribution to a minimum.

Jenny turned to the six women and three men of the jury, and told them that they had been summoned to decide the cause of death of Adam Patrick Jordan, aged thirty-two, whose body was found at the edge of the southbound carriageway of the M5 motorway beneath a bridge from which he appeared to have fallen. Having heard the evidence, they would be required to return a verdict of accident, misadventure (meaning that the deceased had died whilst freely undertaking a risk), suicide, unlawful killing, or, if what they heard proved inconclusive, an open verdict.

Adam Jordan had been an aid worker in the turbulent border territory of South Sudan, Jenny told them, he had helped to raise crops from the arid scrub and had saved countless lives, but that was the least remarkable thing they would hear about him. Here, in this hall, in this quiet corner of the Welsh countryside, it would fall to them, nine ordinary men and women, to listen to and assess some quite extraordinary evidence that nothing in their day-to-day lives was likely to have prepared them for. The coroner's court, she explained, was a unique institution: it may be small and without the funds to reside in the splendour of its cousins the criminal and civil courts, but for eight hundred years coroners and their juries had provided answers to unnatural deaths, no matter how bizarre or unexpected their circumstances. This was a court made up of ordinary people, and its only duty was to the truth.

Her opening remarks concluded, she did the job that Alison would always have done, and called for the first witness: Detective Inspector Stephen Watling.

Watling cut an evasive figure, in the chair between Jenny and the jury that served for a witness box, and rattled through his evidence with the impatience of a man eager to be elsewhere. He described the discovery of Adam Jordan's mangled body at the side of the motorway as matter-of-factly as if he had been reading a schedule of exhibits. The discovery of two-year-old Sam, wandering alone in a nearby woodland cemetery, was also relayed in the same dispassionate tone. Jordan had left no note; his phone records had revealed nothing except business and domestic calls; his wife was at a loss for an explanation; nothing he had learned suggested either a motive for suicide or evidence of foul play.

He paused, as if to gather strength, before concluding his testimony with a statement that gave a clue to his determination not to let the names in his narrative become human beings. 'In my experience, which is more extensive than I would wish, men who kill themselves tend to do so violently and without warning. In that respect, I see nothing at all unusual in Mr Jordan's case.'

Jenny let his words go unchallenged. He didn't know what was to come, or how radically his version of events would be overturned.

Dr Andy Kerr was next to come forward. He opened with a description of Adam Jordan's body when it arrived in the mortuary. As a result of a massive impact with a fast-moving vehicle, there was little remaining of the head and face above the lower jaw, and the pelvis and legs had been crushed by the wheels of several vehicles. The nature of the injuries was such that it was impossible to say whether he had landed head or feet first on the carriageway, or whether he was killed by the fall or as the result of being run over. He had

had no alcohol or drugs in his system, which was unusual in male suicides: it placed him in an exclusive 10 per cent.

Jenny prompted him to tell the jury what had subsequently happened to Jordan's body in the mortuary. He related the events of Sophie Freeman's and Elena Lujan's deaths and described his accidental discovery that Sophie's vital organs, along with Jordan's, had been removed without permission.

Sticking to her agreement with Fitzpatrick to keep mention of the activities of his officers to a minimum, Jenny steered Dr Kerr past the events of Sophie Freeman's inquest, and asked him whether he later had cause to take further tissue samples from Jordan's body.

'I did,' Dr Kerr said, in his deadpan Belfast accent.

'And what did you find?'

'In Mr Jordan's stomach contents there were present meningitis bacteria of the identical strain to that which killed Miss Freeman and Miss Lujan. It's most unusual. I can only presume that shortly before death he consumed some contaminated liquid; whether he did so voluntarily or not, I couldn't say.'

There was a sound – a muted exclamation – from the cluster of waiting witnesses. It had come from the slender figure of Ayen Deng, who was seated between Harry Thorn and his unnaturally beautiful girlfriend. Gabra put a comforting arm around Ayen's shoulder. Harry stared straight ahead, pretending not to have noticed Ayen's momentary distress.

'Thank you, Dr Kerr,' Jenny said. 'Unless you have any questions, Mr Brightland, I'll call Mr Harry Thorn.'

The solicitor shook his head and returned his attention to the file in which he had been absorbed. No doubt he was performing the neat lawyer's trick of billing two clients at once.

Thorn marched forward. He refused the Christian oath and chose instead to affirm. The lines that gave his features the appearance of cracked earth on a drought-stricken plain had been gouged even deeper by his recent ordeal at the hands of Webley's interrogators. The defiant spirit had left him, along with his profane eloquence. He wouldn't have smoked a joint in days, and he was moody and monosyllabic as a result. But Jenny was persistent and determined, and unrelentingly dragged the story of what had happened in Ginya out of him.

For nearly six months he and Adam had been working at a Dinka village named Anakubori, some forty miles from the newly drawn border that separated the mostly Muslim Sudan to the north from its largely Christian and animist neighbour, South Sudan. Decades of civil war had given way to an uneasy and patchy peace. The violence that persisted was mostly tribal: in the absence of civil authority, old scores and property disputes were often settled at the point of a gun. But the feared Arab militias, the ruthless, rag-tag Muslim mercenaries from across North African known as the Janjaweed, had largely vanished from the scene.

AFAD's project involved installing a trickle-irrigation system that would enable a village of five hundred Dinka, who for centuries had scratched a Stone Age living from the dust, to feed themselves and generate an income. Three-quarters of the crop was maize, and a quarter, Thorn admitted, was marijuana that was bought by middle men who shipped it north to Egypt and Morocco.

'I didn't see it as a moral issue,' Thorn said. 'These people needed dollars for medicine and solar panels. They weren't going to be buying Ferraris.'

'How did Adam Jordan feel about that?' Jenny asked.

'He took some persuading, but that's Africa,' Thorn said

with a shrug. 'It attracts idealists and creates realists. Adam was still on the journey.'

Jenny would have liked to have known more about Harry Thorn's adventures in the African drugs trade, but much as she might have tried to squeeze him, he wasn't obliged to answer questions that might prove incriminating. Keeping instead to Adam's story, Jenny took him back to a day in early May. Thorn had been busy negotiating with contractors who'd come from across the border to drill a new well and there was a disagreement over money. Harry was at full stretch keeping angry villagers and irate Muslim workers apart when a government water tanker and a jeep drove in. He sent Adam to deal with them. The two drivers had been dispatched to deliver the tanker to the village of Ginya, fifty miles further down the road, where the solar pump drawing water from their borehole had failed. Engineers were on the way, but the village was without water. The tanker driver was reluctant to go there, frightened that his face might be remembered from a skirmish he had fought in during the civil war. He was angling for someone else to drive the tanker the last leg and was willing to offer a day's wages in return. Adam was keen to deliver the tanker himself, fearing that there might be a lot of thirsty and distressed people at Ginya in need of medical help, but Thorn needed him, and persuaded a local man with kin in Ginya to deliver the truck instead.

The round-trip over dirt roads took the best part of twenty-four hours. The man Thorn had sent returned in the jeep with the second of the two drivers sent by the government, happy to report that he had arrived just in time; the people had been a day and a half without water – they were thirsty and had jostled to fill their buckets – but there had been no casualties. He went to collect his payment from the first government driver who had been too frightened to make the trip to Ginya, but he was nowhere to be found. Meanwhile, his colleague who had been driving the jeep took off on his own. Thorn and Adam had been too busy supervising the rebellious drilling crew to pay the disappearance much attention, but the next morning a rumour swept the village that a group of Janjaweed had been seen camping a couple of miles to the north in the bush. The boy who had stumbled on them said they had AK-47s.

Adam smelt a rat and wanted to drive back to Ginya straight away, but Harry needed him to help keep the peace in what was still a tense situation. If the Anakubori well wasn't sunk within the following few days, they risked missing that year's growing season altogether.

Adam made the journey to Ginya four days later. On his return he would say that he was greeted by a vision of hell. The village was a collection of large thatched huts surrounded by a wooden stockade. As he approached along the dirt road he was struck by its unnatural quietness. No swarm of excited children came running out to meet him; thirsty, emaciated livestock were wandering freely. He drove through the entrance to the stockade and into a wall of flies. There were bodies everywhere – men, women, children, babies – all of them bloated and disfigured beyond recognition. They lay in contorted positions that could only have been caused by agonizing death throes. There were no signs of violence and no damage to the buildings, which led him to wonder if they had been poisoned by the water. He went from hut to hut searching for survivors, but found none. He was heading back out of the village, having given up hope, when he saw a solitary young woman walking across the scrub from a cattle shelter that stood outside the village perimeter. It was Ayen. She told him she was the only person left alive. Adam's assumption was right: she claimed that the water had poisoned everyone except her.

A tremor of emotion entered Thorn's voice; a glimpse of the man he must once have been before. He paused to take a drink with an unsteady hand before continuing his story.

Adam brought Ayen back to the village, but Thorn insisted he take her straight to the hospital in the nearest city, Malakal, and that for his own safety he not come back. Thorn realized that as soon as the villagers found out what had happened, his life would be in danger, too: there were blood ties between Anakubori and Ginya, and outsiders could all too easily become scapegoats in the search for revenge. He left that night, only a few hours after Adam, and hadn't been back since.

'Do you know who sent that tanker?' Jenny asked.

'Not for certain,' Thorn replied. 'But during the civil war there was a notoriously bloody battle near Ginya. Nearly a hundred Janjaweed were captured and massacred. I heard stories that the Southerners decided to give them a taste of their own medicine and killed them the sharia way: buried them up to their necks and stoned them to death. It's not too much of a stretch to imagine a party coming back over the border to settle the score.'

'Who did you tell about this incident, apart from the local police?'

'That was it.'

'Didn't you think it was worthy of further inquiry – a massacre of innocent people?'

Thorn was defiant. 'My organization has saved the lives of tens of thousands. No one wants us to succeed. No one wants to give us money. All anyone ever wants is to profit from us or use us for political ends. I don't believe it was a mistake they came to our village. Whoever it was, whatever they represented, they wanted to destroy our work and our reputation beyond all hope of redemption. I told Adam to leave the girl in Malakal –' he glanced over at Ayen – 'a pretty girl, she'd find a husband, but he wouldn't do it. He hadn't grasped the fundamentals. We were there for the many, not the few. You start caring about this person or that person, you're no longer an aid worker, you're a social worker, you're a street cleaner, not a street *builder*.'

It was an impassioned speech that shook the hall like a peel of thunder, but one that left Thorn standing stooped and hollow. He had paid a high price for his tough brand of compassion. The man who counted the value of lives in numbers had had the love burned out of him by the African sun, leaving him as pitted and dry as bones in the desert.

Jenny let him end his evidence there. The later events at AFAD's offices were still under joint investigation by detectives from the Metropolitan Police and agents from Ruth Webley's department, and fell outside the agreed scope of the inquest. All that Jenny knew was that Eda Hincks had been working in the office when two men of Middle Eastern appearance had burst in demanding to know the whereabouts of Ayen Deng. When she refused to talk, they had violently assaulted her, slashed both her breasts and left her for dead. Detective Superintendent Williams had found her, alive but unconscious. If he'd been fifteen minutes later, Eda Hincks would surely have been dead. In a short statement she had given from her hospital bed, Eda had confirmed that she knew nothing about the events in Ginya and had never heard of Ayen Deng.

Jenny called the young African woman sitting between Harry Thorn and Gabra forward to give evidence. Ayen Deng was slightly built, with hair knitted in tight cornrows, her eyes permanently wide and startled. With one hand grasping the Bible and with the other pressed to her chest, she spoke her oath in English that carried a strong hint of an Irish accent. When Jenny asked if she had understood the proceedings so far, Ayen said she had understood them perfectly. Until the age of twelve, she had been educated by Irish nuns, the Sisters of Charity, who had run a mission school in Ginya. They had stayed for much of the war, but when the fighting got close, the villagers had made them leave; the Janjaweed would have slaughtered white nuns like goats.

Jenny could picture Ayen as a child sitting straight-backed in the mission school classroom. She delivered her evidence with the same earnestness and attention to detail that she must have shown in her studies. Despite all she had seen, she remained rigorous and attentive, rooted in something deep and substantial Jenny could only assume was the faith inculcated by the Sisters. Having spoken just a few sentences, Ayen had the jury – and Jenny – captivated.

She had lived in Ginya all her life, she said, and had four brothers and two sisters. When she was young and at school, she had hoped to leave the village and train to be a nurse, but then the war came. Many of the men, including two of her brothers, were killed by the Janjaweed, their throats cut and their bodies left unburied. There was no hope of leaving after that. Life became a little easier when, a year or so ago, the old well was replaced by a borehole that went deep into the earth. It was wide enough only for a thin pipe through which water was sucked by a solar pump, but there was always sufficient to drink. It had always worked without a problem until one morning the pump was found broken. A young man was sent to the next village, where there was a telephone from which he could call the government office in Malakal. For nearly two days they went without water until a tanker arrived. It was like a gift from God.

The tanker water had tasted good: clear and cool, far nicer

than the water they drew from the well. Everybody drank until their bellies were swollen and could hold no more. It was some hours later during the night that people started to fall ill. At first it was the children and the very old. It began with headaches and fevers, then their skins erupted in rashes, their faces and limbs started to swell and the whites of their eyes turned black. They started to fit as if devils were dancing inside them. By morning adults were falling sick, too, even the strongest men. Ayen prayed with her sisters just as the nuns had taught them, but it was no good. One by one they were all struck down. Some of the old people were saying it was a curse, others said the water had been poisoned. Ayen hadn't known what to believe: she had drunk the water and felt fine. By the second night she was the only person left in the village who wasn't sick, and more than half the people were already dead. None of her family survived till morning. She waited for death to take her, too. But it didn't come.

'I went out of the village to pray,' she said. 'I remembered the stories of Lazarus, and of Legion and the swine; I prayed the evil spirits would leave us and go into the cattle.' Ayen paused, raising her hand to her mouth as if she might cry, but no tears came. 'Then I saw the jeep coming. I saw Mr Adam.'

Her account grew sketchier as she tried to recall the events of the bewildering days and weeks following her rescue from Ginya, a place she had left only twice in her twenty years of life. Jenny extracted the barest details of her journey to the hospital at Malakal, where the doctors could find nothing wrong with her. She had nowhere to go and asked Adam to help her find the nuns who had run the school in Ginya. She wanted to go to their convent in Juba, but he told her he wanted to take her back to his country. He said he would look after her and that she could help to find out what had killed all the people in her village.

They stayed in Malakal for several weeks, getting her papers and a passport, then Adam brought her to England to the house in Bristol. He told her she wouldn't have to wait long, that he was going to find out what caused the disease in her village and then she would tell her story. When people heard it, he told her, there would be no more people dying like they had in Ginya. One morning he came to find her and said they were going to meet a man, a doctor, who would scrape her mouth to find out why she hadn't died like the others. They travelled a long way in Adam's car. She sat with his son, Sam, in the back seat.

'Is the man you met that day with Mr Jordan sitting in this room?' Jenny asked.

'Yes,' Ayen replied. 'That's him.' She pointed to Guy Harrison.

They had met beside a petrol station. He scraped the inside of her mouth with a cotton bud, then handed something to Adam that looked like a silver bottle. They drove again, this time to the place where Adam's father was buried. His father had been very precious to him, Adam had told her, and he wanted to talk to him before they told the story of what had happened in Ginya.

She had left him by himself and was walking with Sam in the field when the men came. There were three of them in a big vehicle. She heard shouting and saw Adam running towards his car. He managed to get inside, and she saw him drinking down the contents of the silver bottle as the men beat on the windows. One of them saw her and chased her into the woods, where she managed to lose him.

Ayen dipped her head in shame. 'I ran away. I left the baby and I ran away through the trees. It was like the war again.'

She spent the night hiding, sure that she was going to be hunted down and killed.

'Why did you think you would be killed?' Jenny asked.

'The men who took Adam spoke the language of the Janjaweed.'

'They were speaking Arabic?'

'Yes. I heard them shouting. I had heard that tongue during the war.'

'Did you see them take Adam Jordan away?'

Ayen nodded. 'Yes. They pulled him from the car and drove him away.'

She had woken to the sound of voices. From the cover of the trees she watched policemen arrive and saw them take Sam. Too frightened to show herself, she stayed hidden until late in the morning, when the policeman standing by Adam's car walked away from it along the road. She ran to the car to fetch the doll she had given him as a present when he rescued her from Ginya. She had carved it herself.

'Why did you do that?' Jenny asked.

Ayen looked at her, puzzled, as if the answer were obvious. 'While people were dying, I held it in my hand and the sickness didn't touch me. There were good spirits for me in that doll.'

The good spirits had continued their work. A car stopped for her on the road and the woman driving it had taken her to Bristol. Frightened to tell her story and not knowing who to trust, Ayen had pretended not to be able to speak English and told the woman nothing. For days she hid in her room, too frightened to leave, even to fetch food, then Mr Thorn arrived. He told her he was taking her to Ireland, to the Sisters of Charity who had taught her in school. She went in his car with Gabra, but in the hurry to leave she had forgotten her doll and there were no spirits to guard her. The police caught them before she could get on the boat.

Jenny reached down into her briefcase and brought out

the figurine that had been lying on the floor of the abandoned bedsit. 'Would you like it back?'

Ayen's eyes lit up. Jenny got up from her seat and handed it to her. She seized hold of it in outstretched hands and pressed it to her lips.

'Thank you, Miss Deng. You may step down.'

Clinging to the doll, Ayen made her way back to her seat.

Honouring her agreement with Fitzpatrick, Jenny asked the single reporter present to leave the hall while the next witness gave evidence. Stirring from a semi-doze, he dutifully did as she asked.

Every bit as gawky as she remembered him, Guy Harrison kept his eyes fixed on the floor, too shy to look directly at the jury, as Jenny led him through his evidence. He had been working for Combined Life Systems first as a lab technician, then as a senior technician, since its establishment by the late Professor Roman Slavsky ten years earlier. From the outset, a premium was placed on security. All employees were required to sign a strict confidentiality agreement containing punitive penalty clauses: leaking company secrets wouldn't only cost your job, you would be sued for everything you owned. The quid pro quo was that everyone down to the receptionist was granted generous share options: Slavsky convinced them he had a vision that would make their company one of the richest pharmas in the world; they were all going to be millionaires.

The concept was simple and, as Slavsky often repeated to them, a perfect example of beating swords into ploughshares. As a Soviet military scientist, he had spent many years developing work first commenced by his American counterparts in the 1960s. In its first incarnation, the idea had been to study populations that showed immunity to certain common viruses and bacteria, with a view to developing weapons that would attack only certain ethnic groups. The work had limited success, but in the early 1980s US biotech companies started perfecting cheap laboratory techniques that allowed DNA from one organism to be spliced into any other. The fruits of much of this work filtered back to Slavsky and his colleagues in Moscow, who began to see new possibilities for targeted biological weapons. What if an agent like botulism could be adapted to attack only the cells of a person who carried a given set of genetic characteristics? It was a tantalizing prospect for military planners, but Slavsky's work hadn't progressed beyond the theoretical stage when he fled across the Iron Curtain in 1989.

Theory made the leap to practical reality in the early 2000s, when it became possible to decode vast sections of the human genome quickly and cheaply. Slavsky's idea was to put an ethical spin on his earlier research. He would isolate the genetic code for ethnicity not to develop smart weapons, but to create smart vaccines and medicines that would be effective only on certain populations. He saw it as a huge joke on rich Western governments, who had used their financial muscle to drive down the price they paid for drugs, beyond the point at which the manufacturers could afford to discount them for poorer countries, thus depriving the neediest of badly needed medicines. But if you could develop an Aids vaccine or a cancer treatment that would operate only on West Africans or Indonesians, they could have it for a dollar, while Americans and Europeans would have to pay ten for a version engineered to treat their populations. If he could perfect the technique, every major drugs company in the world would want to license the technology.

Their efforts were stunningly successful. The DNA of individuals from hundreds of different ethnic groups was compared for minute variations. Within six months it became apparent that in among the three billion base pairs of DNA that make up the human genome there was a region containing fewer than a hundred pairs, in which the code varied significantly among different local populations.

The work then progressed to the much slower task of identifying and precisely analysing the proteins expressed by these genes, for only when they were understood could a mechanism be reverse-engineered that would allow a drug to activate only in the presence of that tiny sequence.

'Imagine a very complicated set of molecular keys and locks,' Harrison said. 'Our technology was designed to create locks that could be opened only by the key created by each specific ethnic gene.'

By 2008 work had already begun on a meningitis vaccine that would operate only on populations sharing a gene sequence common to 80 per cent of sub-Saharan Africans. The end was in sight, but Slavsky had worked himself to exhaustion. Word of their work had leaked out. Slavsky suddenly found himself bombarded with offers to buy the business. He resisted, but following his sudden death, his daughter became the majority shareholder and sold to the highest bidder, Mohammed Al-Rahman, a Saudi business-man who had invested his family's oil wealth in biotech.

During the period of Al-Rahman's ownership, everything had changed. Many senior personnel had been replaced, and Harrison had found himself demoted to menial tasks and excluded from the regular strategy meetings. Within the past eighteen months, a whole new lab within a lab had been established, and dark rumours had circulated about the nature of its research.

One of those absorbed into the new secretive team was Katya Toluev, a gifted young woman whom Slavsky had personally recruited from St Petersburg University. Harrison had worked closely with her until she had joined the inner circle, but their friendship picked up again when they found themselves working alongside one another at the Diamond Light Source. It was obvious to Harrison that Katya was deeply troubled and unhappy. Near the end of their stretch at Diamond she finally took him into her confidence and told him that she and her team were working on a contract to create BWs. Al-Rahman had refused to tell them who the buyer was or even to assure them it was legal. She suspected the customer was a Middle Eastern or North African government: they were developing a strain of meningitis designed to activate in the presence of the sub-Saharan gene, which they had named SS1, and another which they had isolated amongst Ashkenazi Jews, named, unimaginatively, AJ1.

Katya's concerns weren't only ethical: she knew the work was illegal. She confessed to Harrison that she had been contacted by an Oxford academic, Sonia Blake, who was surprisingly well informed. She had known that Slavsky had been developing ethnically targeted medicines, and she also claimed to have information that some of the staff imported from the Middle East were known to have been working on BW programmes in Saudi Arabia and North Africa. It was a crude attempt at blackmail: Blake offered Katya the choice of turning whistleblower or taking her chances once Blake made her evidence public. Katya hadn't needed much persuasion. Nor had Harrison.

He agreed to help her obtain evidence: a live sample of the recombinant meningitis that could be independently analysed. Several weeks passed during which Katya hadn't mentioned the subject again, but late one evening she had called him in great distress, saying that she had heard from Blake that there had been a mass death from meningitis in South Sudan that bore all the hallmarks of their pathogen. A British witness had reported that an entire village had been wiped out, leaving only one survivor, who had been brought to the UK. Sonia Blake was preparing to make formal allegations based on a dossier of evidence, and had given Katya a last chance to cooperate.

The plan was to smuggle a sample of meningitis out from the lab that could later be independently analysed. The whole operation was organized like a spy ring, with Sonia Blake sitting at the centre, the only person who knew the identities of all those involved. Katya was to bring the sample out of the lab and Harrison agreed to act as courier. The initial stage all went according to plan: he collected a flask Katya had left in a concealed spot in the Savernake Forest and took it home, where he stored it in his refrigerator. After a gap of several more days, he received an email from Sonia Blake instructing him to hand the flask to Adam Jordan, who would meet him at a filling station in Great Shefford. He was also told that the survivor of the attack in South Sudan would be present, and that he was to take a DNA swab. It would be an easy task for him to run her sample through the lab to see if she carried SS1: hundreds of such analyses were being conducted every day.

Harrison's rendezvous with Jordan and Ayen Deng had been over in a matter of minutes. He had handed Jordan the flask, run a cotton bud around the inside of Ayen's mouth and gone on his way. Twelve hours later he had a result: she was negative for SS1. She could have drunk a gallon of infected water and not suffered so much as a headache. Her failure to inherit the gene, while her sisters had, was less a lucky accident than an indication that her own biological father had probably come from outside the area.

Jenny glanced out at Ayen, now sitting arm in arm with Gabra, and was grateful to see that she had failed to register the meaning of what Harrison had just said. She saw no need to explain it.

Jenny said, 'Do you have any idea who the men were that Miss Deng saw abducting Adam Jordan?'

'Al-Rahman had security staff, Saudi guys he'd brought in
to keep an eye on the employees. It was rumoured they were
ex-secret police – they certainly behaved like it. We would
all get called in for random checks. They would ask you
whether you had been approached by anyone asking questions about your work, or whether you had said anything
you shouldn't have online. They knew their business all
right.'

'How do you think they caught up with Adam Jordan?'

'They didn't come after me that day, so my best guess is
they picked up on an indiscreet phone call. From what I've
heard today it wouldn't surprise me if Rahman's people
knew Jordan had witnessed the massacre at Ginya and had
been keeping tabs on him. You can plant a device the size of
a penny piece in someone's car, listen in on their conversations and track their location to within a few feet. It's easy
when you know how.'

Jenny had only one more question: 'Why Ginya, Mr
Harrison?'

He looked up from the floor and met Jenny's gaze for the
first time during his evidence. 'It was a testing ground. No
one's going to buy without due diligence. Rahman chose the
most obscure corner of Africa he could find to prove his
technology worked.' He gave a slow, thoughtful nod. 'It
worked all right. Just like Professor Slavsky knew it would.
I'm just glad he knew nothing about it.'

The evidence was almost at an end. The lone journalist
re-entered the hall and returned to his seat, and Jenny read
a short statement that had been forwarded to her by Dr
Verma.

In their search for a link between Sophie Freeman and
Elena Lujan, the HPA had found meningitis bacteria in a
throat swab taken from a thirty-five-year-old paramedic at
the Vale Hospital named Gavin Evans. Evans had been one

of a team of three who had removed Adam Jordan's body from the motorway, and at the time he had been suffering from a bad head cold. His partner was a theatre sister, who in the days after Jordan's death had been working alongside Ed Freeman. Evans, it seemed, had picked up bacteria on his hands and inadvertently transferred them to his mouth. He had become the means whereby bacteria spread from person to person, but finding no receptive host other than Sophie, they had quickly died off. Evans had denied ever having visited the Recife sauna, but shown his photograph, several of the staff had claimed to recognize him as an occasional customer. Evans had since been placed in isolation while undergoing treatment to ensure any live bacteria were eradicated.

Attached to Dr Verma's statement were the results of DNA analyses Jenny had requested with Harrison's guidance. They confirmed that both Sophie Freeman and Elena Lujan carried the short sequence of genetic code Combined Life Systems had identified as AJ1. This tiny footnote in their genetic history meant that among the hundreds and thousands exposed to the bacteria incubated and spread by Evans, only Sophie and Elena had been vulnerable to full-blown infection.

Dr Verma had tactfully made no reference to the fact that, as Sophie had been infected via her father, who like his wife had failed to contract the disease, the likelihood was that neither parent carried AJ1. There was no question that Fiona Freeman was Sophie's mother, which left Ed unlikely to be her biological father.

Jenny watched Ed Freeman turn to his wife as the realization dawned, but she refused to meet his eyes, and in a moment understood by no one in the room except the three of them, Fiona Freeman stifled a guilty sob in her sleeve and hurried, head-down, from the hall.

Jenny waited until her footsteps had died away before beginning to sum up the evidence to the jury. She would invite them to return a verdict of unlawful killing and was confident they would oblige. But as Karen Jordan took hold of her mother's hand and stared into a future without the father of her child, Jenny knew that even if his killers were found and brought to justice, their knowledge could not be undone.

Many more Ayens would emerge alone from a wall of flies before some method, as yet unknown, might neutralize the threat.

It was just the way it was, as inexorable as the cycle of life and death: human beings only truly learned from their most catastrophic mistakes.

TWENTY-EIGHT

THE BIRDS GREW QUIET IN AUGUST. There was no riotous chorus at sunrise, no exultant clamour to greet the day. They had switched their attention from reproduction to survival, and were silently gathering strength to defy the winnowing of winter. The wheel ground on. Life would endure, but individual life would not.

Saturday mornings always seemed to bring such thoughts to the fore, and today Jenny felt them keenly. They had been with her since before she woke, needling and goading her. A brief exchange from her final conversation with Dr Allen – almost forgotten in the frantic rush of the previous weeks – played over and over in her mind: 'Remember that life is precious, Mrs Cooper. It exists by chance but thrives by will. Always keep hold of your purpose.'

Even the full blast of the shower couldn't silence his persistent voice. What did he mean, *purpose*? Wasn't it enough that she had delivered her verdict of unlawful killing? That Karen Jordan's son would grow up knowing that his father hadn't abandoned him? That she had beaten Webley and all the others to the truth? How much more could he expect of her? Did he really think she could make herself *happy* as well? Happiness lay with other people's decisions, not with hers. All she could do was prepare the ground and hope – and my God, she had tried.

After several weeks of silence, she had finally persuaded Michael to talk. They had turned their lives inside out, examined them from every angle. There was so much that they could have had together, but one great stumbling block hadn't gone away: Michael really did want to be a father. Jenny had searched deep inside herself, questioned herself a thousand times over, but each time arrived at the same answer: she had brought one life into the world, and that would be the extent of her contribution to the continuance of the human race. Had she lost Ross, who knows what elemental forces would have stirred in her, but she hadn't. Michael was welcome to share her life – she hoped more than anything that he would – but she alone would have to be enough. It was over to him. He was the one who had to find a purpose beyond fatherhood if they were to have a future.

She carried the coffee pot to the table in her long-neglected garden along with her mobile. There were darting swallows, fat dragonflies the colour of peacock feathers hovering by the stream, and somewhere nearby a deep, persistent hum that said bees were swarming, but Jenny's eyes kept flicking to the screen in her hand, hoping for a message from Michael saying that he had decided to be with her. But none came. She refilled her cup and turned her face up to the sun, closed her eyes and tried to unwind. It began to work – the tension that had gripped her shoulders slowly eased, her breathing settled to a slow, steady rhythm – but one short buzz from the phone and her heart leaped as violently as if it had been a gunshot. It was an email. She hit the screen with impatient fingers, only to find that it was from Ruth Webley: *I thought you might find the attached interesting. I turned it up in the notes of Slavsky's Berlin debriefing in '89. No luck with Slavsky's book, however. All copies gone from the second-*

hand market. Not our doing, I assure you. Suspect Al-Rahman and friends.

The attachment was a scanned image of a heavily edited page of typescript. All of the text had been blacked out except for a short passage:

Asked how he came into possession of the file from
Genix, a biotechnology company in Scottsdale, Arizona,
Slavsky replied that he had indirectly procured it. He
knew Genix's leading research scientist to be Roy Emmett
Hudson, a man who had worked on the US Army's
biological weapons programme at Cornmill Creek in
the late 1960s, and had suggested the KGB target him.
Hudson was duly approached by an undercover agent
claiming to be acting for a rival company, but rejected
even the most generous financial offers. Hudson's wife
proved more persuadable, however. An agent posing
as a radical journalist befriended and seduced her, and
persuaded her to copy and hand over several batches of
her husband's technical documents with the suggestion
that his work might have sinister military applications.
The techniques they revealed had accelerated Slavsky's
work in recombinant DNA by at least five years. It had
been the committee's decision to eliminate Hudson when
his wife expressed nervousness that he was growing
suspicious of her. Slavsky claimed he felt no remorse
for the death of a man who had been involved in BW
research at the start of his career. In his words, 'We
were scientific combatants and bore the same risks as
the military.'

Jenny looked up from the document and thought of Sonia Blake's unhappy childhood. Slavsky had held the one piece of information that might have enabled her to make sense of her life, but hadn't the courage to confess it to her. Jenny forwarded the email to Alex Forster and then to Henry Blake in the hope that they might gain a little peace, even if it had been too late for the tormented woman they had both tried, unsuccessfully, to love.

Morning slipped into afternoon. Michael wasn't going to call. She wasn't enough. *To hell with him.* Time to move on and forget him, time to forget about men altogether. That was why she was unhappy, the lousy men she had chosen, none of them able to see beyond themselves, none of them prepared to make the kind of sacrifice every woman took for granted. She felt tears of self-pity threatening and pushed them away. No. No crying. *What was she thinking?* She had far more important things to deal with than her hurt feelings.

Jenny had grown to recognize each one of the ICU nurses over the past few weeks. It was Maria, the Filipina with bright, child's eyes, she had to catch hold of. The others were sticklers for visiting time, but Maria was always guaranteed to let her through. Jenny hovered in a doorway along the corridor until she appeared from the nurses' station, waited for her nod signalling the all-clear, then slipped across to the ward and into the curtained-off bay.

She was lying exactly as she had been three days before on Jenny's last visit, eyes partially open, as if staring at the ceiling. Jenny slowly passed a hand in front of her face.

'Alison. It's Jenny.'

There was no response.

She was breathing without a ventilator, which the consultant had assured her was a positive sign, but he couldn't say when the return to consciousness would come, or even if it would. Her hair, grey at the roots, was starting to grow back where it had been shaved from the crown of her head to the top of her forehead, slowly covering the U-shaped seam of stitches that enclosed much of the front portion of her skull. It had taken three separate, painstaking operations to reconstruct the shattered bone. She hadn't been wearing a seatbelt. If she had, she would have emerged from the wreck with nothing but a few broken ribs. Alison, who fastidiously wore a belt even in the back seat of taxi, had flown at the Range Rover unprotected and hit it head-on. In the intervening days, Jenny had often wondered whether she had done so on purpose. In a cruel twist, her oncologist had revealed that her most recent biopsies were clear. What he had feared was an aggressive secondary tumour was nothing but benign, fibrous tissue, a harbinger of approaching old age, but not of death.

What could you do for someone in a coma apart from sit and wait for a sign of life? Jenny stared at her in tongue-tied silence, feeling more than helpless.

'It's good to talk to her. Sometimes it can work miracles.' Maria appeared with a fresh bag of saline drip and hooked it up to the stand. 'It doesn't matter what you say. It's just hearing the voice.' She picked up one of Alison's hands. 'Her nails could do with filing.'

'I'll see to it.'

From the depths of her handbag Jenny dredged up a file that she seldom found time to use on herself. Pulling up a chair, she cautiously took hold of one of Alison's hands and was surprised to find that her fingers were warm and perfectly relaxed. She set to work, filing each nail in turn – short but not mannish, wasn't that how Alison liked them? Silence was too awkward, too *intimate* now they were touching, so she tried to keep up a flow of small-talk, the kind of chatter the girls in the hair salon she occasionally visited managed to maintain all day. But Jenny lacked their gushing spontaneity; the words dried up before she had finished the first hand. So instead she spoke to her about the office, the things Alison would have been fretting about had she been conscious. The pile of neglected files was down to half its previous size, Jenny assured her, but another big case had come in on Friday: the bodies of five Bangladeshi stowaways had been discovered in a container at Avonmouth docks. She would be spending most of the week trying to trace their families – the kind of task Alison would have dealt with in a morning with the help of all her contacts.

She had done a good job – nails filed, cuticles pushed back – but Alison's manicured hands slipped from where Jenny had placed them across her middle and flopped like those of a corpse, either side of the bed. She lifted her arms again, feeling their full weight, and tucked them inside the sheet.

Jenny found herself with nothing left to say and was seized with fear that this might be her last opportunity.

'You'd better not die on me, Alison.'

No answer. The blank expression now looked accusatory, as if Jenny had somehow stolen the life out of her.

'Go on, then. See if I bloody well care.'

From the corner of the eye she saw the heart monitor flicker: two high peaks, close together.

Maria reappeared between the curtains.

'Look,' Jenny said, pointing to the monitor. 'Her heart . . .'

The nurse glanced at the monitor, then back at Jenny. 'It does that now and then.' She gave a patient smile. 'I'm going to be busy here in a minute. I think you probably ought to go now.'

'Will she live?'

Maria gave a gentle smile. 'We can't say. She might be lucky, she might not. Who knows how these things are chosen?'

Who knows indeed?

Jenny whispered a final goodbye and made her way across the ward and along the interminable corridor that led eventually to the exit. She stepped out gratefully into the warm late-summer air. She looked up at the chestnut trees waving in the breeze and felt the life in them. A life majestic but uncaring, which existed only for its own sake. To hell with purpose. Life was life, and every scrap of it was miraculous and beautiful, and when you weighed it against the alternative there was no contest.

NOTE

MY INTEREST IN THE MACABRE and terrifying subject of biological weapons was first stimulated when I was a student in the 1980s and chanced on a second-hand copy of a book entitled *A Higher Form of Killing: The Secret History of Chemical and Biological Warfare*. It had been published in 1982 and was co-authored by the journalist Jeremy Paxman (now an eminent TV presenter) and Robert Harris (now an equally eminent novelist). The authors related the existence of a US biological weapons programme during the Vietnam War, and described failed attempts to create a biological weapon that would afflict only enemy combatants.

In the intervening years, I had followed developments in genetic science with great interest. DNA, the blueprint for life, consists of only four amino acids – known by the shorthand initials A, C, G and T – arranged in a coded sequence. Over the course of the last three decades, science has learned to cut and splice it with tremendous efficiency. Human DNA can now be decoded very quickly and cheaply and on an industrial scale. The hunt is now on to discover precisely what each DNA sequence codes for, and how this knowledge can be exploited for the development of medical treatments and, of course, for generating profit. Could all these advances, I wondered, be turned to darkly sinister purposes? On reading a revised 2002 edition of *A Higher Form of Killing*, I saw that Paxman and Harris had had the same thought: 'The very success of the project to map the human genome opens the theoretical possibility of weapons designed to target sectors of the populations whose only offence is to share a race, gender or genetic predisposition.'

Eager to know if practising scientists shared this fear, I consulted with an eminent microbiologist, who explained to me in simple terms that it was theoretically possible to create an ethnic weapon, though the practicalities would present a considerable technical challenge. He used the analogy of keys and locks to explain the complex chemical interactions between bacteria and the cells they attack. But in theory, if you are able to isolate the proteins expressed by a gene specific to a particular ethnic group, you will have taken the first and most difficult step in the process of creating a bacterium engineered to attack only hosts containing that precise sequence of DNA.

Interestingly, while my contact was willing to talk about theoretical possibilities, he became more circumspect when it came to discussing what specific disease might be used as the basis for a weapon. I could see that he wouldn't want to be associated with a story that took for its subject a highly emotive pathogen such as meningitis, so I didn't trouble him again, and hence I am not quoting any experts by name as the sources of my information. I have learned that research into these highly dangerous organisms is an extremely delicate subject and, quite understandably, not one which those working in the field wish to be sensationalized or treated lightly. I hope I have not done so, but I nevertheless respect the wishes of scientists to remain squarely within the realms of present and practical reality.

The field of human genetics is moving so quickly and in so many unexpected directions that it is impossible to say what wonders may emerge over the next fifty to a hundred years; the possibilities – from smart drugs to treat cancer to therapies that promise to extend life to a span of several centuries – seem limitless. But almost more intriguing to me is whether the forces antagonistic to life will develop with equal alacrity and cunning. The most obvious example of how we have escaped one horror only to be faced with another is the evolution of superbugs, which have in effect been created by the antibiotics we developed to counter bacterial infection in the first place. In researching these phenomena I have been fascinated to read the scientific and philosophical debate over how and why life-threatening bacteria and viruses have evolved: they serve no function other than to make us ill; they are not part of any wider ecosystem; there is no *need* for them to exist. Having weighed the principal arguments, I was left asking myself whether the existence of these organisms is in fact evidence of an anti-life force in the world? I haven't yet arrived at an answer, nor has science, but I've a feeling it's a question that may be receiving a lot more of our attention in the future.

ACKNOWLEDGEMENTS

I would like to thank my editor at Mantle, Maria Rejt, for her wise and perceptive comments on the manuscript and for being such a reassuring presence throughout the process: no writer could hope for better. Thank you also to my agent, Zoe Waldie, whose honest opinions and sound advice I value greatly. I am also indebted to my publicist, Katie James, and to Sophie Orme and all the unfailingly friendly team at Macmillan. I am extremely grateful to my wife, Patricia, for her help in editing and to all my family for the support they give me every day. Those who helped with my research into very sensitive areas of science and medicine have chosen to remain anonymous, but they know who they are and I thank them very much. Lastly, I would like to express my gratitude to all the readers who have written to me during the last year – your warm words are a constant source of inspiration and encouragement.

If you enjoyed *The Chosen Dead* you'll love *The Burning*, the new Coroner Jenny Cooper novel.

Out in Hardback February 2014

A dense, bitterly cold fog has settled over the Wye Valley when Bristol Coroner Jenny Cooper is called to the scene of a dreadful tragedy: in the village of Blackstone Ley, a house has burned to the ground with three members of a family inside.

Though evidence of foul play is quickly uncovered, it isn't long before the police investigation is drawn to a close. It seems certain that the fire was started by one of the victims, Ed Morgan, in a fit of jealous rage. Their infant son still missing, Ed had left a message for his surviving wife, Kelly Hart, telling her that she would never find the child . . .

But as Jenny prepares the inquest, she finds herself troubled by the official version of events. What could have provoked Ed's murderous rampage? How might the other, guarded inhabitants of the village have been involved? And what could the connection be with the mysterious abduction of a little girl ten years ago?

An extract follows here . . .

The morphine was supposed to make her sleep through the night, but for a little over a fortnight now, Clare Ashton had slept for only two hours before waking again at eleven. It was the same pattern each night. As the grandfather clock on the landing beat out its inexorable rhythm, she would lie cold and restless with the dull pain mounting in her chest and spine while her mind flooded with long-forgotten memories as vivid, sometimes more vivid, than the original events themselves. Tiny, irrelevant details – a stain on her sundress, a patch of unshaved stubble on her father's cheek – would manifest with dazzling clarity. Smells, too: her mother's scent, the smoke from the woodstove in the living room, the damp wool of her winter coat. The odd thing was, these recollections were only of childhood. Her body, and she was always conscious of her body, was flat-chested and slender-hipped. A boy's body, her grandmother had once said in gently mocking tones that still rung hurtfully in her ears. A little girl with the body of a boy until she was nearly fourteen years old. The last among her friends to grow breasts. The last to bleed.

Yet in most other important respects she had been first. The first to marry. The first to give birth. The first – and only one among them – to lose a child. And soon, aged only thirty-five, she would be the first to die. Something had gone wrong somewhere along the line. Not something that had *happened* to her, but something in her make-up; in her wiring. For as far back as her memory stretched she had always felt more than a little off-kilter. As a girl she had found no words to express it. As an adult nearing the end of her life, Clare had found the perfect encapsulation: it was as if she had always been a reluctant visitor to this world. Part of her, she had come to realize, had never wanted to arrive here in the first place. If the prospect of death in two months' time held any consolation, it was in the hope that she would finally get to meet that reluctant part of herself, and to understand who in fact she really was. And if there was nothing to come, if the lights simply were to extinguish, then none of it mattered anyway. Everything from beginning to end would have been meaningless. A monstrous joke.

It was nearly 11.30 when she heard Philip's footsteps on the lane and the creak of the gate as he returned from one of his increasingly frequent late-night runs. The closer Clare came to the end, the more restless her husband seemed to become. More often than not he would sleep in the spare room. 'I didn't like to disturb you,' he would explain softly, but it was he who was disturbed, not she. A man who ran marathons and began each day with 200 press-ups was never going to feel comfortable lying next to a dying woman. Who could blame him? Besides, he had students to teach in the morning. A classroom full of bright-eyed private-school teenagers brimming with hope for the future. He was too considerate not to meet them each day with energy and optimism.

Of the two of them, it was Philip who had always been the selfless one, the coper, the one who had kept up the daily routines in the bleak months after they lost Susie. Without Philip's strength Clare was certain she wouldn't have lasted one year, let alone ten. Sometimes she pictured him as a widower, alone in the house, quiet and stoical, his hair cut shorter as it slowly turned grey, his body even leaner and harder as he doused his inevitable guilt at surviving her with an ever more punishing exercise regime. There would be women, of course, but she couldn't imagine him falling in love again. He had already done that twice in his life and each time it had brought him nothing but unhappiness. No, despite his best intentions the women he let into his bed would never possess him as she had done, and it would trouble him deeply that he couldn't give the devotion they craved.

Perhaps when he was old, when she had become nothing more than a faded photograph, he might let down his defences again and lay himself open, but by then he would be a stranger about whom, imagining him now, she found it hard to care. That was another thing she had noticed about dying: it was making her selfish. As her life force diminished so did her capacity for empathy. With a little luck, by the time she reached the end, the process would be complete. It would be a small blessing, but a blessing nonetheless, to be allowed to die without pity for those left behind.

Clare closed her eyes and tried to banish a procession of uninvited mental images of her nursery school in the small village on the Welsh borders where she had grown up. She had loathed the place and all but erased it from her mind, yet here was the outdoor sandpit with its weathered boards and plastic buckets and spades; now the grey lumps of Plasticine stored in a biscuit tin and the red-and-white chequered apron with her name embroidered across the chest; now the tightly crammed coat pegs, the beanbags in the reading corner. And here came Miss Allsop, or at least her fat calves and ankles stuffed into heavy brown shoes. Her smell: sour milk and face cream. 'Which book shall we read today?' Miss Allsop's voice cut through her tiny child's body, demanding and judgemental.

Clare slipped in and out of a shallow doze with the childhood memories still unbanished, trapped inside the emotions of a fearful four-year-old. Monsters and other unknowable horrors lurked around each corner. Miss Allsop led her along the corridor and into her office. She produced scissors from her cardigan pocket. 'Now give me your fingers, Clare.'

She jolted awake. Her heart was racing. Her pyjama top was glued to her body with sweat. The dark was frightening her. 'Philip? Philip?' she called out faintly, hoping that if he had left his door ajar he might hear her. There was no reply. She called louder and was met with the implacable silence of a still and empty house.

A sensation of rising panic began to overwhelm her, but the stubborn quietness of the night was interrupted by the distant sound of a siren; no, several sirens. They were drawing closer, heading into the village from the Thornbury Road. She reached for the lamp at her bedside, and fighting the pain, forced herself to her feet and limped stiffly to the window. She drew back the curtain and lifted the blackout blind to see a column of flames on the far side of the three acres of common around which the dozen or so houses of Blackstone Ley were randomly arranged. The lights from numerous flashlights were converging from several directions. She dimly made out excited voices and wondered if the villagers were having a bonfire, but for what? New Year? Wasn't it three days too early for that?

There was a sudden and violent explosion. A spectacular fireball erupted just to the left of the burning house. The rolling flames surged upwards and lit up the entire common, exposing a small crowd of horrified onlookers whose hands flew simultaneously to the exposed skin of their faces. Seconds later, Clare felt an intense wave of radiant heat travel through the cold glass and in the same moment realized that it was Kelly and Ed's house that was alight, and that the explosion must have been the large tank of propane gas that stood alongside it in the garden. She thought of Kelly and the three children and wondered if they had escaped the inferno. Then of Philip.

Had she seen him among those on the common? She hoped he hadn't tried anything heroic. It would be just like him. *Please, no. Not now. Not like this.* She pressed her face to the pane, praying for a glimpse of him. She waited and waited, growing more and more desperate, until at last she saw him captured in the headlights of a fire engine. *Thank God.* He was standing absolutely still: tall, lean, strong, staring into the flames. Even as the fire crew busied themselves all around him, he remained unmoving. Clare could read his thoughts as if they were her own: he was seeing their own lost child among the flames. Their Susie. And after ten long years, he was wondering if this place might at last be about to give up its secrets.

*Also in the Coroner
Jenny Cooper series . . .*

The Coroner

When those in power hide the truth,
she risks everything to reveal it

When lawyer, Jenny Cooper, is appointed Severn Vale District Coroner, she's hoping for a quiet life and space to recover from a traumatic divorce, but the office she inherits from the recently deceased Harry Marshall contains neglected files hiding dark secrets and a trail of buried evidence.

Could the tragic death in custody of a young boy be linked to the apparent suicide of a teenage prostitute and the fate of Marshall himself? Jenny's curiosity is aroused. Why was Marshall behaving so strangely before he died? What injustice was he planning to uncover? And what caused his abrupt change of heart?

In the face of powerful and sinister forces determined to keep both the truth hidden and the troublesome coroner in check, Jenny embarks on a lonely and dangerous one-woman crusade for justice which threatens not only her career but also her sanity.

'A brilliant, original and gripping crime novel – I can't wait for M. R. Hall's next one!'
Sophie Hannah

The Disappeared

Two missing students.
One sinister cover-up.

Two young British students, Nazim Jamal and Rafi Hassan, vanish without a trace. The police tell their parents that the boys had been under surveillance, that it was likely they left the country to pursue their dangerous new ideals.

Seven years later, Nazim's grief-stricken mother is still unconvinced. Unable to understand why the police failed to investigate the suspicious circumstances surrounding the boys' disappearance, or the mysterious involvement of the Security Services, she has exhausted every avenue in her search for the truth. Jenny Cooper is her last hope . . .

'As premises go, this one's a killer . . . It's a terrific series, meticulously researched, sharply plotted and peopled with sympathetic characters'   *Financial Times*

The Redeemed

A mystery from the past.
A deadly secret in the present.

A man's body is discovered in a churchyard, the sign of the cross carved into his abdomen. Later he is identified as Alan Jacobs, a troubled nurse at a local psychiatric facility. To Jenny Cooper, Severn Vale District Coroner, it seems likely to be an open and shut suicide case, but something tells her to probe a little deeper.

Then enigmatic young priest, Father Lucas Starr, arrives on Jenny's doorstep, entreating her to hold an inquest into the death of Eva Donaldson, a reformed porn actress turned campaigner. A young man has recently been sentenced for Eva's brutal murder, but Father Lucas is convinced of his innocence.

Jenny's investigations into Eva's death lead her to a powerful new religious group: the Mission Church of God, and to those who control it. Meanwhile, Jenny finds herself finally having to confront the demons of her past, which have tormented her for so long. And as her private life threatens to shatter, she is put under intense pressure, from all angles, to cease her investigations. But to Jenny Cooper, whose whole life has been governed by deception, the truth is everything . . .

'Intelligent and intricate, and grips from the beginning to end'
Woman & Home

The Flight

A tragic accident or a terrible crime?

When Flight 189 plunges into the Severn Estuary, Coroner Jenny Cooper finds herself drawn into the mysterious fate of ten-year-old passenger, Amy Patterson.

While a massive and highly secretive operation is launched to recover clues from the wreckage, Jenny begins to ask questions the official investigation doesn't want answered. How could such a high-tech plane – virtually impregnable against human error – fail?

Under pressure from Amy's grieving mother, and opposed by those at the very highest levels of government, Jenny must race against time to seek the truth behind this terrible disaster, before it can happen again . . .

'Fasten your seatbelts for a quality thriller . . . Hall's Gold Dagger-nominated books, quite simply, get better each time'
Independent on Sunday

extracts reading groups
competitions books new
discounts extracts extracts
competitions events
books new reading groups discounts
events new books
reading groups extracts books
new titles reading groups
interviews extracts
new reading groups books events
books discounts interviews
new books events events
books events new interviews
discounts extracts discounts now

www.panmacmillan.com

extracts events reading groups
competitions books extracts new books